Ever a Princess

Awakened one night by her father's most trusted servant, Princess Giana is given her father's ring—signifying her as ruler of Saxe-Wallerstein-Karolya. Her parents have been slain by her treacherous cousin in a coup to seize the throne. But with the princess still alive, no one can claim the crown. With only a handful of loyal servants left to attend and protect her, Giana flees to an abandoned hunting lodge in Scotland to hide.

Adam McKendrick is a successful hotel owner from Nevada—and the unfortunate subject of a series of embarrassing dime novels. A stroke of luck at poker wins him a Scottish hunting lodge giving him the excuse he needs to leave the States and his infamous reputation for a while. To his surprise, he finds the lodge has a domestic staff, headed by a very clumsy, yet quite beautiful maid named Giana. . .

Turn the page for acclaim for Rebecca Hagan Lee . . .

A Hint of Heather

Gossamer

"*Gossamer* is a tender treasure of a book."
—Teresa Medeiros

"Warmth, love, tenderness and humanity fill the pages to overflowing in another beautifully rendered romance. Following an original plotline, tackling important themes and creating memorable characters ensure Ms. Lee a place among the finest writers." —*Romantic Times*

"Beautifully written and very touching . . . if you're looking for something a little different from the norm, this is the one to read." —*Old Book Barn Gazette*

"Outstanding and unforgettable." —*Bell, Book & Candle*

"A moving and emotional love story." —*All About Romance*

"*Gossamer* is an incredible diamond." —*Affaire de Coeur*

Ever a Princess

Rebecca Hagan Lee

JOVE BOOKS, NEW YORK

This is a work of fiction. Names, characters, places, and incidents either are the product of the author's imagination or are used fictitiously, and any resemblance to actual persons, living or dead, business establishments, events, or locales is entirely coincidental.

EVER A PRINCESS

A Jove Book / published by arrangement with the author

PRINTING HISTORY
Jove edition / February 2002

Visit our website at
www.penguinputnam.com

ISBN: 0-515-13250-0

A JOVE BOOK®
Jove Books are published by The Berkley Publishing Group, a division of Penguin Putnam Inc., 375 Hudson Street, New York, New York 10014.
JOVE and the "J" design are trademarks belonging to Penguin Putnam Inc.

PRINTED IN THE UNITED STATES OF AMERICA

10 9 8 7 6 5 4 3 2 1

For Maria Isabel Fernandez Marrero.
Here's your story, Mari.
Enjoy!

Codicil to the Last Will and Testament of
George Ramsey, fifteenth Marquess of Templeston

My fondest wish is that I shall die a very old man beloved
of my family and surrounded by children and grandchildren,
but because one cannot always choose the time of one's Departure from the Living, I charge my legitimate son and heir,
Andrew Ramsey, twenty-eighth Earl of Ramsey, Viscount
Birmingham and Baron Selby, on this the 3rd day of August
in the Year of Our Lord 1818, with the support and responsibility for my beloved mistresses and any living children
born of their bodies in the nine months immediately following
my death.

As discretion is the mark of a true gentleman, I shall not
give name to the extraordinary ladies who have provided me
with abiding care and comfort since the death of my beloved
wife, but shall charge my legitimate son and heir with the
duty of awarding to any lady who should present to him, his
legitimate heir, or representative, a gold-and-diamond locket
engraved with my seal, containing my likeness, stamped by my
jeweler, and matching in every way the locket enclosed with
this document, an annual sum not to exceed twenty thousand
pounds to ensure the bed and board of the lady and any living children born of her body in the nine months immediately
following my Departure from the Living.

The ladies who present such a locket have received it as a

promise from me that they shall not suffer ill for having offered me abiding care and comfort. Any offspring who presents such a locket shall have done so at their mother's bequest
and shall be recognized as children of the fifteenth Marquess of
Templeston and shall be entitled to his or her mother's portion
of my estate for themselves and their legitimate heirs in perpe-
tuity according to my wishes as set forth in this, my Last
Will and Testament.

George Ramsey,

Fifteenth Marquess of Templeston

Prologue

The first duty of a Princess of the Blood Royal is to serve the House of Saxe-Wallerstein-Karolya.

—FIRST MAXIM OF PROTOCOL AND COURT ETIQUETTE OF PRINCESSES OF THE BLOOD ROYAL OF THE HOUSE OF SAXE-WALLERSTEIN-KAROLYA, AS DECREED BY HIS SERENE HIGHNESS, PRINCE KAROL I, 1432.

April 18, 1874
PALACE AT LAKEN
BALTIC PRINCIPALITY OF
SAXE-WALLERSTEIN-KAROLYA

"*You must wake up, Your Highness!*"
Her Royal Highness Georgiana Victoria Elizabeth May heard the whisper, recognized the voice, and placed her hand against the soft fur at her side to quiet the low, menacing growl coming from the throat of Wagner, the huge wolfhound sharing her bed. She opened her eyes and found Lord Maximillian Gudrun, her father's private secretary, standing in the dim glow of the lamplight beside her bed.

"Thank the All Highest," he whispered reverently. "I've reached you in time."

Alarmed by the old man's reaction, Princess Giana pushed herself into a sitting position, leaning against the mound of feather pillows propped against the headboard of the old-fashioned half-canopied tester.

"What is it, Max? What are you doing here? You're supposed to be in Christianberg with Father and Mother."

A sheen of tears sparkled in Lord Gudrun's eyes and ran unchecked down the weathered planes of his face. The old man clutched at his side, then dropped to his knees by the side of the bed and bowed his head. "Something terrible has happened at the palace, Your Highness."

A frisson of foreboding prickled the fine hairs at the back of Giana's neck, and her voice echoed her terror. "Max?"

Lord Gudrun reached across the fine snowy-white linen and thick eiderdown comforters to clasp Giana's right hand. His hand left a dark smear of blood on the covers, and Giana drew in a sharp horrified breath as he slipped a heavy gold signet ring onto her right thumb.

"His Serene Highness Prince Christian Frederick Randolph George of Saxe-Wallerstein-Karolya bid me bring this to you, Your Highness."

"No." Giana began to tremble as she stared down at the gold ring Max had slipped on her thumb. The royal seal. The seal of state worn by every ruler of Saxe-Wallerstein-Karolya since the principality's beginnings in 1448—a gold seal now stained with blood. "My father . . . Max?" She glanced up at him. "He can't be . . ."

Lord Gudrun bit down on his lip to stop its quivering, and then gave a sharp affirmative nod. "I'm afraid so, Your Highness."

Although she understood the meaning of the transfer of the royal signet ring, and had always known that one day, this day would come, Giana couldn't bring herself to utter the words. To do so would be to confirm the thing her heart and her mind could not accept. Her beloved father was dead. She was now ruler of the principality.

A sudden rush of hot, salty tears stung her eyes as Giana pushed back the covers and scrambled to her feet. The wolfhound bounded to his feet beside her. "We must go to the palace at Christianberg at once. My mother will . . ." Her mother would know what to do. Her mother would put aside her own deep overflowing grief and help Giana get through the ordeal ahead; to do what must be done.

Lord Gudrun struggled to stand, then gripped Princess Giana's hand with his left one and squeezed it hard. "I'm sorry, Your Highness, but your mother . . ."

Giana wrenched her hand out of his and shook her head. "No, Max, please . . . Not my mother, too."

"I'm sorry, Your Highness."

"How?" she asked. Giana was willing to admit that a healthy, hearty man in his early fifties might meet an untimely death, but she could not concede that his wife might meet the same fate. Unless . . .

"Treachery, Your Highness. Your father and your mother were stabbed this evening by hired assassins."

Giana's breath left her body in a rush. "Why? Who?"

"Prince Victor has been inciting the young men of the ruling class, denouncing your father's support of a constitution and a Declaration of Rights for the Masses. Victor has been promising estate grants, titles, and funds to the foolish younger sons of aristocratic families to gain their support, and he has convinced these young traitors that your father's aim was to reward the poor with the landed estates of the rich."

"Victor?" Giana struggled to comprehend the meaning of Max's words. "My cousin assassinated my parents?"

"Yes, Your Highness," Max confirmed. "Your parents were murdered in their bedchamber after retiring from the state dinner celebrating the opening of Parliament. The palace has been overrun. Your father's loyal servants are being slaughtered, and Victor's men are searching for you."

"How did you escape?" She asked the question, though she dreaded hearing the answer.

"I was delivering the nightly dispatch box to your father's bedchamber. I heard Prince Christian cry out a warning as your mother entered the room. I entered your mother's chamber from the south door through the dressing room and hid the dispatch box under a bonnet in one of the princess's hatboxes, then I drew my dress sword and entered your father's bedchamber." Lord Gudrun took a breath. "Your father lay on the floor, bleeding from several wounds. Your mother lay dead beside him. One of the traitors was attempting to remove the seal from the prince's hand. He turned and discharged his pistol as I entered the room."

Giana suddenly realized Max was bleeding—that the blood from the seal hadn't belonged only to her father. "How badly are you injured?"

Max shrugged. "A minor wound, Your Highness. The ball glanced off my rib." He uncovered the wound in his side so Giana could assess the damage.

Giana's face whitened at the sight of the spreading red stain. Please, don't let me faint, she begged, please; let me do what must be done. Her stomach muscles clenched and her head began to spin, but she refused to give in to the weakness. Stiffening her resolve, Giana reached across the bed for the nearest pillow, stripped off the pillowcase, and pressed the white linen into Max's hand to help staunch the flow of blood. She found, to her amazement, that the task was what she needed to help dispel her light-headedness. "It may require stitching." She bit her bottom lip. "But for now, I think it best if we wrap it."

"Yes, Your Royal Highness."

Giana met Max's gaze. His eyes were dark and shadowed with pain as she withdrew her hand from the makeshift bandage at his side. Giana wiped her bloody hands on the sheets, then took a deep breath to steady herself. She reached for another pillow, removed its case, and bit a hole in the seam, tearing the fine linen into strips of bandage. She repeated the procedure with another pillowcase, then helped Max remove his waistcoat and jacket. He lifted the bandage as Giana unbuttoned his shirt, then placed it back over the wound as she wrapped the strips of linen around his chest. She talked as she worked, speaking in the clipped and precise regal tone that was as much of an imitation of her father as she could manage, hoping her questions would keep the old man's mind off his pain. "The traitor who shot you?"

"I ran him through, Your Highness."

Giana tightened the last strip of linen, knotted it into place, and stepped back to view the results. "And Papa? Did he suffer?" She knew the answer. She knew her father had suffered terribly, but she wanted Max's reassurance, so she had to ask.

"No, Princess," Max answered, softening his tone and reverting to the familiar form of address. "Nor your mother. She died instantly. Your father tried to save her and when he could not, he bid me to deliver his seal to you, to get you to safety, and to guard you with my life. Those were his final orders to me." Prince Christian had given him one other order before he died, but Max could not muster the strength to deliver it yet. *Tell Giana never to be afraid to follow her heart. Promise me, Max. Promise you will help her find a way.* His voice broke on a sob and his rounded shoulders shook from the force of his grief. "And I shall, Your Highness, I will not fail you again."

Max buttoned his shirt over the bandage and struggled into his brocade waistcoat and wool jacket. He stared at the princess. To him, she was still a girl—barefoot, dressed in a demure white lawn nightgown with her long blond hair plaited into a single braid. She was too young to be the ruler of a wealthy principality. Too young to bear the crushing burdens of the state. Her blue eyes were darkened with sorrow and redrimmed from the sting of tears she refused to let flow. She stood tall and looked him in the eye, her gaze unflinching as she accepted responsibility for her country and for her people. She was a girl on the brink of womanhood, a princess and rightful heir to the throne, filled with strength and courage and compassion.

Her Serene Highness Princess Georgiana Victoria Elizabeth May of the house of Saxe-Wallerstein-Karolya.

Max knelt before her, kissed the ring that had belonged to her father, and swore to serve her as he had served her father and as his father and grandfathers had served the rulers of Saxe-Wallerstein-Karolya for four hundred years.

Giana reached down and buried her fingers in the soft brindle-colored fur just above her wolfhound's shoulders. She held on to Wagner, bracing herself against the tide of anguish that threatened to overtake her. She was the sovereign ruler of her country, and she was alone and terribly afraid. She wanted to throw herself into Max's arms and weep as she had done many times as a child, but she stayed the impulse. The ruler of Saxe-Wallerstein-Karolya could not succumb to emotions. She couldn't behave like a grief-stricken daughter. She had to behave like a princess—like the ruler of her country. She had to behave as her father would have behaved, so she accepted her due, nodding regally as she helped Max to his feet. "Wake the others," she ordered. "We must prepare for the journey to Christianberg."

"Your Highness, you cannot return to the capital," Max told her. "Your cousin will kill you if he finds you."

"Finds me?" Giana asked. "The fact that I'm on holiday here is common knowledge. My program is published each month. Victor knows I'm at Laken."

"No, Your Highness, he does not. Your schedule was altered before it was made public."

"By whom?" Giana demanded.

"Your father."

"But why?"

"Prince Christian knew of the unrest among the young aristocrats in the capital and suspected your cousin might be behind it. Prince Christian received word of your cousin's traitorous activities shortly after he refused to consider Victor's request for your hand in marriage."

"Victor offered for me?"

Max nodded. "Your father knew Victor was plotting to overthrow him. He refused his offer for your hand because he feared Victor would use you to gain the throne. But Victor was incensed by Prince Christian's refusal, so your father suggested this trip to Laken in order to get you out of the capital and away from possible danger."

Giana's eyes widened at the revelation. "Papa sent me away? On purpose?"

"Yes," Max confirmed. "He suspected Victor might try to use the opening of Parliament to incite rebellion."

"He sent me away. But he allowed Mother . . ." Giana couldn't finish the thought.

"You were the heir apparent," Max reminded her.

"But—"

"Prince Christian tried to send your mother away. He begged her to accompany you, but Princess May refused to leave him. She refused to allow him to face the traitors alone."

"Oh, Mama." Giana tried mightily to keep her sorrow in check, tried to keep the tears at bay, but one solitary droplet slipped through her lashes and rolled down her cheek. While her father had ruled the principality, her mother had been the glue that held everything together. Prince Christian was the hereditary leader of Saxe-Wallerstein-Karolya, the embodiment of goodness, justice, and might, but Princess May was the heart and soul of the country—the mother of its heir, the champion of the common people, keeper of centuries-old traditions, and social arbiter. Without her mother to guide her, Giana was lost. Overwhelmed. Terrified. Unequipped to rule. She didn't understand government; she didn't understand the nuances of negotiating treaties, or foreign trade rights. Giana had always known that the continued beating of her father's heart was all that kept her from assuming the throne, but somehow the knowledge hadn't seemed real. She had never seen herself ascending the throne, had always assumed her role as heir apparent was temporary—until a brother came along. She didn't know how to do her father's job. She wasn't prepared to be a ruler. She only knew how to be a princess. She glanced at Max. He had been her father's confidant and adviser for more than twenty years. Surely he would know what to do. Surely he would have all the answers.

"How many people do we have, Max?"

"Only myself, Your Highness, and those serving you here at Laken."

Giana frowned. The permanent staff at Laken was kept to a minimum. Those presently serving at Laken were Langstrom, the butler, and Isobel, his wife, who served as housekeeper, Josef, the stable master, and Brenna, Giana's personal maid. Everyone else lived in the village and came into work on a daily basis. "That gives us four," Giana said. "Six counting you and me. Seven with Wagner." She glanced down at her beloved wolfhound. "Seven against Victor's traitors."

"There are many landowners and men in the government and the army who will remain loyal to your father," Max assured her.

"Then we must return to Christianberg to rally them."

"You cannot, Your Highness. I swore a solemn oath to your father that I would see you to safety. The palace isn't safe and neither is the capital."

"But we can't let Victor win," Giana protested. "We can't stand idly by and allow Victor to ascend my father's throne. To get away with murder—with regicide."

"We must for now," Max assured her. "The tide of rebellion is running high. Victor will not risk losing his chance to gain the throne—however briefly. We cannot risk your life. We cannot risk the life of the rightful heir to the crown."

"The crown," Giana breathed slowly, reverently, as understanding dawned. "The crown. If Victor wishes to wear the crown of Saxe-Wallerstein-Karolya, he must abide by the Law of Succession. He must endure the wait. He cannot marry until the traditional period of mourning for the late ruler is over. And he cannot be crowned until he is married. Until that year is over, Victor can govern the principality, but he cannot be recognized as its rightful ruler."

Max managed a slight smile. "And because you are recognized as your father's successor, not Victor, the People's Parliament of Karolya will require him to marry a princess of Karolyan blood."

"There are no princesses of Karolyan blood left to marry. I am the only one." She looked at Max. "Unless he marries one of his sisters."

"An act none of the other European ruling families could or would condone." Max shook his head. "No, Your Highness, in order to be crowned His Serene Highness, Prince Victor IV of Saxe-Wallerstein-Karolya, your cousin must marry you."

"Or produce my body," Giana reminded him. "And my father's seal of state."

"Then we have no more time to waste. We have only one year."

"We must leave the country before Victor closes the borders. For the time being, we must bide our time, go to ground like the fox, and endure the wait."

Max studied his princess, marveling at the strength and sense of determination he heard in her voice. He knew, even if she did not, that until the year was up there was no safe haven left to them, knew Princess Giana's life was forfeit if her cousin found her, knew she would never agree to marry her parents' murderer, and he also knew that Victor would search the countryside for the princess and post spies in every remaining monarchy in Europe in an effort to find her. "Where shall we go?" he asked. "What is to be our destination?"

Giana's mouth thinned into a firm hard line. "I don't know. But it must be a place where no one would ever think to look for a princess."

Chapter 1

The Bountiful Baron never refuses a woman in need.

—The First Installment of the True Adventures of the Bountiful Baron: Western Benefactor to Blond, Beautiful, and Betrayed Women written by John J. Bookman, 1874.

June 18, 1874
USS *Yankee Belle*
From New York to London

"*Call.*"

Adam McKendrick studied the cards in his hand for a moment longer before spreading them out on the table. "Full house. Gents and ladies."

Ignoring the groans and the round of good-natured teasing, Adam pulled a gold watch from the pocket of his waistcoat, flipped open the lid, and stared down at the face. Squinting through the blue haze of cigar smoke that hovered over the tables and seemed to swirl beneath the prisms of the crystal chandeliers, he made out the time. Three forty-seven A.M. In a couple of hours the first light of dawn would begin to break the horizon, but none of the men in the Gentlemen's Gaming Salon would see it.

The man across the table from him picked up the deck of cards. "You in or out?"

"Out." Adam grabbed his hat from the hat rack and raked his earnings into it. He left his hat sitting on the table while he stood up and stretched his arms over his head, easing the tension in his neck from the long hours at cards. His head ached from the smoke he'd inhaled and the whiskey he'd consumed, and his body was stiff and sore from sitting at a card table all evening. "It's late, gentlemen. I'm calling it a night."

"What about you?" The dealer nodded toward Murphy O'Brien, Adam's friend and traveling companion.

Murph glanced at Adam and winked. "I need to recoup my earnings. I'll play another hand or two before I turn in."

"Suit yourself." Adam shrugged into his jacket and picked up his hat. No one else at the table looked up as he crossed the room to the cashier's window.

Adam helped himself to an expensive cigar from the humidor while he waited for the cashier to exchange his poker chips for currency. He snipped the end off the cigar and struck a match to it while the clerk counted out his cash. Adam pulled a bill from the pile and handed it to the clerk, then recounted the bills, folded the money, and tucked it into his pocket.

Opening the door to the Gentlemen's Gaming Salon, he stepped into the passageway and made his way to the purser's office, where he deposited the bulk of his cash into the safe. Once he had his receipt in hand, Adam left the purser's office and climbed the steps to the deck. He circled the deck twice, then leaned against the rail of the ship to breathe in the cool air and study the stars as he smoked his cigar.

Half an hour later Adam left the deck and made his way back down the passageway to his stateroom.

A steward smiled broadly and greeted him as he unlocked the door. "Have a good evening, Mr. McKendrick."

"Thanks," Adam replied as he stepped through the door and into his room.

"Shall I light a lamp for you, sir?"

Adam shook his head. "That won't be necessary. I can manage." He closed the door behind him and fumbled for a match. The odor of sulfur filled his nostrils as he scraped the match against the striking plate. He lifted the lamp globe and touched the flame to the wick, then turned toward his bunk. "Aw, hell! Not again!"

A curvaceous blonde, naked except for the bedsheet, lay in the center of his bunk. "Hello, handsome," came the husky voice. "I've been waiting for you."

"Dammit!" Adam crossed the room in four angry strides. "This is the third time this week. How did you get in?"

"I bribed the steward."

Adam managed a half-laugh. "No wonder he was smiling. If this keeps up, he'll be a rich man."

The woman stretched luxuriously like a cat and allowed the sheet covering her breasts to slip lower, giving Adam an enticing view.

"Get your clothes and get out."

She pouted. "I thought you helped women in need."

"You don't need my help," he reasoned. "Or you wouldn't be bribing the steward."

"A woman doesn't have to be financially destitute to need help." She smiled a meaningful smile. "I require a different sort of assistance."

Adam looked her in the eye. "You've got the wrong man."

"But you're Adam McKendrick," she purred.

"Let me put this another way," he said firmly. "Madam, I'm not interested."

"Helena," she continued, undaunted. "Helena Compton."

"Mrs. Samuel Compton?"

"The same." She wet her lips with the tip of her tongue in a move too practiced to be an accident. "I could be very good to you, you know."

Compton. Adam raked his fingers through his hair. He'd just spent most of the night playing poker with Samuel Compton, a Chicago railroad tycoon, almost twice her age. "I don't want you to be good to me, Mrs. Compton," Adam told her. "I don't want you to be anything to me. And I don't want to come back to my room and find you in my bed again. Understand?"

"No." She pouted prettily.

"Too bad." He glanced around the stateroom. "I don't mind winning a man's money, but I draw the line at winning his money and bedding his wife. Now, where are your clothes?" he asked.

"I didn't wear any."

Adam raised an eyebrow at that. "How did you get from your room if you didn't have on any clothes?"

"I had an accomplice. She came with me, waited while I undressed, then took my clothes back with her."

"The woman who was here the other night?" Adam guessed.

"My cousin." She shrugged. "We figure one of us will get lucky sooner or later. And we don't mind sharing."

"I do." Adam rang for the steward, then leaned down and scooped Helena Compton into his arms, sheet and all.

"Won't you at least give me reason to hope?" She wrapped her arms around Adam's neck and pressed herself against him.

"Nope."

The steward knocked on the door almost immediately, and Adam invited him to enter. "You rang for me, sir?"

Adam carried Helena Compton across the room and deposited her in the steward's arms. "This lady has mistaken my room for hers," he said, removing a crisp fifty-dollar bill from his pocket. "Please see that she finds her way back to the correct one."

"But, sir, the lady assured me that you and she—"

"Please bring another sheet for my bunk." Adam folded the money and tucked it into the steward's breast pocket. "As you can see, the lady was mistaken. I know she can rely on your discretion in rectifying her error." He stared at the other man. "And I'm sure her husband would appreciate it if you'll see that this sort of mistake doesn't happen again." Adam backed the steward into the passage and closed the door in his face.

How the hell was he going to face Samuel Compton over the poker table again? And how in the hell was he going to explain if the older man learned of his wife's escapade and took exception? Adam stripped off his jacket and shirt, tossed them over the nearest chair, and sat down on the edge of the bunk. His unwanted notoriety was beginning to be a pain in the ass.

He blew out the breath he'd been holding and rubbed the throbbing spot on his temple. There were days when he'd give every penny he'd ever made to find a place where no one knew or cared who he was.

Today was shaping up to be one of them.

Chapter 2

The Bountiful Baron defends the weak and helps the poor.

—THE SECOND INSTALLMENT OF THE TRUE ADVENTURES OF THE BOUN-
TIFUL BARON: WESTERN BENEFACTOR TO BLOND, BEAUTIFUL, AND BE-
TRAYED WOMEN WRITTEN BY JOHN J. BOOKMAN, 1874.

Later that morning
USS *YANKEE BELLE*
FROM NEW YORK TO LONDON

*A*dam started as a dime novel sailed past his shoulder and landed on the table in the main dining room, rattling his cup and saucer. He looked up from the newspaper he'd just opened and frowned at his friend. "What the . . . ?"

"You're famous, my friend," O'Brien replied. "Your reputation has preceded you."

Adam sat at his usual table, nursing a scalding hot cup of strong black coffee and battling the effects of a wicked hangover while he watched a group of fellow travelers file into the room for breakfast. He folded his newspaper and laid it aside, then picked up the small book and glanced at the title. *The Second Installment of the True Adventures of the Bountiful Baron: Western Benefactor to Blond, Beautiful, and Betrayed Women.*

"What do you think of that?" Murphy asked.

Christ! There was another one! Adam opened the novel, scanned the first couple of pages, and let out a derisive snort. One good deed, he thought. If the truth were known, he'd probably never done an entirely unselfish deed in his life—including the one that was currently causing so much trouble. He'd been furious at his sister Kirstin's husband because the bastard had beaten her for attending a suffragette rally. Adam shoved his fingers through his hair. The truth was that he'd been angry enough at his brother-in-law to kill him, and he'd taken his frustration out on a cowboy he'd caught slapping a saloon girl around. Adam let out another snort. He'd done one good deed, protected one saloon girl from an abusive customer, and this was the result. He flipped through the pages. The pen and ink drawings in the first installment had depicted him as a gentleman defending a saloon girl from a ruffian; this installment appeared to have expanded upon the theme with drawings of women from all walks of life—rich and poor—escaping tyranny and neglect, turning to him for help.

Adam groaned. Instead of confining his good deed to the defense of one saloon girl, this installment depicted him as an avenging angel defending blond womanhood everywhere. Well, at least that explained Helena Compton's uninvited appearance in his bed. She'd seen the book and wanted to share a pillow with the Bountiful Baron. "I think that if I'd eaten breakfast, I'd be losing it about now."

Murphy laughed, then reached over and helped himself to the pot of coffee on the table.

"Need my cup and saucer?" Adam cocked an eyebrow at his friend.

"No, thanks." Murphy held up a thick mug. "I brought my own. I figured that since the *Bountiful Baron* would provide the coffee, the least I could do was bring my own cup." He commandeered the chair across from Adam and sat down.

"*Very* funny." Adam shoved the book back across the table and glared at Murphy. "Where'd you get this?"

"From one of the dudes at the poker table last night."

"Which one?"

"The one with the foreign accent and the fancy embroidered vest," Murphy replied.

Adam narrowed his gaze, wrinkling his forehead and drawing his brows together in a concentration.

"You won't remember him. He came into the salon with three companions—all foreigners—after you raked up your winnings and left."

"It was nearly four before I left the table," Adam told him. "I thought you were right behind me."

O'Brien chuckled. "I couldn't help myself. I had to stay awhile longer and pad my winnings. You'd left the table and I couldn't stand the thought of anyone else winning the cash those foreigners were flashing around." He smiled at Adam. "And when one of them started showing this"—Murphy picked up the dime novel and stared at the cover—"around the table and asking if any of us had ever heard of him, I became curious." He dropped the book on the table and turned back to Adam.

Adam rubbed his forehead in a futile effort to rub away his headache. "Did anyone answer?"

Murphy shook his head. "Fortunately, no one else at the table had seen a copy of the book and the foreigner referred to you as the baron instead of by name. But you're a passenger on this ship and your name is on the manifest. If they want to find you, it won't take them long."

"Jesus, Joseph, and Mary! How many of those are there?" He nodded toward the dime novel. "I've bought up as many copies of the first installment as I can find. Am I going to have to buy the publisher just to put an end to this? Why did"— Adam stared at the author's pseudonym—"John J. Bookman print my name? He doesn't use *his* real one." He muttered a curse beneath his breath. "It was bad enough when the first one came out. Now there are two of them." His reputation for lending a helping hand to women in need had spread like wildfire through the mining camps to Virginia City, Sacramento, and San Francisco before the publication of the first installment. Now a second installment had appeared. At least there was some truth to the first installment. The second one was pure fiction. "You're the Pinkerton. Do something useful. Find out where these things are coming from." He picked up the book and slapped it down on the table. "This is almost as bad as having a reputation as a gunslinger. I can't turn around without tripping over someone who's read all about me. . . ."

Murphy commiserated. "Yeah, beautiful blondes every time you turn around and all of them desperately seeking aid and succor. Damn the luck."

"Luck and beauty have nothing to do with it," Adam protested. "There will be women and girls of all shapes and sizes, from sixteen to sixty looking for help. My life is going to be living hell when I get back home."

Home for Adam McKendrick was Queen City in the Nevada Territory, a town built from the fortunes made on the silver ore of the Comstock Lode. Adam owned the largest hotel in town and the Queen City Opera House, a fancy name for a saloon and gambling house, but one the city council insisted would lure moneyed visitors to town. Adam doubted that the grand name he'd given his saloon had as much to do with the draw as the fact that new silver strikes occurred in Queen City on a regular basis and the fact that it was the last large town on the main stage line to Virginia City and San Francisco. But the city fathers were right about one thing—business was booming.

"If you get back." Murphy took a sip of his coffee.

"If? What do you mean, if?" Adam demanded.

Murphy shrugged. "You're going to the Scottish Highlands to check out the hunting lodge you inherited. You might decide to stay and be lord of the manor."

Adam snorted. "I didn't inherit the lodge. I won it in a poker game. And why would I decide to stay in Scotland and be lord of a manor when I've got several perfectly good businesses to run back home?"

"The Highlands are known for their wild and desolate beauty. And McKendrick is a Scottish name. You may develop a fondness for the auld sod."

"I don't give a damn how beautiful the Highlands are or what the name is. I'm an American. And any fondness I develop for the auld sod will come from the fact that there's money to be made there."

"Not to worry, then." Murphy laughed. "You won't be forming any undue attachment to Scottish soil. They may be beautiful, but there's nothing in the Highlands but poor people, shaggy cattle, heather, and sheep. If there was a way to turn that into money, surely someone would have found it by now."

"Maybe they weren't looking at it the right way." Adam reached over and cuffed Murphy on the shoulder. "The world is changing, my friend. Wealth isn't confined to the aristocracy anymore. Men are making fortunes in gold and silver mining, in railroads and steel mills. There's a whole new class of millionaires looking for new ways to spend money and new things to spend it on." He grinned. "I earned my first fortune breaking my back digging silver from the Comstock, and I can tell you that the money pouring into the hotel and the opera house is a hell of a lot easier to make. That's why I decided to see if the hunting lodge has potential."

"Potential for what?"

"For recreation. Manly recreation that relies heavily on hunting and fishing, drinking whisky, and playing cards, polo, and golf."

"Golf?" Murphy raised his eyebrows as if he'd never heard the word before. "I know hunting and fishing and playing cards and drinking whisky. And I've heard of polo. But what the hell is golf?"

Adam smiled. "A game Scotsmen like to play."

"Where did you hear about this game?"

"From an old Scotsman who worked the claim next to mine. He always talked about going back to Scotland and building a gentleman's club where men could play golf."

"Is it an indoor or an outdoor game?" O'Brien asked.

"Outdoor," Adam answered.

O'Brien threw back his head and laughed so hard that he had to wipe tears from the corner of his eyes. "It's so damned cold and windy in Scotland that a man would have to be a fool to pay good money to play any kind of game outdoors."

"McTavish swore his kinsmen loved it."

O'Brien continued to chuckle as he looked at Adam. "Are you sure that old Scotsman was right in the head?"

"Absolutely," Adam replied without hesitation.

"This I've got to see."

"That's why I asked you to come along," Adam told him.

O'Brien helped himself to another cup of coffee. "You didn't just ask me to come along. You're paying me to come along because you wanted someone other than your sister to talk to during the crossing."

Adam grimaced. "That's true. I love my sister, but she gets on my nerves." He did love his sister. There was no one in the world he loved more than his mother and his four older sisters, but there was no doubting the fact that they could try the patience of a cathedral full of saints. And Adam was no saint. Still, he'd grown up with them. He knew what to expect. Conversing with his other three sisters could be a trial, at times, because they were so opinionated and stubborn, but talking to Kirstin about anything of importance or of real interest was next to impossible. His mother and his other three sisters might be budding suffragettes, but they hadn't succeeded in converting Kirstin. She didn't understand what the fuss was all about. Kirstin was just as beautiful, but she wasn't as smart as his mother or his other sisters. Learning to read had been difficult for her and schoolwork, a chore. But their mother had always preached about using the talents God gave you, so Kirstin used hers—a beautiful face and body and stubborn persistence—to get what she wanted out of life.

Unfortunately, she had wanted an English lord for a husband. And she had gotten one.

Kirstin had never had any intention of preaching equality of the sexes to the ladies of London. She didn't care about equal rights. She cared about prestige—the kind of prestige that could only be achieved by being the wife of a peer. Kirstin didn't talk politics all the time, but her conversation began and ended with fashion and gossip. And that, Adam discovered, was a mixed blessing. Because there was a limit to the number of times a man—even an adoring and indulgent brother— could listen to her rapturous descriptions of bows and frills. And unless the lodge proved to have commercial potential, Adam didn't care a fig for the gossip of London society. Although he could successfully avoid constant association with Kirstin during the day, society demanded she have a suitable escort at night.

Adam heaved a sigh. Wrestling with a dozen forks and

spoons and knives and the dizzying array of plates and glasses included in the twelve-course dinners was such a chore, he and Murphy cut cards each night for the dubious honor of escorting her. So far, Adam had won the cut more than he'd lost and Murphy was suffering through the gossip and the fashion reviews. Still, Adam was honor bound to pay the man for his trouble and provide other amenities like cigars and fine liquor to make it up to him. Because the truth was that he liked Murphy O'Brien and he would have died of boredom on the crossing if Murph hadn't taken him up on the offer. Adam reached for his coffee cup, took a tentative sip and studied O'Brien over the rim. "Which reminds me, it's your turn to escort her into dinner tonight."

"If you hate the job so much, how did you allow yourself to get talked into taking her back to her husband?"

"You know what they say." Adam met O'Brien's gaze. "No good deed goes unpunished."

"How's that?"

"It all started with the party my oldest sister, Astrid, planned for my mother's sixtieth birthday. We all made the trip to Astrid's house—including Kirstin and her husband, the English lord . . ."

"Like mother, like daughter." O'Brien chuckled.

"Not quite." Adam pinned O'Brien with a look that told him he could do without the commentary. "The difference is that Kirstin wanted one. Even if the English lord was strapped for cash and looking to marry an heiress. Unfortunately, he's turning out to be the bad penny that turns up every so often asking for more. My father was just the opposite. He had plenty of money and he didn't stay around long after he married my mother because she encouraged him to go. She says she knew their marriage was a mistake from the start because they were so different. Personally, I've always thought he left before I was born because the thought that I might be a twin and a girl probably scared the bejesus out of him."

Adam laughed. He had to admit his family was unique. All four of his sisters were twins. The two older ones were twins and the two younger ones were twins and they all looked alike. Like his mother, his sisters were all blonde and blue-eyed. He was the odd man out. The youngest child. The only boy. The only one in the family with dark hair and the one whose father decided a return to London was preferable to remaining in an ill-advised marriage to a widow with four daughters. "Anyway, Kirstin and His Lordship made the trip to Denver to celebrate my mother's birthday."

"So it was a nice family gathering," Murphy commented.

"It was hell," Adam said. "My mother is as stubborn and independent as ever. She's still running the farm in Kansas and worrying about the weather and the price of corn and wheat and she's become a leader in the women's suffragette movement." He smiled at the mental image of his mother carrying a placard. "I've always been proud of her strength and independence and I'm certainly in favor of women's suffrage, but I sometimes wish my mother . . ." He'd been about to say that he wished his mother hadn't been quite so independent, wished that she hadn't chosen her first husband's legacy over her second husband's love, but Adam shrugged off the thought. His mother was who she was and he loved her. She wasn't the type to show affection. It wasn't in her nature to boast or to coddle. Her nature was to push, to work hard to succeed, and to see that her children succeeded. And she'd been successful. "My sister, Astrid, is helping her husband expand his medical practice into a hospital, despite the fact that she's pregnant with her seventh child. And Erika has hired three new teachers—all suffragettes—for her school. Her husband is an engineer with the railroad. He travels a lot and Erika spends her energy on the school." Adam shrugged. "Greta and her husband purchased the farm adjacent to Ma's, and Greta gave up her position at the newspaper in town, but she's publishing a weekly bulletin for female farmers. And now, Ma, Astrid, Erika, and Greta have formed a Women's Temperance League with other local suffragettes." He glanced over at Murphy. "The other three of my sisters' husbands don't seem to find their politics threatening, but *His Lordship* . . ." Adam shook his head and swore viciously. "His bloody Lordship has turned out to be a real bastard. The legitimate kind. He beat the hell out of Kirstin because she dared—she dared—accompany my mother and sisters to a temperance rally. Kirstin was sporting a black eye when I arrived. And all because *His Lordship* is afraid she might take her suffragette ways back to England—to the wives and daughters of his House of Lords friends. The irony is that Kirstin only went to the rally because all of the other women in town were going. She didn't care about temperance or the suffragette movement; she went because she didn't want to be left out. But His bloody Lordship beat the hell out of her anyway."

"Sheesh!" Murphy ran his fingers through his thick brown hair, shuddering at the thought of ugly bruises marring Kirstin Marshfeld's gorgeous flesh. "But I hate English lords. Bloody arrogant bastards, the lot of them." He looked over at Adam. "With one notable exception."

"Don't make an exception on my account," Adam told him. "I agree with you."

"But you're a . . ."

Adam shook his head. "My father is the younger son of an English lord. He was supposed to inherit money and property instead of a title, but he'd never claimed his inheritance. Ma said he didn't need it. She said he had the Midas touch and loads of charm to go with it. He could have made a go of anything he tried, but when she met him, he was living for adventure. He wanted to see the world and although my mother loved him, she refused to give up the farm she inherited from her first husband in order to explore the world. At any rate, they parted company. Eventually my father had the marriage annulled. Although I wasn't born one, technically I became a bastard when my father dissolved his marriage to my mother in order to marry someone else." He paused. "Ma didn't get anything out of the marriage except me. But that was her choice. After she wrote to tell him I'd been born, he sent passage money to England for all of us and an old gold locket he told her to give to me." Adam pulled out his watch chain to show O'Brien the locket he wore as a fob. "She kept the locket and returned the money. *This* was my inheritance. When the marriage was annulled I was no longer entitled to bear the McKendrick name, but Ma insisted I keep it. She says it's the name I was born with and neither the law nor the church has the right to take it away." He shoved the watch back into his pocket and continued his story. "Kirstin's husband is the real English lord. I tried to persuade her to leave him, but she wouldn't consider it." Adam traced the rim of his coffee cup with his index finger. "There was nothing I could do except promise His Lordship I'd kill him if he touched my sister in anger again. And I promised him I'd be watching from now on."

"Did he believe you?" O'Brien asked.

"He believed me enough to leave Kirstin to visit with Ma while he took the next train east and a boat back to England," Adam answered. "And so did the guy slapping one of the girls around in the Gold Nugget Saloon later that night."

"Hence the first installment of the true adventures of the Bountiful Baron . . ."

Adam nodded. "There must have been a journalist in the saloon. Someone who heard me offer the girl a job and a place to stay. She turned down the offer of a job, but she accepted a train ticket back home to her parents' farm in Indiana."

"The girl might have sold her story to the dime novel."

"Could be." Adam refilled his coffee cup, and then signaled to the waiter for a fresh pot. "Or Kirstin's decided on a novel way of earning pin money. However it came about, it's a pain in the ass."

"Speaking of which," O'Brien said. "Where is Her Ladyship?"

"Breakfasting in her stateroom," Adam replied. "She says it isn't done for a viscountess to be seen before one or two in the afternoon."

"What does she do in there all morning?" O'Brien asked. "She can't be primping. She's already gorgeous enough to stop clocks."

"I don't know and I don't care as long as I don't have to listen to one more description of the new gowns she's ordered for the Season." Adam waited until the waiter removed the empty coffeepot and replaced it with a fresh one. He refilled his cup and took a swallow. "Thank God we'll be docking in a few days. Her husband can listen to her for a while." He glanced at Murphy. "Don't get me wrong about this. I despise the man. I think Kirstin made a big mistake in marrying His

Lordship and is making another one in going back to him. But it's her life and her decision. I worry about her. But my hands are tied unless she changes her mind about being a viscountess." He thought for a moment. "If she does, I'll only be as far away as Scotland."

Murphy murmured an agreement. He'd spent enough time in Kirstin Marshfeld's company to know that she wasn't about to give up the prestige that went with an old and honorable title—even if that meant suffering beatings at the hands of her husband. And he knew Adam well enough to know that he felt duty bound to protect her—even if that meant protecting her from her own ambition. "Look at the bright side." He picked up the dime novel and waved it at Adam. "Nobody in Scotland will know about the Bountiful Baron."

Adam saluted O'Brien with his coffee cup. "I won't have to look at that thing every time I turn around."

"Or attempt to live up to his reputation." Murph grinned.

Adam matched Murph's grin with one of his own. "You can bet on that. I've had my fill of blond, blue-eyed darlings. If they have 'em in Scotland, I don't want to know about it."

"You're sure about that?" O'Brien teased.

"Completely," Adam pronounced. "You can have 'em all."

Chapter 3

"*There is trouble, Your Royal Highness.*"

Giana sighed. "Max . . ." She had reminded him a thousand times that it did no good for them to travel incognito, pretending to be a family, or to remain in hiding if he insisted on speaking Karolyan and using her title every time he addressed her. She was supposed to be the daughter of a well-traveled cook and butler. Max was supposed to be her paternal uncle, and Josef and Brenna, her cousins. They had come to Scotland on holiday from their jobs in the household of a recently deceased Slovenian countess to visit Gordon, her mother's brother. English was to be spoken at all times, but Giana had learned to make allowances when she and Max were alone.

Max glanced over his shoulder to be certain no one overheard. The habits of a lifetime were difficult to break. "We're alone, Your—Giana."

She dropped the dress she had started mending into the basket sitting on the stone floor of the massive gathering room. It was too dark to sew. The daylight had faded with the gloaming and a soft mist had begun to fall and the fire in the huge hearth gave meager light. The gathering room had become her favorite room in the lodge. The stone walls, high ceilings, and exposed timbers of the gathering room reminded her of the summer palace at Laken. Giana squared her shoulders and prepared for the worst, as she calmly waited for Max to explain. He didn't have to announce bad news. She could tell by the expression on his face that the news he bore wasn't good. "Is there news of Victor?"

Max shook his head. "No, Your Highness."

"Then what?"

"We must find another hiding place," he told her. "The owner of this one is on his way here."

Giana frowned. After spending six weeks crisscrossing the back roads of Europe from Karolya to the Mediterranean and up through Spain and France, Giana and Max had finally felt safe enough to lead their little band of refuges to their current hiding place—an uninhabited hunting lodge hidden deep in the highlands of Scotland where Isobel's brother, Gordon, was gamekeeper and caretaker. The empty hunting lodge had been a godsend. Isobel had lived in Karolya for more than twenty years, and the fact that she and Langstrom lived and worked at Laken, away from the capital, made the likelihood of any of Victor's minions realizing that she had a brother in Scotland remote. "But Gordon said Lord Bascombe hadn't come to the lodge in years. He hates the place."

"Gordon was correct," Max told her. "Apparently, Lord Bascombe hated the lodge enough to sell it. There was a telegraph awaiting Gordon in the village saying the new owner is on his way to inspect the property. He instructed Gordon to make the lodge habitable."

"When?" Giana breathed.

"Any day now," Max said. "The telegraph operator waited for Gordon to come into the village to collect his mail and messages instead of riding out here to deliver them." He glanced at the princess. "I'm afraid that doesn't give us much time to find another place, Your Highness."

Giana worried her bottom lip with her teeth. "Do we know if the person who purchased the lodge is someone who might recognize us?"

"The origin of the name is Scottish," he said. "But according to the telegram, the gentleman is from America."

Giana smiled. "Then we need not worry about finding a new place to hide, Max."

"Why not?"

"We shall be safe and comfortable here until it's time to return to Karolya and reclaim the throne." She hoped she sounded more confident than she felt.

"How can you be so certain Highness?"

"It has become common knowledge, among royals, that Americans pay little attention to our goings-on."

"But, Princess, we cannot remain in a lodge the new owner expects to find uninhabited," he protested.

She thought for a moment. "We can if we're the staff."

Max groaned. He recognized the look of determination in her eye. "The staff? Highness, please . . . I beg you to reconsider."

"It's perfect, Max." Giana smiled. "We'll become the staff."

He bit back another groan, but he couldn't prevent his wince. Princess Giana's last attempt at domesticity had been an unmitigated disaster. She'd set herself and the palace kitchens in Christianberg on fire in a failed attempt to master the art of French cuisine. She hadn't been burned, but in her efforts to gain practical experience in homemaking skills, the princess had reduced the goose she'd been preparing to ash, and her skirts and the oven had suffered irreparable damage. The palace chef, always temperamental at best, had refused to continue the princess's cooking lessons and had forbidden Her Royal Highness from entering his domain. Even Isobel, who was the most forgiving of souls, forbade the princess to try her hand at meal preparation, saying they could not afford to sacrifice the lodge's only working cookstove.

Max tried again. "Your Highness, I beg you to remember your Sixteenth."

Giana's smile faded. According to Karolyan custom, young girls born to common families could not marry until they reached the age of six and ten. In order to prepare for that momentous rite of passage, they spent their fifteenth year learning the skills they would need to care for a husband and family. Although the custom excluded females born to the nobility, who were often betrothed before they reached the age of consent, Giana was the exception. As heir apparent to the throne, she was expected to set an example and encourage every girl born in the principality of Karolya to prepare for her Sixteenth by learning to cook and sew and clean. Prince Christian and Princess May had arranged for the palace chef to teach her to cook and for individual members of the staff to teach her ordinary housekeeping skills. "That was an accident, Max."

"Of course it was, Your Highness, but the fact remains that you have no practical experience in staffing a hunting lodge."

"I've greater practical experience, Max. *I* grew up in a palace."

"Growing up in a palace and working in a palace are two very different things."

She frowned at the secretary. "I am aware of that. But I've watched the staff. And I do have some experience aside from cooking. I learned to perform other vital tasks in preparation for my Sixteenth. I swept and mopped the floor and dusted furniture and helped beat the rugs, and I washed dishes and clothes."

She neglected to mention that those lessons had come to an end when she left her lawn nightgowns and delicate undergarments soaking in lye and forgot to rinse the floor of the entry to her father's reception hall after washing it. The lye soap had eaten holes in all of her underclothes, and the palace seamstresses had had to work around the clock to make new ones, and a German ambassador had slipped and fallen on the hard marble floor leading into the reception hall, sending two Papal emissaries skidding across the floor, where they'd landed at the feet of the Chancellor of the Exchequer. Papa had laughed about it later, saying the ambassador had rolled through the emissaries like a bowling ball through pins, but he'd declared her lessons in scrubbing floors and doing laundry at an end.

Her other lessons continued, and two days later she accidentally demolished several pieces of her mother's priceless Venetian crystal by plopping them into scalding hot dishwater.

A week after that she'd unpropped the lid of the grand piano, dropping it onto the fingers of the Russian counsel while practicing her dusting in the Music Room, and shattered one Ming Dynasty horse when she knocked it off its pedestal while beating the dust from a tapestry chair. The next day her father had instructed that her lessons be confined to sewing, then immediately revised that order to exclude sewing done by machine. From that day forward, her homemaking skills were directed toward the traditional ladylike arts of the nobility—menu planning, flower arranging, embroidery, and gardening. The palace topiaries had suffered slight damage, the goldfish had been fed more often than usual, and a few of the roses had been pruned too enthusiastically, but her name was read along with all the other girls in Christianberg who marked their Sixteenth with a bouquet of white flowers and a silver pin in the shape of a bouquet, inscribed with the year and the Karolyan motto: *love, duty, family.* The silver pin had been her mother's idea—a commemoration given to all the young women in the land upon the occasion of their sixteenth birthday.

Giana had worn hers ever since. She cherished her pin, placing as much value on it as she did the Karolyan Crown Jewels. With the exception of that silver pin and the locket her mother had given her on her twentieth birthday, everything she had— her wealth, her titles, her position in life—had all been awarded to her by virtue of her birth. But her silver pin had been earned. She had worked for it. She reached up and traced the familiar contours through the bodice of her gown. She didn't dare wear it where anyone might see it and inquire about it, so she wore it pinned to her chemise, just above the edge of her corset, close to where her locket hung around her neck, suspended from a fine gold chain. The Seal of State hung on a sturdier chain fastened about her waist where no one would ever see it. "I earned my pin."

"Yes, Your Highness, but . . ." Max stared into his princess's shining blue eyes. He couldn't, in good conscience, recommend a course of action that he feared might expose her identity and compromise her safety. But he couldn't refuse her, either.

"We can do this, Max."

"Princess, have you considered that by taking the work meant for the surrounding villagers, you may deprive them of wages and the livelihoods they need to survive?"

Giana hesitated. She hadn't considered that. And, in truth, she had no wish to deprive the crofters of badly needed wages. She had had no idea, when she arrived, that Scottish Highlanders were so impoverished or that her godmother, Queen Victoria, had failed to provide her beloved Highland people with a means of earning a sufficient living. Giana looked at her adviser. "We—I—" She was trying to learn to use the singular pronoun, but it was very hard to remember to be an "I" rather than the "we" she had always been. "I shan't accept wages."

"Oh, but you must, Your Highness," Max informed her. "To do otherwise would raise suspicions. These days no one works as a domestic except as a means of earning wages."

"Then we—I—shall donate my wages to charity. You and Gordon shall arrange for them to go to the needy so that I might become an anonymous benefactor."

"Very good, Your Highness." Max didn't have the heart to tell her that the meager wage she would earn as a domestic would do very little to alleviate the suffering of the poor.

"The staff, of course, shall keep whatever they earn. Isobel and Langstrom shall resume their roles as housekeeper and butler. Josef shall be in charge of the stable. Brenna and I shall be the maids, and you shall be the lodge steward."

Max cleared his throat. "I believe that is the position Gordon currently holds, Highness."

"Oh." She thought a moment. "Then you shall be the . . ." She frowned, searching her brain for the common equivalent for the title of Lord Chamberlain, the head of the royal household. "Overseer."

"I beg your pardon, Your Royal Highness, but *paid* employees do not require an overseer. I believe that, in English, the term is most commonly used to describe the taskmasters assigned to direct slaves and convicts."

Giana felt the heat rise in her cheeks. "We didn't mean to insult you, Max. We—I—only meant that you shall be whatever it is that Scottish commoners call the Lord Chamberlain," she pronounced. "You shan't be just the Master of the Household, you shall be the person responsible for the maintenance and staffing of the royal residence—wherever that may be—in exile and when we return to Karolya."

Her announcement brought tears to Max's eyes. For nearly four hundred years Gudrun men had been assigned to the Prince of Saxe-Wallerstein-Karolya's household, and not one of them had ever risen above the position of Private Secretary to His or Her Serene Highness. His princess had, in one sentence, promoted him to the highest office any member of his family had ever achieved. Or ever hoped to achieve because the Lord Chamberlain was the highest-ranking member in the royal household, answering only to the royal family.

He bowed his head. "I am deeply honored, Princess."

Giana managed a sad smile. "You deserve far better," she said. "The position of Lord Chamberlain isn't much of an honor at the moment. We've only a borrowed royal residence and a staff of six for you to supervise, but we hope to make it up to you when we return to the palace at Christianberg."

"You need not worry about making anything up to me, Your Highness," Max told her. "I'm honored to serve you in any capacity."

"And *I* am honored to have you." She stood up. "I shall require help," she said softly. "Although I earned my Sixteenth pin, I do not, as you reminded me, have quite enough practical experience to attend to all of the duties necessary to run a hunting lodge. Although I'm extremely proficient in mopping and dusting, my skills in cooking and laundry are not as proficient. You may secure additional staff from among the crofters to instruct and assist us."

Max winced again. "Of course, it shall be as you command, Princess. But may I suggest that Your Highness might put her skills to better use in a supervisory capacity?"

Giana shook her head. "I cannot occupy a higher position in the household than Langstrom and Isobel," she said. "They are supposed to be my parents. I fear that having a daughter supervise their activities might arouse suspicions as to our identity."

Max bowed. "You are correct, Princess."

"Then assemble the other guests and inform them of the owner's arrival." Giana reached out and placed her palm against Max's cheek.

"Guests, Princess?" He looked up and lifted an eyebrow in surprise.

"Guests for one more night," she explained. "For tomorrow we become staff." She gifted Max with mischievous smile. "I may be a Princess, but even *I* noticed that none of the staff normally occupied bedchambers on the same floor as the family." Giana didn't know about the accommodations of the other members of her little entourage, but she suspected that the rooms they occupied bore little resemblance to the room she had chosen for herself—the one with the large marble fireplace and a massive four-poster bed piled high with feather mattresses.

"There is still time for you to change your mind, Your Royal Highness, and avoid the attic." He winked at her. "The position of housekeeper includes a private room."

"I'm tempted," she replied honestly, "because I shall hate to give up that wonderful bed, but Isobel will be a better housekeeper than I."

"Isobel will have no need of the housekeeper's quarters. She's Langstrom's wife. She'll share his bedchamber."

"And I will share a bedchamber in the attic with Brenna."

Max shook his head. "If you feel you must, Your Highness."

"I must." She laughed. "But not until tomorrow."

Chapter 4

A Princess of the Blood Royal never disagrees with those of higher rank, or expresses a difference of opinion to those of lesser rank.

—MAXIM 201: PROTOCOL AND COURT ETIQUETTE OF PRINCESSES OF THE BLOOD ROYAL OF THE HOUSE OF SAXE-WALLERSTEIN-KAROLYA, AS DECREED BY HIS SERENE HIGHNESS, PRINCE KAROL I, 1432.

"*Open up!*" *Adam banged his fists against the* solid oak front door, and then began a rapid tattoo with the brass doorknocker. "Open up!"

By the time he reached the front door of Larchmont Lodge, the light mist that had greeted him in at the train station in Glasgow had become a torrential downpour with wind gusts that threatened to sweep him off the steps. Holding on to the doorknocker with one hand to brace himself against the gale-force winds, he fumbled in his coat pocket for the front door key. Bascombe hadn't had the key on him when he'd lost the deed to the place to Adam in a high-stakes poker game during his tour of Nevada and the American West. Adam hadn't wanted to accept the deed in the first place. He enjoyed winning his opponents' cash as long as he knew they could afford to lose it, but the thought of winning family property made him uncomfortable. His attempts to excuse Lord Bascombe's debt had been rebuffed. The man had insisted he accept the lodge as payment for his losses, and Adam had been compelled to do so. He'd filed the deed away in his safe and had all but forgotten about it until a key to the front door arrived by mail some three months later along with a note detailing the out-buildings and the furnishings and informing Adam that although the lodge was no longer fully staffed, a caretaker named Gordon Ross remained in residence to look after the place.

When he'd ridden onto the grounds, Adam had thought the lodge was empty. He'd sent a telegram to the caretaker from London instructing him to hire a staff and make the lodge ready for his arrival, but that didn't mean the man had done it or if he'd received the telegram telling him to do it. Murphy had tried to warn him when they left the train in Glasgow, suggesting they spend the night in a hotel in the city and send another telegram before continuing the journey into the Highlands, but Adam wouldn't hear of it. He'd been cooped up long enough—first on the ship, then in London, and finally on the train. He was ready to see the countryside, ready to see Larchmont Lodge and weigh its commercial appeal.

Because he didn't want to be shot for trespassing, Adam had planned to go to the Ross's cottage first to apprise the man of his arrival. He'd meant to ride around to where he knew the caretaker's cottage sat some distance from the main house at the back of the property, but a flicker of light through the window of the lodge caught his eye. It was late, and although no one hurried across the yard with an umbrella and a lantern to greet him, the light at the window and the smell of chimney smoke told him that lodge was inhabited. It seemed that Gordon Ross had gotten his telegram after all. The staff—if there was staff—had most likely retired for the night, but someone was inside the lodge, and he might as well join whoever it was—after all, he owned the place.

Adam let go of the brass knocker, reached up, and readjusted the brim of his hat and the collar of his mackintosh in an effort to redirect the steady stream of rain dripping down his neck. He shivered as a gust of wind blew across the lawn, but he managed to fit the front door key into the lock. He was wet, cold, and thoroughly road weary and had spent the last few miles of the journey looking forward to a roaring fire, a hot meal, and a bed. Adam knew that he might have to do without those comforts tonight, but not without a fight.

"I know you're in there." He lifted his hand to bang on the

door once again. "Open up!" Adam shouted one final warning, then turned the key in the lock and pushed open the door.

The door flew open, crashing against the interior wall with a thud that shook the frame. The key bounced out of the lock and skidded across the marble entry while a man and a woman dressed in nightclothes leapt back to avoid the torrent of cold rain. Adam stepped over the threshold, grabbed hold of the front door, and slammed it shut. He leaned his back against it, breathing heavily as he removed his hat and raked his fingers through his hair.

"I'm Adam McKendrick." Adam dropped his hat on the marble-topped table in the entry hall and offered his hand to the other man. "You must be Gordon Ross."

The older man retreated, shaking his head as he stepped away from Adam's outstretched hand.

Adam withdrew his hand and frowned. "Then, who?"

The woman stepped forward, responding with the answer to Adam's question before the man could form a response. "Staff," she replied in a thick Scottish burr. "I'm Isobel Langstrom and this is my husband, Albert. We're part of the staff."

"Staff . . . ," Adam breathed a sigh of relief. "Thank God." He removed his mackintosh, shaking the water from the folds as he glanced around for a place to hang it.

Albert took the coat from him.

"Thanks." Adam left the couple standing in the foyer and started up the staircase. He took the stairs two at a time. "I've been traveling all day. I'm wet, cold, and tired. I'd like a roaring fire and a soft bed as soon as possible. And please see that my horse is tended to right away." Pausing at the top of the landing, he asked, "Where's the master suite?"

"Last one on the left," Isobel replied automatically, "but, my lord . . . wait . . ." She started up the stairs behind him.

Adam waved her off. "No need to show me," he said. "I'll find it."

He heard the low noise and recognized it as a warning growl seconds before he opened the door of the master suite. "What the devil—" The air left Adam's lungs in a rush and a series of white-hot stars danced against a black background as the base of his skull thudded against the hard floor.

He couldn't see his attacker until he was flat on his back with a hundred plus pounds of a massive animal—an ugly shaggy-coated brute that appeared to be some sort of missing link—a cross between a dog and a Shetland pony—standing on his chest. The soft glow of the lamplight illuminated the brindle-colored fur on the dog's legs and the white fur of his underbelly. A flash of light sparkled off the dog's neck, and Adam realized he was staring at a black velvet collar trimmed with gold braid and studded with what appeared to be paste diamonds. He lifted his head to get a better look, and the dog growled another warning.

"Wagner! Cease!"

The beast was obedient, responding immediately to the command. Unfortunately, he responded instantly by lying down. Adam's head connected with the floor once more. He let out a groan and another whoosh of air as the dog's elbows pressed against his stomach.

"Wagner, you may have killed him!"

The animal whined at the rebuke, shifting his weight as he buried his nose in the hollow beneath Adam's left ear and his elbows deeper into Adam's ribs.

"Not quite." Adam gasped the words.

"Good," she breathed. "You are alive."

Blinking hard to clear the stars from his eyes, Adam looked up and beheld his savior standing in the center of the bed. He groaned again, this time in abject disappointment. His savior was blond and beautiful and female, and if the length of her legs was anything to go by, very nearly tall enough to look him in the eye. Her body, silhouetted through her long white nightgown by the light from the table lamp behind her, was slim and curved in all the right places. A thick rope of tightly braided hair hung past her hips and she bore the delicate, classical facial features that had graced the canvases of great painters for centuries. He couldn't see her feet, buried as they were in the mound of bedclothes, but he supposed they were as classically beautiful as the rest of her. "What the hell is this? Who the hell are you? And what are you doing in my bed?"

Her eyes widened in shock. "Wagner is one of the finest

wolfhounds ever bred, and I am Her Ser—" she began in a haughty tone that set Adam's teeth on edge.

"Our daughter!" The shout echoed through the room, covering whatever it was the girl was about to say.

Adam turned his head in time to see Isobel rush through the doorway. He looked from Isobel to the Amazon standing on the bed. The top of Isobel's head was several inches below his chin, and Albert was only an inch or so taller than his wife. "Your *daughter*?" Adam's tone of voice held a healthy measure of disbelief.

"Yes," Isobel and Albert nodded in unison. "Our daughter, Georgiana Langstrom." Isobel turned to the girl. "Georgiana, meet Mr. Adam McKendrick from America, the new owner of Larchmont Lodge."

"How do you do, Mr. McKendrick?" she asked.

He stared at her as she extended her hand with the grace of a prima ballerina and waited patiently for him to take it. Adam rolled his eyes. Beauty appeared to hold an entitlement all its own. His sister, Kirstin, would have responded in exactly the same manner. All the world was a stage—populated by blondes aspiring to be great tragediennes. Adam didn't know whether to laugh or to cry, to shake hands with her or crawl to his knees and pay homage. He settled for indignation. "How do I do? How do I do?" He sputtered. "I'm lying flat on my back in the middle of the floor with a hundred-pound dog on my chest. How do you think I do?"

"Rude." Georgiana narrowed her gaze at him. "And there's no need to be rude, Mr. McKendrick."

"Really?" He tried to shove the dog off him, but the beast refused to budge. "I can think of a dozen reasons—beginning with him." He glared at the wolfhound.

"Wagner! Off!" She pointed to the dog, then patted her thigh. "Come!"

Wagner obeyed, first by standing on Adam, then stepping over him in order to hurry to his mistress's side.

Adam pushed himself to his feet.

Wagner growled in warning once again and Adam growled back.

Georgiana clucked her tongue at him. " 'Manners maketh man,' " she quoted. "William of Wykeham."

" 'She speaks, yet she says nothing,' " he retorted. "William Shakespeare." Adam smiled. "And if we've concluded this war of quotations, I'll take the opportunity to remind you that you haven't answered my question."

"What question was that, Mr. McKendrick?" Georgiana pretended ignorance.

"What are you doing in my bed?"

"We didn't know when to expect you, sir," Isobel hastened to explain. "The attic quarters need cleaning and repair and the beds are short and narrow . . ." She sighed. "And, as you can see, our Giana is taller than most girls. So tall that her feet hang off the mattresses." She shrugged her shoulders. "But the master suite has a huge bed, and we saw no harm in allowing her to sleep in comfort until you arrived. If that has offended you, then I beg your pardon, sir."

"You must not blame my parents for wanting to provide the best for me," Giana told him.

"Why not?" Adam lifted an eyebrow in query.

Giana smiled her most angelic smile and fluttered her eyelashes at him. "To do otherwise would be against their nature."

The smile and the fluttering lashes almost worked, but Adam had been raised in a household of consummate actresses. Wheedling and coy feminine wiles no longer had the power to sway him. Especially when he sensed that employing them wasn't part of the Amazon's nature. He liked her better when she challenged him. "Is its size the only reason you happened to be in my bed?"

Giana blinked. "What other reason could there be?"

"I'm a very wealthy man," Adam said.

"How very nice for you," Giana politely replied.

Adam inhaled sharply, swallowed his breath, and began to cough.

Giana waited patiently for him to recover from his fit of coughing. She stared at him with an expectant look on her face.

"I'm also young and healthy."

"Then you are to be congratulated, Mr. McKendrick, for I

understand that Scotland can be a very harsh land. You are very fortunate to have youth and health on your side, for one cannot overestimate their importance. I feel quite certain that those qualities will go a long way in alleviating the hardships one encounters here."

Adam was fascinated by the words that came out of her mouth each time she spoke. Her words sounded like English, but he couldn't quite grasp the meaning. Nor did she appear to grasp the meaning of his. Maybe it was because he was American and she was . . . well . . . foreign . . . but the Amazon couldn't take a hint. "I'm also generally considered to be reasonably attractive," he informed her.

She cocked her head to one side and studied him. "I do not agree."

"You don't?"

"No, I do not." She sighed. "I do not wish to find fault with the opinions of the people who have commented on your appearance, but I would have to say that you are more than reasonably attractive—"

Adam grinned. "More?"

"Of course," she replied matter-of-factly. "I have only just made your acquaintance, and know nothing of your character, but I would judge your outward appearance to be *very* attractive."

"Is that so?" Adam gave her a slow, appraising glance.

"Yes, Mr. McKendrick, it is so." She frowned, unable to understand why he insisted on questioning her answers or why he appeared to have difficulty understanding her English. Although it was not her native tongue, Giana knew her command of the English language was exceptional because her mother had taught her to speak it, and her mother had been a cousin to Queen Victoria.

"You must have been aware that I'm a bachelor."

"No, Mr. McKendrick, I know nothing of the details of your private life." Giana frowned even more. "What have they to do with me?"

"Let's see," Adam drawled sarcastically, raising his hand and pretending to count on his fingers. "What *could* the details of my private life have to do with you?" He paused for effect.

"Especially since I'm young, healthy, wealthy, and reasonably—no, make that *very*—attractive, unmarried, and the owner of the bed you're currently occupying." He looked up at her. "I would have to be extremely unenlightened not to realize that, in most circles, I'm considered to be quite a catch."

"In most circles, perhaps," Giana informed him. "But not in mine."

Adam cocked an eyebrow once again. "Indeed?" He'd have to be an extremely unenlightened man not to realize that the daughter of his new housekeeper and butler had just declared her circle closed to him. Adam had deliberately baited her, but her answer still stung, and Adam didn't know whether to find the idea amusing or pathetic.

Isobel stepped forward. "Come, Giana, we'll leave the McKendrick to settle in here while we find you another bed."

"Wait." Adam glanced from mother to daughter. "Tell me what you've heard about the *Bountiful Baron?*"

Isobel was clearly puzzled by the demand. "I don't understand."

Adam turned to Giana. "What about you?"

Giana lifted her chin. "That baron is not among my acquaintances."

"Then you can stay where you are," he said. "For tonight. But tomorrow you and the dog find someplace else to sleep." Adam lifted his chin and gave her his most winning smile. "You're welcome to sleep indoors, but fancy collar or no, the dog sleeps outside."

Giana glared at him, her nostrils flaring in anger. "You cannot . . ." she sputtered.

He grinned. "Sorry, sweetheart, but I outrank you. You may be tall, but I'm taller and I own the place." Adam turned his back on Giana and headed for the bedroom door.

The other occupants of the room gasped.

"What?" Adam paused in the doorway and glanced over his shoulder at the Amazon standing in the center of his bed. Her mouth gaped open, and he noticed for the first time that the ribbons threaded through the neckline of her nightgown were black and untied.

Giana was stunned. She knew, even if he did not, that he was in the presence of royalty, and one simply did not turn one's back on royalty. Since she could not bring her royal status to his attention, she settled for chastising him for his rudeness. "Manners, Mr. McKendrick," she called out in a too-sweet singsong voice. "Shall we find you some? Along with your warm fire and comfortable bed? Because you seem to have forgotten yours again."

"Not at all." Adam put his thumb and forefinger up to his forehead, inclined his head, and pretended to tip his hat to her. "Pleasure meeting you, George."

Chapter 5

A Princess of the Blood Royal calmly addresses the concerns of her loyal subjects.

—MAXIM 104: PROTOCOL AND COURT ETIQUETTE OF PRINCESSES OF THE BLOOD ROYAL OF THE HOUSE OF SAXE-WALLERSTEIN-KAROLYA, AS DE-CREED BY HIS SERENE HIGHNESS, PRINCE KAROL I, 1432.

"*George!*" Isobel propped her fists on her hips and sniffed her disapproval to Giana and the rest of the staff as they huddled around the kitchen table discussing the night's events.

The new owner of Larchmont Lodge had been fed and comfortably settled into a room in the opposite wing of the lodge more than an hour ago. Isobel and Albert had returned from tending to McKendrick's needs and promptly awakened Max, who insisted on rousing the rest of the staff in order to hold a family meeting to determine the best way to avert a crisis and proceed with the plan.

Giana politely covered her yawn with her hand. As far as she was concerned, the best way to proceed with the plan was to proceed. She saw no reason to rob the others of a few hours' sleep by holding a midnight meeting. But Max had wanted to make certain everyone knew of McKendrick's arrival and understood their roles, and Max had always been cautious and a stickler when it came to planning. Giana swallowed another yawn. If holding an urgent meeting on the crisis eased his mind, then she was willing to comply. But the fact remained that the crisis, if one could call it that, had already been averted. McKendrick had willingly accepted their explanations, and as long as McKendrick believed they were staff, they were safe. And McKendrick had no reason not to believe them. Isobel and Albert had made certain that he'd been fed and made comfortable in his room, and Josef had seen to the care and feeding of his horse in the barn.

Still, the family had been surprised and upset by McKendrick's unexpected arrival, and the least she could do as their leader was to listen to their worries and do her best to reassure them.

"The McKendrick called you George, Your Highness," Isobel repeated.

"So he did." A half-smile played at the corner of Giana's lips. Her mother had called her Fleur when she was growing up because, she said, Giana was the most precious bloom in the principality. Her father's name for her hadn't been quite as elegant. To him, she had always been Monkey. Her father had said it was because she'd come out of the womb all arms and legs, red-wrinkled face, and grasping hands. He'd told her that she hadn't looked like a princess at all and had more closely resembled the monkeys in the Christianberg zoo.

Giana sighed. She hadn't been called anything except Giana or Your Royal Highness since the night her father was mur . . . her father died. How she missed hearing her father's voice. Missed hearing the sound of his footsteps echoing down the marble halls of the palace at Christianberg, the clink of his dress spurs and the rattle of his scabbard as he hurried from room to room, greeting guests and attending to business. Her Royal Highness Princess Monkey. Her father was the only person who had ever called her that. And she'd loved it because it made her feel special. Because she was the heir apparent to a crown, everyone else in the world addressed her by her given names or by the title she held. Only her parents dared to call her anything else. Until now . . .

"And he insulted you," Albert said.

Giana frowned. He might have seemed insulting to Isobel and Josef, but she preferred to think of his manner as challenging rather than insulting. Except on rare occasions when Max did it, there was no one to question her decisions or challenge her ideals or opinions the way her parents had done.

There wasn't anyone to tease her or chastise her for her royal hauteur or remind her that her position in life existed so that she might serve, rather than be served. "When?"

"He deliberately turned his back on you, Your Highness," Albert explained.

"Oh, that." She'd dismissed his action as thoughtless and unintentional. He hadn't known he was in the presence of royalty or that turning his back on royalty was the height of insult, so the sight of the three of them—Isobel, Albert, and herself—standing in stunned silence with their mouths agape must have seemed quite strange. Giana smiled at the memory. "I rather doubt that Mr. McKendrick's *practical experience*"—she used her father's favorite expression—"with royalty is as great as yours or Isobel's."

"Turning his back on you wasn't the only insult he paid you, Your Highness," Isobel continued her list of grievances against the American. "He stared at you in a most impolite manner."

"Did he?" Giana asked.

Isobel nodded. "He stared at you as if he thought you were something on display in a sweet shop window. How is it that you did not notice?"

Giana smiled her mysterious princess smile—the one that said she knew a great deal more than she was telling. "Let's see," she said, mimicking Adam's drawl, "could it be because most everyone we've—I've—ever met stares at me as if I'm something on display in a shop window? And the fact is that I have *been* on display like merchandise in a shop window since the day I was born. Over the years I have grown quite immune to impolite stares. How is it that you failed to notice that?" She teased, reaching over to pat Isobel's hand.

"You've only us to protect you." Isobel glanced around the table and nodded at each of her companions, all of them subjects who had remained loyal to their beloved princess and the memory of her late parents. "We must have Max speak to the McKendrick about his presumptuous and forward manner toward you," Isobel said.

"No," Giana said. "Max must not speak to the McKendrick." She looked at the older woman. "Would you have had Max or Albert speak to my father or any other gentleman about his manner of speaking to a member of the female staff?"

"Of course not," Isobel answered. "But Prince Christian was the sovereign ruler of Karolya."

"Adam McKendrick is the sovereign ruler of Larchmont Lodge and all the land surrounding it," Giana replied. "We have no where else to go. We cannot risk discovery."

Isobel grudgingly admitted Giana was right, but she didn't have to like it. "That is true, Your Highness, but you should not allow him such familiarity."

"I could do nothing to prevent his familiarity. You told him that my name was Georgiana and that I was your daughter." She softened her tone of voice. "He's an *American*, Isobel, and unaccustomed to royalty." She shrugged her shoulders in a gesture her mother would have declared most unbecoming a princess. "As long as he thinks I'm a servant in his employ, you cannot expect him to address me properly or hold his ignorance of my royal heritage against him."

"Maybe not," Isobel conceded, "but we can certainly hold his *familiar* manner against him, Your Highness."

"I have already taken the man to task for his lack of manners, Isobel," Giana reminded her.

"I understand, Your Royal Highness, but as you said, he is an American ignorant of our ways"—she turned to the other members of the staff—"but we are not. We are Karolyan citizens. We cannot put any job above our duty to our princess and our duty is to serve and protect our princess first and foremost." Isobel narrowed her gaze. "One of the ways we shall protect our princess is by keeping watchful eyes on the McKendrick."

Chapter 6

The men and women in the Bountiful Baron's employ sing his praises.

—The First Installment of the True Adventures of the Bountiful Baron: Western Benefactor to Blond, Beautiful, and Betrayed Women written by John J. Bookman, 1874.

"*Good morning, sir.*"

Adam automatically grabbed at the bedclothes and yanked them from his waist to his chest. Good lord! His new housekeeper was as bad as his mother—barging into his room and waking him up without so much as a knock in warning. Keeping one hand on the covers to ensure his modesty remained intact, Adam raked his hand through his hair to smooth down the locks he knew, from experience, were standing on end.

Isobel struggled to keep from smiling. "I brought your breakfast, sir. And your clothes." She plopped the breakfast tray across his lap and pointed to the neatly pressed suit hanging on a brass hook on the open door of the mahogany wardrobe.

He frowned at her. "You're the last person I expected to see this morning, ma'am. Where is Albert? Why didn't he bring my clothes?"

"Albert is meeting with Max in the library. They're discussing the refurbishing of the servants' quarters and the hiring of additional staff from among those available in the village."

"Who is Max?"

"Private secretary to Her . . ." Isobel caught herself. "Your private secretary."

Adam shook his head. "I don't have a private secretary."

"Of course you do, sir," Isobel said. "Owners of hunting lodges always have private secretaries to attend to their correspondence and the correspondence of their guests."

"I attend to my own correspondence," Adam replied. "It's more private than employing a private secretary, and I prefer it that way."

His answer came as a surprise to Isobel. "But what of your guests, sir?"

Adam shrugged his shoulders. "If they wish to correspond with anyone, they'll have to write the letters themselves," he said. "I'm not going to do it."

"Of course not, sir," Isobel replied. "That would be an unthinkable breach of protocol—especially since it is Max's duty to attend to it for you."

"Max has no duty to attend to for me," Adam told her. "Because I don't have a private secretary."

Isobel turned and gestured toward the china pot sitting upon the breakfast tray. "How do you take your tea, sir?"

"I don't drink tea."

Isobel frowned. I can fetch you a cup of hot chocolate from the pot I made for Giana."

"Giana." Adam repeated aloud, rolling the name around on his tongue, liking the sound of it.

"Our daughter," Isobel reminded him. "You met her last night."

George. The Amazon. How could he forget? He smiled at the memory of the young woman standing in the center of the bed. He thought of her as an Amazon, not because she was masculine in any way, but because she was tall and beautiful and able to look a man in the eye. "I thought her name was . . ."

"Georgiana."

"George."

They spoke in unison and the housekeeper narrowed her gaze and frowned at him. "We call her Giana."

Adam lifted an eyebrow. "And you prepare a pot of hot chocolate for her each morning?"

"Of course, sir," Isobel replied. "Hot and frothy, just the way she likes it."

Adam snorted. "And deliver it on a tray to her bed."

She nodded. "Just as I delivered this one to you."

"Quite the little princess, isn't she?"

Isobel froze. "Sir?" The single query came out as a high-pitched squeak.

"I thought my mother spoiled my sisters, but you . . ." He shook his head. "You treat your daughter like a queen."

Isobel looked puzzled. "That is a mother's duty, is it not?"

"But your daughter . . ." He paused for a moment, as if he couldn't believe what he'd heard. "Georgiana gets the master suite, the largest bed, and chocolate hot and frothy just the way she likes it every morning."

"That's right, sir. Shall I fetch you a cup?" Isobel ventured.

Adam shook his head. "I prefer coffee."

"I'm sorry sir, but I didn't bring coffee. Only tea."

"Then I'll take tea," Adam replied, wincing as he did so.

"Very good, sir." She turned to the tray, filled a cup with steaming liquid from the china pot, and handed it to him.

He accepted the cup and saucer she handed to him but refused the milk and sugar she offered. "I take it straight." He swallowed a sip of the strong brew. It wasn't coffee, but it was hot and since it was all he could do to keep his teeth from chattering with cold, he drank it. "Thank you."

"You're welcome, sir."

"Not at all, sir," she replied. "I made an exception this morning because I thought you might appreciate having your clothes. But now that your man has arrived, I'm certain he will assume that duty."

"My man?" She had surprised him once again.

"Your valet, sir."

"I don't have a valet."

"Of course you do, sir. All gentlemen have valets to see to their wardrobes. Although I've never met an Irish one before." She thinned her lips in a disapproving line. "O'Brien, I believe he said. Murphy O'Brien. He arrived early this morning in a coach piled high with your luggage."

Adam laughed. "O'Brien isn't my valet," he replied. "He's

my friend." He poured himself another cup of tea, then lifted a piece of bacon from the rasher on the tray and scooped up a forkful of eggs.

Isobel sniffed. "You could ha' fooled me."

"Why do you say that?"

"Because the only men I've ever known who fussed that much over luggage were valets," she said.

Adam laughed again. "O'Brien has reason to be concerned about the luggage," he told her. "Because over half of it is his, and he spent a small fortune to procure it in time for the journey."

"Then he's a gentleman like yourself."

"I'm not sure either of us qualify for the title of gentleman," Adam said. "But he's my friend nonetheless. My closest friend." His voice held a warning note to remind Isobel that O'Brien was a friend and she was staff.

"Very good, sir." Isobel understood the warning. "I'll prepare a room for Mr. O'Brien." She bobbed a slight curtsy.

"Thank you."

"The staff will await you in the library, sir, when you've finished your breakfast and completed your morning ablutions."

Adam quirked an eyebrow in question.

"They expect to be presented, sir."

"Please ask the members of the staff to assemble in the library in half an hour," Adam instructed. "And ask Mr. O'Brien to join me here."

"Very good, sir."

Adam waited until the sound of the housekeeper's footsteps faded on the stairs before he lifted the breakfast tray off his lap and placed it on the table beside the bed. He flipped back the covers and climbed out of bed. Pulling the coverlet off the bed, Adam wrapped it around his waist, holding it with one fist as he padded barefoot across the cold floor to the privacy screen in the corner of the bedchamber.

He answered the call of nature, then made his way to where his suit hung on the door of the wardrobe. The top drawer of the wardrobe was opened, and his shirt and linen undergarments were dried and neatly folded inside it. His boots stood beside the wardrobe, and his leather saddlebags hung on a brass hook inside the wardrobe door.

Adam let the coverlet fall to the floor as he removed his trousers from their hook. He stepped into his underwear and trousers and pulled his shirt over his head. Still shivering with cold, he retrieved his boots and saddlebags, silently thanking the brave soul who had ventured out in the cold rain to tend to his horse and claim his belongings. Adam hopped from one foot to the other as he crossed over to the fire and set his boots on the hearth to warm. He stoked the peat fire, stirring the embers into a small flame before he made his way back across the room to the washstand. Christ! He was so cold his teeth were chattering. No wonder Bascombe sold the place. The rest of the world was enjoying a moderately warm summer, but a man could freeze to death in Larchmont Lodge in Scotland unless he kept a close proximity to the fire, and Adam had already learned that peat fires tended to smoke more than they heated.

Sucking in a breath, Adam broke the thin film of ice on the water in the china pitcher on the washstand. He poured the icy water into the bowl, gritted his teeth, removed his mug and brush and a bar of soap from his saddlebags, and prepared to shave. Adam managed a grim laugh. He thought he'd put this particular brand of discomfort behind him. When he'd struck it rich working his silver claim, he vowed he'd have hot water to shave in every morning for the rest of his life. But he hadn't counted on winning a hunting lodge in the wilds of Scotland. He washed his face in the cold water and grimaced at his reflection in the mirror. What good was a staff when no one thought to provide him with hot water for shaving? Unless that was one of the duties of a valet . . .

"Where are you, McKendrick?"

Adam recognized the sound of O'Brien's hearty chuckle before his friend opened the bedroom door. He dipped his shaving brush in the basin of water and rubbed it across the bar of shaving soap. Murphy announced his arrival by entering the room.

"Hold it!"

Adam froze.

"Yer handsome face will look like raw meat if you shave in water from that." He nodded toward the bowl. "Especially if it's been sitting overnight. Besides, the bossy little woman downstairs told me I should do my duty and bring this up to you." O'Brien held up a kettle, its handle wrapped to keep from burning him.

Adam reached for it.

"Careful, boyo, it's boiling," Murphy warned as he handed the kettle over.

"Thank God," Adam breathed. He poured hot water into the basin, tested the temperature, then added some more. "I was ready to sell my soul for hot water."

"Good." Murphy grinned. "You can pay me for it later."

Adam met O'Brien's grin with one of his own. Trust Murphy to take him up on his offer to pay. He turned his attention to the mirror and began to lather his face.

"Well, boyo, what do you think?" O'Brien asked. "I don't know about it's commercial appeal, but this is some setup you've got here." He gave a low whistle of admiration and lifted a scone from one of the plates on Adam's breakfast tray. Murphy slathered the scone with butter and marmalade, swallowed the biscuit in three bites, then crossed the room and stretched out on Adam's bed. He stacked his hands beneath his head and watched while Adam shaved. "Have you seen the place?" Murphy whistled again.

Adam frowned. "I arrived during a storm. I saw gale-force winds, freezing rain, the outside of the lodge, and the shadow of a barn."

"I don't know how to break the news to you, but you didn't win the deed to a hunting lodge," Murphy told him. "You won the deed to an estate that takes up half the bloody county." He scratched his forehead. "I should be so lucky."

"Why aren't you?" Adam deadpanned. "I thought the Irish were famous for their luck."

Murphy chuckled. "It never applied to the common Irish, only the wealthy landlords."

Adam finished shaving, wiped his face on a length of toweling, then pointed to a garment hanging in the wardrobe. "Hand me that waistcoat, will you?"

Murphy reached up and lifted the waistcoat off its hook and tossed it to Adam.

Adam caught the waistcoat in one hand and shrugged into it. "Thanks."

"Anything for you, Your Lordship," Murphy replied in an exaggerated British accent.

"I'm not Your Lordship."

"All right, then, Mr. McKendrick, what say we saddle up and spend the morning surveying your estate, evaluating its potential?" O'Brien rolled off the bed and onto his feet.

"Can't," Adam answered.

"Too sore to ride?" O'Brien speculated.

Adam shook his head. "I have to inspect the staff," he answered in a near perfect imitation of Murph's exaggerated English accent.

"Inspect the staff?" O'Brien nearly doubled over laughing.

"A place this size has to have staff," Adam reminded him. "And I've been informed that they're waiting for me to pass judgment."

"Well, lead on, boyo, I wouldn't miss this for the world."

"Of course you wouldn't," Adam agreed. "Because I believe you've just become a part of it."

"What?" O'Brien's mirth died a quick dead.

"The bossy little woman who sent you up here with the hot water is the housekeeper," Adam explained. "And she thinks you're my valet."

"Your *what?*"

"My gentleman's gentleman."

O'Brien cast a suspicious glance Adam's way. "And just how would she get an idea like that?"

Adam held up his hands. "Don't look at me. You're the one who gave her the idea."

"Impossible!" Murphy scoffed.

"And I quote, 'The only men I've ever known who fussed over luggage that much were valets.' "

"Criminy," Murphy swore. "That luggage cost me a bloody fortune!"

"I explained that," Adam said. "And I told her you were my friend and traveling companion, but apparently she chose to believe otherwise." He clucked his tongue. "It's amazing, really. I thought she'd take one look at you and know."

"Why should she?" O'Brien demanded. "What's wrong with the way I look?"

"Nothing," Adam teased. "Except your clothes, your hair, and your manner." O'Brien's clothes were the latest fashion and made of fine cloth, but he would never be considered stylish. He was too big, too brawny, and too ruggedly handsome to fit the image of a valet.

"What about them?"

"There's no way in hell you'll ever pass inspection."

Chapter 7

A Princess of the Blood Royal is obliged to attend all court presentations.

—MAXIM 8: PROTOCOL AND COURT ETIQUETTE OF PRINCESSES OF THE
BLOOD ROYAL OF THE HOUSE OF SAXE-WALLERSTEIN-KAROLYA, AS DE-
CREED BY HIS SERENE HIGHNESS PRINCE KAROL I, 1432.

And all other mundane and tedious presentations...

—ADDENDUM TO MAXIM 8: HER SERENE HIGHNESS, PRINCESS MAY,

1850.

The staff of Larchmont Lodge weren't the only
ones under scrutiny. Adam couldn't walk down the halls
of the lodge without feeling the fine hairs on the back of his
neck prickle in reaction. The walls lining the central corridor
were hung with massive portraits of long-dead ancestors of the
previous owners, and dozens of pairs of painted eyes seemed
to follow his progress as he made his way from his bedchamber to the library.

And the sensation of being watched increased as he entered
the comfortable oak and leather confines of the lodge's magnificent library and glanced around to find eight—nine, if he
counted Murphy O'Brien's—pairs of actual eyes staring at
him.

Albert Langstrom stepped forward, bowed to Adam, then
turned to another slightly older gentleman with jet-black hair
liberally streaked with silver and a ramrod-straight posture. He
spoke in a language Adam didn't understand, which seemed

odd for a Scottish staff. Odder still, since Adam thought he understood English—even English spoken with a Scot's burr. When he finished speaking, whatever he was speaking, Langstrom took his place in line beside his wife.

The older man turned to Adam. "My name is Maximillian . . . umm . . . Langstrom," he said. "I am Your Lordship's private secretary. You may call me Max. My brother"—he paused ever-so-slightly—"Albert begs your pardon for his failure to perform his duty as expected, but his English is limited. He asks that you allow me to stand in his stead and perform the required introductions." Max's English was heavily accented, but Adam had no trouble understanding it. "May I present to you the remaining staff of Larchmont Lodge?"

They stood in a line in the center of the room—obviously according to position and rank, rather than height.

"You're not Scottish?"

Max shook his head. "Gordon and Isobel are Scottish. They are brother and sister. The rest of us are from continental households, most recently from the late Countess of Brocavia's household."

"There are only eight of you?" Adam's tone of voice mirrored his surprise at finding the lodge so thinly staffed.

"Eight at present, my lord . . ."

Adam held up his hand. "I know you're accustomed to addressing Lord Bascombe as my lord, but I'm an American, not a lord."

"But, my lord—"

"McKendrick," Adam told him, extending his hand for a handshake. "Adam McKendrick."

Max glanced at Adam's outstretched hand. Adam clamped his teeth together as the older man accepted his hand in a brief handshake, then quickly released it and stepped away. Max's discomfit at being asked to shake his employer's hand was patently apparent.

"Jesus!" Adam swore beneath his breath. "You'd think I was contagious. Haven't they heard that 'all men are created equal'?"

"Easy, boyo," O'Brien whispered, placing a hand on

Adam's shoulder to steady him. "You're in the old world now."

Adam shot him a look of disbelief. "I realized that."

"Then you should realize that here America is a distant dream. It's not you. In America all men are created equal. Here, they occupy different stations in life," Murphy told him. "Act like a bloody lord and they'll respect ya. Act like an American and they'll look down on ya."

Adam focused his attention on Maximillian Langstrom. "Sir." He didn't raise his voice, but spoke in a firm tone loud enough for everyone to hear. "Not my lord. I prefer to be called sir."

"Yes, sir." The male members of the staff bowed their heads, and the female members of the staff bobbed a brief curtsy—with one notable exception.

George stood straight and tall with her shoulders back and her head held at a regal angle. Unusual in a girl so tall. His sisters had tended to hunch their shoulders and to slouch to keep from appearing taller than the boys they knew from school and church. That habit had been a continuous source of concern in the household. Adam remembered his mother commanding his sisters to stand straight and tall and to look a fellow right in the eye, forcing them to walk around the house with books on their heads to make certain they did so. Unfortunately, looking the fellows right in the eye was the problem, since like George, his sisters tended to tower over their would-be beaus.

But George appeared to have no qualms about standing straight and tall and looking a fellow right in the eye. Even when she wasn't supposed to. Adam bit the inside of his cheek to keep from smiling as a younger, smaller girl elbowed George in the ribs and motioned for her to curtsy.

Langstrom rushed to cover George's gaffe by clearing his throat and resuming the inspection. "Would you care to introduce your man, my . . . sir . . . and have him join us so that we might continue our inspection?"

He couldn't be serious. He couldn't really believe that O'Brien was a valet. Or could he? Adam glanced at Maximillian and realized that Langstrom was entirely serious. Ap-

parently, Isobel hadn't believed him when he'd told her that
O'Brien wasn't his valet because she hadn't seen fit to pass
the word along to her husband or brother-in-law. "O'Brien is
my friend. He's not my—"

"I'm honored that you consider me so, sir," O'Brien interrupted smoothly. Leaving his place beside Adam, O'Brien
crossed the Turkish carpet and stepped into line with the rest
of the staff. Turning to Langstrom, he replied in a thick Irish
brogue, "My name is Murphy O'Brien and I'm proud to serve
Mr. McKendrick not just as his valet, but as his gentleman's
gentleman."

Adam lifted an eyebrow at Murph's bold claim, but he
didn't dispute it.

A couple of inches shorter than Adam, O'Brien stood at
least a head taller than everyone else in line except George,
who stood at the end of the line, with the dog seated beside
her. O'Brien gingerly took his place on the other side of the
dog. He and George stood shoulder to shoulder with the wolfhound sandwiched between them. Adam watched as O'Brien
cautiously patted the wolfhound on the head and winked at
the girl peeking around George to get a better look at him.

Adam was doing his best to give the introduction ceremony
the attention Max and the rest of the staff thought it deserved,
but his stomach tightened at O'Brien's flirtatious manner and
Adam gestured for the older man to precede him down the
line. "Shall we continue?"

"Very well." With one quick nod of his head Maximillian
Langstrom acknowledged O'Brien's introduction and dismissed it. There was, after all, a hierarchy and a schedule to
maintain.

Max gave another of his characteristic bows. He cleared his
throat and walked to Albert. "Sir, may I present to you Albert
Langstrom, butler at Larchmont Lodge, last in service as head
of household to the late countess of Brocavia."

"Albert." Adam acknowledged the butler.

"Sir." Albert inclined his head.

Max stepped down the line to the next person. "Sir, may I
present to you Isobel Langstrom, housekeeper at Larchmont

Lodge, last in service as housekeeper to the late countess of Brocavia."

"Mrs. L.," Adam said.

"Sir." Isobel bobbed a curtsey as Max and Adam moved to the next person.

Max continued down the line introducing Isobel's brother the gamekeeper, Gordon Ross.

His official title was houndsman and gamekeeper, but Gordon Ross had been responsible for taking care of the lodge in the absence of its previous owner, Lord Bascombe. He was the man Adam had telegraphed requesting that the lodge be suitably staffed. It came as no surprise to Adam that, upon such short notice, the gamekeeper would turn to his family for help in staffing the house, but it came as something of a surprise to learn that an experienced household staff with such sterling qualifications and references had been available.

Unfortunately, there weren't enough former members of the countess of Brocavia's to go around. The grounds and stable staff consisted of two men: Gordon Ross and the master of the stables, Josef Langstrom, who was Max's son.

Adam turned to Gordon Ross. "I'd like a tour of the grounds and the stables as soon as possible. If the property proves suitable for my purposes, you'll need to hire more men to tend the grounds and the horses." He glanced at Josef. "There will be more work than the two of you to handle."

"Understood, sir."

Adam nodded in reply and moved to stand before the two remaining members of the household staff: Brenna and Georgiana Langstrom, Albert and Isobel's daughters, who worked as housemaids.

The younger petite Brenna looked nothing like her sister. She was short and small-boned with brown hair and eyes. She appeared shy and favored her mother more than her father.

Adam knew that sisters didn't necessarily have to look alike to be sisters, but coming from a family with four sisters who were pairs of identical twins made the other reality seem strange. In his family Adam was the different one. In George's family she was. It gave them an unexpected bond.

And Adam supposed the bond also extended to the dog, which

bore no resemblance to any breed of dog he had ever encountered. He stared at the animal sitting quietly beside George. Beauty and the beast.

"What about the beast?" He asked the question of Max, but Adam kept his gaze on George to see if she would speak for herself and for her pet.

The girl opened her mouth, but Max smoothly interrupted. "The beast, as you call him, sir, is an Irish wolfhound. The countess of Brocavia was a great lover of dogs. She gave this one to my niece, Giana, when he was orphaned at birth. Giana raised him, and as you can see, he's as devoted to her as she is to him."

"With the exception of the beast, the countess of Brocavia's loss appears to have been my gain," Adam commented.

"He isn't a beast. He's a dog. His name is Wagner." Unable to contain herself any longer, George ignored her uncle's warning look and challenged Adam's authority. "And he goes where I go."

"I trust you have no objections." Max's response wasn't a question but a statement.

Adam ignored Max and focused all of his attention on the girl. "That depends."

"Upon what?" she retorted.

"Upon whether the two of you intend to occupy my bed again tonight."

Chapter 8

Adam ignored the gasp that echoed through the massive library like the collected breath of a cathedral choir. He kept his attention focused solely on George. "I trust you found it to your liking."

"We found it very much to our liking." Giana tangled her fingers in Wagner's fur and lifted her chin a fraction higher than usual in order to meet McKendrick's gaze.

"Sir," Adam reminded her.

Giana frowned.

"We found it very much to our liking, *sir*," he repeated, emphasizing his proper address.

"Sir." She uttered the word through clenched teeth.

Adam grinned at her. "There," he said, "that wasn't so hard, now was it?"

Giana glared back at him. "I do not understand your meaning."

"You're a clever girl," he answered. "You'll figure it out."

The tension between Adam and Giana crackled like lightning across the sky, and everyone in the room felt it.

Adam recognized the tension for what it was. He knew lust when he felt it, and he felt it whenever he was around George. His nerve endings sizzled with awareness, and his body responded to her presence in a way that wreaked havoc on his peace of mind. He was playing a dangerous game and knew that he was in danger of being burned. He'd never subjected any of his other female employees to the sort of forward and ungentlemanly behavior he'd displayed toward George. But he'd never found himself attracted to any of his other female employees. And all he could think to do was to make her family aware of his unwanted feelings and hope that they would help keep her safely out of harm's way. Out of *his* way.

Adam was honest enough with himself to admit that he didn't want to be attracted to her or approve of the way he was handling his unwanted emotion. But he was also honest enough to admit that he seemed to have no control over it or his behavior.

Nor did he understand how George's family could stand by and allow him to flirt with her or to engage her in unsavory wordplay. Anyone with half an eye could see that despite her ability to defend herself, George was an innocent who didn't understand the sexual undertones in his manner. But that was no excuse for his behavior or for her parents. Albert and Isobel had to understand what was happening. His meaning must be as apparent to them as it was to him. It couldn't lose that much in translation. So why didn't her father or brother or uncle put a stop to it? Why didn't they protect George by boxing his ears or punching him in the nose? Why weren't they looking out for her?

Giana shivered. Until she met Adam McKendrick, no one except her mother and father had ever spoken to her in an irreverent manner. She liked the change. She liked the tingle in her blood and the way her senses seemed to go on alert whenever he was near. She bit her bottom lip to keep from laughing aloud at the sheer joy of engaging him in a battle of wits. Giana liked the way he talked to her, liked the way he took it for granted that she was his intellectual equal and that he was hers. And she enjoyed knowing she was able to challenge him without fear of reprisal.

His words reminded her of her parents' witty, flirtatious teasing—teasing that almost always led to passionate embraces and time spent alone behind locked doors. Yes, she liked the

McKendrick's teasing. She liked it enough to encourage more of the same. She glanced up at him from beneath her lashes. "Are you going to allow us to occupy your bed once again?" she asked.

"*Your* presence in my bed is most welcome," Adam told her. "But I'd prefer the dog sleep elsewhere."

There was another collective gasp from the assembled staff. Adam prepared himself to face her father's or uncle's or cousin's wrath, but it was not forthcoming. Apart from the audible gasp, the Langstrom men did nothing to defend George's honor.

But then, Georgiana Langstrom was perfectly capable of defending her own honor.

"That is not possible," Giana answered. "For Wagner sleeps where I sleep."

Adam shrugged his shoulders. "I suppose I could make an exception for you."

"There is no need for you to make such a sacrifice, sir." Giana favored McKendrick with a smug smile. "For Wagner and I have already made our bed elsewhere."

Adam shook his head and clucked his tongue in mock sympathy. "I can't say that I'll miss Wagner, but not having you in my bed again is something I'll truly regret."

"I feel for you." She looked him in the eye. "Because, I fear, it will be a terrible waste for a gentleman like you to mourn what will never come to pass. *Sir*."

"You've been in my bed once," Adam reminded her, enjoying their verbal sparring much more than he cared to admit. "And you could easily be there again." He grinned at her. "Never is a very long time. You may be surprised by what the future holds for you."

She glanced at Max, then turned to Adam and shook her head. "I do not think so," she answered honestly. "My future was decided the day I was born."

The flash of sadness in her eyes startled him. "Fortunes change, George," he replied. "Lady Luck smiles on everyone once in a while." He shrugged his shoulders. "Even housemaids."

Giana reacted to the innuendo and the arrogance behind his

words. "It is possible," she retorted, holding his gaze for a long moment. "But not very likely, *sir*."

Although he'd tried to mask it, Adam knew she'd seen his empathy mirrored in his eyes. He knew the expression on his face had given him away the moment George looked down at the floor and bobbed a respectful curtsey.

Adam gritted his teeth. Her respectful curtsey was harder for Adam to swallow than her saucy impertinence. George was tall, blond, and blue-eyed, and she bore more than a passing resemblance to his four sisters. The sad look in her eyes and that slight, almost imperceptible tremor in her voice shouldn't bother him. But it did.

Her unexpected subservience tore at his conscience and left a hollow feeling in the pit of his stomach.

Adam turned to the staff. "Everyone except Josef and my valet, Mr. O'Brien, is excused to return to their duties."

No one budged.

Adam tried again, waving the staff toward the library door. But the staff remained where they were, and Adam turned to Max Langstrom for help. "Thank you for introducing me to your family. And to you, Mr. Ross"—he looked at Gordon Ross—"for hiring them. Now, I'd like you to dismiss everyone except Josef and my valet."

"Have you any instructions for the rest of us?" Max asked.

"Brenna and George can return to their daily chores while you assist Albert and Isobel with the hiring of a cook, a kitchen staff, and a few more maids to help Brenna and George," Adam replied. "Mr. Ross can see to the recruitment of additional staff for the stables and grounds, and Josef can see to the saddling of horses so that Mr. O'Brien and I might ride out over the estate."

"But, sir, you cannot!" Max sputtered in protest.

Isobel said something in a language Adam didn't understand, and Albert began vigorously shaking his head.

"I can't ride out over my estate?"

"You cannot ride out with your valet," Max corrected.

"Why not?"

"Gentlemen do not ride out with their valets." Max leveled a firm look at O'Brien. "And valets do not accompany their employers on pleasure jaunts unless they are needed to attend to wardrobe or luggage."

O'Brien raised an eyebrow at that. While he was familiar with many of the ways of the aristocracy, he hadn't expected to be mistaken for a valet or taken to task by Adam's new private secretary. O'Brien exchanged amused glances with his friend. Such was the life of a Pinkerton agent. "Is that so?"

Max nodded. "Sir, it simply isn't done."

"Gentlemen don't ride out with their valets in Scotland," Adam told him. "But they do ride out with their friends. Murphy O'Brien is a friend first and a valet second."

"Your friend, sir?" Max gave voice to his confusion. "I've never met a gentleman who would call his valet or any servant a friend."

"You have now," Adam replied. "Tell me, Max, have you ever been to America?"

"No, sir."

Adam smiled. "Well, in America, gentlemen ride out with their valets or anyone else they call friends—no matter what their station in life. That's why I'm going to ride out and look over my estate with my friend, Murphy O'Brien." He gave Max a firm look that brooked no further protest and walked over to stand in front of the stable master. "Do you understand English?"

Josef didn't respond.

"How about French?" Adam repeated the question in French.

Josef smiled. "*Oui.*"

"*Bon,*" Adam answered, continuing to speak the universal language of aristocrats. "Please saddle my horse and Mr. O'Brien's horse, as we'll be riding out momentarily."

Adam waited for the stable master to leave the room, and when he didn't, Adam attempted to hurry him along. "*Au revoir,* Josef," he said. "Mr. O'Brien and I will join you in the stable shortly."

Josef backed toward the doorway, paused long enough to receive an almost imperceptible nod from George and from Max, then left the room.

Adam glanced at his private secretary and the Amazon. "Thank you for your assistance, Max, and for yours, Miss Langstrom. . . ." he acknowledged George's unspoken interference. "I'll call if I need you. *Au revoir.*" He waved his arm and shooed the staff out the door.

Chapter 9

The Bountiful Baron always behaves in a gentlemanly fashion. He treats all women as if they are ladies.

—The Second Installment of the True Adventures of the Bountiful Baron: Western Benefactor to Blond, Beautiful, and Betrayed Women written by John J. Bookman, 1874.

"*That was enlightening,*" Murphy commented wryly as he and McKendrick rode out of the stable yard.

Adam glanced over at Murphy to gauge his measure. "Was it?"

O'Brien chuckled. "I always knew the English—above- and belowstairs—considered the Irish to be beneath contempt." He winked at McKendrick. "But I didn't realize the European Continent followed suit until today."

"Don't take it personally," Adam advised. "You may be Irish, but at least you're from the Old Country. Those of us born in the New World rank lower than the Irish because we don't understand the aristocracy or its class system—above- or belowstairs."

Murphy agreed. "Americans are a threat. Not because you don't understand the aristocracy or class system, but because you hold the aristocracy and the class system in greater contempt than they hold you."

"There's no doubt about it." Adam loosened his grip on the reins and urged his horse into a faster gait. "We're rough and ready, unrefined and unrepentant. America is bursting at the seams with people escaping the class system in search of a better life—people who have no respect for centuries of cultural refinement and superiority."

"Some of whom should have had better taste than to become *nouveau riche*," Murphy pronounced in his best upper-crust accent.

"You sound like my brother-in-law, the Legitimate Bastard," Adam said, reverting to the title he'd given Kirstin's husband, the Viscount Marshfeld.

O'Brien shuddered. "God forbid."

Adam laughed. "You know the main difference between the Bastard and me?"

"He enjoys slapping women around and you don't?" O'Brien quipped.

"That's part of it," Adam replied.

"You're rich and he's not?"

"You know as well as I do that in America, anyone can become *nouveau riche* if he's willing to work hard and get a little dirt under his fingernails. The men and women who struck it rich during the Rush of Forty-nine and the Comstock got lucky—sure—but they worked hard to make that luck possible." Adam grinned at his friend, then took off, cantering his horse up a hill.

"Like you," Murphy shouted.

"Like me," Adam answered. He topped the rise of the hill and waited for O'Brien to catch up. "The difference between me and the Bastard is that the Bastard can't understand why I got lucky and he didn't. He's supposed to be lucky. Because he has a much better pedigree than I have and a far superior place in society. *He* was given every advantage—an old family name with land and titles, a guaranteed place in society, and an expensive education. I had none of those things. My only advantage was being born in America to a mother who taught me the value of hard work and big dreams.

"But my brother-in-law, like his father and grandfather before him, was too bored, too sophisticated, and too lazy to work or to dream. He squandered what was left of his inheritance and wasted his advantages.

"I didn't. I made the most of my advantages. That's the

primary difference between the Legitimate Bastard and me."

O'Brien disagreed. "Character. That's the main difference between the two of you. You have it and he wants it."

"He wants my money." Adam snorted. "He doesn't give a fig about my character."

"I disagree," O'Brien said. "The Bastard wants to be you. Hell, Adam, a lot of men want to be you! John J. Bookman wants to be you! Most of the time even *I* want to be you!"

Adam laughed out loud.

"It's true!" O'Brien protested. "Who do you think is buying *The Second Installment of the True Adventures of the Bountiful Baron: Western Benefactor to Blond, Beautiful, and Betrayed Women?*"

"Too damn many blondes for my comfort," Adam joked. "And let me tell you, that they aren't all beautiful, betrayed, or natural blondes."

"Yeah, well, there are suckers like me, who ought to know better, buying 'em, too."

"What?" Adam turned to his friend, a look of pure astonishment on his face.

"That's right, boyo," O'Brien confirmed. "I gave the dude at the poker table a five-dollar chip for it."

"Good god, why?"

"Because I'd already read the first installment and I wanted to see what else Bookman had to say about you."

"That's a hell of a reason."

O'Brien gave him a sheepish grin. "The fact is that you inspired someone to write a book about you."

"A dime novel, Murph, not a book," Adam reminded him. "If I hadn't been at the wrong place at the wrong time, he'd have found someone else to inspire it."

"Yeah, well, I'm a Pinkerton agent and nobody's written a dime novel about me," Murphy grumbled.

"Thank your lucky stars," Adam breathed.

"I don't have lucky stars," Murphy said. "I wasn't willing to do what it takes to get them. You were. That's the point." He grinned at McKendrick. "That's what men admire about you. You have dreams. Dreams you work hard to make come true. Most of us simply take the easy path."

"You work hard," Adam said. "And you stand up for the things you believe in."

"That's right," Murphy agreed. "I stand up for what I believe in and I work hard. But I work hard for Allan Pinkerton, not Murphy O'Brien, because it's easier. And safer than risking everything." He paused to see what Adam would say. "No wonder the Bastard envies you. Think how hard it must be to be a poor aristocrat. Because it's hard enough to be poor without carrying the expectations that come with the pedigree."

Uncomfortable with the topic and unable to sit still any longer, Adam urged his horse forward. Murphy followed and the two of them rode over the estate, admiring the scenery without saying a word until Adam crested another hill and stared out at the moors below. "Christ! This place is beautiful. Too damn cold. But beautiful. And it's perfect for what I have in mind."

"Then it's a good thing that you're the lord of all you survey," O'Brien said.

"Yes, it is." Adam exhaled. He paused for a long moment. "That was enlightening."

"Was it?"

Adam chuckled. "I always knew the English—above- and belowstairs—considered the *nouveau riche* to be beneath contempt." He winked at O'Brien. "But I didn't realize the European Continent followed suit until today."

"Don't take it personally," O'Brien advised. "You may be *nouveau riche* and beneath contempt, but the girl likes you."

Adam lifted a brow and pretended ignorance. "The girl?"

"Yeah, the tall, blond Valkyrie," O'Brien answered.

"Valkyrie, eh?" Adam looked at O'Brien with new eyes. "I thought of her as an Amazon."

O'Brien shrugged. "I like opera. Her dog's name is Wagner. I made the connection."

Adam shook his head. "I can't quite see her as a Brunnhilde. My mother—even Erika or Astrid—yes. But George—no." He was thoughtful for a moment. "I see George not just as an Amazon warrior, but as Artemis."

"And how long have you known this Artemis?"

"I met her last night," Adam told him. "She and the dog were in my bed when I arrived."

"I gathered as much from your earlier exchange." O'Brien made a face. "The question is: Did she and the dog remain in your bed after you arrived?"

"Yes."

"Did you?"

"No," Adam answered.

O'Brien snorted. "Would you tell me if you had?"

Adam shot him a meaningful look. "Have I ever?"

"No."

"And I'm not going to start now. You should know that discretion is the mark of a true gentleman, and that means that a gentleman doesn't kiss and tell."

"Ah, but you're no gentleman." O'Brien's tone of voice took on a more serious note. "Or else she's no lady. . . ."

"She's definitely a lady."

"She's a housemaid, Adam."

"Who cares? Jesus! O'Brien!" Adam took off his hat and raked his fingers through his hair. "Didn't you hear a word I said to Maximillian Langstrom? Didn't I defend my friendship with you? Didn't I tell them that you are my friend? Do you really think I care that she's a housemaid or that you're my valet?"

"No," Murphy replied. "But then, I'm not your valet."

"The rest of the staff thinks you are."

"But you know I'm not."

"That's right," Adam said. "I know you're not my gentleman's gentleman. But the point is that it wouldn't matter to me if you were. You would still be my friend."

"So, why didn't you tell them who I really am?"

"I did," Adam protested. "I told them you were my friend. They chose not to believe me."

"You told them I'm your friend who works for the Pinkerton Detective Agency?"

"No, I told them you were my friend." Adam met Murphy's unwavering gaze.

"Why didn't you set them straight about what I do for a living instead of allowing them to believe that I'm your valet?"

"I tried. You're the one who volunteered to step into the role of my valet," Adam countered. "Why did you do that? You had as much of an opportunity to correct their misconception as I did."

Murphy shrugged his shoulders. "I don't know."

"Neither do I," Adam admitted. "Other than the fact that something simply doesn't feel—"

"—quite right." They answered in unison.

"Exactly," Murphy pronounced. "I can't put my finger on what's bothering me. But I know something is bothering me. I'm not entirely comfortable with this situation."

"Neither am I." Adam paused. "Did you notice the way everyone looked to Max or to George before they moved?"

"I noticed," O'Brien said. "I didn't know if you did."

"I kept telling myself that it was because they didn't understand me, but Max and Isobel and George and Gordon Ross all speak English, so that couldn't be the reason." Adam scratched his forehead. "So why didn't anyone try to help defend her from me?"

"Who?" O'Brien asked.

"You know who," Adam snapped. "The Valkyrie. The Amazon. George."

"You said you didn't sleep with her." Murphy O'Brien enjoyed ruffling Adam McKendrick's feathers, loved seeing him loose some of his control, so he relished his role as devil's advocate every chance he got.

"I didn't," Adam repeated.

Murphy narrowed his gaze. "You wouldn't speak to the Valkyrie the way I heard you speak to her this morning unless you didn't think she was a lady or an innocent or unless you intended to find out."

Adam was thoughtful. "I can't deny that," he said softly. "I spoke to her in a way no gentleman should ever speak to a lady—especially one who is still an innocent."

"How do you know she still innocent?"

Adam shot O'Brien a look that spoke volumes about the continued wisdom of playing devil's advocate or of asking patently stupid questions. "She's still innocent. I'd bet my life on it."

"So would I," O'Brien agreed.

"Then why didn't her father or brother or uncle punch me in the nose?" Adam stared at his friend. "You would have defended your sister's honor. God knows I've defended my sisters' honor often enough." Adam frowned. "So why didn't George's family defend her honor? There's no excuse for it."

"Unless they've something to fear," Murphy suggested.

"Such as?"

"Losing their positions."

"I'm more inclined to dismiss them for *not* defending her honor than I would be *for* defending it," Adam said.

"You know that and I know that," O'Brien replied. "But they don't know that because they don't know you. You heard them, Adam, their employer died. They're starting over in a new place. Maybe they were afraid of jeopardizing their positions here."

"I hope so," Adam fervently replied. "I hope it's as simple as that."

"Would you dismiss them?" Murphy asked. "Knowing they may have nowhere else to go?"

"Who me?" Adam put on his most innocent face. "I'm the Bountiful Baron, remember? Western Benefactor to Blond, Beautiful, and Betrayed Women everywhere."

"Ah, criminy," Murphy swore. "I knew it!"

"Knew what?"

"You're preparin' for a third installment."

Adam grinned. "Then let the adventures begin. . . ."

Chapter 10

The Bountiful Baron is a man of action and few words.

—THE SECOND INSTALLMENT OF THE TRUE ADVENTURES OF THE BOUN-
TIFUL BARON: WESTERN BENEFACTOR TO BLOND, BEAUTIFUL, AND BE-
TRAYED WOMEN WRITTEN BY JOHN J. BOOKMAN, 1874.

*O*nce Adam decided the lodge was ideally suited
for the purpose he intended, plans for the building and
the grounds got under way.

No one knew exactly what the McKendrick had in mind for
the lodge, but everyone wanted to watch the progress and share
in the process. The word went out that the McKendrick was a
rich, eccentric American who paid top wages to workers willing to help renovate the lodge and construct a private golf
links. McKendrick was looking for permanent staff, and that
was all that was needed to entice the men and women in Kinlochen and the surrounding crofts and villages to travel to
Larchmont to offer their services as craftsmen and day laborers
and as housemaids, laundresses, cooks, and kitchen and scullery maids; as stewards and footmen, gardeners and gardeners'
helpers, stable boys and caddies. Permanent staff lived in and
was allowed one day off a week, paid holidays, and time off
for sickness and emergencies. They were guaranteed perqui-
sites at Easter and Christmas and the end of every year of
service. A permanent position in a house like Larchmont
Lodge was the best form of employment one could hope for
in the Highlands, and dozens of applicants vied for every position.

Adam had never lived or worked in a house the size of

Larchmont Lodge. He didn't know everything he needed to know in order to run a huge household, but he owned and operated a hotel and saloon back home in Nevada, and he knew enough to hire the best people he could find and allow them to take pride in doing their jobs. At Larchmont Lodge the man charged with the task of finding the right people for the jobs was Gordon Ross. Gordon quickly learned that Adam McKendrick was a man who held his staff to high standards. In that regard, he was like every aristocrat and royal Gordon had ever come across, but unlike most royalty, the McKendrick expected and was willing to pay well for quality service.

And Adam believed in allowing a man the opportunity to pursue his dreams. No one employed at Larchmont Lodge had to remain in his current station simply because the men in his family had always held that position. If a gardener aspired to become a butler or a stable boy or stable master or valet, Adam McKendrick believed in allowing him the opportunity. He believed in providing the men and women who lived and worked on his domain with opportunities for advancement and the means to live a better life.

To that end, Adam asked Gordon to create as many jobs as possible, and to arrange to have a roster of additional help available at all times. The additional staff would earn quarter day wages for agreeing to work at the lodge when needed and would receive full day wages to supplement their regular income for substituting for permanent employees on off-days, holidays, sickness, or emergencies. This meant that the local farmers, craftsmen, shop owners, housewives, and crofters could continue to work for themselves, but would also have the opportunity to receive training in other positions and to earn additional wages by working at the lodge or on the grounds. Max, Isobel, and Albert were in charge of training all household workers, and Gordon and Josef were in charge of training all outside workers.

Except children. Adam specifically instructed Gordon not to hire children. Any young man or girl hoping to work at Larchmont Lodge or for the McKendrick had to have reached their sixteenth year. Children could be paid for helping with the daily chores like running errands or sweeping steps and walkways, for walking ponies, mucking stalls, and weeding borders and flower beds, and other traditional childhood tasks so long as they worked no more than a half day.

Gordon agreed, and although the grounds of the lodge echoed with the sounds of children, it was the sound of laughter and play. Once the staff and the day laborers were in force, the creation of the golf links began near one of the old stone gatehouses that was being renovated to include a bar and wine cellar overlooking the eighteenth green.

Adam sent to St. Andrew's, the oldest golf links in Scotland, for help in designing the one at Larchmont. He also sent for instructors and craftsmen to fashion the clubs and balls used in the game. Because he was paying top wages, men who loved the game of golf flocked to Larchmont looking for work. That influx of workers dictated that the next step in the renovation was the refurbishing of the staff quarters.

Adam's decision to begin with the women's wing of the servants' quarters was a result of a simple but earnest desire to remove George Langstrom's wolfhound from the second floor—and his close proximity to Adam's bed. Work began at the top. Laborers repaired the leaking roof and ceiling by installing new slate roofing tiles and a new plaster ceiling. Oilskin shades and thick wooden interior shutters were added to the windows to help keep out the cold night air and interior walls removed so that bats of thatch and straw could be stuffed between the wooden timbers and the stone exterior wall as additional insulation.

The dormitory-style quarters, though efficient and practical for children, allowed little privacy for adults, so Adam ordered the room partitioned off into private areas that each contained a bed with feather mattresses, a nightstand, a chair, a washstand and a mirror. One larger, separate, more spacious area contained a bed long and wide enough for a very tall woman and an Irish wolfhound to sleep on. Two water closets with twin sinks and bathtubs, hot and cold running water, and two toilets were added.

No one in the village of Kinlochen had ever seen a water

closet, and workers had to be brought in from Glasgow, along with the supplies, in order to construct them. But Adam felt it was worth the expense and the effort.

In his journeys to England escorting or visiting his sister, Kirstin, Adam had discovered that the water closets, if they existed at all, left a great deal to be desired. Those with running water worked intermittently, and the others weren't water closets at all, but earth closets or worse, chamber pots in wooden cabinets. Wealthy gentlemen expected better facilities, and the employees who provided service for wealthy gentlemen deserved better.

Unfortunately, the construction of the water closets and the bathing facilities was proving to be more of a challenge than Adam had anticipated. The employees and the locals who kept stopping by the construction site to gawk hampered the craftsmen and laborers from Glasgow.

The only employees who seemed immune to gawking were Gordon Ross and the Langstrom family. The women's wing was in chaos, but the rest of the house ran as smoothly as clockwork. It didn't run to suit him, but it ran smoothly.

It was hard to believe. Especially in light of the fact that the only members of the staff who followed his instructions were the laborers working on the renovations. He was the undisputed head of the household, but nothing in the household ran according to his directions.

In the three weeks he'd been at Larchmont Lodge, Adam discovered that breakfast was never served when he ordered it. Nor luncheon or dinner. None of his domestic instructions were followed as he issued them—all of them seemed to be circumvented by someone—either Isobel, or Albert or Max— but Adam had to admit that the household ran smoothly—with or without his instructions.

His sister Kirstin had told him once that England's great country houses were run for the convenience of the staff and not for the convenience of the owners. Adam had scoffed at the notion, but now he wasn't so sure. He didn't like it, but he didn't seem to be able to do very much about it. He couldn't even control the dog.

Adam entered his bedchamber to find the wolfhound lying

in the center of his bed. The dog lay snoring on his back with all four paws in the air. Careful not to wake the beast, Adam backed out of his bedroom and closed the door. "Miss Langstrom!"

A door down the hall opened. Shy, dark-haired Brenna stepped onto the threshold and covered a yawn with her hand.

"Not you." Adam pointed toward his bedroom door. "The other Miss Langstrom."

Brenna frowned at him.

Adam frowned back at her. "George. I want George. Your sister Georgiana . . . Where is she?"

Brenna pointed to the valet's room across the hall.

Adam crossed the hall and opened the door. "Miss Langstrom!"

The Langstrom in question sat before the coal grate, a pair of leather work gloves, a pail of ashes, and a container of lead black beside her. She turned at the sound of his voice and Adam noticed several things at once—she wore a black silk moire gown—a Worth from the look of it—covered by a plain white cotton pinafore. The black set her blond hair and her figure off to perfection, much better than the soot streaked on her right cheek and across her forehead.

"Yes?"

"We need to talk about your dog."

"Oh?" George wiped her hands on her skirt and jumped to her feet so fast she stepped on the hem of her dress, lost her balance, and fell against the mantel. A porcelain shepherdess toppled off her pedestal and crashed to the hearth.

Adam moved as quickly as possible, but he wasn't fast enough to save the delicate bone china. The shepherdess figurine splintered against the marble.

A look of sheer horror crossed George's face as she dropped to her knees and began collecting the pieces of the broken shepherdess. It wasn't the first object she'd broken in his presence. Yesterday she had dropped a tray of dishes she'd been carrying to the kitchen when she met him in the corridor, and three days before that she had broken one of the collection of clay pipes in his study, and the day before that she had lost her grip on a china cup and saucer when he walked into the dining room.

"I am too sorry," she apologized.

"It's all right." Adam bent to help her. He took several large pieces of the figurine she'd retrieved from the hearth out of her hand and placed them in the ash pail.

"But . . ." Embarrassed beyond belief at her unprincesslike clumsiness, Giana resumed her hurried attempt to gather all the bits of the broken shepherdess. She collected the largest pieces of china, then unthinkingly swept her palm across the hearth to corral the smaller pieces.

"No!" Adam grabbed hold of her wrist to stop her. The touch of his fingers on her hand sent a jolt of electricity through him, but he was so intent on preventing the mishap he knew was coming that he barely noticed. But he was too late.

Adam flinched almost as badly as Giana as a piece of one of the lambs that had adorned the base of the figurine sliced through the fleshy portion of her palm.

"Oh." She gasped in pain and surprise and instinctively closed her hand to halt the flow of bright crimson blood that ran from the cut down the side of her hand.

"Don't!" Adam eased his grip and gently caressed her wrist with the pads of his fingers, feeling the steady throb of her pulse against them, as he gently pried open her fist. "Please." He looked into her eyes. "Let me."

Giana opened her hand, relaxing her grip and allowing the McKendrick to inspect the wound.

There were blisters on her palm and a jagged wound. Adam ran his thumb over the cut, wincing as he felt the sliver of china from the shepherdess protruding from her hand. The wound was small, but fairly deep, and droplets of blood pooled around his thumb, staining the nail.

George sucked in a breath.

Gritting his teeth, Adam carefully removed the porcelain shard. It had to hurt, but she didn't complain.

Adam noticed the tears sparkling on her lashes and the incredibly fragile feel of her hand in his. He was immediately struck by the contrast of their skin tones—his dark, hers so pale and translucent that he could see the fine network of blue veins beneath her skin.

Reaching for the handkerchief in his breast pocket, Adam carefully dabbed at the bloody cut, before wrapping it around her palm to help stanch the crimson flow. The expression on her face tugged at his heart. It was filled with equal amounts of bewilderment and betrayal. She looked like a lost child who can't understand how she came to be that way. Adam impulsively pressed a kiss against her palm to make the hurt go away the way his mother and sisters had kissed away his childhood wounds.

Giana shivered at the rush of warmth flooding her body when Adam gently pressed his lips against her hand. A shock of awareness jolted her. She stared up at him. The flicker of deep emotion in his dark eyes pleased her. She held his gaze for what seemed like an eternity, reluctant to let it go. The look in his eyes sent a tingle of awareness down her spine. "I am too sorry about the little shepherdess."

"It doesn't matter," Adam told her.

"Oh, but it does," Giana insisted. She recognized the fact that the little shepherdess had been a priceless bit of sixteenth-century porcelain.

"I will pay for it and for all the other things I have damaged."

"There's no need." He shrugged his shoulders. "I'm as much to blame for the accident as you are. I startled you. If I hadn't burst in here shouting at you about the dog, you wouldn't have knocked the shepherdess off the mantel. Besides, it was only a bit of pottery."

"But it was Meissen porcelain . . ." Giana murmured.

That caught his attention. Adam lifted an eyebrow in query. "How did you know it was Meissen?"

Giana bit her bottom lip. "We . . . I . . . She . . . had a collection of Meissen shepherdesses."

"Who?" He asked.

"The countess of Brocadia." Giana glanced at him from beneath her lashes. "I dusted them."

"Brocavia," Adam corrected, caressing her wrist with his thumb.

"Pardon?"

Her pulse fluttered beneath his thumb. "The countess of Brocavia," he explained. "You said you dusted the countess of Brocadia's Meissen shepherdesses."

Giana lowered her gaze. "I meant the countess of Brocavia. My English is not—"

"Your English is fine," Adam told her. "It's your countess I question." He also questioned the countess's wisdom in allowing George to dust her collection of little shepherdesses. But that was supposing the countess actually existed and Adam wasn't so sure.

"I do not know what you mean," she said.

"I think you do."

Giana's eyes momentarily flashed fire as she pulled her hand from his grasp and scrambled to her feet. It was the second time the McKendrick had accused her of telling an untruth. And the fact that he was right only made it worse. Before her parents' death, Giana had never knowingly told a lie, but her parents' death had necessitated a huge deception and an intricate web of half-truths. But she wasn't a liar by nature, and Giana couldn't help but take exception to the fact that Adam McKendrick believed she was.

Adam didn't get to his feet right away. He stayed where he was, kneeling on the hearth, wishing he didn't have to force the issue, wishing he didn't have to acknowledge what he knew must be the truth. But wishing didn't change the truth or make the confrontation any easier. Adam let out a breath and pushed himself to his feet. He expected to tower over her and was pleasantly surprised, once again, when he was able to look her in the eye. "There was no countess of Brocavia."

Giana crossed her fingers behind her back and hid her uninjured hand in the folds of her skirt. "O-of course there was."

Adam studied her closely, then slowly shook his head. "Was there? If I were to look through a few of those European lineage books in the library, would I find any reference to the countess of Brocavia? If I send for letters of reference from the countess's family, will I get them or will they be forged by one of your family members?" The blood seemed to drain from her face. Adam reached out to steady her. "That's it, isn't it?" he asked.

Giana couldn't answer. She bit her bottom lip and sat perfectly still, barely breathing as she waited for his next move.

The fact that she didn't offer to defend herself or to offer an argument sent a quiver of alarm up his spine. Adam took a deep breath, then slowly exhaled. The wounded look in her eyes twisted his gut into knots. He didn't think he could feel any worse if he'd spent the morning robbing defenseless widows and orphans. Adam was suddenly deeply, inexplicably ashamed of himself. "I'm not going to check.

She didn't respond.

"I'm not going to investigate the countess, George. Do you understand? I don't care about references. You and your family have done a wonderful job here so far. I have no complaints."

Her eyes lit up and she managed a brief smile. "Truly?"

"Well . . ." He hesitated.

Too long. He hesitated too long. "It's me, isn't it?" Giana glanced down at the handkerchief wrapped around her hand. "Because I am so clumsy." She picked at the edge of the linen. The bleeding had ceased.

"You aren't clumsy."

"I am like the bull in the teapot," she confided.

Adam furrowed his brow, unable to comprehend her logic.

She returned his frown, unable to understand why he didn't understand her perfectly correct English. The way he frowned one would think that she was speaking Karolyan to him. She unwrapped his handkerchief and handed it to him. "I am as efficient and careful as the other members of the house . . . of my family . . ." She gave a most unprincesslike shrug. "But it seems that the more careful I am, the more I break things."

Like a bull in a china shop. It took a moment for him to grasp her meaning. Adam bit the inside of his cheek to keep from laughing at her mangled idiom. Adam handed the handkerchief back to her. "You keep it. You may need it again should the wound reopen."

Giana recognized the wisdom of that advice. "Very well."

She gave him her most regal nod. "But I will pay you for the shepherdess."

"Forget the shepherdess!" Adam burst out. "I don't care about the shepherdess! I care about finding that blasted beast of yours in my bed again!"

Chapter 11

"*Wagner?*" *Her voice held a note of panic.* She sat back on her heels and looked up at him.

"Yes, Wagner," Adam retorted. "Who else?"

Giana glanced around. "Where is he?"

"When last I saw him, he was snoring soundly."

"Was Brenna with him?"

Adam frowned. "Brenna? What does Brenna have to do with anything? She wasn't there. He was alone and stretched out in the center of my bed."

"When I began cleaning Mr. O'Brien's room, I left Wagner with Brenna. Where was she and why was he not with her?"

"Perhaps it's because your sister finds her bed more comfortable than mine," Adam commented, remembering Brenna's half-hearted attempts to cover her yawns and the sleep marks on her face. "Unlike the dog. Or maybe it's because she prefers a human sleeping companion to a canine one."

"Wagner sleeps only with me."

Adam snorted in amusement. "Apparently, he's more selective in his choice of bed partners than he is in his choice of beds."

"On the contrary," Giana told him. "He is equally selective in his choice of beds. It was my bed until you arrived. He returns to it because it retains my scent."

"Of orange blossoms and woman," Adam muttered beneath his breath. He couldn't argue with her logic. Although the linens had been laundered several times since she'd removed to another bedchamber, his bed still retained the scent of her perfume. He had thought the fragrance came from something the laundry staff added to the final rinse when they washed the sheets. He hadn't realized, until this moment, that the tantalizing perfume originated with George. But now he recognized the surprisingly erotic scent of orange blossoms and musk that emanated from her hair and her skin—a scent that was still faintly detectable despite the pungent metallic smell of fresh blood, coal ash, and lead blackening.

Adam had always appreciated the fresh, clean scent of orange blossoms, but never more than he did now. And the scent of her wasn't all he found appealing. He was fascinated by George's words and even more fascinated by her mouth, so much so that he found himself staring at it. Everything about her mouth intrigued him from the perfect shape of her upper and lower lips to the subtle pattern of textures imprinted there.

Giana had spent her entire life as an object of curious speculation. She was accustomed to having people stare at her and generally found it easy to overlook their rudeness, but Adam McKendrick's intense blue-eyed gaze disturbed her in a way she had never expected because it made her feel things she had never known existed. For the first time in her life she felt like a woman instead of a royal princess. But awareness of new feelings brought another kind of awareness—an awareness of Adam McKendrick as a man—a man who had an uncanny knack for making her forget who she was and the responsibilities she had been born to bear.

Forcing herself to look away, Giana turned and reached for the pair of leather gloves balanced on the rim of the ash pail. "Pardon me."

"No." Adam took the gloves from her and stuck them in his jacket pocket.

"Excuse me." Assuming her English was to blame for his failure to understand her, Giana politely repeated her request, then picked up the pail and tried to move past him, but the McKendrick refused to let her by.

"What do you think you're doing?" This time Adam reached for the ash pail.

"I have to collect Wagner," Giana answered. "And complete my work."

Adam set the pail out of her reach. "Your work day is finished."

"But there is more to do. . . ." she protested.

"That may be. But you're not going to be the one to do it. You've a nasty cut on your hand. Someone else can finish cleaning the grates." Adam was suddenly struck by the notion that while Giana had been cleaning and polishing the coal grates in the second-floor bedrooms, Brenna had been napping. "Someone like your sister."

Giana shook her head.

"Why not?" he demanded.

"Brenna's duties do not include work of this sort."

Adam lifted an eyebrow at that. "But yours do . . ."

"Yes, of course."

"Why?" He asked. "Why are you cleaning fireplaces while your sister sleeps? Other than watching the beast, which she has failed to do, what exactly are her duties?"

"Brenna is a lady's maid," Giana explained.

"Which means . . ."

"Her duty is to attend the lady of the house. To personally dress and undress her, arrange her hair, attend to needlework and repair personal items of clothing, and serve as companion."

"There is no lady in the house for Brenna to personally attend," Adam reminded her.

Giana had never behaved coyly in her life, but she supposed there was a first time for everything. She turned her mysterious princess smile on the McKendrick and glanced up at him from beneath the cover of her lashes. "There will be."

"Oh?" Adam gave her another speculative look. "How so?"

"When gentlemen begin extensive and costly repairs to their homes, it is generally supposed that they mean to settle down and begin their families. . . ." Giana pretended to knowledge of the ways of the world that princesses of the blood royal were supposed to inherit at birth. "Naturally, we supposed that once the renovations to the lodge are concluded, you would do likewise. . . ."

"You supposed that?" Adam hadn't grown up with four sisters without learning more than he had ever wanted to know about the way their minds worked. He recognized a blatant fishing expedition when he saw it, and he also recognized the fact that none of his four sisters would ever had tried such an obvious ploy to gather information. His sisters were experts at toying with a man's sensibilities. George was a rank novice. Adam decided to respond in kind, gifting her with a devilish grin and an equally devilish reply, "Surely, you're not naïve enough to think that renovating a building has anything to do with whether or not I intend to begin a family or that beginning a family necessarily includes marriage or having a lady in or of the house."

She opened her mouth to reply, but no words came out.

Unable to resist, Adam reached out and smoothed a smear of soot off her cheek with the pad of his thumb. "Who are you? And what have you done with George?"

Giana's felt the color leave her face as she straightened her backbone, stiffened her spine, and prepared to have her deception revealed. "I do not understand what you mean."

Adam exhaled. She had proved to be such a stimulating adversary in verbal sparring he'd forgotten that, for all her pretense to the contrary, she *was* a naïve young woman for whom English was obviously a second language. "I mean that coyness doesn't become you, George."

Giana moistened her lips with the tip of her tongue. "Nor you, sir."

"I've been called many things, George, but never coy." He smiled to show that there was no censure in his words. "When a woman answers the way you did, it's generally thought that she's deliberately being coy. When a man answers that way, it's generally *supposed* that he's being evasive."

"Are you?"

Adam's smile widened into a grin. "Now, there's the George I know and lo—" He broke off abruptly.

Jesus, Mary, and Joseph! Adam wiped his hand over his face. Where had that thought come from? He was in trouble. Big trouble. George was everything he had always said he didn't want in a woman. But his preferences no longer seemed to matter. God, she was a beauty. And worse than that, she was a beauty who sent his pulse racing. He was definitely in trouble. He recognized the warning signs, but he wasn't sure he could prevent the damage. He might be too late to prevent the damage. He might be too late to save himself.

Unless . . .

He'd never before been tempted by a woman like George. He'd always preferred more demure women. . . . He tended to be attracted to petite, dark-haired, dark-eyed beauties. Never blondes. Which made those damned dime novels so laughable. But he hadn't shared a bed with a woman since he'd left Nevada. There was always the chance that he might simply be attracted to the novelty of kissing a woman who could look him in the eye. . . .

Adam bent his head and leaned closer. There was always the chance that kissing her would prove to be nothing more than a pleasant distraction—an enjoyable way to pass the time while in Scotland. . . . And there was always the chance that he was a bigger damned liar than she was. He'd have to be a fool to find out. . . .

And he had never been a fool. Until now . . .

Adam made one last valiant attempt to save himself. He tried to back away, tried to give her room to retreat, but George showed no signs of retreating. Standing on tiptoe, she leaned toward him, lifted her chin, parted her lips, and closed her eyes. . . .

He stared down at her face, at her softly parted lips, and was lost. . . . Adam covered her mouth with his and licked at the seam of her lips. She gave a startled gasp at the intimacy of that gesture. He took advantage of the opportunity and slipped his tongue inside her mouth.

And discovered he was both a liar and a fool. George was sweet and innocent and incredibly tempting. Although he used his tongue to tease, tantalize, and seduce, it was quite apparent to Adam that the woman he held in his arms had never had anyone kiss her the way he was kissing her. And it was equally apparent to Adam that he never wanted anyone else to have the chance.

The idea scared him so much, Adam broke off the kiss. He stepped back and fought for control, but he knew he was fighting a losing battle when George looped her arms around his neck and pressed herself against him.

"God help me!" He murmured the heartfelt prayer moments before he bent and traced the delicate contours of her cheekbones with the pads of his thumbs. Leaning forward, Adam pressed a gentle kiss on her eyelids, then worked his way down her face, back to her lips. He kissed her again and again, paying particular attention to her plump bottom lip, savoring the texture, flicking his tongue over it, touching the roughness of the myriad tiny abrasions she made with her teeth each time she bit her bottom lip. He lavished her mouth with attention, sucking on her lower lip, teasing her, tempting her to open her mouth and allow him further access.

She yielded to temptation, and the touch of his mouth was a revelation, producing an avalanche of hidden emotions. Giana parted her lips, allowing him to deepen the kiss. He complied, moving his lips on hers, kissing her harder, then softer, then harder once more, testing her response, slipping his tongue past her teeth, exploring the sweet hot interior of her mouth with practiced finesse. As he leisurely stroked the inside of her mouth in a provocative imitation of the mating dance, George followed his lead. She moved her lips on his and kissed him back. Her abundant talent and enthusiasm inspired him as much as it surprised him, and Adam made love to her mouth, teaching her everything he knew about the fine art of kissing.

And George was an excellent pupil. She progressed rapidly, mirroring his actions and inventing a few of her own as she moved from novice to expert in the space of a few heartbeats.

The jolt of pure pleasure he felt as she used her newfound talent with her tongue and teeth and mouth to entice him shook him down to his toes, threatening to steal his breath away along with his suddenly tenuous control.

"Stop." Adam let go of her. He needed distance. He needed space. He needed to let go of her before he took her on the floor of O'Brien's bedroom.

"Why?" Now that she'd discovered kissing, Giana meant to continue practicing it for as long as possible. "I like it."

"I'm gratified to hear it," he answered curtly. "But your lesson is over." He clenched his fists to keep from touching her.

"I do not want the lesson to end," Giana informed him in the imperious tone she had long ago learned to use in order to get her way. Being a princess of the blood royal did have its uses, and one of them was being able to order people of lesser rank to obey one's commands.

Adam stared down into bright blue eyes. "You probably don't want to end up on the floor on your back with your skirts over your head, either, but that's what's going to happen if we don't stop kissing."

"Truly?" Giana had no idea why she'd be on the floor on her back with her skirts over her head, but the notion of such a thing happening to her intrigued her. "How extraordinary!"

"Yes," Adam agreed, "it's extraordinary. So extraordinary that millions of people do it every day."

"Do they?"

Adam shook his head in wonder. "Yes, they really do. Why do you think there are so many babies?"

He could tell from the expression on her face that he had finally succeeded in shocking her.

"Babies?" She stared up at him in awe. So that was how babies were born. She knew, of course, that babies were a natural result of marriage, just as she knew that her duty as a princess of the blood royal was to marry for the good of her country and provide her husband and country with an heir. After kissing Adam McKendrick, Giana could finally understand how children might come to be born out of wedlock. "I had no idea."

The expression on her face was so appealing that Adam fought an almost overwhelming urge to kiss her again. "You still have no idea," he told her. "And I intend to keep it that way. For both our sakes." He turned and started toward the door. "Stay out of my way, George. Stay out of my room and out of my bed and keep that beast of yours away as well."

Giana attempted to point out the fact that he had come in search of her and not the other way around. "But, sir . . ."

Sir. She had called him sir. After kissing him senseless and nearly causing him to lose control of his *extraordinary* control, she'd called him sir. He'd become a caricature of every lusty landowner who'd ever tumbled a serving wench in his employ. He wiped a hand over his forehead. Christ! He couldn't feel any worse if she'd kicked him in the groin. "Adam," he said softly. "When a man teaches a woman to kiss, the least she can do is call him by name."

"And the least a man can do, after teaching her, is to continue, *Adam.*" Giana didn't wait to hear his reply. She simply turned and walked out of the bedroom, leaving Adam McKendrick staring after her.

Chapter 12

The Bountiful Baron hates a mystery or a riddle and feels duty bound to solve it.

—The Second Installment of the True Adventures of the Bountiful Baron: Western Benefactor to Blond, Beautiful, and Betrayed Women written by John J. Bookman, 1874.

"There's something strange going on here, boyo." O'Brien swirled his whisky around the bottom of his glass before taking a hefty swallow.

"Oh?" Adam quirked an eyebrow at him and gave an ironic chuckle. "What makes you think so? The fact that every man-servant in this household has taken the lord of the house to task for daring to drink whisky instead of brandy after dinner or for sharing the bottle with his valet?" He and Murphy had retreated to the library after dinner and remained there long after the other members of the household had retired for the night. Neither Albert's frowning disapproval or Max's pointed comments had dissuaded Adam from treating Murphy like the friend he was instead of the gentleman's gentleman he was pretending to be.

"All you're subjected to is a few frowns and a comment or two," O'Brien reminded him. "While I'll have to endure another in a series of lectures regarding my lack of training in the proper etiquette for a gentleman's gentleman."

"What?" Adam asked.

"Some lord of the manor you are," O'Brien teased. "Don't ya know that your private secretary feels he's duty bound to lecture me following breakfast in the upper servants' quarters each morning?" He spoke in an exaggerated Irish brogue. "Of course you don't." He answered his own question. "But it's time you opened your eyes, boyo, and paid attention to what's going on inside the walls of the lodge, instead of outside them."

"What does he lecture you about?"

"The usual topic is the relationship between a particular gentleman's gentleman and his employer and why said gentleman's gentleman should maintain a proper distance between his employer and himself and not attempt to overreach his station in life by believing he is his employer's equal." O'Brien drained the last of mouthful of whisky from his glass and set it down on the table beside his chair.

"Despite his employer's words and actions to the contrary."

O'Brien laughed. "Despite that."

Adam joined in the laughter. "I have complete faith in your ability to handle Maximillian Langstrom."

"That's good," O'Brien told him. "Because I'm beginning to lose faith in yours."

Adam stopped laughing.

"Face it, boyo, you've been spending too much time outdoors supervising the building of that golf track. . . ."

"Links," Adam corrected automatically. "It's called a golf links."

"Track. Links. No matter," O'Brien said. "Whatever it's called, you've spent so much time there that your instructions carry little weight with the indoor staff around here."

"My words and actions carry *no* weight with any of the staff around here," Adam corrected. "Except the day laborers from the village, the workers from Glasgow, and the men from St. Andrews . . ."

O'Brien shook his head. "The workers from Glasgow and St. Andrews maybe, but the villagers are taking their orders from Isobel and Gordon, who take them from Max, the reigning head of the household. You may own the place, boyo, but you've been usurped."

"I can't have been usurped." Adam gave a self-deprecating snort. "Because I've never been in control of the household staff." He poured himself another finger of whisky, offered some to O'Brien, then set the bottle aside when O'Brien refused. "I haven't even managed to gain control over that damned dog."

"Caught him on your bed again, eh?"

"On his back with all four paws in the air, snoring loud enough to wake the dead."

"Where was his owner?" O'Brien asked.

"On her hands and knees cleaning the ashes and soot from the fireplace in your room," Adam replied.

Murphy knew that one of the many duties of a housemaid was to clean and blacken the fireplace grates, but he could not reconcile the image of Georgiana Langstrom on her hands and knees scrubbing like a charwoman. "You're joking."

"I wish I were," Adam answered honestly. "But seeing George on her hands and knees cleaning the hearth in a Worth gown was no joke."

O'Brien wondered suddenly if he'd heard correctly or if Adam had simply consumed too much whisky. "Did you say Worth gown?"

Adam nodded. "A black silk moiré day dress with jet beading, a small bustle and short train."

"How do you know it was Worth?"

"I crossed the Atlantic with Kirstin, the Honorable Lady Marshfeld." Adam smiled. "So did you. And I happen to know that we were treated to the latest Parisian fashions including several by Monsieur Worth. I recognized the style."

"I've always said that you were a man of many talents," O'Brien retorted.

"Talented enough to know that the white pinafore George wore over her gown was not Worth. It was ordinary, run-of-the mill, standard housemaid attire."

"How many other households can lay claim to a housemaid who wears Worth gowns?" O'Brien couldn't control his smirk. He pushed himself to his feet and sketched an elaborate bow. "You are, indeed, the Bountiful Baron."

Adam shook his head. "I'm not *that* bountiful. I didn't supply the staff with Worth gowns."

"Then who did?" O'Brien set his whisky glass aside and exchanged glances with Adam.

"Certainly not the Langstroms," Adam answered. "If they could afford Worth originals, there would be no need for them to work as domestics."

"Maybe the gown was one of the countess of Brocavia's castoffs."

Adam paused for a moment, debating whether or not he should confide his suspicions about the countess of Brocavia, but thought better of it. Murphy O'Brien was the soul of discretion, but Adam had promised George he'd keep silent. "I don't think so," he said at last. "Brenna is the lady's maid, and as a lady's maid, she would be entitled to any of her mistress's cast-off garments."

"But Brenna's not wearing Worth originals," O'Brien finished Adam's train of thought.

"That could be because she hasn't done anything to merit them," Adam grumbled.

O'Brien shrugged. "You said it yourself. Brenna is a lady's maid. What is there for her to do?"

"She could be helping her sister with the dusting and cleaning," Adam told him.

"Not so, boyo."

"Why not?"

"Belowstairs doesn't work that way. Belowstairs has its own hierarchy. A lady's maid ranks higher than a housemaid. Ordinary dusting and cleaning is beneath her."

"I know what a lady's maid does and I understand her place within the household," Adam retorted. "George explained it. But it galls me to know that while George is on her hands and knees scrubbing hearths, Brenna does nothing to earn her keep except watch the dog." Adam snorted. "And she's a dismal failure at that."

O'Brien laughed. "The dog sleeps all the time. He must not be very interesting to watch, because Brenna is much better at watching her sister and her mother and me work."

"You?" Adam was surprised.

O'Brien winked. "Shy Brenna isn't as shy as we thought. She watches me as I go about my duties as your gentleman's gentleman."

"That is interesting," Adam mused.

"It may not be as interesting as you think," Murphy said.

"She may not be watching me, so much as hoping to keep an eye on you."

"Unless the Langstroms have Brenna watching you because they know you're not what you pretend to be."

O'Brien shrugged. "They have no doubt that I'm a vastly inexperienced valet," he said. "But I don't think they know I'm only masquerading as one—or that I'm a private detective. And there's no doubt that Brenna is watching us—but whether she's been instructed to or whether she is doing it on her own—or whether she's watching me or you—remains to be seen," O'Brien said.

"In your role as a valet you're a more likely prospect for a lady's maid than I am," Adam reminded him.

"That's true. But you're better looking and a better catch."

"I think she finds you attractive. . . ." Adam teased.

"She might," O'Brien agreed. "Or she might have decided to use me to get to you." He shrugged his shoulders once again. "I don't know. Unfortunately, my French is worse than her English, and I can't begin to guess what her other language is. I do know that Brenna isn't as lazy as you think," O'Brien added. "Or as unfeeling. She may not help Georgiana take care of the housework, but she helps in other ways."

"What other ways?"

"According to Max, Brenna practices her lady's maid skills by taking care of George—by drawing her sister's baths and attending to her clothes and hair."

Adam got up out of his chair and began to pace the length of the library. "You mean to tell me that I'm paying one member of the staff to take care of another?"

"I hear she needs it now that she's sliced her hand."

"She cut her hand"—Adam stopped his pacing and turned to face his friend—"on a shard of broken porcelain. She didn't slice it."

"Isobel and Albert and Max made such fuss over the wound while Isobel was cleaning it and dressing it with salve, you would have sworn that it was mortal." O'Brien gave a sharp whistle as he reached over Adam's abandoned chair and helped himself to another whisky. "I don't know what they found more shocking—the fact that Georgiana cut her hand or the fact that you refused to allow her to continue to work until it healed. Let me tell you, boyo, there was quite a family discussion when Georgiana appeared for the noonday meal, all pink-cheeked and rosy-lipped, presenting her cut and your soiled handkerchief to Isobel." O'Brien took a sip of whisky, then refilled Adam's empty glass and held it up to him as Adam resumed his pacing. They kept their voices low and I didn't catch more than a word or two of the conversation, but your name and the word *porcelain* came up more than once."

"Thanks." Adam snagged the glass of whisky as he walked past.

Murphy winked and pretended to tip his cap. "At your service, sir." He grinned as Adam swallowed a mouthful of liquor. "I gathered from those two bits of information and the wound on Georgiana's hand that there was more breakage. . . ."

Adam laughed. "I seem to have that effect on her."

"What was it this time?" O'Brien asked more out of curiosity than anything else.

"The little shepherdess that used to sit upon the mantel in your bedchamber."

Recalling the pretty little porcelain figurine, O'Brien frowned. "Was she valuable?"

"The ones in Kirstin's house are."

"Ouch."

"Yes, ouch," Adam agreed. "That brings the breakage total to a tray of dishes, a clay pipe, a cup and saucer, and a porcelain shepherdess."

"It's a good thing Georgiana doesn't work at your saloon," O'Brien joked, "or there would be a severe shortage of beer mugs by now."

"Yes, but the value of the breakage would be much lower."

"Did she offer to repay you?"

Adam nodded. "She's offered to repay me for all of it. But it's out of the question," he said. "Worth gown or not, she doesn't make enough to replace what she's broken. Besides, there's no need. And it doesn't matter. The loss of a few pieces of expensive china isn't going to break me."

"What about the girl?" O'Brien asked, turning his unflinching stare on Adam.

Adam sighed. "The china is of no consequence, but George may prove to be the death of me."

Chapter 13

A Princess of the Blood Royal of the House of Saxe-Wallerstein-Karolya understands and willingly accepts the personal sacrifices she must make in order to do her duty to her country.

—Maxim 2: Protocol and Court Etiquette of Princesses of the Blood Royal of the House of Saxe-Wallerstein-Karolya, as decreed by His Serene Highness, Prince Karol I, 1432.

He had kissed her. Adam McKendrick had pulled her into his arms and kissed her. She had felt the heat of his body penetrating the fabric of her white cotton pinafore and the silk of her black dress beneath it. But the heat of his body had been nothing compared to the heat of his mouth.

Giana remembered the taste of him, the rasp of his tongue against her teeth as it slipped between her lips into her mouth. She recalled the urgency of his kiss and the way she had echoed it, moving her lips under his, allowing him further access. Giana moved her own tongue, then experienced the jolt of pure pleasure as it found, and mated with, Adam's. She had looped her arms around his neck, and her hands had somehow found their way onto his broad shoulders. She remembered the feel of the superfine of his coat against her fingertips. She had traced little circles against the fabric before trailing her fingers up the column of his neck to caress his thick, silky black hair.

As she lay in her bed staring up at the ceiling, Giana knew that as long as she lived she would remember the thrill, the sweetness, the romance, the absolute terror of her first kiss. It would remain firmly embedded in her heart and on her soul until her dying day. She pressed her fingertips against her mouth. A man had kissed her, and her life would never be the same.

Wagner moaned in his sleep, and Giana wiggled her toes against his back as he slept at the foot of her bed. Adam McKendrick complained about finding Wagner on his bed every time he turned around, but she didn't understand why. She preferred the comfort and companionship of a warm body cuddled beside her—even a canine one—because it kept her from feeling so alone and being so lonely.

She had always been alone. Her mother and father had had each other, and in many ways they had never needed anyone else. When she outgrew the nursery and her nanny, Giana had been alone. She was a princess surrounded by people, yet isolated from them by her position and rank. But for a few precious moments while Adam McKendrick was sharing his life's breath with her, she had felt as if she were a part of him. She, who had always felt apart and different, had felt as if she finally belonged, not to the people of Karolya, but to him. In his arms Giana had found the safety and security that had eluded her since the night she had learned that her parents were gone.

She reached up and traced the outline of the gold locket that lay beneath her nightgown, nestled in the valley between her breasts. It had belonged to her mother. Princess May had taken it from around her own neck and presented it to her daughter on the anniversary of Giana's twentieth year of life. Inside the locket was a miniature of her maternal grandparents copied from their official wedding portrait and a miniature of an informal portrait of her father and mother and herself on the day of her christening. Giana had always loved the expression on her parents' faces as they gazed down at the child their love had created. She swiped at a tear with the back of her hand and managed a tiny smile.

Her father had often said that he'd taken one look at her mother and known that May was the woman God sent to share his life. They had fallen in love and married despite the objections of her father's ministers, clergy, and the high aristocracy.

His Serene Highness Prince Christian of Saxe-Wallerstein-Karolya had married for reasons of the heart instead of for reasons of state. And because he had married for love, he had married beneath his rank.

Giana sighed. Now she understood why her mother had never explained how wonderful kissing could be. It was a feeling that couldn't be put into words. It could only be experienced. It could only be felt. And her parents had felt it. They had known that incredible feeling of wonder and the sense of belonging to someone else and to each other.

But Giana was a princess of the Blood Royal and princesses of the Blood Royal were not permitted to belong to anyone except their subjects, nor were they permitted to kiss a man until they had been pronounced man and wife. As to enjoying the experience, Giana suspected that that depended a great deal on the man chosen to be their husbands. She shuddered. Now that she knew what it was like to kiss and be kissed by Adam McKendrick, she found it impossible to imagine kissing any of the royal suitors who had petitioned her father for her hand in marriage or allowing them to kiss her—and sharing a bed with any of them was out of the question—especially her cousin Victor.

Unfortunately, princesses of the Blood Royal of the House of Saxe-Wallerstein-Karolya historically had little or no say in the man chosen to be their husbands. But in this Giana had been exceptionally lucky. Her father had not only refused her cousin Victor's suit, but had kept it a secret from her. The fact that he had done so had been a blessing because the idea of marrying her first cousin was so abhorrent to her it made her skin crawl.

Giana rolled onto her side and hugged her pillow closer. When she was a little girl, her mother had kept her entertained for hours with stories of how she and Prince Christian had met and fallen in love. But as she grew older, her mother had grown more and more reluctant to regale her with those romantic tales. And now she understood why.

Her mother wouldn't discuss the particulars of the marriage bed with her because her mother's tutelage in the intimacies to be found in the marriage bed had come from a loving husband. They were precious and private, not meant to be shared with anyone—even a daughter. Especially when the daughter's introduction into the intimacies of the marriage bed would most likely come from a stranger—a husband chosen by her father and his cabinet ministers for state reasons.

Giana exhaled the breath she hadn't realized she was holding. Her parents' marriage was unique in Karolyan history. They had been allowed to marry for love—not out of sentimentality, but because her father, as sovereign, had had the power to make the match he wanted. But her father was a man.

She was a female, and while the "Female Provision" of the Karolyan Charter allowed Giana to assume the throne, it did not allow her the complete freedom to rule as she saw fit. Giana suddenly realized that the sadness she had seen in her mother's eyes when she had begged to hear the romantic stories of her parents' courtship and marriage was there because Princess May had known that her daughter might not be as fortunate.

Princess May hadn't been born a princess, she became one when she married Prince Christian. She hadn't even been born Karolyan. Lady Caroline Frances Alexandra May, only child of the elderly marquess of Barracksford and his young marchioness, Lady May—as she preferred to be called—came into the world as the sole heiress to a tidy fortune.

There had been whispers surrounding the birth of Barracksford's heir, but none of that meant anything to the marquess and marchioness. Let the gossips speculate and whisper about the fact that Lady May bore no resemblance to the marquess. She was born a Barracksford and nothing could change that. The marquess and marchioness held their heads high and ignored the gossip. Antoinette Barracksford had married the marquess without regret and she had been rewarded with a daughter who became the light of her life and who exceeded her grandest expectations by marrying Prince Christian of Saxe-Wallerstein-Karolya, becoming a princess, and presenting her adopted country with an heir.

An heir who was currently working as a chambermaid in a hunting lodge deep in the Scottish highlands and sharing a bed with an Irish wolfhound while she built girlish fantasies around a man with dark hair and sky-blue eyes who kissed like a dream.

A dark-haired, blue-eyed man who had not only kissed her lips, but had kissed away the pain of the cut on her palm. A man who overlooked her embarrassing spate of clumsiness and the destruction of his objets d'art and household china. Although he refused to accept payment for the damages, Giana intended to find a way to repay him. And she knew, without a doubt, that if she thought about it long enough, she would come up with a way.

A Princess of the Blood Royal of the House of Saxe-Wallerstein-Karolya had been kissed by a man who was not her husband. A miracle had occurred. Anything was possible.

Chapter 14

"*How dare you stand before me and announce* that you have failed to locate her!" The white dueling scar that bisected Prince Victor Lucien of Saxe-Wallerstein-Karolya's left cheek stood out in stark contrast to the vivid scarlet hue staining the rest of his face as he berated the captain of the guard standing stiffly at attention before him.

"I regret that I must do so, Your Highness, but after searching every city, town, village, and encampment in Karolya from Christianberg to the mountains beyond Laken, we have failed in our quest to locate Princess Giana or Lord Gudrun." Captain Peter Tolsen betrayed no emotion as he stood before the regent and reported that the anarchists holding their beloved princess had eluded His Highness's Royal Palace Guard for nearly three months.

"He must have sent her out of the country," Prince Victor said.

"He, Your Highness, or they?" the captain asked.

"He, you incompetent cur!" Prince Victor exploded.

"Lord Gudrun?"

"Not Lord Gudrun! My uncle, Prince Christian!" Prince Victor forced himself to rein in his temper. It wouldn't do to let the earnest young captain know that he was playing an unwitting part in a scheme to cover up the identity of Princess May's and Prince Christian's real murderer or to lay the blame for their deaths at Gudrun's feet. "Maximillian Gudrun is nothing more than a glorified scribe. He has neither the skill nor the courage to spirit the princess out of the country."

"According to the reports of those of your household guards who attempted to aid my men, Lord Gudrun had the skill and the courage to murder Prince Christian and Princess May and abduct Princess Giana."

"And you lacked the skill to keep him from escaping with our princess." Prince Victor snapped at the captain.

"He could not have abducted or escaped with the princess," Captain Tolsen announced. "Because Princess Giana wasn't in the palace on the night of the murders."

Victor whirled around to face the captain. "How do you know that?"

"Your personal guard reported that the anarchists killed the guardsman on duty outside the princess's apartments."

"Which of my personal guard reported this? And to whom?" Victor tried to sound mildly interested, but he was seething inside.

"I sent word from the hospital that I wanted to speak to the guard who found my guardsman's body. Captain Mareska presented himself and related the details of the incident," Tolsen answered.

Victor stared down at his right hand. The finger that should have been home to the royal seal of state was bare. He did not have the seal or the princess and the only witness to Prince Christian's murder was still alive. Victor clenched his hand into a fist. "Did Mareska report anything else? Anything that might help us find the princess?"

Captain Tolsen shook his head. "He told me that the rabble broke into her rooms, forcing the doors, only to find her apartments unoccupied."

Mareska had reported too much. Tomorrow he would be replaced. And weeks from now, his family would receive word that he had died in the line of duty protecting the Prince Regent. The Karolyan people would learn that the anarchists who had murdered Prince Christian and Princess May and abducted their princess had also attempted to assassinate the Prince Regent. The same would be true of Captain Tolsen when his usefulness ended. Victor focused his gaze on the captain. "My uncle must have suspected something. He must have gotten wind of the anarchists' plot and sent Princess Giana to safety somewhere outside the border. But where? Where would he send her? And why hasn't she come forward?"

"I do not know, sir," Tolsen admitted.

"Why not?" Prince Victor asked. "You're captain of His Highness's Royal Palace Guards. You must have escorted her somewhere. . . ."

Captain Tolsen shook his head. "The Royal Guard did not escort her. If she left the country, she did so by force or by traveling incognito."

"You had no orders from Prince Christian? Or Lord Gudrun?"

"No, Your Highness." The captain looked up and met the prince's unnerving gaze.

"How do you explain her absence?"

"I cannot explain it, Your Highness. The surviving members of His Highness's guard were told that our princess had been taken hostage by anarchists." Captain Tolsen frowned. After escorting Prince Christian and Princess May to their apartments, the members of the Royal Guard not standing guard outside the doors leading to Prince Christian's and Princess May's private chambers and Princess Giana's private chambers, had retired to their barracks for the night. Most of those guards had never awakened. The anarchists had set upon them while they slept. Captain Tolsen had been fortunate. He'd recovered from his stab wounds, but many of his friends and fellow guardsmen had not.

Prince Victor's contingent of guards had escaped the massacre. Their barracks were in the Tower at the opposite end of the palace close to Prince Victor's apartments. Victor's guards had raised the alarm after the Prince and Princess were murdered.

Victor narrowed his gaze at the captain of the guard. "And so she was," the prince regent agreed. "But we have it on the highest authority that the anarchists were in league with Lord Gudrun. We must assume that Lord Gudrun ordered the princess taken."

"Whose authority, sir?" Captain Tolsen forgot himself long enough to demand an answer. "I should like to speak to the person from whom you've received this information."

Prince Victor stared at Tolsen, daring him to continue. "The identity of the informant does not concern you, Captain Tolsen."

"You charged me with the investigation into Princess Giana's disappearance, sir. If you have information as to her whereabouts, it concerns me." The young captain stood his ground, refusing to allow the prince regent to intimidate him.

"I did not charge you with the duty of *investigating* my cousin's disappearance! I charged you with the duty of *locating* her and with rescuing her from her abductors," the prince told him. "The princess is gone! That much is quite apparent! How she disappeared is of little consequence now!" He pointed a finger at the captain of the guard. "You are charged with the task of finding her! And soon! Time is running out, Captain. For both of us!" Prince Victor drew his dress sword from its scabbard.

Captain Tolsen remained silent. He had failed in his mission to find and rescue the heir to the throne and in so doing had angered and frustrated the volatile prince regent. Up until this moment Captain Tolsen believed that the anarchists who had murdered Prince Christian and Princess May had abducted Princess Giana, but now, he wondered. . . .

As he stared at the Prince Regent, Captain Tolsen understood that if it pleased him to do so, Prince Victor could dispense with the niceties of military protocol and dispatch the current captain of the royal guard with one clean thrust of his sword and replace him with someone more loyal to the prince regent than he appeared to be.

Tolsen looked into the prince regent's eyes and saw death. He drew himself up to his full height and stood ramrod straight, waiting for the thrust that would end his life—and conceal his failure.

But he was granted a reprieve. A knock sounded on the

salon doors as the prince regent's equerry announced the arrival of his savior, "The special envoy from the Court of St. James has arrived, Your Highness."

Prince Victor growled his frustration, then wielded his sword against the household furnishings, severing the legs of a dainty French cabriole table, sending it crashing to the floor.

Captain Tolsen breathed a silent, heartfelt sigh of relief, but Prince Victor wasn't finished with him yet.

"Find her!" Victor ordered. "Find Princess Giana and find her fast, or I will find a captain of the guard who can!"

Captain Tolsen gave a crisp nod, clicked his heels together, and backed out of the salon, withdrawing from Prince Victor's presence before the prince regent could change his mind about allowing him to escape. He passed the British Special Envoy, Lord Everleigh, on the way into the room and wondered how the prince regent would explain the splintered gilt table.

Lord Everleigh greeted Prince Victor with a brief bow. He did not slight the prince regent intentionally, but neither did he show the deference usually reserved for ruling heads of state.

His action angered the prince regent, but Lord Everleigh ignored the prince's displeasure.

A handsome man, in his late fifties, the marquess of Everleigh had spent more than thirty years in the diplomatic corps as ambassador to the Habsburg court in Vienna and as special envoy to Russia, Crimea, and the Balkans. In his current role as special envoy to Saxe-Wallerstein-Karolya, Lord Everleigh was acting on personal instructions from the Queen's Most Trusted, Loyal, and Special Advisor, the sixteenth marquess of Templeston.

Lord Templeston had charged Lord Everleigh with the task of discovering what happened in Christianberg and if the prince and princess were murdered by anarchists or by someone hoping to usurp the throne. As godmother to Princess Giana, Queen Victoria felt it her duty to assist the Karolyan government in finding her. Although she knew Prince Victor was hoping for official recognition from the British government, the queen refused to grant it. If Princess Giana was still alive, she must have a country and a throne to return to. If Princess Giana had been abducted and murdered, the prince regent, according to the Karolyan State Charter, must present her body or the state seal in order to be proclaimed ruler.

"Our beloved queen sends her greetings and her deepest condolences on the deaths of Prince Christian and Princess May and the disappearance of Her Serene Highness Princess Giana," Lord Everleigh offered.

Prince Victor lowered his gaze and inclined his head. "Please relay our deepest thanks to Her Majesty."

"Of course, sir." Lord Everleigh studied the prince. "Her Majesty and Her Majesty's government is quite alarmed by the state of affairs in Karolya. . . ."

The prince regent took umbrage to the special envoy's statement. "I assure you, sir, so that you may assure your queen, that she has no cause for concern about the state of affairs in Karolya."

"I beg your pardon, Your Highness," Lord Everleigh replied, "but Her Majesty disagrees. Anarchists who seek to abolish all monarchies have apparently murdered the hereditary ruler of Karolya, and his wife. That is reason enough to concern our gracious queen. The fact that her goddaughter, Princess Giana, is missing only adds to her concern. You are second in line to the throne of Karolya, behind the heir apparent. You are regent because Princess Giana has yet to be found. The government is in complete disarray and you lack the support you require in the parliament." He paused. "Those facts give Our Gracious Majesty plenty of reason to be concerned and plenty of reason to express it."

Prince Victor attempted to conceal his anger and failed miserably. Lord Everleigh noted that the prince regent's dueling scar gave him away, serving as a barometer for his moods. "I am quite capable of governing the country in my cousin's absence."

"And the Karolyan Charter gives you that right," Lord Everleigh commented. "But as prince regent, you are acting in Princess Giana's stead and on her behalf until she is returned."

"We have been searching for the princess for weeks now—

to no avail—and we fear that something terrible has happened to her."

"Something terrible *has* happened to her," Lord Everleigh replied. "She has been kidnapped by the person or persons who murdered her parents and is being held against her will."

"Our cousin, Princess Giana, was kidnapped by anarchists in league with a traitor. We have evidence that suggests that Prince Christian's private secretary, Lord Maximillian Gudrun, conspired with the anarchists to arrange the deaths of Prince Christian and Princess May and the abduction of the heir."

"For what purpose?" Lord Everleigh asked. "Why would Lord Gudrun betray his country?"

"For Karolya's iron ore deposits," Prince Victor responded promptly. "His Highness, Prince Christian, refused to barter or sell the iron ore deposits that would greatly enrich Karolya's coffers."

The consummate diplomat, Lord Everleigh gave no hint as to his political leaning or partisanship. "It is our understanding that Karolya's coffers are already full. Prince Christian was a very wealthy man, and the country has one of the highest standards of living in Europe. There was no need for Prince Christian to sell the iron ore deposits or rape the landscape in order to add to the country's already overflowing treasury."

"That may be true," Victor agreed, "but the fact remains that we have uncovered evidence that Lord Gudrun engineered the deaths of the prince and princess and the abduction of the Princess Royal in order to gain control of Karolya and the iron ore deposits."

"Then it is fortunate for the people of Karolya that your life was spared, Your Highness." Lord Everleigh met the prince regent's unwavering gaze.

"It was, indeed, most fortunate," the prince regent agreed.

"A great deal more fortunate than the other members of your family." Lord Everleigh didn't blink as he asked the barbed question, "Why do you suppose that came to be, Your Highness?"

Prince Victor's complexion was a mottled mix of red and scarlet hues. "I beg your pardon?"

"Anarchists aren't ordinarily so discriminating," Lord Everleigh responded. "They usually kill as many royal personages as possible. And generally do not leave a member of the ruling house in a position to take over the country." He paused for effect. "Our Gracious Majesty, Queen Victoria, held the late Prince Christian and Princess May in the highest regard and felt very deep affection for them. She is eager to honor our country's alliance with Karolya and assist your government in its efforts to locate Princess Giana. . . ."

"That will not be necessary," Prince Victor replied. "We thank Her Majesty for the offer, but we are quite capable of negotiating with the anarchists for Princess Giana's safe return."

"Then you have located the anarchist leader?"

Victor faltered for a moment. "No, we have not."

"With whom will you negotiate?"

"The anarchists have made their demands known."

"Have they?" Lord Everleigh pursed his lips in thought. "We were not aware . . ."

"The anarchists made their demands known through the democratic newspaper," Prince Victor answered in a flash of brilliance.

"I see," Lord Everleigh said. "It was our understanding that the publication of Karolya's democratic newspaper had been suspended since the night of the murders so as not to further alarm the people about the disappearance of the heir apparent."

"The official newspaper has been suspended," Victor recovered. "But we have continued to issue bulletins informing our people of our efforts to locate our beloved princess. The anarchists contacted the editor to make their demands known. They've assured us that the princess is alive and well cared for. Of course, the editor immediately contacted the military police."

"Why the military police?"

"Because Karolya is under martial law until the negotiations are completed and the princess royal is returned."

"I see." Lord Everleigh nodded his head in understanding. "And what have these anarchists demanded?"

"That we not add a Declaration of Rights for the Masses to the Karolyan Charter and that ownership of Karolya's iron ore deposits be surrendered to them as representatives of the people."

Lord Everleigh paused. "That's odd. One would think that anarchists would support any legislation created to provide and protect the basic rights of the common people." He looked at Prince Victor. "So, they wish to exchange the princess for the iron ore."

"Yes."

"I do not envy you, Your Highness. That is a terrible decision for a ruler to have to make." The empathy in the special envoy's words sounded entirely genuine. "The loss of either one will have a profound effect on Karolya's future."

"Yes, but our cousin would be the greater loss." Prince Victor didn't flinch as he looked the older diplomat in the eye.

"One would imagine that if sold to the highest bidder, the iron ore deposits would be worth an enormous sum of money."

"Yes, one might imagine that." Victor glanced down at his right hand.

Lord Everleigh followed his gaze. "It is a great deal to lose."

"No more so than the Crown." Prince Victor gave Lord Everleigh a brilliant smile. "But that is not going to happen. I am most confident that our cousin, Princess Giana, will be found and that the people and the parliament will unite behind its new ruler. I hope that is what you shall report to Her Majesty."

"Most definitely, Your Highness," Everleigh agreed. "I shall be most happy to report that you have everything in Karolya under control and that your efforts to secure Princess Giana's release from her captors is currently under way."

"Will that satisfy Her Majesty?"

Lord Everleigh smiled. "I've no doubt that Lord Templeston and Her Majesty will be most satisfied to learn that they need not worry about Karolya's future. Your assurances, Your Highness, have left us with no doubt as to who is responsible for these heinous and cowardly acts against the Crown, and I am sure Her Majesty and her most trusted adviser will be as relieved as I am to know that you have proven yourself to be a completely formidable adversary—"

Victor took a step toward the special envoy.

"For the anarchists," Lord Everleigh continued. He shook his head. "Until today I would never have believed anyone so close to Prince Christian and Princess May could be capable of such treachery. Nor could I ever have imagined Maximillian Gudrun in the role of anarchist leader or thought to point a finger at him. But you, Your Highness, have managed to make me see things in their true light."

"Have we?"

"Yes, indeed. I seldom mistake a person's character." Lord Everleigh sketched another bow.

"We are very glad we were able to help." Victor grinned.

"I'm sure Her Majesty will be most grateful to know that you have been so forthcoming."

"Will you be sending your report soon, Lord Everleigh?"

"I shall have it ready for the next post," he answered.

Prince Victor nodded. "If there is nothing more—"

"There is one other thing," Lord Everleigh told him.

"Yes?"

"I must confess to a certain amount of curiosity as to what happened to that small gilt table. I thought I heard a crash upon my arrival. . . ." Lord Everleigh nodded to the remains of the French cabriole.

The prince regent attempted a boyish shrug. "You must have been mistaken. You see, the anarchists invaded this part of the palace and wreaked havoc the night our aunt and uncle were murdered. It remained closed and sealed until we chose to use it for this meeting. We did not realize it had not been properly cleared and cleaned."

The special envoy glanced around the room. Except for the gilt table that lay splintered on the marble floor, the room was clean, the surfaces of the furniture, dusted. If the anarchists had wreaked havoc upon the room, they had done it very neatly, for nothing else was disturbed. No china smashed or paintings slashed. No obvious signs of looting. "Thank you for indulging my curiosity, Your Highness."

"Good day, Lord Everleigh." Prince Victor dismissed him.

Lord Everleigh bowed to the prince regent, then respectfully backed out of the room.

❧

Three quarters of an hour later the marquess of Everleigh sat down at the desk in his borrowed office in the British Embassy to write his report. He would follow up his written report with a face-to-face audience with the queen and the marquess, but first he had to relay the details of his audience with Karolya's acting ruler to the marquess of Templeston.

"Lord Everleigh? Am I disturbing you?"

Lord Everleigh looked up from his writing to find Lord Sissingham, the British ambassador in Karolya, standing in the doorway. "No. Please, come in, Sissingham."

"How did it go?" Sissingham asked.

Everleigh put down his pen and invited the ambassador to sit down and help himself to the tea tray. "I believe you have accurately judged the situation."

Sissingham raised an eyebrow. "Then you agree?"

"Most definitely," Lord Everleigh replied. "There are no anarchists."

"We were suspicious when we heard rumors that Prince Victor was inciting young men of the ruling class to denounce Prince Christian's support of a constitution and a Declaration of Rights for the Masses."

"Your suspicions appear to be correct," Lord Everleigh said, grimly. "Prince Victor has usurped his uncle's throne."

"Have we any idea what has become of Her Serene Highness Princess Giana?"

Everleigh shook his head. "Prince Victor is a desperate man. Desperate to hold on to the Crown—a Crown he has stolen first from his uncle and from his cousin, Princess Giana."

"Do you think he has her?" Sissingham asked.

Everleigh thought for a moment before he replied, "I don't think so. He wasn't wearing the royal seal."

Sissingham was impressed. "You noticed."

"Victor didn't appear nervous, but he kept glancing at his right hand. It struck me as odd until I recalled that Prince Christian shook hands with me at a meeting in Geneva once and the state seal cut into my hand. Prince Christian apologized by saying that he rarely shook hands because the seal tended to bruise him and maim the handshake recipient. He laughed and said he'd made an exception in Geneva because he didn't want to appear to be a stuffy old monarchist at a meeting on the modernization of Europe. He always wore the seal of state on his right hand. Victor's right hand was bare."

"Have you had an occasion to read a copy of the Karolyan Charter?" Sissingham asked.

"On the journey here from London."

"Then you're aware that Victor cannot be crowned unless he abides by the Law of Succession. He cannot marry until the traditional period of mourning for the late ruler is over and he cannot be crowned until he is married."

"The traditional period of mourning is one year," Everleigh said. "He can govern for seven more months before he's required him to marry a princess of Karolyan blood."

"The only available princesses of Karolyan blood are Victor's sisters and Princess Giana."

"In order to be crowned His Serene Highness, Prince Victor IV of Saxe-Wallerstein-Karolya, the prince regent will have to marry Princess Giana or submit proof of her death and produce the seal of state." Lord Everleigh ran his fingers through his hair. "He's desperate to find her."

"So are we," Sissingham said.

"Yes, but he wants the crown and the iron ore deposits. We only want to see that she is safely returned so that we can help her reclaim her country and her crown."

"How much damage can Victor do to the country in seven months?" Sissingham wondered.

"If he finds Princess Giana before we do, Victor could force her into marrying him."

"I don't think the princess would ever agree to marry her parents' killer," Sissingham said.

"Under normal circumstances, I don't think she would either. But these aren't normal circumstances. If she is being held captive somewhere, she may not know who is holding her or who is responsible for her parents' deaths," Everleigh expounded. "And if she's in voluntary hiding and Victor finds her, she may not have a choice. Marriage and the opportunity to regain your country are preferable to death."

Sissingham frowned. "And even if he chose not to marry her, Victor could coerce her into handing over the seal . . ."

"We are, of course, assuming that she is still alive and that the seal is in her possession," Everleigh interrupted. "And that she wants to regain her crown . . ." Deep in thought, Everleigh rested his elbow on the desk, propped his chin on his thumb and lightly tapped his lower lip with the tip of his index finger.

"We might try negotiating," Sissingham volunteered.

"With imaginary anarchists?"

"No, with Victor."

Everleigh looked askance at the ambassador.

"Hear me out," Sissingham said.

Everleigh nodded.

"Suppose the princess is in voluntary hiding and suppose the price of her freedom is her signature on the rights to the Karolyan timber and iron ore deposits, do you think there is any chance that she might come forward?"

"Would you with every newspaper in Europe and Britain, including *The Times*, carrying the latest news of Victor's search for the missing princess?" Everleigh asked.

The ambassador frowned. "What if we promised to protect her?"

"We can promise," Everleigh admitted, "but I don't know if we can ensure her complete safety if Victor sets assassins on her. And if we were successful in our negotiations, what is the likelihood of Prince Victor honoring such an agreement with her?"

"None." Sissingham admitted. "Her life would be forfeit."

"Agreed," Everleigh said. "The only way Victor can rule is if she's his wife or if she's a corpse." He glanced at Sissingham. "You are more familiar with the princess than I am. Do you think she is politically well-versed or intelligent enough to arrive at the same conclusion we've come to?"

Sissingham nodded. "Especially if Maximillian Gudrun is with her."

"Suppose she is alive and Lord Gudrun is with her. Where

would they go? Is there anyone in Europe—any relatives she can trust?"

The ambassador met the special envoy's gaze. "Princess May was an only child and all of her family, except distant cousins, are gone. The only close relatives Princess Giana has left are Prince Victor, his mother, three sisters and two younger brothers."

"She wouldn't turn to them. And even if she did, it's doubtful that any of them would hide Princess Giana from Victor." Lord Everleigh sighed. "What about her paternal aunt? Prince Christian's older sister?"

"Princess Pauline lives in Saint Therese's Convent outside Salzburg."

"Could Princess Giana seek asylum there?"

The ambassador shrugged. "I don't think so. Women seeking sanctuary at Saint Therese's are admitted only if they intend to remain there. Princess Giana has no immediate relatives to turn to except Victor's family and a few distant cousins who've married into the other royal families of Europe."

"Some of whom are negotiating to buy iron ore and timber and who may or may not be in league with Victor," Lord Everleigh said.

"That leaves her godmother. Our gracious queen."

"Who remains secluded at Windsor." Everleigh looked at the ambassador.

"If Victor is searching for her, he's sure to have men in London and around Windsor."

"What about Scotland? The queen will make her annual trek to Balmoral in August. Do you think Princess Giana is aware of the queen's schedule?"

"Of course she is," Sissingham said. "She and her parents have visited the queen at Balmoral." He met the special envoy's gaze. "But so has Victor."

"True," Lord Everleigh nodded. "But if I were Princess Giana and I were hiding from my enemies, I'd do my damnedest to obtain an audience with someone I knew I could trust and someone I knew could protect me and who better than my godmother, the queen of England?"

"And it would be a great deal easier to obtain an audience with the queen in Scotland than it would be at Windsor . . ." the ambassador agreed.

"I think we would be remiss if we didn't begin a discreet investigation of the towns and villages within a day's journey of Balmoral."

Several blocks away at the Christianberg Palace, Prince Victor Lucien sent for his equerry. "Find a goldsmith," he ordered.

"Sir?"

"Find a goldsmith," Prince Victor repeated his order. "And every tall blond female bearing a resemblance to our princess that you can find." He pointed to a miniature of Princess Giana that sat on what had once been Prince Christian's desk. "Take that with you for comparison."

"I do not understand," the equerry replied.

"What is there to understand?" Prince Victor demanded. "We've given an order we expect you to follow. We require a goldsmith." He stared as his equerry. "The British government is snapping at our heels. Time is running out. We need the Karolyan State Seal, and if we cannot locate the original, we must produce a well-crafted replacement. The same is true of the princess."

Chapter 15

The Bountiful Baron is a man who is keenly aware and always in control of his surroundings.

—THE FIRST INSTALLMENT OF THE TRUE ADVENTURES OF THE BOUNTIFUL BARON: WESTERN BENEFACTOR TO BLOND, BEAUTIFUL, AND BETRAYED WOMEN WRITTEN BY JOHN J. BOOKMAN, 1874.

"*Wake up, boyo, or you'll be missing your* breakfast." O'Brien burst into Adam's bedchamber carrying a tray with a pot of tea, a kettle of boiling water, and a cup and saucer on it in one hand and a pair of Adam's trousers and a white linen shirt over his arm. He set the tray on the table beside Adam's bed, then tossed his trousers and his shirt at him.

Adam shoved his shirt off his face and sat up. "What time is it?"

"Half past six." O'Brien poured Adam a cup of tea and handed it to him, then carried the kettle of water to the basin in the shaving stand and filled the bowl.

Adam accepted the tea. "Where's yours?" he grumbled, glaring up at his friend and drinking companion, who was perfectly groomed and showing no ill effects from the previous night's indulgence.

"I had mine earlier this morning."

"What are you doing up? I ordered breakfast served at half past eight."

"The staff eats before they begin their workday," O'Brien recited. "In a well-run household a proper gentleman's gentleman rises with the rest of the staff to prepare for his employer's awakening."

"Was that the topic of this morning's lecture?"

"Aye."

"And you stood for it?"

"I suffered through it," Murphy replied. "I am supposed to be a proper gentleman's gentleman, remember?"

Adam took a sip of tea, grimacing as the hot, sweet liquid burned its way down his throat to his stomach. He wasn't sure what had happened to the cook, because he specifically remembered asking the woman if she knew how to brew coffee. But if someone didn't teach her how to make a pot of coffee soon, he was going to have to give up drinking coffee and learn to drink the scalding and disgustingly sweet tea she sent up to him every morning—or find another cook. "Where do I have to go to get a cup of coffee?"

"Kinlochen."

"Why is that?"

"Because proper households serve tea."

"I don't care about being proper. I want a cup of coffee. I need a cup of coffee!" Adam growled. "And so do you. You couldn't have had more than three hours of sleep."

"Closer to two," O'Brien admitted. "But your proper household is running smoothly. The question is who does it run to suit? Because it does not run to suit Adam McKendrick."

"No, it does not," Adam replied. "And it's about time I did something about it."

O'Brien smiled.

Adam swung his legs over the side of the bed, but kept his grip on the covers, anchoring them across his lap. He was naked except for a pair of dark woolen socks.

"You're wearing socks."

"Of course, I'm wearing socks," Adam said. "It's as cold as an icehouse in here." He shot his friend a dirty look. "So get the hell out of here so I can cover the rest of me before I freeze to death."

"A proper gentleman's gentleman assists his employer with his dressing."

"I can dress myself," Adam reminded him. "I've been doing

it for quite a while now. I'm going to get breakfast. You go back to bed."

"And miss all the fun when you take on the household staff? Not on your life."

"At least have the decency to turn your back."

O'Brien obliged.

Adam stood up, stepped into his trousers, and pulled his linen shirt over his head. He walked over to his shaving stand and dropped a towel in the hot water. He took out his razor, removed it from its case, and stroked it against the razor strop. When he finished stropping his razor, he laid it aside, then wrung the hot water from the towel and placed the steaming linen over the lower portion of his face. "Ah . . ." He closed his eyes and allowed the heat from the cloth to clear his head, penetrate his pores, and soften his whisker stubble.

"Shall I attend to your shaving, sir?" O'Brien couldn't keep the note of laughter out of his voice when he asked the facetious question.

"It may surprise you to learn that I can dress and *shave* myself," Adam shot back. He removed the cloth and opened his eyes. "I've been doing that for quite some time now, too." He stared into the mirror as he dipped his shaving brush in the basin of hot water, then into his shaving mug where he worked the spicy sandalwood soap into a frothy lather. Adam coated his beard with the soap, then lifted his razor and began to carefully scrape away his whiskers.

"You're the one who accused me of being a valet." Murphy still loved baiting Adam over the whole valet misunderstanding. It was practically a daily ritual now. He went to the armoire and took out a collar and tie from one drawer and a waistcoat from another, then turned his attention to the selection of coats and jackets. O'Brien held up two coats—a dark green and a heather tweed.

"I didn't accuse you of being a valet," Adam corrected. "I told you Isobel thought you were my gentleman's gentleman." He glanced at the jackets O'Brien held.

"You could have set her straight," Murphy said.

"I did set her straight, but she chose not to believe me because you arrived with a wagonload of new and expensive luggage—something she said only a valet would do. You decided to masquerade as one." Adam finished shaving and donned his collar and tie.

"And I'm becoming quite good at it, don't you think?" He winked. "Solid or tweed?"

Adam shrugged into a brown waistcoat that contrasted very nicely with his buff trousers. "Tweed."

O'Brien took the jacket off its hanger and held it out for Adam to slip into, then tilted the cheval glass so Adam could inspect his appearance.

Adam raked his fingers through his hair and laughed at his reflection. "Well, what do you think? How do I look?"

O'Brien grinned. "You look like the lord who's about to retake his manor."

"Good morning, sir," Albert greeted Adam as soon as he entered the dining room.

"Good morning." Adam took a plate from the stack on the sideboard and filled it with an array of food warming in the silver chafing dishes, then walked over to the dining table and sat down.

Albert filled a cup with steaming hot tea and set it down beside Adam's plate.

Adam picked up the cup of tea and handed it back to Albert. "I don't drink tea."

The butler took the cup of tea, removed it to the sideboard, then returned to the dining table and silently placed a cup of hot chocolate beside Adam's plate.

Adam frowned at it. "I don't want chocolate." He looked up at Albert. "I drink coffee."

Albert shook his head. "No coffee."

"Why not?" Adam demanded. "I drink coffee. Hot, black coffee. Every morning. Not tea. Not chocolate. Coffee." He knew he was running the risk of sounding like a spoiled child, but it was time he began enforcing his authority in his home and now was as good a time as any to begin.

"No coffee," Albert repeated.

"Then find some," Adam ordered, raising his voice loud enough to be heard in the next room. "Can't a man get a cup of coffee in his own house?"

Max came running. "Good morning, sir."

Adam acknowledged him with a quick nod. Trust Max to come translate Adam's simple, but largely ignored, instructions for his brother.

"A mail packet arrived for you from London," Max continued. "I placed it on the desk in your study, and I took the liberty of giving the newspapers to Albert to iron for you." Max turned to Albert and questioned him in a language Adam didn't understand.

Albert nodded.

"He says he ironed them well so there's no need to worry about the ink smearing your hands or clothing. They are neatly stacked on your desk. I hope that meets with your satisfaction."

Adam smiled. "As a matter of fact, it's the first thing he's done that meets with my satisfaction."

"Sir?"

Adam waited while the clock on the mantel chimed seven times, then focused his attention on his private secretary. "It's seven o'clock in the morning."

"Yes, sir," Max answered with a puzzled look on his face.

"Max, why am I sitting down to a breakfast of scrambled eggs at seven o'clock in the morning?" Adam asked. "When I ordered it to be served at half past eight?"

"The household runs on a schedule, sir," Max replied stiffly.

"Yes, it does," Adam agreed. "But not at the expense of its owner. I'm eating scrambled eggs because I don't like kidneys, blood pudding, or ptarmigan, and the steak I ordered isn't on the menu. Nor is the coffee I drink."

"Sir?"

"This household will be run to suit me." Adam's voice held an unyielding note of steel resolve. "Me. Adam McKendrick. No one else. Is that clear?"

"It is very clear. But I fail to understand the reason for your displeasure, sir." Max faltered for a moment, then cast a speculative look at Adam. "With the exception of Her—Giana's—

unfortunate accidents with the china, the household has been run to suit you."

"Really?" Adam quickly finished eating his scrambled eggs, then laid his fork aside and pushed back his chair and stood up. "Let's go see."

"Sir?" Max was clearly taken aback.

"Let's take a look," Adam reiterated. "We'll start with the kitchen." He turned and led the way out of the dining room, down the corridor to the kitchen, where he stopped in the doorway and stared at the cook. He was male and, from the looks of it, French. "Where's Mrs. Dunham, the cook I recommended Mrs. Langstrom hire?"

"Mrs. Dunham was a local woman who cooked local fare," Max explained. "She did not cook in the French style."

"I know," Adam said. "She cooked good, plain, hearty fare. That is why I recommended that Mrs. Langstrom hire her."

"I'm sure she is a wonderful cook," Max said, "but the food she cooks is not the sort of food Her—to which we were accustomed. We were among the staff of the countess of Brocavia, which set an exquisite table. That is why Isobel—I mean Mrs. Langstrom—hired Monsieur Henri."

The temper Adam had been struggling to contain exploded. *"Henri!"*

"Oui?" The chef glanced up as he answered.

"Do you speak English?" he asked in French.

"Non."

Adam exhaled and slowly counted to ten, then asked if Henri could make coffee. *"Est-ce que vous pouvez faire le café?"*

"Oui," Henri replied in his native tongue. "but, there isn't any."

Adam ordered, "Find some, or find someplace else to cook, because from now on I expect a pot of hot coffee every morning. Understand?"

"Oui." The French chef nodded to show his understanding.

Adam turned to Max. "Find Mrs. Dunham and hire her back right away."

"Sir, how will I explain to Henri?"

"Explain that from now on, Henri and Mrs. Dunham will share the kitchen duties. For breakfast, I'll expect a variety of Scottish and French dishes. Mrs. Dunham will prepare luncheons and tea and Henri will be responsible for dinner and desserts. Larchmont Lodge will offer its owner, guests, and staff a choice of fare."

"Chef Henri will not be happy," Maximillian warned. "He prefers to be in control of his kitchens."

"And I prefer to be in control of my household," Adam replied. "If you can't manage to run it to my satisfaction, without countermanding my orders, I'll find a staff who will." With that, Adam turned and stalked out of the kitchen, his long legs eating up the distance as he left the kitchen and made his way to his library.

Maximillian followed close on his heels, managing to cross the threshold before Adam slammed the door in his face.

"Out!" Adam ordered.

"Sir?"

"That will be all, Max," Adam said.

"But, sir . . ."

Christ, but he was tired of having all of his instructions and decisions questioned and circumvented! "Please leave, Max." Adam struggled to rein his temper in. "I want a few minutes alone."

Max opened his mouth to protest, but Adam cut him off. "Perhaps I was remiss in not explaining my purpose in renovating Larchmont Lodge. But I plan to open it as a gentleman's club. A place of refuge for men of wealth and stature—businessmen, aristocrats, and world leaders—to come to—" Adam broke off as a slight noise caught his attention. It sounded as if someone had drawn a quick breath. He turned toward the sound and noticed a triangle of black silk on the carpet behind the leather sofa. There it was again, another almost imperceptible noise, only this time it sounded like a mouse crawling across the open pages of a book. Adam suspected it might be a very big mouse—one who stood nearly six feet tall in her stocking feet. He bit the inside of his cheek to keep from smiling.

The older man blanched. Max had heard it, too. "Do I understand, sir, that you intend to open the doors of Larchmont Lodge to the public?" Max asked.

Max sounded as if Adam had just announced that he intended to assassinate the queen. "I intend to open the doors of Larchmont Lodge to the well-paying public." Although the links required another six months or so of work to become established, Adam had decided to extend an invitation to preview the lodge to a few select guests during the week of the Cowes Regatta. "The best way to turn this pile of stone into a profitable enterprise is to convert it into a place where the rich and famous can rest and relax far away from the pressures of everyday life. I hope it will be a place men will come to hunt and fish, to ride and walk the moors, to golf or lounge around playing cards or reading. I've already issued private invitations for the week of the Cowes Regatta." He gave a little snort. "You needn't worry about riffraff, Max. They won't be able to afford to holiday here."

Adam waited until the private secretary regained some color in his face before he waved him back over the threshold. "Thank you, Max, that will be all." He closed the door to the library, barely missing the highly polished toes of Max's shoes.

Adam turned the key in the lock, then closed his eyes and leaned against the door, resting his forehead against its cool, wood grain surface. His body ached from hours spent overseeing the construction of the golf links and from hours of instruction in the game of golf. For what was the use of building a golf links to entice the richest and most powerful men in the world if he didn't know how to play the game with them? His head was pounding from too much drink, too little sleep, and no coffee. He pushed away from the door and eyed the long leather sofa.

Adam glanced at his desk where a packet of mail and a pile of neatly ironed newspapers lay stacked on the blotter just as Max had left them. He should attend to his correspondence, but he couldn't concentrate on the mail or the newspapers with an aching head. He had to admit the sofa was more enticing than the mail. A brief nap would do him a world of good. Besides, Adam reasoned, he hadn't planned to get up before half-past eight anyway. But there was the small problem of George. What to do about her? Adam covered a yawn with his hand, then slipped the key to the door inside his waistcoat pocket and stretched out on the sofa. She was the interloper. Let her wait. He just needed to close his eyes for a few moments. . . .

Chapter 16

A Princess of the Blood Royal of the House of Saxe-Wallerstein-Karolya respects the privacy and the property of her subjects.

—MAXIM 803: PROTOCOL AND COURT ETIQUETTE OF PRINCESSES OF THE BLOOD ROYAL OF THE HOUSE OF SAXE-WALLERSTEIN-KAROLYA, AS DECREED BY HIS SERENE HIGHNESS, PRINCE CHRISTIAN I, 1864.

Giana leaned against the back of the long leather sofa and reread the article printed in the bottom corner of the front page of the *Times of London*. Shocked by the deaths of Their Serene Highnesses, Prince Christian and Princess May of Saxe-Wallerstein-Karolya at the hands of anarchists, Britain's Queen Victoria had sent a special envoy to Christianberg, the capital of Karolya, to assist Prince Victor, the prince regent, in the investigation of the murders and in negotiating the return of Her Serene Highness Princess Georgiana, who had been taken hostage and was currently being held for ransom by the anarchists, whom it was believed were in league with the late prince's private secretary.

She had stumbled across the newspaper while cleaning the McKendrick's office, and although she had been taught to contain her curiosity and ignore the reams of official documents she saw lying scattered across the surface of her father's massive desk, Giana couldn't ignore a newspaper article about her family. Not when it affected her future and the futures of the men and women who had risked their lives in order to save her.

Giana swallowed her tears and bit back a sob. Victor had accused Max of being in league with anarchists who were supposed to have murdered her parents and kidnapped her! But the anarchists were a figment of Victor's imagination. Victor had murdered her parents and was trying to murder her, and now he had enlisted the help of her godmother's government in finding her.

Giana glanced at the date on the paper. It was more than a fortnight old, and although this edition had been lying on the top of the stack, she didn't know whether or not it was the most recent one. McKendrick had arrived before she had had time to look through the rest of the stack. She had grabbed the newspaper and hidden behind the sofa to read it. She hadn't intended to eavesdrop on his conversation with Max any more than she had intended to neglect her household duties by reading the newspaper instead of cleaning the library, but there had been no way to avoid overhearing the McKendrick's conversation with Max.

And the conversation she had overheard was as shocking as the newspaper article. She was so shocked by what she'd heard she hadn't been able to prevent a gasp of surprise—a gasp that had almost led to her discovery. Adam McKendrick intended to open Larchmont Lodge to the public—to the wealthy male public. Time was running out. The regatta was only a few weeks away. If she didn't think of some way of reaching Balmoral or of delaying the preview, there would be no place for her to hide.

Giana bit her bottom lip. Max had been horrified by the news and must be beside himself with anxiety for her safety. To think that the one safe place they had been able to find was about to become a haven for the very men she was trying to avoid! She needed to talk to Max, needed to consult with the rest of her entourage before they panicked. She needed to come up with a plan.

Unfortunately, she couldn't do anything until she made her way out of the library without waking McKendrick. McKendrick. Giana ground her teeth together and looked up at the ceiling. She hadn't expected McKendrick to remain in the library. She had expected him to follow Max out the door, but McKendrick had slammed the door almost in Max's face and decided to take a nap. A nap! Who would have thought that he'd decide to take a nap so soon after breakfast?

Folding the newspaper as quietly as possible, Giana lifted her skirts and tucked it in the waistband of her drawers. She didn't like the idea of borrowing McKendrick's newspaper, but she needed to show it to Max, needed to share her fears with the one person who had as much to lose as she did. Giana took a deep breath, screwed her courage to the sticking place, and crawled around the sofa.

The McKendrick—Adam—was sleeping soundly. His breathing, deep and even. Giana knew she should keep moving, but she couldn't help but stop and look at him. At Adam McKendrick. At the man who had given her her first kiss.

She liked the way he looked when he slept, liked the way his dark eyelashes fanned against his cheekbones and the way his nostrils flared ever-so-slightly as he breathed. And Giana especially liked the way his lips remained slightly parted. His lower lip was slightly plumper than his upper lip, but both were exquisitely shaped. Giana leaned closer—close enough to study the subtle pattern of lines on his lips. She remembered the taste and touch and feel of his lips on hers, his warm breath, and the way he had used his tongue to tempt and torment her. Had there ever been anything quite as enticing as the soft, rough feel of Adam McKendrick's tongue mating with hers?

Fighting an almost overwhelming urge to press her lips against his, Giana took one last look and began the long crawl across the library. She inched her way across the Aubusson carpet, past his desk and the last wall of bookcases to the door where she reached up and stealthily turned the brass doorknob.

But the door didn't open. It was locked. She felt for the key that had been in the lock when she entered the room. It was gone. Giana pushed herself to her knees and stared through the open keyhole. She was locked in the library with Adam McKendrick. There was no way for her to escape unless she located the missing key—and Giana wasn't at all sure she wanted to. But duty compelled her to look.

She tiptoed over to his desk and began looking for the key.

She searched his desk from top to bottom, carefully opening each drawer and rifling through the contents in a futile search for the key. She had never plundered through anyone else's private belongings, and the idea that she was invading *his* privacy made her feel slightly queasy. And the fact that she failed to locate the key to the library door only served to increase her queasiness.

If the key was not to be found in the McKendrick's desk, then it had to be on his person. Giana tiptoed back to the sofa and knelt beside it. She slipped her hand beneath his jacket and began a stealthy search of his pockets.

Adam moaned in his sleep and moved his head against the arm of the sofa. He smoothed his hand over the fabric of his waistcoat and his fingers met hers. He closed his hand over around her wrist. "Looking for something, Miss Langstrom?"

The sound of his voice startled her. Giana jumped back, upsetting a table and the lead crystal vase of hothouse flowers sitting on it.

"Oh!" She grabbed for the vase, but Adam was quicker. He reached behind his head and caught hold of the vase seconds before it hit the ground or spilled its contents over his head.

"Is it me?" Adam chuckled. "Or do you have something against fragile household objects?" He righted the vase, then caught hold of Giana's hand before she could do further damage.

"I-it is you," Giana replied. "I am not normally so clumsy. But I become clumsy around you."

Her honest answer surprised him. When she tried to withdraw her hand, Adam wouldn't let go. He let his gaze roam over her. His seat on the sofa gave him a unique view of the underside of her black silk and white cotton pinafore-covered breasts. They were magnificent. "Why do you think that is, Miss Langstrom?" he asked.

"I think it is because you kissed me."

Adam lifted an eyebrow at that. "You were breaking the china and the crockery before I kissed you."

Giana answered him with her most mysterious smile. "Why do you think that is, Mr. McKendrick?"

"I think it's because you were trying to get my attention," he teased. "Because you were hoping I'd kiss you."

She opened her mouth to deny his charge or protest it, but she was too honest to deny the truth. She swallowed hard, inhaling the scent of him. She loved the way he smelled and the way he tasted and she did want him to kiss her. She did want to taste him again.

Adam watched as she parted her lips until her mouth formed a perfect circle. A perfectly kissable circle. "Are you waiting for more of my kisses? Is that why you locked yourself in the library with me?"

"I did not lock the door, sir. You did," she pointed out. "I was seeking the key."

"What are you doing in here?"

He gave her hand a little tug. Giana lost her balance and fell forward, sprawling across his chest. "I appear to be locked in."

Adam turned his most devastating grin on her. "You *are* locked in," he told her. "The question is why."

Her china-blue eyes widened in surprise, and her pink, pouting lips were slightly opened and quiet, for a change.

"What's the matter?" he asked, placing his hands on her waist and pulled her closer to his face. "Cat got your tongue? No? Maybe that's because I have," he murmured sympathetically an instant before his mouth found hers.

Giana inhaled the spicy sandalwood scent of him, allowing it to engulf her as she felt the exotic touch of his tongue on hers. She felt the heat of his body penetrating through her pinafore and her dress, but it was nothing compared to the heat of his mouth. She tasted him, feeling the rasp of his tongue against her teeth as it slipped between her lips into her mouth. She felt the urgency of his mouth and she echoed it, moving her lips under his, allowing him further access. Giana experienced the jolt of pure pleasure as her tongue mated with his.

Adam caressed her back through the fabric of her dress. The fabric hampered him, frustrated him. He wanted to feel the softness of her flesh beneath the layers of clothing. He wanted to move his hands over her, count her ribs, and test the weight of those wonderful, pear-shaped breasts, but all he could really feel was fabric. Too much fabric, masking the curves pressed against him. He moved his hand down her back, over one firm buttock, to the back of her thigh. Fumbling with her skirts, he reached beneath them, then ran his fingers under the lace of her drawers, caressing the bare flesh of her knee while his mouth ate at hers. Over and over again.

The twin pinpoints pressing into his chest were hard and tight and driving him mad. Adam reversed their positions, shifting his weight until George lay on the sofa. He stopped kissing her mouth long enough to roll her onto her back, then began pressing warm, wet kisses against her line of her jaw, her neck, and beneath one ear.

Giana gasped when Adam's probing tongue explored the contours of her ear. She was hot, breathless, light-headed. She whimpered.

Adam took that as a sign of encouragement. He became bolder, slipping his hand farther up the lace-edged leg of her drawers and higher along her thigh.

Hearing a slight rustle and remembering the newspaper she had secreted in the waistband of her drawers, Giana pulled away. "What are you doing?" she murmured against his lips.

"I was touching you," Adam answered, caressing her thigh once more with his fingers before he withdrew his hand. "Because I want to undress you and spend the rest of the morning touching you all over."

"I have never been undressed by anyone except my"—she almost said lady's maid, but she recovered in time—"Brenna when she's practicing her lady's maid skills." Giana bit her bottom lip and shyly averted her gaze. "I did not realize that a man might choose to undress a woman or that she might allow him to do it."

"The privilege is usually reserved for a husband or a lover," Adam whispered. "And if a lady decides to allow it, the man chosen for the privilege is honored to make sure the lady enjoys it."

"Is that permissible?"

"It's not only permissible, it's desirable," Adam whispered.

Giana shivered as his warm breath caressed her ear. "For ladies as well?"

"As far as I'm concerned," he said. "When a woman grants me the privilege of undressing her, I like to touch all of her. Beginning with her eyes, her lips, her breasts, and continuing until I know all her secret places." He touched each part of her with his gaze as he explained his preferences. "Shall I demonstrate?"

Giana's eyes widened with each husky word, then darkened to a deeper blue as his meaning became clearer. "Adam!"

"George," he breathed, bending closer to kiss her mouth, hard.

She kissed him back, stopping only when she felt him deftly unhook the bodice of her pinafore and unbutton the top button of her dress.

"Yes?" he queried.

She was tempted. Tempted in a way that Princesses of the Blood Royal should never be tempted, but the newspaper stuck in the waistband of her drawers wasn't the only thing she was hiding. She couldn't allow Adam to unbutton her dress because she was wearing a fortune in family heirlooms concealed in the bodice of her dress, and that wasn't all. . . .

Giana was a walking, talking jewelry safe. There were gems sewn into the lining of her corset cover, the padding of her corset and the hems of most of her skirts. About the only thing not sewn into her clothing was the tiara she wore during official functions. It was concealed in the false bottom of her traveling case. There would be no way to conceal her identity if she allowed him to continue, for how would a chambermaid ever explain the presence of a king's, or in her case a princess's, ransom in precious stones.

"I cannot," she whispered.

"I should not," he admitted as his conscience returned with a vengeance. The girl lying with him on the leather sofa was an innocent in his employ. An apparently willing innocent, but an innocent nonetheless. And he knew better than to turn his attention to innocents. Especially innocents who looked like George.

He knew better. But that didn't seem to matter. He wanted her. And what was worse than wanting to make love to her was knowing that she was everything he had always avoided in a lover. Adam exhaled.

What was it about George that fascinated him so? He had never been attracted to tall, leggy, blondes before. They tended to remind him of his family. But he was attracted now. He wanted George. He couldn't seem to keep his gaze off her. He'd made a valiant effort, but he'd failed. She excited him. She challenged him. She fascinated him.

He wasn't breaking the china and the crockery, but she was having a similar effect on him. It was all he could do to keep his hands off her. He wanted to taste her, to feel her. And that made him very nervous.

The best thing he could do for the both of them would be to make her forget about him by turning his attention to someone else. Someone different. Someone safe. Someone like her sister, Brenna.

Adam shifted his weight off her and helped her sit up. Reaching into his waistcoat pocket, he removed the door key and handed it to her. "I believe this is what you were looking for."

Giana accepted it. "Thank you, sir." She stood up, walked over to the library door, and unlocked it.

"My pleasure," Adam said. "Thank you most kindly for a very entertaining morning, Miss Langstrom."

Giana opened the door, then glanced back over her shoulder to look at him. She was blushing. "You are most kindly welcome, sir."

Adam grinned back at her. "Am I?"

She met his gaze and gave him her most regal look. "More than you know." Giana glanced back one last time, then slipped through the doorway and disappeared.

Chapter 17

"*This cannot be!*" *Max's hands shook as he read* the article in the newspaper Giana had borrowed from Adam's office. He sat at the table in the housekeeper's room and covered his face with his hands. "This simply cannot be."

Giana studied his hands—the raised blue veins, the swollen joints, and the dark blotches on his skin—and suddenly realized how much Max had aged since her parents' deaths. He had spent more than thirty years of his adult life in Christianberg Palace and the strain of living a lie in a country far from home was beginning to show. Although their sojourn at Larchmont Lodge had been safe and uneventful, life in exile did not agree with him.

"I was certain that you had seen it and that you had kept silent in order to spare me." She and Max were meeting in Isobel and Albert's room because the housekeeper's room was larger than Max's and because it offered complete privacy from the rest of the staff. Although Isobel laid out a tea table for the staff, no one entered without permission.

Max was shocked. "I would never keep important information regarding matters of state from you, Your Highness."

"I apologize, Max, but I thought that you collected the mail."

"Yes, I did, Your Highness. I placed the mail packet on the McKendrick's desk and gave the bundle of newspapers to Albert to iron."

Giana nodded her understanding. Foreign languages were not Albert's forte and despite having lived with Isobel for nearly a quarter of a century, his grasp of English was rudimentary. The butler had performed one of his many daily chores, ironing the newsprint without realizing that one of the articles on it could have a profound affect on their futures.

"What about the other editions?" Max asked. "Do they contain similar articles?"

"I do not know," Giana replied. "McKendrick arrived before I had the opportunity to read the other editions."

"We must find out," Max said. "We must discover a way to get our hands on those newspapers."

"The newspapers are only a part of our worries," Giana reminded him. "You heard what A—McKendrick said. He intends to open the lodge to several very rich, very powerful, very important guests during the week of the Cowes Regatta. We haven't much time." She was more terrified by the possibility of having Victor or someone else she knew, visit the lodge than she was by the prospect of Adam discovering her true identity.

Giana sighed. Having Adam discover her true identity might be more of a relief than a hardship for her because she disliked lying to him. But the same might not be true for the rest of her staff and until she was certain she could trust him completely, Giana would not risk it.

"I think the time has come for us to send Gordon to London to seek an audience with the queen," Max said.

"The queen remains in seclusion at Windsor," Giana said. "And the courtiers around Queen Victoria will never grant a simple gamekeeper an audience," Giana said. "It's time *I* left our cozy little nest and sought an audience with the queen."

Max nodded. "You cannot go to Windsor alone. I will accompany you."

"You cannot go," Giana told him. "I will not allow it."

"But, Princess . . ." Max resorted to the less formal use of her title.

"You have been accused of murdering my parents and of kidnapping me. I will not risk having you arrested."

"That would not happen, Princess, as long as you are there to explain."

"What if I am not there to explain? What if something should happen to me to prevent me from explaining? Who would bear witness to the truth then? Who would tell the world of the murders of my parents or denounce Victor as the murderer? Who would prevent him from becoming Prince Regnant?" Giana shook her head. "I cannot fulfill my duty to my country and my people unless I am certain that you are safe and that you will bear witness for my parents if I cannot. And you will not be safe until I am able to speak to the queen."

Max opened his mouth to protest, but Giana held up a hand to silence him. "Please, Max. I could not bear to lose you. You're not just my private secretary, you're my Lord Chamberlain and you are the only witness to my father and my mother's murder. You are the only one who saw the assassins—the only one who can identify them as part of Victor's entourage. I trust you, Max, and I need you." She smiled at him. "I need to know that you are here with me."

"If the McKendrick invites his guests to the lodge before Regatta week begins, it may be too dangerous for us to remain. We may have to leave before the queen arrives in Scotland."

"Then we will leave," Giana assured him, "and if we leave, we will find a way to contact our ambassador in London."

"Princess, have you considered that we may not be able to trust our ambassador—that he may be in league with your cousin?"

"Of course, I've considered it." She frowned at Max. "I've also considered that while Queen Victoria may be perfectly willing to offer me protection and to support my claim to the throne, her government might not."

Max lifted an eyebrow in surprise.

"You still see me as a child, Max. And because you still see me as the little girl in pinafores and plaits, you forget that I cut my teeth on politics and government. I learned from the best. From the time I was old enough to sit at my father's knee. I am not a naïve little girl. I realize that some of my father's policies were unpopular. I know there were those in our country who were against creating a modern constitution and a Declaration of Rights for the Masses. I know they feared the loss of power. My father spoke to me about it. He explained that there were those in power in Karolya who wanted to harvest our timber and extract our rich iron ore deposits in order to add more gold to their coffers and that there were those in power in other countries who would be only too happy to assist in the harvesting of timber or the mining of iron ore or in the buying and selling of it. And while I don't know who all of the traitors in our country were, I can guess. I am not entirely sure where our ambassador's loyalties lie, but I cannot let that dissuade me from claiming my crown. I am the rightful heir to the crown of Saxe-Wallerstein-Karolya. My father died preserving my heritage and I don't intend to allow his murderer to steal what is rightfully mine or to exercise control over my subjects any longer than necessary. If that means I must put my faith in the fact that our ambassador is loyal to us and that Queen Victoria's government is as well, then I will do so. I am more than willing to risk my life for my country, but I prefer to do it once I know my godmother has arrived on Scottish soil." Giana felt safe at Larchmont Lodge, but she would be safer at Balmoral under the protection of the British government. Giana had known from the beginning that her stay at Larchmont Lodge would be temporary—simply a place to rest and regroup until she was able to present herself to the world and rescue her people and her country by proving her cousin, Victor, was the murderer and usurper she knew him to be.

But knowing her stay was temporary wouldn't make it any easier to leave. It wasn't home, but the lodge had served her well. It had become a place of refuge and sanctuary and even though she didn't want to admit it, even to herself, Giana knew in her heart of hearts that the primary reason she was reluctant to leave Larchmont Lodge had nothing to do with safety or security and everything to do with Adam McKendrick.

"What shall we do, Your Highness?"

Giana took a deep breath, then slowly expelled it. Max expected answers. He expected her to be the leader of her country, not just a figurehead, but the heart and soul and common sense of her country. "We must find a way to prevent the McKendrick from inviting guests during Cowes." She worried her bottom lip with her teeth. "And we must find a way to do it without alarming the McKendrick."

"Have you something in mind?"

"I suggest we do what we do best," she told him. "We simply do more of it."

Max frowned.

Giana grinned. "Instead of discouraging Albert from attempting to institute a proper dress code and rules of conduct for the workmen renovating the lodge, we encourage him to do so. I will begin by encouraging him to be the butler he would be if we had stayed at Laken." She turned to Max. "Your mission will be to take over as much of McKendrick's correspondence as you possibly can. Move into his office and do the same job for him that you would do for my father or for me if we were in Christianberg."

Max's smile began at one corner of his mouth and grew. "What of the rest of the staff?"

"We will simply instruct the members of our household to pretend they are back home and attend to their duties accordingly. We can issue specific instructions as we think of them." In a very unprincesslike gesture, Giana propped her elbows on the table and propped her chin on her hands. "Brenna presents a problem," she said at last, "because her traditional duties require that she take care of me. But I am sure that with a bit of thought, I will be able to discover Brenna's skills and her finest qualities." She snapped her fingers. "Since she cannot perform physical labor that does not include taking care of me, we will concentrate on allowing her to supervise the redecoration of the lodge."

Max winced. The McKendrick was sure to disapprove for like most lady's maids, Brenna's tastes tended toward flowers and frills—not at all what the McKendrick had in mind for Larchmont Lodge. "The McKendrick is already angry. You heard him threaten to dismiss us all if we didn't run the household according to his wishes."

Giana turned her most proper princess smile on Max. "That is another risk I am willing to take."

"When do we tell the others?" Max asked.

"Tonight at dinner in the housekeeper's room," Giana answered. "After the rest of the staff has gone home or retired."

"What about Mr. O'Brien?"

"I'll take care of Mr. O'Brien," she promised.

Giana was as good as her word. She knocked on Murphy O'Brien's bedchamber door a quarter of an hour before the rest of the upper staff were to meet in the housekeeper's room.

"Yes?" O'Brien opened the door to find Georgiana standing in the corridor holding a butler's table loaded with a variety of dishes under silver covers.

"I have brought your dinner, Mr. O'Brien," she announced, thrusting the table at him.

Afraid his dinner was about to hit the floor, Murphy grabbed the tray in self-defense. "I see that. Thanks."

"You are welcome." Giana gave him a brief nod and whirled around to leave.

"Wait a moment!" Murphy set his dinner tray on the floor inside his room.

Giana paused. "Yes, Mr. O'Brien?"

The expression on her face and her tone of voice told him that she hadn't expected him to question her. O'Brien felt the corner of his mouth curve upward in the beginning of a smile and he fought to conceal his amusement. "Are you delivering dinner trays to all of the other members of the staff or might I conclude that I'm the only one?"

"We thought it best if Henri prepared a tray for you, Mr. O'Brien," Giana explained.

"We, Miss Langstrom?" he asked.

"The family, Mr. O'Brien," she replied. "The housekeeper's room is reserved for members of our family tonight. We are dining together *enfamile*."

"Is there some special occasion of which I should be aware?" O'Brien asked.

Giana shook her head. "No, Mr. O'Brien."

"Just a quiet Langstrom family dinner?"

"That is correct."

"Fine." Murphy heaved a dramatic sigh in an effort to win her sympathy and gain more information. "I guess I'll have to make do with a tray. I can't change my name. O'Brien isn't Langstrom."

Giana felt a surge of guilt. O'Brien had the right to feel left out and hurt. He had the right to feel slighted. She understood how it felt to be the odd fellow out, but she didn't know O'Brien well enough to trust him—not with her life or the lives of the other members of the "family." "We regret that we must exclude you, Mr. O'Brien. We did not intend to injure your feelings or cause harm, but we have family matters to discuss and these things must remain private."

The note of distress in her voice was real and Murphy decided to let her off the hook. "I understand, Miss Langstrom," he said. "Enjoy your *family* dinner."

"And you, Mr. O'Brien."

"I'm sure the food will be excellent. But I am not a man who enjoys solitary meals," he said. "Now, if you or your lovely sister would care to join me . . ." He made the suggestion to see how she reacted.

"Thank you most kindly for the invitation," she replied. "I am sure that my lovely sister and I will be honored to join you for dinner tomorrow night in the housekeeper's room."

O'Brien laughed as Georgiana saw through his invitation and called his bluff.

Giana smiled at him, then turned and made her way down the stairs to the housekeeper's room.

Murphy was mesmerized by her smile. It was the kind of smile to which men dedicated sonnets. Murphy thought that he might easily fall in love with a smile like that, if she hadn't already caught the eye of his best friend. It didn't matter that Adam had freely relinquished his rights to all the blond, blue-eyed darlings in Scotland. O'Brien smiled. He might not want to be attracted to Valkyries and Amazons, but Adam McKendrick had grown up in a family of extraordinarily lovely women. He would never be happy with the plain, petite, timid women he chose to squire around. Once Adam realized he was hopelessly attracted to the tall, blond, blue-eyed and beautiful Miss Langstrom, he would want her back. The Bountiful Baron was nothing if not predictable.

Chapter 18

O'Brien related the incident to Adam an hour or so later when they met in the library for their customary after-dinner whisky and cigars.

"George brought your dinner to your room?" Adam asked.

O'Brien nodded. "Yes. On a butler's table that she handed over to me without rattling a dish."

"You were witness to a miracle," Adam commented dryly.

O'Brien laughed. "It's a fairly commonplace miracle." He shot a pointed look at his friend. "But *I* don't affect her the way you do."

"*I* make her nervous."

"Of course you do," O'Brien said. "Because you look at her as if she's the rabbit and you're the fox."

Adam lifted an eyebrow at that.

"And she looks at you as if you're a rabbit and she's the fox."

"You've been paying attention."

"I'm a Pinkerton agent," O'Brien reminded him. "I'm supposed to pay attention."

"Yet you have no idea what the family meeting was about?" Adam poured a glass of whisky for each of them.

"I imagine it was about you," Murphy said. "But I can't

prove it. Despite my attempt to appeal to her sense of fair play."

Adam smirked. "You're losing your touch, *boyo*." He handed O'Brien a glass of whisky.

"Not quite," O'Brien retorted. "She felt sorry for me and she felt guilty about excluding me from the family gathering, but not enough to induce her to tell me what the meeting was about."

"You tried."

"Yeah, well, I tried to entice her into having dinner with me, too."

"What?"

It was Murphy's turn to smirk. "That got your attention."

"What are you talking about?"

"I'm talking about you, boyo, trying to ignore your attraction to the Valkyrie, when anyone with half an eye can see it's impossible. When's the last time you took any notice of the women I invite to dinner?"

Adam glared at his best friend. There would be hell to pay if O'Brien found out just how attracted to the Valkyrie he was. And if Murph got wind of the kisses he and George had exchanged behind the library's locked doors, he would never let him hear the end of it. "You needn't worry about it," Adam said. "I'm sure that any attraction I might be tempted to feel for the Valkyrie will die a quick death once we return to London."

"London?" Murphy choked on the mouthful of Scotch he'd just swallowed, coughing until his eyes watered.

"That got your attention." Adam reached over and pounded O'Brien on the back.

"Did you say we were going to London?" O'Brien asked in a high-pitched voice that sounded nothing like his normal baritone.

"That's what I said."

"Why?"

Adam pulled a white linen envelope from the pile of mail stacked on the corner of his desk and waved it in the air. "I received a letter from Kirstin today."

O'Brien frowned. "Is *His Bastard Lordship* up to his old tricks?"

"She doesn't say." Adam pulled the letter out of the envelope and handed it to O'Brien.

O'Brien read Kirstin's letter, then folded it and handed it back to Adam. "Any idea why she wants you to come to London?"

Adam shrugged his shoulders. "Nope. Unless she's missing us already," he joked.

"She saw us three weeks ago," Murphy said. "I wouldn't think she'd be missing us so soon." He winked at Adam. "But it's possible. I've always believed Lady Marshfield harbors a *tendresse* for me."

Adam bit the inside of his cheek to keep from smiling as the whisky loosened O'Brien's tongue. He had always believed that O'Brien harbored a deep *tendresse* for Kirstin. Not that Kirstin would ever notice since O'Brien didn't come from a prominent family or possess either fortune or title. But O'Brien had always exhibited much more patience with Kirstin than she had ever exhibited toward him or toward anyone else. She was his sister and Adam loved her dearly. Although she was the elder by two years, Adam had always felt protective of her and Greta, her twin, and there was nothing he wouldn't do for her—including journeying to London simply because she asked him to. "You know Kirstin nearly as well as I do," Adam said. "What do you think?"

"I think I'd better call it a night." Murphy set his glass on the side table and pushed his chair back. "I've got some packing to do."

❧

Down the hall, in the housekeeper's room, another meeting was taking place. Giana showed everyone the newspaper she'd found in McKendrick's library, passing it around the table, before she carefully folded it and laid it on the seat of one of the chairs. After everyone at the table had an opportunity to look at the article in the newspaper, Giana explained their other dilemma—that Adam McKendrick planned to open the lodge to the public—and not just any public, but the wealthy, aristocratic public. A public that could jeopardize their lives.

Giana outlined her ideas for delaying the opening of the lodge to guests until Queen Victoria arrived in Scotland for her Balmoral holiday. If they could delay the opening of the lodge long enough for the queen to reach Scotland, Giana might be able to request an audience with her godmother without risking her discovery by Victor's spies.

The trick would be to delay the opening without risking their positions. Adam McKendrick meant to make the lodge profitable, and he would not allow anyone to stop him. They ran the risk of losing their jobs if they angered the McKendrick. But losing their jobs was better than losing their lives. And the risk was worth the taking.

Giana took a deep breath, then faced her "adopted" family. Everyone had specific roles to fulfill, and each role was dependent upon the other in order that they might succeed. "We must rely on each other," Giana reminded them. "For we do not know who else to trust."

She looked at Albert. "We must be able to read McKendrick's newspapers. As butler, you are responsible for ironing them before you give them to McKendrick. But the newspapers carry stories about us and about Karolya. You must confiscate those papers."

Albert nodded in agreement.

"We cannot hazard the chance that McKendrick will read those newspapers. We must think of a way to get them before he sees the photograph of me and puts the pieces of the puzzle together. If he recognizes me, our masquerade is over." As if in answer to her prayers, Giana heard the soft sound of paper ripping. She looked down at her feet to find that Wagner had pulled the newspaper from the seat of the chair beside her and was systematically shredding it. Giana smiled. Although he was nearly three years old, Wagner still exhibited occasional bouts of puppy behavior. And one of his favorite vices was the destruction of newspapers and shoes. Her father had twice scolded her for allowing Wagner access to his office and his closets. On both occasions Wagner had chewed the toes of his

boots and had created a whirlwind of destruction by ripping
newspapers and a batch of state papers into hundreds of tiny
pieces that littered the floor of his office. It seemed her pet
wolfhound adored the taste of newsprint and of the mink oil
used to polish and waterproof her father's boots.

Now Giana realized that Wagner's bad habits could aid in
preventing Adam from reading his morning papers. From now
on she would grant Wagner access to the newspapers.

But doing so was not without its risks. For it meant that
from now on, she and Wagner would have to bear the full
brunt of Adam's wrath at the dog. She sighed. Wagner spent
his life protecting her. She would learn to protect him. And
she would begin just as soon as this meeting concluded. There
were more newspapers on the desk in the library, and she had
to get her hands on all of them.

Giana turned to Max. "Do you all understand what we are
asking you to do?"

Everyone nodded.

"Good," she pronounced. "We begin tomorrow."

The library smelled of expensive cigars, leather
book bindings, the lemon beeswax she used on the furniture,
and Adam McKendrick. She tiptoed over to his desk and carefully lifted the globe on the lamp and struck a match to the
wick.

"Returning to the scene of the crime? Or for another lesson
in kissing?"

The globe rattled against the base of the lamp.

"Easy," Adam cautioned. "If you break that, you're liable
to set the whole place on fire." He got up from the leather sofa
and walked over to Giana.

"How did you know it was me?" she asked.

Adam gently removed the lamp globe from her fingers and
placed it back on the lamp. "Orange blossoms."

"Pardon?" She looked up at him from beneath the cover of
her lashes.

"You smell of orange blossoms," Adam said softly. "You're the only one here who does."

"And you are the only one here who smells of sandalwood and cigars."

"You noticed." He sounded more pleased than surprised.

She glanced toward the leather sofa. "How could I not?"

Adam heard the unspoken meaning behind her question. He stepped forward and opened his arms.

She knew she should obey his earlier directive and stay away from him, knew she should stand her ground, but it was impossible to keep her distance. How could she obey his command to stay away from him when he paid it no heed? She took a step forward and found herself held firmly against his chest as he bent his head and kissed her for the second time in as many days.

And this time she had a better idea of what to expect and how to respond. She kissed him back, silently granting him permission to deepen the kiss. And Adam obeyed, tightening his embrace around her waist, pulling her closer until it was impossible to tell where he stopped and she began.

Giana sighed. His kiss was everything she remembered and more. It was soft and gentle and tender and sweet and enticing and hungry and hot and wet and deep and persuasive at once. It coaxed and demanded, asked and expected a like response, and she obliged. She parted her lips when he asked entrance into the warm recesses of her mouth. She shivered with delight at the first tentative, exploratory thrust of his tongue against hers. She met his tongue with her own, returning each stroke, practicing everything she had learned in her first lesson in kissing him and began a devastatingly thorough exploration of her own.

She grabbed a fistful of his shirt and held on, losing herself in Adam's kiss. She hadn't thought it was possible for a man's kiss to steal her heart and her soul, but she learned it was more than possible—it had happened. She wasn't just a princess anymore, but the princess in the fairy tale—sleeping for years—waiting for her handsome prince to come along and awaken her. Adam McKendrick kissed her as if she were the most desirable woman in the world and reawakened the dreams and desires Giana had put aside the night her parents were murdered.

Adam teased. He coaxed. He promised. He held her as if she belonged in his arms. And that was exactly where Giana wanted to be.

As he held her, Giana suddenly realized how great the sacrifice her position demanded of her. She was a princess of the House of Saxe-Wallerstein-Karolya. She could not marry for love if her country required that she marry for political or economic purposes. And while the Female Provision of the Karolyan Charter allowed her to marry a man of lesser rank, it did not allow her to marry a man without a hereditary title. Nor could a female heir apparent marry without the consent of her nearest male relative, and Victor would never consent to her marrying anyone other than himself. He would see her dead first. And since he had already murdered her parents, Giana had no reason to hope that Victor would miraculously decide to spare her or the man she chose to marry. Especially an American. And Adam McKendrick was an American.

She could not marry him. But she could love him. For as long as she remained at Larchmont Lodge and in Scotland, for as long as she remained on the earth, she could love him. Giana loosened her grip on his shirtfront and pressed her hand on his chest over his heart.

Adam immediately broke the kiss and stepped back. He looked down at her and sanity returned. Jesus, Joseph, and Mary! He was at it again! He was kissing a chambermaid. A long-legged, blue-eyed, blond chambermaid who worked for him. What was he thinking? What had happened to his code of honor? What had happened to his morals? What had happened to his sense of self-preservation?

"I thought I told you to stay away from me," he said hoarsely.

"You did," she whispered.

"Then what are you doing here?"

Giana didn't want to lie, so she told as much of the truth as possible. "I came for something to read."

Adam stared at her as if the words she'd uttered made no sense. "Something to read?"

Giana nodded. "Yes. That is what one generally does with books."

He frowned. "I'm aware of that."

She extended her arm to encompass the space around them. "Then you must also be aware of the fact that one generally reads in the library because it is the room where all the books are kept." She paused. "*This* room is the library at Larchmont Lodge."

Adam glanced at floor to ceiling shelves filled with books, then rolled his eyes. "So it is."

Giana laughed. "You are surprised? I am not like other chambermaids. My parents and the Countess of Brocavia value an education."

He shook his head. "Not surprised, just foolish. I didn't realize chambermaids could read." He turned away from her and began scanning the titles on the shelves, noting in passing that several of the volumes that should have been shelved in alphabetical order were not. "What were you looking to read? Milton? Shakespeare? Sir Walter Scott?"

"Newspapers," she answered, focusing on the stack on his desk.

"Newspapers?" he parroted.

"My duty may be to work as a chambermaid, but I like to improve my mind by keeping recent on events."

"Current," Adam translated automatically. "Current on events."

Giana blushed at the mistake. "Current," she repeated. "So I would like to borrow your newspapers. If you have concluded your reading of them." She held her breath.

"I haven't started my reading of them." Adam frowned again. The words sounded strange to his ears until he realized that his speech was beginning to sound like George's.

"Oh."

Adam smiled at her. "But I'm not likely to have a chance to read them before I leave—"

"Leave?" She interrupted. "You are leaving Larchmont Lodge?"

"I'm leaving for London in the morning," Adam confirmed. "So feel free." He walked over to his desk, gathered the stack of newspapers in his arms, and handed them to her. Unable to keep from touching her, Adam lifted her chin with the tip of his index finger. "Don't look so stricken, George. I received a letter from my sister in London—"

"Sister?" It was Giana's turn to repeat his words.

Adam gave a little self-deprecating laugh. "I have a sister," he told her. "Actually, I have four sisters and a mother." He gently tapped the tip of her nose with his finger. "That's right, George. I have a mother and three sisters back home in America and another sister in London. Did you think I crawled from beneath the cabbage plant fully grown?"

"What about your father?" she asked.

Adam shrugged. "I suppose he's in London, too."

"With your sister?"

"Nope," he replied. "With his wife and children."

Giana wrinkled her brow, and Adam reached over and soothed them away with the pad of his thumb. "I never knew the man. He met and married my mother, a widow with four daughters, in America, then returned to England before I was born. When he learned of my birth, he sent for us, but my mother refused to give up her farm and her independence. Several years after that, he had their marriage annulled so that he could marry someone else."

"You never saw him?"

"No."

"And he never saw you? His son and heir?"

"Not to my knowledge."

"How sad for you!" she said. "And how sad for him! I cannot imagine never knowing my father. He was"—Giana caught herself—"is a great man."

"Don't be sad on my account, George," Adam told her. "I've done all right growing up with a mother and four sisters." He grinned crookedly. "One of whom I'm going to visit." He leaned closer and brushed her forehead with his lips, breathing in the scent of orange blossoms and George. "But I'll be back before you know it." Adam took three steps back, then gently turned Giana around and headed her toward the door.

"And George—"

"Yes?"

"Try to keep your beast off my bed and out of my room while I'm gone. He ate the toe from one of my slippers this morning."

Chapter 19

The Bountiful Baron is a man who knows who he is and what he wants from life. He is as comfortable in a roomful of rough miners as he is in a mansion full of millionaires.

—The First Installment of the True Adventures of the Bountiful Baron: Western Benefactor to Blond, Beautiful, and Betrayed Women written by John J. Bookman, 1874.

The train trip to London took ten hours from Glasgow. The first leg of the journey, the trip from Glasgow to Edinburgh, was the slowest, taking nearly four hours. The second leg from Edinburgh to London aboard an express train took a mere six. They traveled in relative comfort in first-class coaches, and Adam said a silent prayer of thanks that the express train they rode had been newly fitted with steam heat.

After pulling into the London station, Adam and Murphy traveled by hansom cab to Lord Marshfeld's Mayfair town house. Although Kirstin had written to beg Adam to come to London as soon as possible, his visit would not be allowed to interrupt the Marshfelds' social calendar. Adam's arrival coincided with an evening musicale and reception hosted by Lord and Lady Marshfeld for the cream of London society. Adam and Murphy O'Brien arrived in time to bathe and dress for dinner.

"And there he is now," Kirstin Marshfeld announced as Adam descended the main staircase of the Mayfair town house and entered the drawing room. "My brother, America's famous Bountiful Baron!"

She beamed at Adam, then at her society friends as they crowded around, politely applauding his approach.

"Christ!" Adam muttered beneath his breath. "Now it's reached London."

Murphy laughed.

Adam greeted his sister, leaning down to kiss her cheek. "I see you're up to your old tricks, sister mine." He stepped back and studied her, peering past the subtle application of cosmetics and rice powder coating his sister's beautiful face. "Has His Lordship been up to his?"

Kirstin glanced at her husband, who had moved aside when Adam entered the room. "He's treated me like a queen since my return to England—especially after the Bountiful Baron stories began to appear." She turned her loveliest smile on her brother. "You are quickly becoming the toast of London nearly as famous as one of Sir Walter Scott's dashing heroes. When my friends started telling me about *The True Adventures of the Bountiful Baron: Western Benefactor to Blond, Beautiful, and Betrayed Women,* I couldn't believe it!" she gushed. "In fact, I arranged this little soirée and invited you here because I knew I was the only hostess in London who could do so. Oh, thank you, Adam, for helping to make my party such a success."

Kirstin turned to O'Brien and cast some of her reflected glory his way. "With the exception of the members of the royal family, I am now *the* premier hostess in London." Kirstin was so pleased with her success that she glowed almost as brightly as the diamonds she wore. "You should be proud of me for discovering a way to increase my stature in London society."

O'Brien winced at Kirstin's thoughtless comment and braced himself for the explosion he knew was coming.

"Proud of you?" Adam was seething, but he kept a smile plastered on his face and spoke to his sister through clenched teeth as he lifted two glasses of champagne from a passing waiter's tray. He handed one to his sister and kept one, leaving O'Brien to fend for himself. "You want me to be proud of you for tricking me into coming to London? And for worrying me half to death, just so you can increase your stature in London society?"

Kirstin squeezed out two perfect tears and allowed them to glisten on her eyelashes before she blinked them away. "I didn't work so hard to become the premiere hostess in London for my benefit alone," she told him. "I did it for Marshfeld and for you as well."

Adam took a long swallow of champagne. "Would you mind explaining how you came to that conclusion?"

"Marshfeld wishes to move in higher circles. Several members of his club have asked him to join them in forming a company to buy and sell forests and mines in other countries. As his wife, it's my duty to help him in any way I can."

"Really? In exchange for what?" Adam whispered. "His promise not to hit you again?"

"He only hit me once."

"He didn't hit you, Kirstin. He beat the hell out of you."

"He lost his temper."

"So what?" Adam demanded. "I lose my temper. Murphy loses his temper. But we don't go around beating women."

"You're not married."

"And you shouldn't be either, if you think marriage gives your husband the right to beat you."

"But it does, Adam. I belong to him."

"You belong to yourself. He belongs in hell and that's where he'll be if he touches you again in anger."

"He won't, Adam. He's changed. He promised he wouldn't hit me again." Kirstin told him what she thought he wanted to hear, but she couldn't bring herself to look her younger brother in the eyes. "He's been so nice to me since the prince began to take an interest in me."

"What prince?"

"Prince Victor of Karolya," Kirstin replied. "He and Marshfeld have business together."

"Christ, Kirstin, you're married. Don't start anything with a prince," Adam warned. "He'll be worse than an English lord. And don't think he'll give you any more consideration than Marshfeld. Because he won't."

Kirstin shrugged her shoulders. "The prince is very nice. A true gentleman." She lifted her chin a bit higher, smiled at Adam and deliberately changed the subject. "My friends are

so excited to have you here. Is it true that you're planning a
preview of your lodge during Regatta week?"

"Where did you hear that?" Adam demanded.

Kirstin ignored his question and asked one of her own. "Is
it true? Because I'm so looking forward to seeing it."

"You won't be seeing it," he told her. "It's a gentleman's
club. No women allowed."

"Adam!" She nearly stamped her foot in frustration.

"All right," he said. "I'll make an exception for you because
you're my sister." He glanced at Kirstin and then over at
Marshfeld. "But be careful, Kirstin. I hope Marshfeld's
changed, but I don't think he has. A polecat doesn't change
its stripe. The only reason he isn't hitting you is because he
has more reason to fear me than he can find to hit you. But
make no mistake about it, Sis, if he ever feels he no longer
has reason to fear me, then you'll become the target for his
anger once again."

Kirstin's eyes flashed fire at him. "Despite what you may
think of me, Little Brother, I am not an imbecile. Whether you
know it or not and whether you like it or not, you need these
people."

Adam glanced at the ladies and gentlemen milling around
the room. "I need these people?" He lifted his eyebrows at her.
"Unlike Lord Marshfeld, I won't need to marry for money in
order to keep myself in the manner to which I've become
accustomed."

"That may be true," she shot back, "but you are in the process of renovating a hunting lodge in the wilds of Scotland.
And if you want to have paying guests when the lodge opens,
you need to cultivate a few of the most influential people here
tonight."

"She got you there, boyo," O'Brien butted in.

"Stay out of this," Adam warned.

"And another thing . . ." She smiled brightly as Lady Carstairs walked by. "I don't need you to remind me that my
husband married me for your money, Adam McKendrick. I
may not have known what kind of man Marshfeld was when
I married him, but I know what he is now."

Adam reached down and lifted Kirstin's chin with the tip of his finger so he could look her in the eye. "Do you love him, Kirs?"

"I did once," she admitted. "I don't now."

"Then why do you stay with him?" Adam didn't understand.

"Because he's my husband and I stood in a church and promised I would," she said. "For better or worse."

Adam smiled at the childish simplicity of her statement. "I don't believe God expects you to put your life and health at risk in order to keep a promise to a man who hasn't kept his promise to love and cherish you."

Kirstin looked stunned. As if that idea had never occurred to her. "Do you really think so?"

He nodded. "Yes, I really do."

She smiled. "Except for Marshfeld's temper, I like my life here, Adam. I dreamed about living like this all my life." She glanced around the glittering drawing room. "I won't allow him to hit me again—ever. But I will fulfill my obligation as Lady Marshfeld—including inviting the famous Bountiful Baron to my party."

"Understood." Adam nodded. "And I'll play along for tonight. But watch yourself. Don't be like the little boy who cried wolf."

Her eyes widened in surprise.

"He lied and cried wolf to get attention so many times that the villagers didn't believe him when a wolf did appear."

"I don't have to worry about that," she replied in a haughty tone of voice. "Because the Bountiful Baron never refuses a woman in need."

"Where did you hear that nonsense?"

"In the *First Installment of the True Adventures of the Bountiful Baron: Western Benefactor to Blond, Beautiful, and Betrayed Women*," she said with a smirk.

"Don't believe everything you read," Adam retorted. "Even the Bountiful Baron gets tired of being used."

"I'm your sister," Kirstin reminded him. "And you love me."

"You're my sister," Adam agreed, "and I love you dearly.

But," he teased, "I have three other sisters who all look like you. I'm not likely to miss the most troublesome one."

Adam kept his word to his sister. For the rest of the evening and long into the night, he acted the part of the perfect gentleman guest of honor. He listened to a Miss Johnstone sing arias from the latest opera and escorted a Miss Caldwell into the midnight supper. After supper he and Murphy donned smoking jackets and joined Marshfeld and a dozen other gentlemen in the smoking salon, where conversation centered on politics and business and fox hunting as well as a dash of society gossip.

As much as he hated to admit it, Kirstin had been right. He did need these people to help make the lodge a success. These men were the power behind the Crown. They were the leaders of government and industry, and Adam hoped that in a few months, they would be making Larchmont Lodge a favorite stop during the Season.

"McKendrick."

Adam glanced over as Lord Bascombe sat down beside him. "Bascombe."

"It's a pleasure to see you again," Bascombe said. "I've heard that you've decided to stay at the lodge."

"Yes."

Bascombe shuddered. "I assume you received my note and the keys to the place and that you found everything in order?"

"The keys arrived safely tucked inside your letter, and everything was exactly as you've described it. Except the staff in residence—" Adam smiled. "The staff came as a surprise."

Lord Bascombe's smile mirrored Adam's. "If there was a staff in residence, it comes as a surprise to me as well. All of the permanent staff of Larchmont Lodge except Gordon Ross was pensioned off two years ago."

"I telegraphed Ross before I arrived and asked him to begin hiring a staff," Adam told him.

"Was he successful?"

Adam nodded. "He hired his sister, Isobel, as housekeeper and her husband, Albert, as butler."

"So Isobel has returned home from Karolya," Bascombe said. "I'm glad to hear it. She's always loved the lodge. She'll take very good care of it."

"She already is," Adam replied. "Tell me, sir, how long was the lodge in your family?"

"Since the reign of Queen Anne. But it wasn't a lodge then," he said. "It was the home of Clan Moray. The earl of Moray was my grandfather."

"Your mother was Scottish?"

"Aye," Lord Bascombe said in his best Scots burr. "A Highland Scot."

"And she married an Englishman?"

"No, she married a Scot from Edinburgh whose family lands lay on both sides of the border," Lord Bascombe explained. "And what of your heritage? McKendrick is a Scottish name, is it not?"

"The surname may be Scottish, but my father was an Englishman."

"And your mother?"

"My mother was born in Sweden. She immigrated to Kansas from Stockholm as a young bride. Three years later she was a widow with four small daughters."

"Four?"

Adam chuckled. "That's right. I have four sisters. My mother is rather extraordinary. She's given birth to two sets of twin girls."

"Then Lady Marshfeld is a twin?"

"Most definitely. Astrid and Erika are the oldest, then Greta and Kirstin. Lady Marshfeld's twin lives in Kansas on a farm near my mother's."

Lord Bascombe did some quick mathematical calculations. "Your father must have died before you were born."

"No," Adam corrected. "My sisters' father was killed in a farming accident. My father met and married my mother while he was visiting America as part of his Grand Tour."

"He settled with your mother in America?"

Adam shook his head. "He returned to England before I was

born. He later dissolved his marriage to my mother and married someone else."

Lord Bascombe cleared his throat. "I'm sorry."

Adam frowned. Lord Bascombe was the second person in as many days to express his sorrow over the fact that he had grown up without a father. "Don't be," he told the older man. "As you can see, I've done quite well for myself."

"You are a credit to your father's name."

Adam met Lord Bascombe's gaze. "I didn't work to accomplish everything I've accomplished so I would be a credit to my father's name. As far as I'm concerned, he's the bastard, not me. I don't give a damn about being a credit to his name, I just want to be a credit to mine."

Lord Bascombe seemed momentarily taken aback, but he looked at Adam and nodded in agreement. "Quite right." He snipped the end of his cigar, lit it, then inhaled and slowly expelled the smoke. "Your sister, Lady Marshfeld, mentioned that you've been renovating the lodge?"

Adam welcomed the change of subject. "Nothing major," he said. "The structure was sound. The roof over the servants' quarters leaked, so we replaced it. We also rearranged the women's quarters, and we're installing plumbing and adding running water and water closets throughout the house."

Bascombe whistled. "That's quite an improvement. Tell me, Adam"—he paused—"may I call you Adam?"

Adam nodded.

"Tell me, Adam, are you planning to take up permanent residence in Scotland, or will you be returning to America?"

"I imagine I'll eventually return to Nevada in order to be closer to my mother. She's getting older, and even though my other sisters and their husbands live nearby, I don't like the idea of having an ocean and most of a continent between us."

"Might there be a chance that your mother would leave her home in Kansas and join you if you decided to remain in Scotland?" Lord Bascombe asked.

Adam gave a short laugh. "It's not very likely. She may be getting older, but my mother is as independent as ever. She'll never leave the farm. It's the only thing she's ever had that belonged solely to her. She will never give it up and I will never try to force her. If that means returning to Kansas one day to look after her, so be it."

Lord Bascombe stared at him. "Your mother has brought up a son who would make any mother and father proud." He finished his cigar, then stood up and held out his hand. "I'm very pleased to have the opportunity to get to know you, Mr. McKendrick." He grinned. "Very glad to have lost my hunting lodge to you."

Adam stood up and shook hands with Bascombe. "Likewise, Lord Bascombe." As he shook hands with the man, Adam realized that he had finally found an English lord he genuinely liked. It was only one man, but it was a start. If Lord Bascombe's friends were anything like him, the opening of the lodge would be a success. "Tell me, Lord Bascombe, don't you feel any bitterness toward me for winning the lodge that has been in your family for generations?"

Bascombe laughed. "Not at all. I wouldn't have wagered it, if I wasn't willing to part with the place. We used to spend the hunting season and Christmas there. I preferred our house in London, so I always hated going to Scotland. To me, Larchmont Lodge was always dark and cold, and aside for the hunting, grindingly boring."

"I sincerely hope I can change *that* situation," Adam said, meeting Lord Bascombe's gaze. "How do you feel about the game of golf?"

"I may live in England, but I'm a Scot as well as an Englishman. I haven't golfed in years, but I was once quite good at it."

"I'm building a golf links on the grounds of the lodge," Adam told him. "And I'd like very much to have you come up and try it out one day."

Lord Bascombe clamped Adam on the shoulder. "Adam, my lad, I'd be delighted."

Chapter 20

The Bountiful Baron always maintains his control, never betraying his anger, disappointment, or discomfort.

—THE SECOND INSTALLMENT OF THE TRUE ADVENTURES OF THE BOUNTIFUL BARON: WESTERN BENEFACTOR TO BLOND, BEAUTIFUL, AND BETRAYED WOMEN WRITTEN BY JOHN J. BOOKMAN, 1874.

"I thought Lord Bascombe had a reputation for being an Englishman of few words," O'Brien commented as he and Adam shared breakfast just after daybreak the next morning.

"I suppose so," Adam replied, slathering a slice of freshly baked bread with jam before taking a sip of his coffee. "Why?"

"You and he spent a great deal of time huddled in the corner of the smoking salon last night talking." O'Brien attacked a rasher of bacon, four scrambled eggs, and half a loaf of bread.

Adam looked up at his friend and grinned. "Jealous?"

"Yer bloody right I'm jealous!" O'Brien retorted. "I had to listen to Marshfeld trying to impress the likes of Lord Carstairs and that dunderhead Viscount Shepherdston while you and Bascombe seemed to get on famously." O'Brien shot him a dirty look. "What was he doing? Trying to talk you into letting him buy the lodge back?"

Adam shook his head. "He doesn't want it back. He had heard I was renovating the place, and he was interested in what I was doing."

"And you gave him a detailed report," O'Brien guessed again.

"I summarized," Adam said. "We talked of many things and . . ."

"And?"

Adam gave another little laugh. "Everything I've learned about Bascombe would lead me to believe that he's smart enough to hang on to his estates."

"Yeah, that puzzles me, too."

"And as surprising as it may sound, I like him, Murph. And so will you."

"When will I have the opportunity to make his acquaintance?" O'Brien asked.

"Sooner than you might think. I invited him up to play golf as soon as we finish building the links."

"Bloody hell, Adam! We're already up to our necks in foreign servants who look down their noses at me for being Irish and you for being a provincial American, and now you want to go and invite Englishmen—the most arrogant bastards who ever walked the earth!"

Adam shrugged. "I liked Lord Bascombe. I didn't find him to be arrogant."

"Well, good for you," Murphy retorted. "But if you don't mind, I'll reserve judgment. Who was it that told his sister last night that a polecat didn't change its stripe?"

"Guilty." Adam raised his hand. "Do you think I was too hard on her, Murphy?"

"No," Murphy answered honestly. "You were a bit more blunt than you probably should have been, but Kirstin is a headstrong young woman. She was wrong to have lied in order to get you down here or to use you for her personal glory."

"She used me to show off for her friends." Adam was still angry about that. But anger was no excuse for cruelty, and he was afraid that he'd been deliberately cruel to Kirstin, who, though selfish and thoughtless, wasn't normally malicious. "I should have showed more understanding. I should have kept my temper and my patience. I know Kirstin. . . ." Adam poured himself a second cup of coffee.

"We both know Kirs—Lady Marshfield—and we both know she could try the patience of a saint."

"Yes, but I grew up with her. I know her strengths and

weaknesses. She can't help being drawn to the cream of society any more than a moth can help being drawn to the flame. I love my sister, but that doesn't make me any less angry with her. Still, it was thoughtless of me to remind her that her husband married her for my fortune first and her charms second."

"It didn't hurt to remind her," Murphy said. "Marshfeld wears a layer of polish, but he's a savage underneath." O'Brien waited until Adam finished his coffee before asking, "Are we going to wait for Lady Marshfeld to come downstairs so you can apologize to her, or are we boarding the morning train and returning to Scotland?"

"We're going back to Scotland." Adam pushed his chair back from the table and stood up.

"Oh, well." O'Brien gave a dramatic sigh. "It's back to being your manservant instead of simply being your friend."

"I'm truly sorry about cutting your holiday short," Adam told him. "And you're welcome to stay if you wish, but I've had all of my sister's hospitality I can stand. She's already invited a half dozen of her lady friends to drop by this afternoon in order to take tea with the Bountiful Baron."

"I'm going with you." O'Brien got up from the table. "Bloody hell! Kirstin is either the most courageous or the most foolhardy woman I've ever met. I'll say that for her."

"At the moment she appears to be the most foolhardy," Adam said. "Because I'm not in a very forgiving mood."

"In order to save Lady Marshfeld's life, it would be best if we got moving before she comes down for breakfast."

"Yes," Adam agreed. He briefly scanned the front page of the newspaper, then folded the copy of the morning edition of the *Times of London* and slipped it in his coat pocket. There was no need for him to rush to read it before the other guests arriving downstairs for breakfast interrupted him. He had ten hours to read it at his leisure on the train. "That would be best."

The return train trip to Scotland took just as long as the first one. Adam did his best to catch up on the hours of sleep that he'd lost the night before, but this time the coach carried its full capacity of six passengers. Sleeping in a coach full of strangers was out of the question.

By the time they arrived at the Kinlochen station and boarded a carriage to Larchmont Lodge, Adam's head ached from hunger and lack of sleep and from inhaling the soot from the smokestack on the train, and his arse ached from too many hours seated on the hard seats of the coach.

He was in a foul temper and not a man to be trifled with. Adam stared out the windows as the carriage made its way from the station through the village of Kinlochen along the post road, where traffic forced the carriage to crawl at a snail's pace.

A throng of people crowded into the tiny village as laborers whitewashed cottage walls and rethatched leaky roofs. A group of carpenters were building fences between the village green and the golf links, and painters were painting signs advertising the local tavern, cobbler shop, bakery, greengrocer, and butcher shops.

Adam was amazed at the transformation of the village. It was bustling with commerce and life. Down the street Old McElreath advertised golfing clubs and gentleman's golfing clothing, and village boys signed their names to slate boards posted beside the stables and the railway station listing themselves as caddies for the golf links at Larchmont Lodge.

Adam nudged O'Brien's ankle with his foot. "Wake up and look at this."

Murphy sat up. "It's the village."

Adam leaned forward. "Those workers painting the front doors of those cottages look familiar. Are they ours?"

O'Brien nodded. "They're all yours."

"From the lodge?"

"Aye." O'Brien smiled. "Didn't you know? Crews of laborers come to the village to work every day."

"On whose orders?" Adam demanded.

"Yours, I thought." O'Brien read the surprise in Adam's face. "Gordon organizes work crews every morning. I thought you knew and approved." Murphy shrugged. "The good Lord knows the lodge has made a difference in this town."

"The lodge hasn't opened yet," Adam reminded him. "Who is financing this?"

"They are." O'Brien nodded toward the men and women in the village. "Now that they have work, they have money to spend, and they see the potential for new business once the lodge opens. But no one wants to holiday in a poor village with nothing to offer. Like you, the villagers of Kinlochen are gambling on the belief that the lodge is going to be a huge success."

"If it ever opens," Adam grumbled. "It's no wonder we're behind on our renovations. Our workers have been renovating everything else."

"Aye," Murphy agreed, "and it's worth it." He shrugged. "Besides, it all belongs to you. The village and the lodge."

He knew it was true, but Adam didn't want to hear O'Brien sing the villagers' praises, or admit that he hadn't given any thought to the village that accompanied the lodge or its commercial potential. All he could think about was crossing the threshold of the lodge and climbing the stairs to his bedchamber, where he planned several hours of uninterrupted sleep.

But opening the front door of the lodge and stepping over the threshold was like stepping into a world gone mad.

The lodge had undergone as much of a transformation in the last twenty-four hours as the village. Workmen were neatly dressed, their clothes pressed and their boots cleaned and polished. They doffed their hats to the maids when they walked by and a chorus of *please*s and *thank-you*s and *pardon me*s echoed throughout the building. It was as if the rough-and-tumble laborers had all been magically transformed into choirboys.

And that wasn't all. Albert greeted them at the door, relaying the news, in a combination of broken English and French, that the plasterers were working on the ceiling of the main salons and that afternoon tea had been moved to the library. Afternoon tea for whom? As far as he knew, the lodge wasn't yet opened for guests. Adam looked to O'Brien for answers, but Murphy looked as bewildered as he was.

"Who is taking tea in the library?" Adam asked.

"The women," came Albert's reply.

"What women?" Adam asked again.

"All of them." Albert turned and led the way. "Follow me, sir."

He hadn't planned to go to the library until after his nap, but curiosity was a force stronger than sleep. Adam had to see it with his own eyes. And seeing was believing because the thing he had sought to avoid in London—a late-afternoon tea party—was in progress, and every maid in the house and every woman from the village looked to be in attendance. And this was no ordinary tea. His sanctuary, his library, had been turned into a ladies' salon where Brenna arranged the hair of a woman seated on the leather sofa while Isobel and George and eight other women sat in nearby chairs plying their needles on several baskets of mending, exchanging recipes and offering advice on fashion and the latest cosmetics.

The remnants of afternoon tea littered the massive library table—at least he thought it was the library table. Covered, as it was, in white linen, crystal and china, and an overflowing vase of flowers, it was difficult to tell.

Adam removed his hat and wiped his eyes with the back of his hand. "Am I seeing what I think I'm seeing?" he asked O'Brien, who had followed him in the front door and now stood at his elbow viewing the scene. After almost no sleep and ten hours on the train, Adam was too tired to judge.

"I'm not sure," Murphy admitted.

"What does it look like to you?"

"It looks like every man's fantasy. Or every man's nightmare." He frowned. "It's a hen party."

"I can see that," Adam growled, "but what the devil is it doing in here?"

"Good afternoon, sir," Isobel greeted cheerfully as she saw Adam and Murphy hovering in the doorway. "Have you just come from the station?"

"Yes," Adam replied.

"Have you had your afternoon tea?" she asked.

"No."

"Would you like to join us? There's plenty."

Adam glanced at the tea table. There was indeed plenty of delicate little sandwiches and light, buttery scones and an array of little cakes and pastries to make a man's mouth water. "No, thank you," he answered, but his stomach growled, loudly betraying him.

Isobel got to her feet. "Here, sir, let me make you a plate," she offered.

Adam shook his head. "I'm going up to my room to lie down until supper, but before I do, I'd like to know the occasion for your gathering and why you invaded—uh, selected—the library."

"The workmen are replastering the ceilings in the main salons," the housekeeper answered.

"What about your room?" Adam demanded. "Isn't the housekeeper's room generally used for the purpose of entertaining staff?"

"Aye, sir," she confirmed. "But the workmen are wallpapering in my room."

"On whose orders?"

"Yours, sir."

"Mine?" Adam was genuinely surprised.

"Aye." Isobel smiled at him. "You told me to do whatever was necessary to make the housekeeper's room my own. I decided to wallpaper."

"I told you that weeks ago."

"Aye, you did," she agreed, "and I decided to wallpaper."

"When? Yesterday?" Adam was trying hard not to raise his voice or lose what remained of his temper.

"It seemed like a perfectly reasonable solution," Isobel told him. "After all, the plasterers were going to be working anyway."

Adam didn't understand the logic in that. What did plasterers have to do with paperhangers? He tried again. "Would you mind explaining the occasion?" He gestured toward the room full of women. There were two new faces, but he recognized the others, having met them when they were hired as kitchen helpers, scullery maids, and laundresses.

"There is no occasion."

"I don't understand," he admitted, looking to O'Brien for

help. But Murphy simply shrugged his shoulders as if to say the answer to the riddle lay somewhere beyond his reach.

"We take tea every afternoon, sir."

Adam was nonplussed by Isobel's reply, and O'Brien fought to keep from snickering. Adam elbowed him in the ribs. "I suppose you do. I just didn't realize everyone did." He nodded toward the two women he didn't recognize. "I don't recall meeting those two ladies."

"You've a good memory for faces, sir." Isobel was impressed. "You haven't met them yet, but they are Martha on the left and Sally on the right." The women got up from their seats and bobbed polite curtsies.

"And what do they do here?" he asked.

"I hired them to help Giana."

Adam automatically turned his gaze on George. She glanced up at him for the merest second before returning her attention to the embroidery in her lap. "I see."

"There is quite a bit for a chambermaid to do," Isobel reminded him. "Giana couldn't do it all alone, and besides . . ." She lowered her voice to a whisper. "I thought it might be a good idea to let someone else dust the breakable items and handle the china."

"Leaving George free to do the hard physical labor . . ." Adam didn't want to admit the idea bothered him as much as it did. But there was no getting around it. He couldn't stand to think of George laboring to clean his house. He'd rather have her break a fortune in china than to have her scrubbing the floors and cleaning fireplace grates.

"I assure you that Giana can manage it," Isobel hastened to reassure him. "She is tall and quite capable."

"What of Brenna?" he demanded.

"You just won't let go of that bone, will you?" Murphy hissed.

Isobel looked at him in surprise and replied, "Brenna is a lady's maid."

"Who arranges the hair and clothing of the other female employees."

"She must keep up her skills else she will be out of practice," Isobel said.

Adam narrowed his gaze at Brenna. How he had ever thought he could prefer her to George simply because of her height and the color of her hair and eyes was beyond him. But she was safe. He knew that. With Brenna, there would be no surprises. One day would be very much like the next. All safe and quiet and dull. Adam exhaled. There was no doubt that she would be the better choice for him if all he wanted was safe and quiet, if all he wanted was a woman who would always defer to his greater knowledge and better judgment. Brenna was shy and retiring, the kind of woman who would never question his choices or push him to greater accomplishments.

Brenna Langstrom was all he'd ever thought he wanted in a helpmate, yet he wasn't the slightest bit attracted to her. She was pretty enough, in a quiet colorless way, while George sparkled with light and color—despite the fact that he'd never seen her in anything except black and white. What was it about George? What was it about her that made him go against his better judgment and want her? She was everything he'd always said he didn't want in a woman, and yet, she was everything he'd always admired. Christ, but he was tired. Adam raked his hand through his hair. Too tired to be debating with Mrs. L. or contemplating the mysterious attraction he felt for George. "Heaven forbid that Brenna get out of practice," he muttered, "even though there's no lady in residence to worry about."

Adam hadn't realized he'd spoken loud enough for Isobel to hear until she answered. "There will be a lady in residence one day, and I'm sure that lady will be pleased with Brenna's skills."

"Of course she will," Adam replied. "How could Brenna displease anyone?" *Except me.* "Now, if you'll excuse me, ladies, I'm going up to my room before I say anything more." His stomach growled again, louder this time.

"What about tea?" Isobel asked. "Shall I have O'Brien take you a plate after he deposits your luggage?"

Adam glanced over at Murphy who was carrying both traveling valises and who was every bit as tired and hungry as he was. "O'Brien has been traveling just as long as I have today. Please see that plates are sent up for both of us."

"I'll send Martha and Sally up directly."

Adam almost requested that she send George but thought better of it and changed his mind. There was no point in embarrassing George if she did break more china. And no point in tempting fate. He was tired and his defenses were weak. He might not be able to keep from kissing her if he had her alone in his room.

"Fine." He backed out of the library and turned toward the stairs with Murphy following close on his heels. Max caught up to them as Adam and O'Brien reached the marble entrance hall.

Adam groaned.

"Good afternoon, sir," Max acknowledged Adam, but typically ignored the fact that O'Brien was standing directly beside him.

"Please, not now, Max. I haven't had more than a couple of hours' sleep since I left here and I'm on my way up to bed."

"Understood, sir," Max empathized. "I simply wanted to inform you that you've nothing pressing on your desk to worry about. I've taken the liberty of handling your correspondence—"

"You what?"

"I've taken the liberty of handling your correspondence with the exception of the personal letter from Lady Marshfeld, of course, since you took care of that one on your own," Max explained.

"You're reading my mail?" Adam was shocked by the idea.

"Of course, sir. And I posted the letters you left on your desk. That is one of the duties of a private secretary. I've separated it for you into matters that must be handled right away and matters that can wait. I've also taken the liberty of rearranging your social calendar and weeding through the various requests for funds from myriad charities. I've made a list of the ones with which I am familiar and the ones I deem most worthy. We shall have to go over the others together—until I become more familiar with your activities and your routine correspondence." Max outlined the tasks he'd performed in Adam's absence, omitting the fact that he hadn't posted the advertisements Adam had written for all of the major American and European newspapers. "Is there anything else you require of me before you retire for your nap?"

Adam frowned. He hadn't required anything of Max to begin with. And he certainly hadn't required that Max imply that he was a doddering old fool who needed a nap every afternoon. He didn't need anyone to manage his correspondence or arrange his social calendar or tend to his charitable requests. "We'll discuss it later."

"Quite so, sir." Max clicked his boot heels together and bowed before withdrawing from the entrance hall.

"What do you make of that?" O'Brien asked as they climbed the stairs leading to their bedrooms.

Adam took his traveling valise out of Murphy's hands. "I can't make sense of it," he admitted. "This is either a bad dream or the whole damned place has turned upside down."

Chapter 21

*D*ownstairs in the library Giana patiently continued sewing as she mentally counted the minutes. She heard Max waylay McKendrick and O'Brien in the marble entrance hall on their way to the stairs and had seen Max walk by minutes later on his way to the room he had appropriated as his office—the room that had once belonged to the bailiff who oversaw the estate. "One thousand thirteen, one thousand fourteen, one thousand fift—"

"Miss Langstrom!"

His roar seemed to shake the rafters, echoing as it did off the marble floors. Giana expected it to rattle the windows in their casements, and knock the fresh plaster from the ceilings.

She looked up and met Brenna's gaze. Giana nodded and Brenna dropped her hairbrush and ran out of the library and across the marble entrance hall. They had worked out a plan. Unless he was specific in his request for her, Giana had decided that Brenna should answer the call. Adam McKendrick had instructed her to stay away from him on more than one occasion, and that was exactly what Giana intended to do for as long as she could.

"Not you!" Adam's shout stopped Brenna at the foot of the stairs. "The other Miss Langstrom. George!"

Giana set her embroidery aside and rose from her chair.

"Take this." Isobel thrust a plate full of sandwiches and tea cakes into her hand. "It might just soothe the savage beastie." Giana glanced down at the plate in her hand. While she appreciated the gesture, she knew it would take more than a few sandwiches and cakes to soothe this savage beastie, but she did not know what that something was.

She met Brenna just inside the doorway of the library and smiled her thanks for Brenna's willingness to beard the lion in his den, then straightened her spine, lifted her chin, and stepped outside the library door. Giana's heels clicked against the marble floor as she crossed the entrance and began the climb up the stairs.

Adam took the plate out of her hand as soon as she reached the landing and pointed through the open door. "What is the meaning of this?"

Giana winced as she peeked inside the doorway. Wagner had been lying in the center of Adam's bed. That much was clear. The pillows and the bedclothes bore the impression of his head and body, and so did the shredded remains of a stack of London newspapers he'd been lying on, but Wagner was nowhere to be found. "What is the meaning of what?"

Adam set the plate on the bedside table and grabbed a square of sandwich. Rather than talk with his mouth full, he shot George a meaningful look that told her he knew she wasn't that stupid. "Try again." He motioned her into the room.

"Wagner?"

"I thought I told you to keep him out of my bed."

An unspoken "or else" hung on the end of his sentence, and Giana decided to challenge it. "Does this mean you are going to flame us?"

"*Flame* us?" Adam wrinkled his brow in frustration. "What the devil does that mean?"

"If you are unhappy with our work, then you must flame us."

Understanding dawned. "I'm not unhappy with your work,"

he told her. "And I'm not going to *fire* you. I just want you to control the beast and keep him out of my bed."

Now that she knew her position and the positions of her "family" were secure, Giana decided to overlook the fact that Adam insulted her by referring to her pet as a beast. "Wagner is not in your bed."

"He was."

She surveyed the room and its furnishings. "Where is he?"

"He was sleeping like a baby with his head on my pillow, his body sprawled across my bed and with all four feet in the air until I shouted. Then he disappeared."

"He hates loud noises," Giana said. She knelt and looked under the bed.

"He *dislikes* loud noises," Adam corrected. "He hates me."

"Oh, no, he likes you." She looked behind the bedroom door and beneath the writing desk.

"That's debatable." Adam snorted. "What isn't debatable is the fact that he continues to like my bed. Tell me, George, did you sleep here in my absence?"

"No, of course not!"

"Just checking." He grinned. "I thought maybe you missed me."

"I did miss—" Giana could have bitten out her tongue for that slip. Well, she decided, there was nothing to do except brazen it out. "I may have missed you," she clarified. "But not enough to sleep in your bed while you were away."

"Just enough to allow Wagner to do it for you," he accused.

The dog whimpered at the sound of his name, and Giana followed the sound to the open door of the armoire. Wagner lay huddled in the bottom. "Wagner?"

He scrambled to his feet, sat up, and thrust his nose through a row of Adam's dark wool suits, peeking out at them. Giana couldn't help but smile, and even though he struggled hard to hide it, she thought she might have caught a shadow of a smile on Adam's handsome face.

"I did not allow Wagner into your room," she answered truthfully, gently caressing the top of Wagner's head. She had instructed Isobel to let Wagner into Adam's room. "It is all right, boy, Adam did not mean to frighten you."

"Adam *did* mean to frighten him, if it meant getting him off my bed," Adam corrected. "Adam is dead on his feet and not at all inclined to sleep with a hundred-fifty-pound canine." He winked at George. "Now, Wagner's master is another story all together. . . ."

Giana bit her bottom lip, unable to decide what he meant.

"Never mind," Adam said. "Just don't let him in here again."

"I did not let him into your room," Giana repeated.

"If you didn't let him into my room, how do you explain the tiny bits of newspaper scattered all over it?" he demanded. "I distinctly recall giving the newspapers to you because you asked to read them."

"I returned the newspapers to your bedchamber after I finished reading them."

Adam watched her as she answered his questions. He knew she was telling the truth because she was so transparent; it was impossible for her to lie. "Why here? Why not the library?"

"I did not finish reading them until late this morning." Giana found it hard to concentrate on his questions or on her answers. She would not be surprised if she heard herself blurting out the truth at any moment because she found herself watching his mouth as he formed his words. Watching. Wondering how it would feel to kiss him again. Wondering if he wanted to kiss her again as much as she wanted him to. "I brought the papers here and placed them on your writing desk because Is—my mother—was readying the library for afternoon tea. He was not in here then, but any one of many people could have let him in," she said. "It is easier to keep Wagner out of your bedchamber than it is to keep him away from the tea table."

"Is it? I hadn't noticed."

She knew she deserved it, but still, his sarcasm cut like the shards of china that had sliced her hand. Giana bowed her head and stared down at the tip of her shoes. "I was wrong," she said. "I am sorry." And she was. Sorry she had to deceive him. Sorry she had allowed Wagner to destroy his property even though the property was only a bundle of newsprint that could jeopardize her future. "I am not the only person who comes into your room during the day."

"You are from now on."

Giana didn't answer or acknowledge that she'd heard what he'd said. She kept her gaze on the floor.

"Hey." Adam reached over and lifted her chin with the tip of his index finger. "I'm sorry, too."

This time she looked at him, and Adam saw the shimmer of tears in her eyes.

"Don't cry," he said softly.

"Do not be impractical," she admonished. "Everyone knows that pri—people in my position never cry."

"Oh, really? Why not?" *Impractical?* Adam searched for a word that meant "impractical" as he wiped a tear off her cheekbone with the pad of his thumb. *Silly. Do not be silly.*

"Because we cannot afford to," she answered. "Besides, crying does not change anything."

"Sometimes it makes you feel better," he told her.

"It does not," she replied. "It makes your eyes and your throat burn, stuffs up your nose, and makes your head ache."

"Sometimes it makes you feel better inside. And how do you know so much about what it does on the outside if people like you never cry?"

Giana gave him her haughtiest, most regal look. "I did not say that I had never cried," she said. "Like everyone else, I cried as a child. And I remember how uncomfortable it was and how little it solved. That is, of course, why I no longer do it."

Adam caught another teardrop with his thumb and nodded. "Of course. It's why I no longer do it, either." He made a face at her and Giana laughed. "There, that's better."

"Is it?" She leaned toward him.

He rubbed his thumb across her mouth. He wanted to kiss her. He wanted very much to kiss her, but Adam was learning just how dangerous to his peace of mind that could be. He had to stop this madness before he was lost. "Yes. I'd like to oblige you, but . . ." Adam shook his head. "At the moment I'm not much of a companion, much less a lover. . . ."

Giana opened her mouth into a perfect circle of surprise.

"It's all right," he told her. "You don't have to say or do

anything. And you don't have to worry about me. I'm not going to do anything. Now, just take Wagner and go."

She tried. She honestly tried. But after a quarter hour of commanding and coaxing and pleading, even bribing with morsels from Adam's plate, Giana was forced to admit failure. Wagner, normally the most obedient and faithful of companions, disobeyed and disappointed her. He simply would not come out of the bottom of Adam's wardrobe. Finally Giana leaned into the opening and attempted to lift Wagner out of his cozy den.

"Oh, no, you don't!" Adam placed an arm around her waist and pulled her back against him. "He's too big and heavy. You'll hurt yourself." Although he'd only meant to prevent her from hurting herself, Adam enjoyed the way his arm pressed against the underside of her breast and the way her bottom fit snugly against his front. They were like spoons stacked atop each other with all the dips and curves and lengths fitting perfectly, complimenting each other.

"Then you must try—"

"Not me." Adam reluctantly let go of Giana, breaking contact as he stepped away and shook his head. "This may seem cowardly to you, but I'm not risking my back or any other part of my anatomy on him." He stared down into the dog's soulful brown eyes. With his big head, expressive eyes, and jeweled velvet collar, Wagner didn't look dangerous, but they weren't called wolfhounds for nothing, and anything that could chase and kill a wolf deserved respect.

"What shall we do?" she asked.

Adam could think of dozens of things he would like to do—all of them with her as a willing partner, but those weren't the kind of suggestions Giana had in mind. Unfortunately for him, they were the only kinds of expressions that sprang to mind. He had no previous experience with removing a recalcitrant dog from a wardrobe, and Adam was quite sure he could do without gaining any. "Leave him where he is."

"Pardon?"

Adam smiled. "You heard correctly. I suggested that we leave him where he is for the night."

"You are certain?"

"Not at all," he replied. "But as long as he stays put, he's not going to bother me tonight." He smothered a yawn with his hand, then turned Giana and headed her toward the bedroom door. "Good night, George."

Giana glanced at the window. It was still light outside.

Adam saw the direction of her gaze. "I intend to sleep through supper and, hopefully, the remainder of the night." He opened the bedroom door and steered her though it. "Bring my breakfast, a pot of coffee, and the morning newspaper when you come to get the dog."

"He goes out quite early," she warned.

"As long as he goes out," Adam said. "And, George, if he does any damage in there—"

Unwilling to listen to any more threats, real or implied, Giana cut him off. "I know," she answered. "Do not concern yourself. If he does any damage, I will pay."

Chapter 22

A Princess of the Blood Royal of the House of Saxe-Wallerstein-Karolya must always be an asset to her name and to her house. She must never do anything that would bring scandal or ruin upon them.

—MAXIM 10: PROTOCOL AND COURT ETIQUETTE OF PRINCESSES OF THE BLOOD ROYAL OF THE HOUSE OF SAXE-WALLERSTEIN-KAROLYA, AS DECREED BY HIS SERENE HIGHNESS, PRINCE KAROL I, 1432.

*G*iana arrived at Adam's bedroom at half-past five the following morning carrying a butler's table containing his breakfast, a pot of coffee, and one slightly scorched morning newspaper. She was grateful that Karolya's missing princess was no longer front-page headline news but had been relegated to a small column on page three. Giana had ironed it herself, putting into practice the skill she had learned so long ago in Karolya. It had been seven years since she'd earned her Sixteenth, and she was quite relieved to know that she only had to iron one paper and to burn only one small section of it. She was also grateful that she was up before the other members of her household. The only members of the staff she had to face were the kitchen staff and Mrs. Dunham, and Henri, who now shared the responsibility of breakfast. If they wondered why she had requested a breakfast tray, they didn't mention it, and Giana thought that might be because the pot of coffee made the answer quite clear. Only three people at Larchmont Lodge drank coffee instead of tea, and those three were: Adam McKendrick, Murphy O'Brien, and Henri Latour. She wasn't taking the chef breakfast in bed, so she could only be taking it to McKendrick or O'Brien. And since most everyone in the household had heard McKendrick shouting for her yesterday afternoon, he was the man most likely to have made such a demand of her.

Giana shifted the butler's table to one hip, then tapped on the door. She tapped a second time, and when there was no answer on the third knock, she turned the knob and eased the door open and discovered that Adam McKendrick was still asleep.

And that he did not sleep in a nightshirt. Or anything else.

His broad back, baked a golden color by the sun, was bare. And Giana wanted to reach out and touch him—to place her palm against his shoulder to see if his skin was as smooth and as warm as it looked.

She glanced around the room. Adam's shirt, waistcoat, jacket, and trousers were draped over the back of the wooden chair of the writing desk and his hat crowned the top of the pile. Giana tiptoed into the room and carefully set the butler's table on the floor beside the nightstand.

One of his tall black leather boots lay beside the cast-iron bootjack where he'd tugged it off. The other lay on the floor beside the footboard of the bed. The toe of that boot, while essentially undamaged, was a bit less glossy than its counterpart and sported recent scuff marks that Giana was certain would match the teeth of the wolfhound that lay curled atop the covers beside Adam.

Giana picked up his boot. There was no disguising the scuff marks on the toe. No hiding the fact that they were there or that Wagner had made them, but she might be able to keep Adam from noticing for a while longer. She studied the boot for a moment, then began polishing the toe with the hem of her apron. The musky odor of mink oil used to waterproof the boots filled her nostrils. She finished polishing and set the boot down beside its mate only to find that the pristine condition of the leather of the right boot made the scuff marks on the left one more noticeable. So Giana put the boot back where she'd found it, placing it on its side on the floor near the foot of the bed. There was nothing to be done about it except to pay for the damage. She unbuttoned the top buttons of her dress, then turned her back and reached inside her corset cover and pulled at a piece of jewelry stitched inside. She thought she had grabbed one of the diamond earrings she had sewn there, but what she pulled out was a gold ring set with a huge black pearl from the South Seas and surrounded by small diamonds. Giana sighed. She had always admired the ring. As a child, she had stood before the portrait of her ancestor, Princess Rosamond, and practiced her counting by counting the circle of diamonds. There were sixteen of them.

Acting quickly, before she could find reason to stop herself, Giana reached down, righted Adam's boot, then dropped the ring inside, shaking it down to the toe, before returning the boot to its place on the floor. Feeling the hot sting of tears, she bit her lip to keep from crying. It was done. She had paid for Wagner's crime and the part she had played in it with a small part of her heritage. She hated that it was one of her favorite parts, but she cared far more for Wagner than she did for a pearl ring. Any pearl ring. And Wagner could not help it.

He was a dog. He could not help being attracted to the scent of mink any more than a bee could help being attracted to the scent of nectar. Any more than she could help being attracted to the man in the bed. Giana sighed. She knew she should not stare at him—especially when he slept, but she simply could not deny herself the pleasure.

He lay in the center of the bed. The cotton sheet draped across his lean hips and over his firm buttocks was the only thing covering him, and the white fabric drew her gaze back to the bed. Lying there, he appeared much younger than he did when he was awake. His hair was tousled in sleep, his jaw shadowed by the stubble on his face. His thick dark eyelashes fanned against his face. But there was nothing boyish about him. The tiny wrinkles marking the corners of his eyes, the powerful muscles of his shoulders and back, and the ridge of a long-healed scar, proclaimed him fully grown. Adam McKendrick was a gloriously healthy man in the prime of his life, and although it seemed to Giana that sleep should have given him a harmless appearance, the opposite was true. He looked dangerous instead. Dangerous to her peace of mind. More dangerous than she'd ever imagined.

Giana bit her bottom lip and clenched her fists to keep from giving in to the wicked, almost overwhelming urge to throw off her clothes and climb into bed beside him. Her whole body quaked with the effort to control it. Heat rushed to her face. Her lips ached to be kissed, and her body begged to be touched.

She wanted to watch him open his eyes, to see those blue eyes darken with desire to a deep indigo. She wanted to feel him run his hands over her naked breasts and on the smooth skin of her thighs the way he had that day on the leather sofa in the library.

Until this moment she had not realized that the desire to hold someone and to be held in return could be so powerful. Living as she had in a sheltered world, she had not understood that such desires truly existed. But now she knew. Now she recognized the urgency—the desire—the need to be with a man. And not just any man, only this one. Only Adam McKendrick. The man who had filled her with these desires. The man she loved.

Loved. Giana shook her head, trying to push the unbidden, unwanted thought aside. Not love. She could not be in love with Adam McKendrick. Princesses did not marry for love. They married for the good of their families or their countries. And she knew that better than most, for she was a princess hiding from the man who wanted her in his bed or dead. Either one, so long as he gained possession of the Karolyan State Seal.

Adam McKendrick was a self-made man. An American. She could not be foolish enough to fall in love with Adam McKendrick. It was desire, she told herself. What she felt for Adam was desire, pure and simple. Lust. Healthy, animal lust. But if that were true, she asked herself, why was it that she had never desired other men, handsomer men, nicer, more suitable men? Giana suddenly began to quake for real. When had she taken the tumble? When had she fallen in love with Adam McKendrick?

"Wagner!" She whispered his name as she quietly made her way around the bed and tugged on his collar. "Time to go outside."

The wolfhound opened his eyes, stretching and yawning, as he stepped off the bed and onto the floor, where he promptly trotted over to the boot lying near the foot of the bed, sniffed, and then pawed at it.

"No!" she hissed.

"George?" Adam murmured her name.

Giana's heart seemed to catch in her throat at the sound of it. Her heart increased its beat, and it seemed that she could hear it rapidly telling her to: follow her heart, follow her heart, follow her heart . . . "Yes?"

He wrinkled his nose against the pillow. "Is that coffee I smell?"

She smiled. "Yes. I brought your breakfast, a pot of coffee, and the newspaper just as you instructed."

"Where are you going?"

"I must take Wagner out before he lifts his leg and christens your bedpost."

Adam rolled onto his back. "Are you coming back to join me?"

Giana watched in fascination and disappointment as the sheet rolled with him, keeping the mysterious part of him covered while allowing a tantalizing view of an arrow of dark hair boldly pointing the way toward the part of him that stood out against the sheet. "Do you want me to?"

He opened his eyes and smiled at her. "I don't think there is any doubt as to what I want. Do you?" He glanced down at the sheet barely covering the lower half of his body

Giana blushed as she followed his gaze. "I am not sure."

Adam frowned. "Not sure you understand what I want or not sure you want the same thing?"

"I do not understand what it is you want exactly," she answered truthfully, "but I know it is something I should enjoy."

"How do you know that?" Adam teased.

Her answer was low and husky, barely above a whisper, "Because I enjoy your kisses."

His erection throbbed beneath the thin sheet, and Adam found himself fighting to maintain control. "Then put the dog outside and come over here so we can share a few kisses and see where they lead. . . ."

Giana bit her bottom lip as she stared at the dark arrow beneath his navel.

"Don't worry," he soothed. "We can start with kisses. And then, I'm open for suggestions."

"Then I will return." She snapped her fingers and Wagner trotted to her side. Giana glanced at the boot near the foot of the bed. The toe was pointing in the opposite direction from the way she had left it, but the ring was still secreted inside.

"Hurry back," Adam replied as he stretched his arms over his head, then yawned, and lay back against the pillows—pillows that carried the faint odor of musk. Adam raked his hand through his hair. No wonder he had awakened hard and as randy as a billy goat! It wasn't enough that he spent the night dreaming erotic dreams filled with images of George in various stages of undress and various stages of arousal. Awakening to the mingled scents of musk, orange blossoms, and coffee were practically guaranteed to do the trick. "And we'll discuss our options and decide the best way for me to negotiate a treaty with the beast."

"You can start by not calling him the beast."

"He's a dog," Adam said. "He doesn't know the difference."

"*I* know the difference." She favored Adam with her mysterious princess smile, then walked to the door. "And he recognizes the tone of your voice."

"Hey," Adam complained. "Aren't you forgetting something?"

"Your breakfast and your coffee are on the table beside your bed."

"And the newspaper?"

"It is on the tray beside your plate." She nodded toward the butler's table.

"You carried that all the way up here by yourself?"

"Yes," she answered proudly. "And your plate and your cup and saucer remain in the single piece."

Are still in one piece. He translated the idiom automatically. "Thank you."

"You are welcome." Giana opened the bedroom door.

"I trust the dog stayed in the wardrobe and behaved himself

last night." Adam knew he was pushing his luck when Giana didn't answer right away.

"George?"

"Wagner, come!" She issued the command, then hurried through the door and quickly closed it behind her.

Adam groaned at her choice of words. He listened for the sound of footsteps and of canine toenails clicking against the floor, but there was nothing until he heard her voice.

"We regret the damage to your boot," she said softly. "He was attracted to the mink oil. We hope you will accept our apology and the payment."

"What happened to my boot?" Adam practically leaped out of bed and across the floor to the door. "George!"

Giana and Wagner were halfway down the corridor when she glanced back over her shoulder and saw Adam McKendrick standing in the door of his bedchamber in all his naked male glory.

Giana swallowed the lump in her throat. The sight of Adam McKendrick standing in front of her as naked as the day he was born practically took her breath away. Her imagination hadn't done him justice. He was beautiful! As beautiful as the statue the cardinals in the Vatican had draped upon her family's last state visit.

She hurried down the stairs to keep from flinging herself at him.

"George!"

She began counting, not daring to look back until she heard his bedroom door slam and open again. "Five, six, seven, eight . . ."

"Wagner! You beast! These boots are handmade! They cost three hundred dollars a pair!"

But Wagner had already disappeared, bounding down the stairs, through the kitchen door, and out into the garden, startling laborers as he hurried to escape Adam's wrath and to relieve himself by the garden gate.

Chapter 23

The Bountiful Baron is a proud man. A confident man. A bold man. Sure of his every move.

—THE FIRST INSTALLMENT OF THE TRUE ADVENTURES OF THE BOUNTI-
FUL BARON: WESTERN BENEFACTOR TO BLOND, BEAUTIFUL, AND BETRAYED
WOMEN WRITTEN BY JOHN J. BOOKMAN, 1874.

She wasn't coming back.

It didn't take three quarters of an hour to let the dog out.

Adam arrived at that brilliant conclusion three quarters of an hour or so after he last saw George hurrying down the stairs as if she feared a lunatic was after her. And the truth was that he had behaved like one. Shouting at her. Shouting at that blasted dog. Standing in the corridor outside his bedroom at six in the morning shouting to wake the dead while wearing nothing but a scowl on his face and his pride of the morning. Good God! How could he blame her for not coming back? He wouldn't if he were in her shoes.

"Adam?"

He looked up to see O'Brien opening his door.

"I knocked but you didn't answer."

"Sorry," Adam muttered a halfhearted apology. "I didn't hear you."

O'Brien chuckled. "That much is obvious." He set the tray he carried on the foot of the bed. "I suppose you've got a lot on your mind. I brought fresh coffee."

"Thanks." He held out his empty cup and saucer, and O'Brien filled it from the fresh pot.

"You're in trouble, my friend." O'Brien didn't waste time getting to the point or mince his words once he got there. "*She's* trouble."

"Yes, I know," Adam agreed.

"The other one would be better for you," Murphy continued. "And she's more your type—the kind of woman you've always said you wanted."

Adam squeezed his eyes shut, then opened them again and looked around the room as if hoping to find it had miraculously changed. He gave a derisive laugh. "Christ! You're not telling me anything I don't already know. There's no doubt that Brenna would be much better for me. Better than George in every way. Less talkative. Less stubborn. Less complicated. Less everything. What I wouldn't give to be able to take Brenna to bed and scratch the itch I'm feeling! What I wouldn't give to get it out of my system. . . ." He let his words trail off as he turned toward the door. "Did you hear that?"

O'Brien shook his head.

Adam shrugged. "I thought I heard something."

O'Brien walked to the door. It was ajar. He pushed it shut, leaning against it, waiting for the latch to click into place. But it didn't click into place. It couldn't because there was a fold of black satin caught between the door and the jamb. He eased the door open and nudged the fabric out of the way, then stealthily pulled the door completely closed. "The little lady's maid, Brenna, is very easy on the eyes."

"She is that," Adam agreed.

"She's petite and ladylike and she has curves in all the right places. Any man would be pleased to have her on his arm."

"I can't argue with that."

"She would make you a much better wife than the Amazon."

"If I were looking for a wife," Adam pointed out. "Brenna is the type of woman I'd want. . . ."

O'Brien gave a low, appreciative whistle to cover the sound of a sudden, sharp intake of breath and the sound of footsteps hurrying down the hall.

"But I'm not dreaming about Brenna. I'm not compromising my morals over Brenna. I'm not having any trouble keeping my hands off Brenna." Adam set his cup and saucer down, then got up from his chair and stalked to the window. "And I'm not making a fool out of myself over Brenna."

"There is that," Murphy agreed.

"Have you ever known me to forget to make sure I was dressed before I ran after a woman?"

O'Brien shook his head. "No." The fact was that Murphy O'Brien had never known Adam to run after a woman. Any woman. At any time. He'd known him to offer assistance or ask them to leave—as the case may be—but he had never run after one before. And not when he was bare-arsed naked. "Can't say that I have, but I'm very happy to see you rectified your mistake."

Adam snorted. He was clean-shaven and fully dressed except for his boots. "It was the least I could do after the show I put on this morning. Jesus, Joseph, and Mary! What a mess! I must be losing my mind," Adam muttered.

"Just your perspective," O'Brien corrected. "And if it makes you feel any better, Georgiana and I were the only ones who witnessed the display, although some of the others may have heard the shouting."

"It doesn't. But thanks anyway." He crossed the room and retrieved his cup and saucer.

"Well, just so's you know, I've seen far worse things than you in yer birthday suit," O'Brien said in his best Irish brogue.

"Yes, but has she?" Adam made no attempt to hide his thoughts.

O'Brien smiled. "She had a slightly different view," he pointed out. "My view was of yer fuzzy arse. And I'd hazard a guess that you probably made a bigger impression on her."

"Yeah," Adam said. "Proud enough to give an innocent young virgin nightmares."

"Or tweak her curiosity . . ."

Adam took one final swallow of coffee and set his cup aside. "As you can see, she hasn't returned."

"She probably has more sense than you." Murphy paced the length and breadth of the room, tidying as he went along. "I take it the dog ate your boots." He changed the subject.

"He chewed the toe of one," Adam confirmed, pointing his foot at the boot in question.

"That's all?" O'Brien bent to get a closer look at the damage.

Adam gave his friend a sheepish look. "I'm afraid my temper got the best of me."

"That's an understatement," O'Brien told him. "Especially when a little boot black and a coat of paraffin should cover the scuff marks."

"What do you use as waterproof?"

"I don't." O'Brien grinned. "*I* pay one of the stable boys to polish your boots as well as mine."

"What does he use?"

O'Brien lifted the undamaged boot and sniffed. "Smells like mink oil."

"That's what I thought," Adam agreed. "Tell the boy not to use it."

"Why not? You can't beat it for waterproofing."

"How about dog-proofing?" Adam looked over at his friend. "He's a male dog. The musk is attracting him."

"Makes sense," O'Brien commented. "Do you want me to have the boy polish it now or wait until Wagner chews the other one?"

"Wait." Adam sighed. "At the rate he's going, it shouldn't take long." He glanced over at the mantel clock. "I was right to get dressed," he announced. "Because she isn't coming back."

"She's probably trying to give you time to eat your breakfast, to cool off, to drink your coffee, and to read the paper you insisted she bring." O'Brien paused long enough to place the silver covers over the dishes on the butler's table, hiding the remains of Adam's breakfast.

"You don't have to do that," Adam told him. "Don't you remember? You're a Pinkerton detective, not a valet."

"Boyo, the first thing you learn as a Pinkerton is to become whatever role you're playing. This is the role I've chosen to play, and as long as I'm at Larchmont Lodge, I'm your gentleman's gentleman." O'Brien picked up the neatly ironed and folded newspaper and tossed it to Adam. "I see she managed to make it up here without breaking the china and that she brought you your newspaper. Since she went to the trouble of ironing it for you, the least you can do is open it."

"How do you know she ironed it?" Adam shot O'Brien a nasty look before unfolding the newspaper. "Never mind," he added before Murphy had a chance to answer.

Adam held the paper up so O'Brien could see the triangular shape of the iron for himself, then shook his head. Two columns on the third page were scorched so badly they were unreadable. "I don't know what her parents were thinking when they trained her as a domestic," he said. "I'm sure she has other talents, but housekeeping isn't one of them." He refolded the paper, tossed it on the bed, and burst out laughing.

O'Brien looked at him as if he was afraid Adam was about to repeat this morning's outburst. "What's so funny?"

"That!" Adam pointed to the paper. "I haven't had the opportunity to read a newspaper since I got here."

"I don't believe it!" O'Brien exclaimed in mock horror. "Adam McKendrick? The man who lives and breathes the financial pages?"

"Believe it," Adam said wryly. "I've been trying to read a newspaper since I got here, but something has happened to all of them. Wagner shredded the batch I got last week, and George's attempt at ironing has ruined this one."

But Murphy O'Brien didn't find the matter amusing. "Have you ever thought that someone might not want you to read the newspaper?"

Adam stopped laughing and focused his attention on O'Brien. "What do you mean?"

"What I mean, me boyo, is that I don't believe in that kind of coincidence." He stared at Adam. "Do you?"

"No, I don't." He met O'Brien's gaze. "Hand me my boots, please."

Murphy handed him the boots.

Adam pulled on the right one, then stepped into the left. "What the devil?" He took his foot out and turned his boot upside down, shaking it a bit until he dislodged the object stuck in the toe. It rolled out of his boot and thudded onto the carpet. "Son of a bitch!"

Beside his foot lay a ring. Adam reached down and picked it up. It was heavy gold and set with an enormous black pearl surrounded by a circle of diamonds. He wasn't a jeweler, but he'd spent years mining silver ore, and he knew quality when he saw it. The ring he held in his hand was worth a fortune. It could only be a family heirloom, and only one person could have placed it in his boot.

Murphy whistled in admiration. "I've never seen anything like it."

"Me either," Adam told him. "Except on the fingers of kings and queens and of the popes in portraits in museums." He stopped. "What would George be doing with a ring like that?"

"She is a chambermaid," O'Brien reminded him. "The obvious answer would be that she stole it."

"She didn't steal it from me," Adam said.

"The countess of Brocavia?" O'Brien asked.

"It's possible," Adam admitted, "but I don't think so. If she stole it, why would she put it in the toe of my boot where I would be sure to find it?" He scratched his jaw. "Besides," he added, "I don't believe there was a countess of Brocavia. I think it's just a name and a story they made up to get the job here."

"How did you come to that conclusion?" O'Brien asked, and Adam related the incident in the library when George had mistakenly called the woman the countess of Brocadia. O'Brien listened to Adam's argument and nodded in agreement. "They lied about the countess. But why?" He looked down at the ring in Adam's hand. "Where do you suppose they came from?"

"Karolya," Adam answered automatically.

"Karolya?" O'Brien frowned. "Is that where . . ."

"Lord Bascombe said that Isobel and Albert had lived in Karolya." Adam handed the ring to Murphy and walked over to his wardrobe, where he began rummaging through the pockets of his overcoat. "There is one newspaper left in this house." He waved the paper triumphantly. "The one I picked up yesterday in London. The one I stuck in my coat pocket to read on the train. But I didn't read it." Adam unfolded the paper, frowning as the ink smeared his hands. "I read the front page and the financial pages and glanced at a few other headlines. But I quit reading when my head began to ache. Still, I thought I remembered seeing something about . . . There it is."

Adam read the headline aloud: " 'Karolyan Princess Missing. Feared Dead.' " He read the rest of the article, studying the small photograph beside it. It was hard to tell, but the picture bore a striking resemblance to George. Adam shoved the paper at O'Brien.

"Do you think it's possible?" O'Brien asked, shocked.

"Yeah, it's possible," Adam replied grimly. "It's not very likely, but it's possible." He gritted his teeth. "Unfortunately, there's only one way to find out."

"Adam?" Murphy's voice was filled with concern. "Are you going to ask her about the ring?"

"In a roundabout way."

"What does that mean?"

Adam exhaled. "If she's that missing princess, she's lied about everything since she arrived. And she obviously has her reasons for hiding here and for lying, but tell me, Murph, what are the odds that she'll trust me enough to tell the truth?"

"If she's that missing princess, she's desperate to remain hidden or she wouldn't be at Larchmont Lodge working as a chambermaid."

"Exactly." Adam met O'Brien's gaze. "But how desperate?"

"Don't," Murphy warned. "Please, Adam, cut your losses. If she's a princess, there's no hope for it. And believe me, boyo, it would be better if you don't have those memories to carry around."

Adam managed a lopsided smile. "I wish it were that simple."

Chapter 24

He found her alone in the newly refashioned women's quarters, lying on her side in the center of her bed, her knees drawn up to her chin, her back curved into a protective posture. Wagner lay beside her.

Adam had half-hoped that he wouldn't find her. And if he did find her, he imagined her looking up and smiling at him or running to meet him, welcoming him with hot kisses and open arms—eager to pick up where they'd left off. But George didn't look up when he entered the room or give any sign of having heard him.

As he drew nearer, Adam saw the movement in her shoulders and recognized the sound echoing hollowly in the empty room and realized why she hadn't heard him. She was crying as if her heart would break. Or as if it had already broken.

Adam's stomach tightened and his heart seemed to catch in his throat. He stopped in his tracks, then silently retreated into the shadows, momentarily stunned, unsure of what to do. Her tears made him uncomfortable, anxious, and willing to do whatever he could to end them. Perhaps because they were unexpected and private. His sisters cried at the slightest provocation. They used their tears or the threat of them to wheedle gifts and favors from him. He was accustomed to those kinds of tears. This was something else.

Only last night George had informed him that people in her position did not cry. *Do not be impractical, she had admonished. Everyone knows that pri—people in my position never cry.*

But she was crying now. And the sight of it tore at Adam's heart. He wanted to sweep her up in his arms and hold her. He wanted to cuddle her close and promise her everything would be all right. He wanted to tell her that her secret was safe with him. He wanted . . . He wanted . . . her. The woman he had come to know and admire. George Langstrom, the chambermaid with the pale blond hair, fierce pride, and determined glint in her eyes.

Adam walked toward the bed.

Wagner growled, low in his throat, as he approached. Adam ignored him and closed the distance between them. He walked over to George's side of the bed and sat down. "George?"

"Go away." She didn't look up but kept her face buried in the pillow.

He tried again and this time he called her by her name instead of the pet name he had given her. "Giana?" Adam placed his hand on her shoulder.

She shrugged it off. "You do not have permission to put your hand upon my person."

Adam snatched his hand back as if she had bitten it, taken aback by the rancor he heard in her voice. He wasn't sure if his shouting at her had brought it about or if there was another cause, but George was definitely in a fine fettle. Having four sisters had taught him to recognize the signs and to know when to advance and when to retreat and when to do both. But he was rapidly running out of options. "Are you crying?"

Giana scrubbed the tears from her cheeks with the heels of her hands, then rolled to her side and sat up. "Do not be absurd. We never cry in front of strangers."

"You give a good imitation of it," he said. "But since I'm no stranger, I think it's fair if you indulge."

"You think not?" she challenged.

"No," he answered gently. "I'm not." He smiled at her. "How can I be a stranger to you when I'm the man who gave you your first kiss?"

"When he had nothing better to do," she retorted. "When he would rather be kissing someone else."

"I don't know where you get your ridiculous notions or what kind of man you think I am. But I am not in the habit of kissing one woman when I would rather be kissing someone else." Adam was stunned by the way she looked at him. Tears glistened on the surface of her blue eyes—eyes that were red-rimmed and bloodshot. Her angry gaze flashed fire at him, and when she spoke, her voice was full of venom. He stood up and began to pace.

"We received our notions from you!"

"From me?" His surprise was rapidly giving way to anger.

Giana wanted him to go away so she could curl up in a tight ball of shame once again with only Wagner for company, but she could not take the coward's way out. "We heard you," she murmured. "We heard you talking to your manservant."

"When did *we* hear that?" Adam demanded, stepping up to the challenge and issuing one of his own just to see how she would react. "And is that *we* you and Wagner or the royal one?"

"Wagner and I." Giana looked him in the eye, daring him to question her veracity. "We—I—returned to your bedchamber. I heard you speaking with your gentleman as I waited outside the door."

"I was waiting for you. Why didn't you make your presence known?" Adam asked.

"For what purpose? Having already assisted you with your toilette, your manservant was going about his duty, tidying the room as you spoke. My presence was not necessary."

Adam knew he was about to tread on thin ice, but he was willing to risk it. "Your presence was very necessary in order to continue what we started—"

"That is what you say now," she accused.

Adam raised an eyebrow in warning. "Twice you've implied I misled you regarding my intentions. Let me clarify things for you. I may not always speak my mind, but I'm not in the habit of misleading women in order to get them to share my pillow. I may not have said it at the time," he conceded, "but I don't believe you mistook my intentions." He glanced at her. "I don't believe I left any room for doubt."

"Humph." She sniffed in disdain.

"Careful, George."

She ignored his warning. "You left no doubt that you wanted someone to share your kisses and your pillow. But I was not that someone. I heard O'Brien say that Brenna would be better for you. You agreed with him."

"Son of a—" Adam raked his fingers through his hair in a show of frustration. "Yes, I agreed with him," he told her. "And it's true."

Giana's heart and all of her lovely dreams of kissing and being kissed, of holding him and being held by him, shattered. His words inflicted so much pain she couldn't speak. She sucked in a breath and fought to keep the fresh onslaught of tears stinging her eyelids from sliding down her cheeks.

"It's true." He twisted the dagger in her heart. "Brenna would be a better choice for me."

"Then go to her!" Giana shouted at him. And the sound of it startled them both. But not for long. Once she found her voice, Giana discovered that shouting could be very invigorating. Very liberating. She tried it again, louder this time. "Find her! Kiss her! You have my permission. But go away and leave me alone!"

"Damn it, George!" he swore. "I don't want Brenna!"

"You said—"

"I know what I said," he snapped. "I agreed with O'Brien when he said that Brenna would be better for me. And do you know why I agreed?" He didn't wait for her to answer. "Because I knew this would happen! Because I knew there was no danger of me falling in love with your sister. She's the image of everything I ever thought I wanted in a woman, and I feel nothing for her. Nothing." He shook his head. "While you make me crazy! You turn me into a raving lunatic! You're shouting because I don't want you. I'm shouting because I do. Damn it, George, I don't dream about Brenna. I don't compromise my morals over Brenna. I don't have any trouble keeping my hands off Brenna." He pointed a finger at her. "And you should have known that. Have you seen me kissing Brenna? Have you seen me chasing after her?"

Giana shook her head.

"That's right. You haven't. And you know why? Because I don't want to take Brenna to bed. I don't want to make love to Brenna. I want to make love to you!" He turned and stalked toward the door. "But you do whatever you want. Run away. Hide. Cry. Feel sorry for yourself. I'm not apologizing for telling the truth. And I'm through explaining."

Giana snapped her fingers and pointed toward the door. "Wagner! *En garde!*"

Before he knew what was happening, Wagner was sitting in front of the door. Adam found himself facing a hundred and fifty pounds of snarling wolfhound. And there was no doubt that the threat was real. If George snapped her fingers and ordered Wagner to attack, the dog could have Adam's bed and his boots all to himself.

"Call him off," Adam ordered.

"No." Giana climbed off the bed and crossed the room to stand beside the dog.

"This isn't funny, George," Adam gritted out.

"No," she agreed. "But I do not want you to leave."

"You told me to go away and leave you alone," he reminded her.

"I was mistaken," she said. "That is not what I want."

Adam eyed her warily. "Then, what do you want?"

"I want you to kiss me and see where it leads."

Her answer sucked the fight right out of him. But her blue eyes were smoldering with desire. "I know where it will lead," he said. "The question is whether or not you'll want to go there."

"Kiss me," she ordered, moistening her lips with the tip of her tongue in preparation. "And I will follow wherever you lead."

"Will you follow if I lead you to bed?" he asked.

Giana moved closer and closer still, until she was able to loop her arms around Adam's neck and press her body to his.

"Kiss me and find out." She followed her invitation with action, pulling his head down so she could kiss him.

Adam returned the kiss. Kissing her thoroughly until one of them came up for air. "I'm not playing games, George. I want to make love to you." He shrugged out of his jacket and let it fall to the floor, then he untied his tie, removed his collar, and unfastened his watch chain, dropping them on top of his wool jacket.

"I want you to do so." She licked the seam of his lips, hoping to encourage him to resume his soul-stealing kisses.

"Then put the dog out," he directed.

"He will not harm you," she told him. "He is simply guarding the door as he was taught to do. His presence ensures us that no one will interfere."

"*He's* watching." Adam smiled. "*His* presence will interfere."

"Oh," she said.

"Send him out," Adam said. "He can guard the outside of the door as well as the inside of it."

Giana snapped her fingers, and Adam opened the door as she issued the command, "Wagner. Outside. *En garde.*"

"Thank you," Adam breathed the words against her lips, before he covered them with his own and proceeded to show her just how thankful he was.

Desire arced between them like a flash of lightning.

Adam bent at the knees and lifted George into his arms, stepped over his garments, and carried her to her bed. Giana thrilled at the feeling. No one had carried her since she was twelve years old and had fallen from her horse and broken her leg. She thought that if it were possible to love him more, she loved Adam for that. She stood nearly six feet tall in her stocking feet, and he carried her as if she were Brenna's size.

Adam placed her on her bed, then followed her down atop the coverlet. He reminded himself that she was a virgin. She deserved gentleness. She deserved tenderness. She deserved his undivided attention, so Adam devoted himself to giving George everything she deserved. He nibbled at her lips, tracing the texture of them, before he touched the seam between her lips with the tip of his tongue, showering Giana with pleasure as he tasted the softness of her lips and absorbed the feel of her mouth; poring over every detail, every nuance of her lips and mouth and teeth and tongue, with the same single-minded determination that had taken him from the bowels of the Nevada silver mines, digging for ore, to Larchmont Lodge in Scotland and a bank account worth millions of dollars.

He leaned into her, pressing the lower part of his body against the cradle of hers and Giana opened her mouth and parted her legs to grant him access. Acknowledging her generous offering, Adam reached up, tangled one hand in her hair, and unpinned the twin coronets of braids, then pulled the ties from the bottom of the braids. He raked his fingers through them, loosening the plaits and breathing in the scent of her as he pulled her closer. He deepened his kiss, delving his tongue into the lush sweetness of her mouth.

Giana's tongue mated with his, mirroring his movements, as she plundered the depths of his mouth, retreating, then plundering again. She sank against him, shivering in delicious response as Adam left her lips and kissed a path over her eyelids, her cheeks, and the bridge of her nose. He brushed his lips lightly over hers once again before continuing his trail of kisses until he reached the pulse that beat at the base of her throat.

There were many times in her life when Giana despaired of the position to which she had been born, but now she was glad of it. Being a princess had taught her how to lead and how to follow, and she discovered that in Adam's arms, she was thrilled to do both. He had much to teach and she had a great deal to learn. And she was a little bewildered to learn that she enjoyed having someone else take the lead for a while. She enjoyed relinquishing her authority, finding incredible pleasure in letting go, becoming an enthusiastic slave to her desires.

Adam rubbed his nose into the hollow below her ear. He inhaled the fresh orange blossom scent of her as he laved the spot where her pulse throbbed with his tongue. He nibbled and teased and coaxed his way from her mouth to her throat, to the dainty pink shell of her ear and back again with a finesse he'd almost forgotten he possessed. A fierce longing flowed through him, making him shudder with the need to touch all of her, to taste all of her.

He remembered the way her breasts had looked beneath the fabric of her nightgown the first time he saw her, remembered the way their pink tips tightened beneath his gaze, and he ached to caress them.

Giana lay back on the bed, watching as he unpinned her apron. He tossed the pins on the night table and pushed the bib down. Sliding one hand beneath her bottom, Adam untied her apron strings and pulled the garment from around her waist. Her dress buttoned in the front, and once he dispensed with her white apron, Adam began unbuttoning the row of tiny jet buttons that held her bodice closed.

Adam opened the bodice of her dress, then cupped her breast with his hand, pushing it up and out of the confines of her black lace corset so that only the fabric of her chemise and corset cover separated her breasts from him. Her chemise, he noticed, and her corset cover were also black. He swallowed hard. He had expected white undergarments and was surprised to find her wearing black.

He felt the tightening in his groin as his erection throbbed against the front of his trousers. Adam smiled. He had never cared much for black lingerie. It held no special attraction for him. He always looked at the woman first and then her undergarments, but this . . . He gritted his teeth. Her choice of lingerie had nothing to do with seduction and everything to do with life and death. Adam hadn't realized, until that moment, that the black dresses George habitually wore had nothing to do with her position as a housemaid. She was in mourning.

Adam ran his hand over the front of her, and all of his worst fears were confirmed. A dozen or more hard lumps and bumps marred the fabric of her corset and corset cover. Suddenly he realized that the black pearl ring wasn't the only family heirloom George kept hidden. And Adam knew that if the ring was anything to go by, she was wearing a fortune in family heirlooms while working as chambermaid in a hunting lodge.

He took a deep breath to help steady his racing pulse, then slowly exhaled. As much as he wanted to undress her, as much

as he wanted to caress her breasts, he wanted—no, needed—
to allow her a few secrets.

Adam kissed the hollow of her throat, along her jaw, and
back to her ear.

"Would you like to remove your corset and corset cover or
shall I?" he whispered, his hot breath caressing the sensitive
lobe of her ear.

Giana squirmed against him, eagerly seeking his lips and
the feel of his hands on her. She started as Adam rubbed the
pad of his thumb over the tip of her breast until it hardened
against the fabric, then moved lower, stroking a place to the
right of it, a place where she had sewn a pair of diamond
earrings. . . .

"Oh!" She opened her eyes, and Adam knew the moment
she realized what he was stroking. He smiled at her, then
kissed his way from her ear to her lips.

"Be my Amazon," he urged in a deep husky voice that sent
chills down her spine and hot liquid pooling between her
thighs. "Bare your breasts for me." Adam covered her lips with
his, kissing her hungrily, thoroughly, before pulling away and
adding, "Show me your hidden charms."

She nodded and Adam gently tugged her into a sitting position.

Giana pulled her arms from the sleeves of her dress, then
took hold of the hem of her corset cover, lifted her arms, and
skimmed it over her head. She tossed the garment on the floor
and reached for the back of her corset. It proved more difficult,
and Giana was forced to seek help.

"Hooks," Giana gasped as he took advantage of her open
bodice and traced the tips of her breasts with the pads of his
fingers. "The hooks are hidden beneath the back flap."

"Hidden?" Adam muttered. "What's the point of hiding
them? You know they're there. And it isn't as if you get to
show all of this beauty off . . ." He didn't have to understand
the fine points of ladies' fashion to unhook it, so Adam duti-
fully reached behind her and felt beneath the flap, groaning
when he encountered a hundred or so tiny hook-and-eye clo-
sures. "Judas Priest!"

It took a few moments. Adam sighed with relief as he finally unhooked the contraption and freed her. Giana scrambled to her knees, then reached down and grabbed hold of the front of her corset and flung it into the air. It landed with a thud near the equally heavy jewel-laden garment she'd worn to cover it.

Her tight-fitting bodice was still buttoned at her waist, so Giana unbuttoned it and let it fall to the bed. Adam sat back on his heels and enjoyed the view as George tugged the hem of her chemise from the waistband of her skirts, pulling it up and over her head, leaving her gloriously naked above the waist.

She smiled at him.

Adam stared in awe. If he lived to be a thousand, he would never forget the sheer beauty of the sight of George's perfectly shaped breasts or the wonder of her smile when she looked into his eyes as she revealed them to him.

He pushed himself to his knees and reached for her, but George danced away. Guessing her game, Adam lay down on his back and waited for her to come to him. He didn't have to wait long.

Moments later Giana leaned over him. Adam raised his head and licked the rosy peak of her breast with his tongue.

Fire, like the fire of a glass of brandy on an empty stomach, shot through her, only this fire was a thousand times better than anything alcohol induced. Giana gasped as the warmth of his breath against her breast made her nipple swell and harden until she ached in the dark mysterious recesses of her body.

"Again," she ordered. And Adam obliged.

"More?" he asked.

Giana nodded.

"Then come closer."

She responded, leaning over him, dangling her exquisite globes above his face, like forbidden fruit.

Adam licked one breast and then the other.

Giana arched her back and moaned.

He reached over, placed his hand on either side of her waist and lifted her atop him, placing her legs on either side of his so that she was pressed against him, straddling him.

She leaned forward and Adam began lavishing her nipple

with attention. He suckled at her breast and thought how much he wanted to touch her, and taste the sweet hot essence of her. He wanted to bury his length inside her warmth and feel the heat of her surrounding him as he throbbed and pulsed within, and he wanted to capture her lips and swallow her cries as they careened toward the heavens on an intimate journey where two became one, where desire and passion were forged like iron and carbon melded into steel, to form an exquisite blend of love and faith and trust.

Adam worked his way from her breasts back to her lips. He plundered her mouth with his warm rough tongue, then slipped a hand beneath her skirts, negotiating a path through the sea of petticoats until he felt the lace of her drawers.

He reached beneath the lace ruffle at her knee and ran his hand up her silk-clad thigh as far as the give in the fabric allowed, then frustrated by his lack of progress, he withdrew his hand from the leg of her drawers and began again. His second foray yielded better results as he ran his hand over the top of her thigh and down into the valley between her legs. Locating the opening in the fabric, Adam gently eased his fingers inside it, caressing the nest of silken curls, finding the damp swollen flesh hidden beneath them.

"Adam!" Giana nearly shouted his name as she thrust her hips against his incredibly talented fingers. Adam traced the contours of her flesh and teased the tight little bud hidden within the folds.

She gasped, unable to describe the myriad delicious and forbidden sensations she felt as Adam worked his magic upon her. He slid his skilled fingers into her petal-soft folds, and Giana felt the impact of those sensations deep inside her womb. Longings she never dreamed she possessed shot to the surface and raged in a most unprincesslike fashion.

Giana knew she should be scandalized by Adam's familiarity with the forbidden places on her body, but he stroked and probed her secret places with such infinite tenderness and such agonizing care that she couldn't be outraged. How could she be shocked and angry when all he gave was pleasure? Incredible pleasure?

"Please . . ." She murmured the entreaty in such a heartfelt tone of voice that Adam couldn't tell if she was inviting him to continue or begging him to stop. He deepened his caress and wiggled his fingers. Giana immediately pressed her legs together in reaction, before opening them again to give him access. And Adam had his answer.

Giana squirmed as pleasure—hot and thick and dangerous—surged through her body. She thrust her hips upward as she moaned her pleasure and gasped out his name in short frantic little breaths.

Adam kissed her, gently at first, then harder, consciously matching the action of his fingers to that of his tongue as he caressed her. He knew she was close, and his body chafed beneath his self-imposed restraint. Adam ached to join her in blissful release, but he took his time, pressing his thumb against her, soothing her aching core with the sweet honey she lavished on his fingers.

George sighed against his lips, then shuddered deeply as her fragile control shattered and she collapsed upon his chest.

Chapter 25

A Princess of the Blood Royal of the House of Saxe-Wallerstein-Karolya must possess virtue beyond compare.

— MAXIM 15: PROTOCOL AND COURT ETIQUETTE OF PRINCESSES OF THE BLOOD ROYAL OF THE HOUSE OF SAXE-WALLERSTEIN-KAROLYA, AS DECREED BY HIS SERENE HIGHNESS, PRINCE KAROL I, 1432.

She opened her eyes and looked up at him with such an expression of sheer wonderment and joy that Adam's breath caught in his throat. He was humbled by the look in her eyes and rewarded tenfold for his unselfish restraint.

Emotion shimmered in her eyes as Giana reached up, placed her palms on both sides of his face. "Thank you," she said simply as she pulled his face down to meet her lips.

"It was an honor," he whispered seconds before he captured her mouth with his own.

Adam kissed her again—this time with all the pent-up passion and frustration and longing he'd been holding in check so long. He kissed her until her breasts heaved with exertion, until her bones seemed to turn to jelly, until all she could do was cling to him while she fervently returned his kisses measure for measure. Adam's mind reeled from the flood of sensations she evoked as her tongue mated with his.

Shaking with need, he pulled away.

"What's wrong?" she asked.

"Nothing's wrong," he answered.

"Then why did you stop kissing me?"

"Because I want you." Adam leaned his forehead against hers and drew a shaky breath. "All of you."

"You have all of me." She looked down at him.

He shook his head. "Not really. Technically, we could stop this now and you would still be a virgin." Adam stared up at her.

Her eyes widened. Adam had kissed her, touched by her in places she had not known existed. How could it be that technically, she remained untouched?

"Do you understand what I'm trying to say?" he asked.

Giana shook her head.

"I'm saying that we could stop what we're doing right now, get dressed, and go our separate ways, and it wouldn't matter for you."

She frowned.

"It wouldn't matter *for* you," he repeated, lifting himself on his elbow so he could kiss her. "My greatest hope is that this will matter *to* you for as long as you live," he said. "But at this moment you can walk away and marry another man or take another lover and no one, except you and I, will ever know what happened in this room between us."

Giana did not understand exactly what he meant, but she knew Adam was allowing her to choose. She was a princess, and she knew that while her parents' marriage had been a true love match, it was also incredibly rare. Royal marriages were arranged for the good of the nations. Princes and princesses understood, almost from birth, that love was not part of the arrangement. Giana sighed. It was her duty to save herself for marriage to ensure a secure succession to the throne. Princess Giana must go to her future husband untouched. But Giana, the woman, wanted Adam McKendrick to continue his lovemaking until no part of her remained untouched. The fact that a match between them was impossible didn't matter. She wanted to be loved for herself. Just once before she was required to fulfill her duty.

Giana decided to forget that she was a princess and decided that for today, she would be only a woman, free to choose, free to love Adam and be loved in return. She reached for Adam and smiled. "I do not want to be untouched. Technically or otherwise."

That was all the encouragement he needed. Adam unhooked

her skirts, untied the waistbands of her petticoats, and unbuttoned her lacy drawers, then untied her frilly black garters. When everything was unfastened, he peeled the garments and her black silk stockings down her slim thighs to where they pooled at the bend in her knees.

"What's this?" Adam fingered a length of thick gold chain encircling her slim waist. A heavy gold ring hung suspended from the chain. He had seen belly bracelets on Egyptian dancing girls in Paris, but he had never seen anything like this one. It was locked around her waist. George couldn't remove it without a key. He wondered, suddenly, who had put it there. There was no doubt that the ring had belonged to a man, for it bore a motto and a coat of arms. "A new kind of chastity belt or a memento from a knight in shining armor?" He kept his hands on the chain, steadying her as she lifted each leg and kicked free of her clothing. He wasn't sure what it was, but it had its uses and there was a certain erotic cachet to making love to a woman with jewelry around her waist.

Giana glanced down. She had forgotten about the seal! Except for the locket she wore around her neck and the gold chain bearing the Seal of State around her waist, Giana was completely nude. "My father gave it to me. It has been in his family for years."

Adam snorted. If her father gave it to her, it had to be some sort of chastity belt. Luckily, for him, it didn't seem to work properly.

Giana blushed bright red and squeezed her eyes shut.

"Open your eyes, George, and see how beautiful you are," he whispered.

She did as he asked, opening her eyes to see if the expression on his face matched his tone of voice and was instantly gratified to see that it did.

"You take my breath away."

She blushed.

"What happens now?" she asked.

Placing the palms of his hands on the undersides of her firmly rounded bottom, Adam urged her up onto her knees, then he grinned as he slid her forward, up his chest. Giana felt the soft, cool satin of his waistcoat and the linen of his shirt against her inner thighs as he moved her forward until her bottom rested against his collarbones. "Now you allow me to see if you taste as good as you look."

Giana looked down and met his unerring gaze.

"Trust me," he said.

And she did. Even so, the feel of his hot breath came as a complete surprise. Giana clamped her legs together. Adam lifted his head and looked at her. "I'm not going to hurt you, George," he said. "I'm only going to love you. If you'll let me."

When he looked at her like that, Giana found she couldn't deny him anything—didn't want to deny him anything. He was the teacher and she, the student. He was the sculptor and she was the clay. As long as he kept his promise to love her, her body was his to do with as he pleased. "Proceed," she ordered.

"My pleasure."

Giana thought she had achieved the greatest level of pleasure when his fingers caressed her, but when Adam pulled her to him, and began to taste the places his fingers had explored, she knew that there was greater pleasure to achieve.

He drove her to the brink of rapture and beyond, then gently rolled her to her side and cradled her beside him, capturing her cries with his mouth as she shuddered back to the earth in his arms. He brushed her damp hair off her flushed face, wiped the tears from her eyes, and murmured love words of praise and encouragement in her ear.

Giana opened her eyes to find Adam staring down at her. "Have you touched me completely?"

He moved his head from side to side on the pillow and laughed. "You're a lot less untouched," he told her. "But a virgin you remain."

"There is greater pleasure?"

"There's a great deal more pleasure," he explained, "as well as a small amount of pain. But the pleasure far surpasses the pain."

Giana eyed him warily. "Pain for whom?"

"You."

"Oh."

Adam leaned over and nipped her bottom lip, catching it

between his teeth, before soothing the bite with his tongue, and kissing her again, making her forget the momentary pain. "What's a little bit of pain compared to this?"

She nipped his lip. "Show me."

"Good Lord!" He laughed. "An autocrat!"

Giana looked shocked and then, dismayed. "I am not an autocrat," she informed him. "I am a constitutional monarchy."

Adam laughed harder. "And I'm a standard-bearer for democracy," he said. "But we'll save that debate for later." He sucked in a breath as his body tightened and the bulge in his trousers threatened to pop his buttons. "At the moment, I have a more pressing problem to discuss with you. . . ."

"What?" She kissed him again.

"The fact that one of us is wearing too many clothes . . ."

She smiled a wicked little smile that played about the corners of her mouth. Her blue eyes sparkled with merriment when she reached for the top button of his shirt. "May I?"

He favored her with a devilish grin and turned her earlier words around on her. "Since you asked so nicely, you have permission to put your hands upon my person."

"I have never before undressed a man," she confided, unbuttoning all of the buttons on his shirt and pushing it open and away from his chest.

"You're doing such a fine job, no one would ever know that you're only a beginner," he praised her.

Giana slid his shirt off his shoulders, down his arms, and over his hands, exposing the hard muscles of his chest and stomach. She rubbed her hands over the mat of hair on his chest, then indulged herself by allowing the tips of her breasts to rub against it.

Adam's blood rushed downward. The hard male part of him throbbed with each beat of his heart. He ached to sheathe himself in George's warmth. He ached to end his exquisite torment.

Wrapping his arms around her waist, Adam gently rolled her onto her back. Giana followed the line of his spine, sliding her hands down his back and over his tight buttocks, then back to the waistband of his trousers. She followed the strip of fabric from his back to the front of his trousers. Adam groaned aloud as she brushed her fingers against him.

She located the buttons of his trousers and carefully undid each one. Adam kicked free of his pants, moaning his immense satisfaction as the hard jutting length of him spilled into her waiting hands. Giana caressed him, marveling at the velvety soft feel of his flesh, and she would have continued her exploration if Adam hadn't gently lifted her hands from around him, then guided her legs up over his hips, and pressed himself against her, gently probing her entrance.

Lost in a frenzy of need, Giana locked her legs around his waist and pulled him to her.

Adam pushed inside her. He closed his eyes, threw back his head, and bit his bottom lip as he sheathed himself fully inside her warmth. His entire body shook with the effort as he fought to maintain his control.

Giana cried out as he entered her and tried to pull away. Adam, realized, too late, that she was no longer a virgin and that he'd just ruthlessly pushed through the veil of her innocence. He held on to her to keep her from squirming and causing herself more discomfort as he soothed her with his words and kissed away the salt of her tears. "It's all right, Giana, the worst will be over in a moment. Lie still. Let me kiss you."

She gasped, then bit his lower lip, hard enough to draw blood. "That was not a little pain."

Adam grunted as they exchanged a bit of his blood for hers. She was entitled. "Sweetheart, the first time for a woman always hurts, but the pain will go away soon, and I promise you, the pleasure will be worth it."

He didn't lie. Her pain gradually disappeared and as it did, Giana began to experiment, moving this way and that, testing to see if it would return. Adam lost his battle to maintain control as her movement forced him deeper inside her. He began to move his hips in a rhythm as old as time. Giana followed, matching his movements thrust for thrust, clinging to him, reveling in the weight and feel of him as he filled her again and again, gifting her with himself in a way she'd never dreamed possible.

She squeezed her eyes shut. Tears of joy trickled from the corners, ran down her cheeks, and disappeared into the silk of her hair. And as she felt the first tremors flow through her, Her Serene Highness Princess Giana of Saxe-Wallerstein-Karolya surrendered to the emotions swirling inside her and gave voice to the passion with small incoherent cries that escaped her lips as Adam rocked her to him and exploded inside her.

He brushed his lips against her cheek as he buried his face in her hair. He tasted the saltiness of her tears, then lifted his head, and looked down at her face. God, but she was beautiful! Adam shuddered as a rush of emotions raced through him. He should have spoken words of love instead of words of passion. He should have cherished her and treated her tenderly instead of using her to slake his raging desire. He'd known she was a virgin. . . . She deserved a wedding night. . . . She deserved to be . . .

Scolded or spanked or . . . loved. . . . Adam sighed. The incredible satisfaction of release also brought the first wave of guilt. Damn it to hell! She had allowed him to seduce her. To take her virginity when she'd had every opportunity to change her mind. What the hell had he done? What the hell had they done? And how would they ever manage to undo it?

Adam stared down at her—into blue eyes shimmering with emotion—and was lost. He wouldn't think about the future. He wouldn't question his good fortune or ask for more than she could give. He'd simply love her while it lasted.

Leaning closer, he touched his mouth to hers in a kiss so gentle, so loving, so precious, it brought fresh tears to her eyes. "Thank you, Adam."

"You're welcome, *Princess*."

Chapter 26

"*You knew?*" *she asked.*

"Not until a moment ago," he admitted. "I suspected, but I didn't know for sure until I looked into your eyes and saw the truth." But he had *known* it. Some part of him *had* known George was different. But he had never suspected how different until he'd discovered the pearl ring and the newspaper. There had been clues all along. So many things that hadn't made sense—the way she talked, the things she said, the way her "family" treated her.

"I can explain."

"Explain what happened or why it happened?" he asked. "Because I know what happened. What I don't know is why it happened." Adam raked his hand through his hair. "You're a princess, for God's sake! I gave you every chance! You were supposed to stop me! You were supposed to say no!" He rolled out of bed and crossed the room. "Damn it! I'm an American. We don't have royalty! I don't even know what I'm supposed to call you!"

"We—I—am Her Serene Highness Princess Georgiana Victoria Elizabeth May of Saxe-Wallerstein-Karolya. I am styled

'Her Serene Highness.' In public you would address me as 'Your Highness' and in private, you may call me George," Giana answered softly, watching as he bent to collect his scattered clothing. "I did not say no because it is not what I wanted to do. I did not want you to stop. Nor did you try very hard to stop yourself."

Adam looked at her and saw that her heart was in her eyes. "You're right. I didn't try to stop myself at all."

"The question is why not?" She pulled the sheet over her breasts and anchored it beneath her arms.

He shook his head. "I don't know. Maybe it's because I wanted the fairy tale. Maybe it's because I wanted to be the prince who saves the beautiful princess. Or maybe it's because for a while there, I truly believed in happy-ever-afters."

A stream of silvery wet tears glided silently down George's face. "You cannot save me from my duty, Adam. Or protect me from my fate." She tried to smile at him and failed miserably. "But you have given me a wonderful gift. A gift I can carry with me for the rest of my life."

"I may have given you more than a gift, Princess," he said bluntly. "It's possible that I gave you a child."

Giana blanched.

"An obviously unwanted child," he remarked cruelly.

Adam wanted to kick himself as soon as the words came out of his mouth. It wasn't her fault. She'd been a virgin. He was the one who should have been prepared. No, he was the one who should have had better sense than to make love to a princess in the first place!

George had enough to worry about without worrying about having a baby. And he could have prevented it, Adam reminded himself, if he'd been thinking with his head instead of that other part of his anatomy. But that was no excuse, and if George were to find herself with child, he'd have to find some way to take responsibility.

"How dare you think that I would not want our child?" Giana threw the pillow at him. It landed squarely, hitting him in the face before bouncing onto the floor.

"You turned as white as the sheet you're wearing," Adam told her.

"Perhaps that is because I forgot such a thing is possible. In my country, children are seldom born beyond the bonds of marriage," she informed him.

"Children are born beyond the bonds of marriage in every country," Adam said. "And royalty is no exception." He carried his clothes back to the bed. "And you're right. I was being unnecessarily cruel, because I was angry, not at you, but at myself." He leaned down and kissed her forehead. "Forgive me."

She nodded. "You are not angry at me?"

"Not for not realizing our lovemaking could have unexpected results," he answered honestly. "That was my fault."

"But you *are* angry at me for the other things." She looked up at him. "Yet you want to kiss me."

"I'd want to kiss you even if I hated you," he said wryly. "Kissing you doesn't mean I'm not angry, it just means that I crave the pleasure you give me."

"Are you still angry about Wagner and the china?"

Adam shook his head. "I believe you paid for Wagner and the china." He reached into his waistcoat pocket and pulled out the pearl ring. "With this." He tried to give it to her, but Giana refused to accept it.

"It's yours," she said.

"No," he corrected. "It's yours or else it belongs to the people of Karolya, in which case, you've no right to give it away." He pressed the ring in her palm and closed her fingers around it.

Giana held it to her heart. "I do not have enough coin to pay for the damages."

"It doesn't matter. I don't want your coin." Adam covered her hand with his. "And I certainly don't require any of the Karolyan Crown Jewels as payment."

Giana looked up at him, and this time he saw that her eyes were full of love and gratitude. "This ring was not part of the Crown Jewels," she told him. "It was part of Princess Rosamond's personal collection, but it has always been one of my favorite pieces." She smiled. "I practiced my counting by counting the diamonds." She proved it by counting to sixteen in half a dozen different languages. "There are . . ."

"Sixteen of them." He leaned over and kissed her tenderly. "I speak French," he reminded her. "And enough Spanish, German, Swedish, and Mandarin to get by."

Giana kissed him back, holding on for dear life. "Mandarin?"

He nodded. "Chinese. I made my fortune building railroads and mining silver. Over half the workers were Chinese, and the other half were Irish." He made a face at her. "Tell me, Princess, how did you come by your fortune?" He pointed toward her corset and corset cover.

"I inherited part of it upon my birth, and I inherited the rest the night my parents were murdered."

"I'm sorry," he murmured sincerely.

"So am I," she said. "They were murdered together in their bedchamber at Christianberg Palace in the capital city of Karolya after retiring from the state dinner celebrating the opening of Parliament." She recited the facts in a calm, unemotional tone of voice. "The palace was overrun and servants loyal to my father were slaughtered."

"By anarchists?" Adam repeated what he'd read in the paper.

But George shook her head. "No, by my cousin, His Highness, Prince Victor of Saxe-Wallerstein-Karolya."

"Your cousin?" Adam struggled to breathe as surprise pushed the air from his lungs. "The man searching for your kidnappers? The man who has been running the country in your absence?"

"The same."

"Son of a bitch!"

"Indeed," Giana said.

"There were no anarchists? Or kidnappers?"

"There may well be anarchists in Karolya," she answered, "but they did not kill my mother and father. Victor was inciting the young men of the ruling class, encouraging them to denounce my father's support of a new constitution and a Declaration of Rights for the Masses. Victor promised estate grants, titles, and funds in order to gain the support of the younger sons of the aristocratic families. He convinced them to become traitors by telling them that my father intended to reward the *bourgeois* for their support by granting them landed estates of the rich. My father and mother were shot and stabbed several times, and Victor ordered it done."

"Why?"

"Greed," she answered simply. "He wants control of Karolya's rich iron ore deposits and its vast acreage of virgin timber."

It took a moment for Adam to comprehend what she was saying. "Your cousin killed your parents to gain control of iron ore and timber?"

"It is a great deal of iron ore and timber," she informed him. "Papa explained the value of the iron ore and the timber to me when other governments began approaching him with offers to secure the rights to them, but I did not understand the role Victor played in the attempts to secure the rights until Max explained it to me after my parents' deaths. Papa refused to sell or lease the rights. Refused to even consider doing so. He believed that Karolya's natural resources belonged to the people. His role as prince of Karolya was to protect those resources for future generations of Karolyans. Karolya is a wealthy country. We do not need to rape the countryside to provide money or jobs for our people."

"Does Victor need money?" Adam asked.

Giana shook her head. "No. Victor needs power. Max told me that Papa learned Victor had made agreements with men of other countries to supply them with Karolyan iron ore and the timber without Papa's consent."

"What did your father do to Victor?"

"I do not know." Giana looked up at Adam. "But Victor asked for my hand in marriage and Papa refused." She dropped the black pearl ring on top of the sheet covering her lap, stared down at her lap, and began twisting the cotton fabric in her hands. "But that will not matter now. Victor will not stop until he finds me."

"Here, let me take that." Adam retrieved the pearl ring and placed it on the nightstand to keep it from being lost among the bedclothes. George surrendered it without a second thought. Adam gave a half smile. He wouldn't have to worry about providing her with expensive jewelry for their anniversaries in the years to come, because George had more than she would ever need and she didn't seem to care. The only jewelry she wore, outside of the fortune sewn into her undergarments, was the locket around her neck, the bracelet around her waist, and a pair of tiny gold earrings. And there was a pin somewhere. He remembered seeing something silver pinned to her chemise. No, George wouldn't require jewelry. She would probably rather have puppies—or children. Lots of children and dogs.

He didn't know Prince Victor, but he had known men like him, and he could well imagine the man's fury when he was forced to give up the iron ore, the timber, and George. And now that he had had the privilege of sharing her bed, Adam knew without a doubt that, even without wealth and power, she was the greater loss. "How did you escape?"

"I was not home," she answered. "My father was afraid for me, so he sent me to our summer palace in Laken." Giana looked up at Adam and spoke in a tiny forlorn voice that first took him by surprise, then frightened him. "I should have been there. I should have been there when they died. I should have been there with my mother and father. I should have died with them, but he sent me away. My father sent me to safety while he and my mother faced their enemies alone. . . ." She began to shake, then burst into tears.

Adam gathered her up in his arms and held her. "Oh, no, my sweet, you should not have died with them. Your father loved you, and because he loved you, he did exactly as he should have done. He sent you to safety, so you would live. So you would marry and have children and continue his line. I would have done the same."

"But they left me. They left me alone!" she cried.

Adam shook his head. "They didn't leave you of their own free will, sweetheart. They had no choice. You were their baby. Their precious daughter and the future of their country. They sent you away because they loved you, because they could not bear to watch you die. And you would have died, George. Make no mistake about it. If you had been home, you would have died and there would be no one to look out for the people of Karolya. You did exactly what your parents expected you to do," he told her, smoothing her hair away from her face, brushing his lips against her forehead. "You survived."

"I survived because no one knew where I was except the staff at Laken."

"Let me guess—Max, Isobel, Albert, Brenna, and Josef."

"No, Max was at the palace in Christianberg with my parents."

Adam took a deep breath. "The article I read in the *Times of London* hinted that Lord Maximillian *Gudrun*, your father's private secretary, masterminded the plot to overthrow Prince Christian and engineered your kidnapping."

"Lord Maximillian Gudrun saved my life," she announced, her voice ringing with pride. "He was wounded in an attempt to save my parents. My father gave Max his Seal of State and charged him to bring it to me and to get me out of Karolya to a place of safety." Giana glanced down at her waist.

Adam reached over and traced the outline of the gold chain at her waist through the sheet. "I take it that this is the Seal of State of Saxe-Wallerstein-Karolya."

"Yes."

"When you said your father gave it to you, I thought it might be some kind of chastity belt," he teased, his blue eyes twinkling with mirth.

"Until I am crowned ruler of Karolya, the Seal of State cannot leave my person. That is why we placed it on a chain and why I locked it around my waist."

"Where's the key?"

"I threw it in the ocean," she said. "We could not risk having the seal lost or stolen, nor could we risk having it recognized. This was the safest place to keep it," she said. "Because no one but Max and Brenna knew of its whereabouts."

"Until today." Adam reached across the bed and retrieved her chemise and handed it to her.

She smiled at him, then let go of the sheet and pulled her chemise over her head. "Until today."

"And now that I know," Adam teased, "I suppose my life is forfeit?"

Giana shook her head. "Not yours. Mine."

Chapter 27

The Bountiful Baron values truth foremost. He does not take well to surprises.

—THE FIRST INSTALLMENT OF THE TRUE ADVENTURES OF THE BOUNTI-
FUL BARON: WESTERN BENEFACTOR TO BLOND, BEAUTIFUL, AND BETRAYED
WOMEN WRITTEN BY JOHN J. BOOKMAN, 1874.

"*What?*" *Adam was paralyzed with terror at* her calm pronouncement.

"In order to succeed the throne of Karolya, Victor must produce the Seal of State and my body or marry me within one year of my father's death." She reached over and caressed Adam's cheek. "Even if I would accept my father's murderer, Victor will never marry me now that I am no longer a virgin."

Her words, spoken in that calm, matter-of-fact way, sent Adam spiraling into anger. "He'll kill you." Adam got up from the bed and began pulling on his clothes. "Jesus Christ! George! This place could be crawling with Victor's spies. If he finds out we made love . . ." He let his words trail off as he stepped into his trousers and shrugged on his shirt. "And it's not as if we have tried to be discreet. We've been missing all morning and anyone who cares to investigate could find us." Adam began buttoning his shirt. "Wagner is posted outside the door. What the devil was I thinking?" He shot her a frustrated look as he tossed her chemise on the bed. "What were you thinking?"

Giana pulled her undergarment over her head. "I was thinking that I did not want to die or to go into another man's bed without knowing what it was like to be in yours," she told him.

His knees gave way and he sat down, abruptly on the edge

of the bed. "You knew? You knew and you were willing to forfeit your life to share my bed?"

"I am a princess, Adam. I do not know if there is such a thing as a happily-ever-after for people in my position. My parents were the only royal couple in Karolya's recent history to marry for reasons of love, instead of reasons of state and a member of their family murdered them. I do not know if I will be able to marry for reasons other than for reasons of state. I only know that if I could choose, I would choose you to be my Prince Consort." She looked at him. "Whatever should happen, please know that for the rest of my life, I choose you."

I choose you. Adam's heart began a rapid tattoo, his breath caught in his throat and the sudden rush of tenderness he felt for her made his legs go weak in the knees. *He loved her.* The unexpected realization struck him like a bolt of lightning from the blue sky. He loved the way she made him feel. The way she touched him. And for now, his love would have to be enough. "Choosing me could cost you your life."

"It will have been worth it."

"Giana, I—"

Giana reached out and placed two fingers against his lips to stop the words she did not want to hear. "George," she corrected. "From you, I prefer George."

Adam gave her a sheepish look. "It doesn't sound very regal."

"I have many regal titles, but you are the only person besides my parents who has ever called me by a pet name."

"Really?" He was surprised and genuinely pleased.

"Yes."

"What did they call you?"

"My mother called me Fleur, but my father called something far more endearing, but not nearly as flattering."

"What did your father call you?" he asked.

"Her Royal Highness, Princess Monkey."

"Princess Monkey?" Adam was intrigued in spite of himself.

"Because I was all arms and legs."

"I think I would have liked your father," Adam told her.

"I think so, too," Giana said. She reached up and fingered

the locket on the thin, gold chain around her neck. "Would you like to see them?"

Adam nodded.

Giana unhooked her gold-and-diamond locket from around her neck, then opened it and held it up for Adam to see.

He stared at the portraits inside the locket.

"This one is my mother's father and mother, the marquess and marchioness of Barracksford." She pointed to the portrait on the left side of the locket. "It was copied from their official wedding portrait. And this one is"—she pointed to the other portrait—"my father and mother and me on my christening day."

"His Serene Highness Prince Christian, Her Serene Highness Princess May and Her Royal Highness Princess Monkey." Adam made a face at her.

Giana giggled.

"Nice portrait," Adam said. "Nice family."

"Yes, we were," she agreed. "I have always loved the expressions on their faces as they looked down on me." Giana's lower lip trembled. She swiped at a tear with the back of her hand and managed a wistful smile.

"You were greatly loved," he said, studying the portraits again. "And who is this?" He touched a tiny clasp at the bottom of the locket and the portrait of her grandparents slipped out to reveal another portrait—one of a handsome gentleman dressed, like her grandparents, in the style of the Regency.

"You have discovered my family's skeleton in the armoire," she told him. "George Ramsey, the fifteenth marquess of Templeston."

"Who was?" Adam remained unenlightened.

"The man who gave my mother life."

Adam raised an eyebrow at that.

"My grandmother was French. A Parisian actress and a commoner. She married very young, to her childhood sweetheart. When she was twenty and he was twenty-two, Grandmama's husband went off to war. He died in Russia fighting for Napoleon and my grandmother found work as an actress on the stage in Paris. She met George Ramsey when he went backstage to present her with a bouquet of flowers and to ask her if she would join him for dinner. Grandmama always said it was love at first sight. Grandmama fell deeply in love with Templeston and he with her. He set her up in a house in Paris and she prayed every day that he would marry her, but Templeston had promised his late wife he would never remarry. And he kept his word. My grandmother ended their affair when she realized that no matter how much George Ramsey loved her, he loved the memory of his late wife more. The marquess of Templeston returned to London and Grandmama returned to the theatre.

"Soon afterward, Grandmama was introduced to another titled Englishman by one of the ladies in the chorus. The marquess of Barracksford was much older than Grandmama. He had never married, but was considered quite a catch and quite a ladies' man. He frequently traveled to Paris on business and for pleasure and was welcomed at all the fashionable Parisian salons. Lord Barracksford fell in love with Grandmama and pursued her. Grandmama tried to discourage him by telling him that she was still in love with George Ramsey, but Lord Barracksford did not care. He continued to court her until my grandmother agreed to marry him." Giana paused, trying to gauge Adam's reaction.

"What happened to Lord Templeston?" he asked.

"He died in a boating accident off the coast of Ireland before my mother was born. He never knew my grandmother was carrying his child."

"Did Barracksford know?"

Giana nodded. "Grandmama told him as soon as she discovered it. She thought Lord Barracksford would change his mind about wanting to marry her, but he did not. Barracksford was in love. He willingly accepted my grandmother and her unborn child as his own. He and Grandmama married and settled in Paris. After my mother was born, Lord Barracksford moved the family to London. George Ramsey had died and his oldest son and heir had become the new marquess of Templeston. My mother was a girl so there was no need for anyone to know the truth of her paternity. Lord Barracksford brought my mother up as a daughter of the house and loved her as dearly as his own, but he was not her father. Lord Templeston was."

"How did you learn of this?"

"It was the story my grandmother told my mother when she gave her the locket and the story my mother told me when she gave me the locket. You see, Lord Templeston made provisions for his mistresses and their offspring in his will. If ever they were in need, they were to present this locket to the current Lord Templeston." Giana smiled. "My grandmother and my mother were fortunate to have married for love and been well provided for. There was never any need to present the locket." Giana knelt on the bed beside him and watched as he replaced the miniature of her grandparents, hiding the likeness of the marquess of Templeston, before he handed it back to her.

"Why haven't *you* presented the locket to the current Lord Templeston?"

Giana fastened the locket around her neck. "I intended to," she answered. "As soon as I reached England, but the newspapers were full of stories of my disappearance and Victor's accusation that Max was responsible." She looked up at Adam. "The papers kept reporting that Queen Victoria's government was assisting Victor in the search for me and the apprehension of Max and his band of anarchists, and that the queen had appointed her adviser, the marquess of Templeston, to act as liaison between the Court of St. James and the Court of Saxe-Wallerstein-Karolya. I was afraid to present the locket until I knew Max was safe and until I discovered if the British government wanted the iron ore and timber more than it wanted me on the Karolyan throne. I could not be sure the marquess would believe my claim or that he was not in league with my cousin . . ."

Adam reached out and touched the gold locket, then the silver pin on her chemise. "Until you are safe, we can never do this again." He turned to kiss her.

Giana looped her arms around his neck and returned his kiss with a passion equal to his own. "And once I am safe, we may never be able to do this again."

"I know," he said, "but nothing is worth risking your life.

Or the life you may be carrying within you. Agreed?" Adam pulled on his waistcoat and jacket.

"Yes." George inhaled, then placed her hand on her abdomen.

He smiled at her and their gazes met and connected. Desire sparked and Adam regretted his earlier words.

"Adam?" she asked, almost as if she had read his mind. "Have you any regrets about this morning?"

He shook his head.

Her eyes sparkled with a sheen of unshed tears. "I apologize for our deceptions and for the delays we caused to the lodge. But we knew we were safe here and we had no where else to go." She walked him to the door.

"There is no need for you to go anywhere," he said. "You can stay here where we can protect you."

Giana gave him a sad smile. "I can only stay until Queen Victoria comes to Balmoral on holiday. She is my godmother. I shall need to see her and explain. Max will not be safe until I've spoken with her . . ."

Adam nodded his understanding.

"I cannot ask anything of you . . ."

"Yes, you can," he answered. "You can ask anything."

"Then, I have two requests."

"Name them."

"I should like to continue our stay here until the queen arrives in Scotland. Their positions here have given the staff a purpose and work to do, something to keep their minds away from the fear and the desire to be home instead of far away in Scotland."

"Done." Adam scratched his chin. "But you might as well know that there are many times when I think your staff leaves a lot to be desired. I've seen you working harder than any of them."

Giana chuckled. "Only because they are barred by Karolyan law from performing any task that might interfere with their traditional duties to the sovereign. While they may work for wages, they must attend to my needs before anything or anyone else."

Adam made a face. "I suppose that explains why my schedule is never followed."

She nodded. "When royalty is in residence, the household staff must attend to them first and to everyone else second."

"Royalty does have its rewards," Adam teased.

"Those rewards always come at great personal sacrifice. Everything has a price."

"And your second request?" Adam asked.

"Will you give thought to my offer?" she asked. "I may not be able to choose, but if I am able to choose, I would choose to have you by my side."

"George, I don't thi—"

"Shh!" She put a finger to her lips. "Do not answer yet. Take the time to think about it. There is much to consider. And your sacrifices would be enormous . . ."

"Are you asking me to marry you?"

She smiled. "I am asking you to accept the role of prince consort of Karolya if I am able to offer it to you . . ."

"I'm a commoner and an American. Is that possible?"

Giana shrugged her shoulders. "It should not be impossible, but I am a woman and it will not be easy . . ."

❧

She sat on the little stool in front of the dressing table staring into the mirror long after Adam left.

Giana thought that she must be losing her mind. She had asked Adam McKendrick to marry her. She could not imagine what she had been thinking to do such a thing. Giana frowned at her reflection in the mirror. That was a lie. She had known exactly what she was thinking when she asked Adam to consider her offer to become her Prince Consort. She had been thinking how nice it would be to wake up in his arms every morning for the rest of her life.

She had been selfishly thinking only of herself. Not of Adam. Giana reached up and touched her lips with her fingertips. How could she ask him to give up his home in America and the Scottish hunting lodge he was working so hard to make a success? How could she ask him to forfeit his businesses in order to take on her problems? How could she ask him to give up his freedom, his way of life, to accept the yoke of a lifetime of obligation and duty to the people of a country not his own?

Giana sighed. She knew better than anyone, the sacrifices Adam would have to make in order to build a life with her. Marrying her would force him to give up everything he loved. Would she be enough for him? Could she give him enough to make up for all he would lose if he decided to accept her offer?

She would be making a sacrifice as well. But Adam didn't know that. And she didn't want him to know. There would be plenty of time to tell him later—if he decided to accept her offer of marriage. Giana bit her bottom lip. She would be heartbroken if he didn't take her offer, but she refused to relinquish all her pride and bribe him to marry her.

Although the Karolyan Charter had abolished the Salic Law prohibiting females from ascending the throne, members of Parliament had added provisos that limited her power to rule.

According to Karolyan law, the heir-apparent had to be married in order to ensure succession. But a princess lost power in the marriage because Karolyan law granted her husband legal jurisdiction over her. By virtue of their marriage, Giana's husband automatically gained equal rights, and in some cases more rights, to everything his wife owned except the hereditary title of Prince. Adam would become prince consort, but a prince consort with more legal rights than his wife.

If she married Adam, Giana risked losing her power over her own country. She wanted to tell him about the Female Provision in the Karolyan Charter, but she was afraid. Afraid that knowing he could gain control of her country might induce Adam to agree to marry her.

Giana didn't know if she could live with the knowledge that the man she had chosen, the man she loved, wanted the role of Prince Consort more than he wanted her. How would she ever know?

Chapter 28

A Princess of the Blood Royal of the House of Saxe-Wallerstein-Karolya must never doubt that the decision she makes is right. She must never show hesitation or weakness.

"**O**kay, boyo, it's time for a talk." O'Brien burst into the library later that afternoon; waving a newspaper he'd gone into Kinlochen to buy. He found Adam seated behind a desk covered with papers.

Adam shook his head. "Not now."

"I'm beginning to think you've found another boon companion," O'Brien teased, "and are avoiding me."

"It's nice to know that you can take a hint." Adam frowned at him. "Besides, I've got work to do."

O'Brien walked over to the desk and picked up one of the papers Adam was laboring over. "I thought you sent out invitations to the private opening of the lodge two weeks ago." He tossed the letter back on the desk.

"I did," Adam confirmed. "And now I'm sending out more."

"Announcing that the opening of the lodge has been postponed?"

"Not postponed, just rescheduled." Adam held up a letter. "I've written to invite the queen," he said. "I hear she'll be coming to Balmoral soon."

O'Brien frowned. "I thought you'd decided—"

"I did. But now, I've changed my mind." He glanced around to see if any of the workers were working close by.

O'Brien followed Adam's gaze to where one of the paper-hangers working in the room across the hall, hovered beside the door of the library. He slapped his thigh. "I met Josef as I was returning from the village, sir, and he asked me to ask if you intended to ride out today."

Adam stood up and grabbed his hat. "I could use some exercise," he said. "And I need to take a look at the progress on the links."

A half an hour later, Adam and O'Brien rode out of the stable yard.

"Where are we headed?" Murphy asked.

"The links," Adam answered. "We can talk there."

They rode in silence until they reached the eighteenth hole of the golf links. They dismounted near the clubhouse and allowed their horses to graze as they walked about what would soon become the putting greens.

"Is she or isn't she?" O'Brien asked, unable to contain his curiosity any longer.

"She is."

O'Brien nodded. "That's the rumor in the village as well. The news of her disappearance didn't mean much to a tiny Scottish village, but now that the renovation on the lodge is under way, people are beginning to put the pieces of the puzzle together." He paused. "The people we've hired to work in the lodge are keeping pretty closemouthed, but there are others who are beginning to believe that the princess is being held hostage against her will at the lodge. And it doesn't help that Prince Victor of Karolya has offered an enormous reward for information leading to her safe return. It won't be long before someone decides to claim it."

"Prince Victor wants her dead."

"Prince Victor is the one paying for her safe return," O'Brien corrected.

"Prince Victor committed regicide," Adam told him. "He wants George returned so his assassins can finish what they started. The only reason she escaped them the night her parents were murdered was because she wasn't in the capital city. Her father got wind of an assassination plot and sent his heir to safety. Nobody except Maximillian knew where she was."

"Shit!" O'Brien took off his hat and began fanning the air with it.

"That about covers it," Adam responded, dryly.

"The newspapers are pointing a finger at Max," Murphy said. "They've named him as the man who organized the anarchists and engineered her kidnapping."

"There were no anarchists and there was no kidnapping. Victor made it all up so nobody would look too closely at what he was likely to get out of having his uncle and his uncle's family murdered."

"What does he get out of it?" O'Brien asked. "As far as I can tell, he's acting as regent for Princess Giana because he can't inherit."

"Control," Adam answered. "Control of George and control of Karolya's iron ore deposits and thousands of acres of timber. He's already trying to broker deals. And the reason Victor is eager to identify Max is because Max witnessed Prince Christian's murder. He recognized one of the assassins as one of Victor's followers." Adam related the story Giana had told him.

"That may all be true, and Max may be entirely innocent of the crime Victor's accusing him of, but how long do you suppose it will be before someone decides to turn Max in?" O'Brien exhaled slowly. "Prince Victor has covered his tracks very well. And Princess Giana is correct. The papers are reporting that the British government is helping him in the search. Although the queen refuses to recognize him as ruler, my sources tell me that Karolya's prince regent is in Scotland to meet with Her Majesty."

"What?" The idea sent a shudder through Adam.

"I telegraphed the New York Pinkerton office for information and received word that the German papers carried the story that the Karolyan government is announcing that His Highness Prince Victor, regent of Saxe-Wallerstein-Karolya has left Karolya in order to pay a visit to Great Britain. There's speculation that the queen has given up hope that Princess

Giana is alive and will use this visit as an opportunity to recognize Victor as Karolya's rightful ruler."

"Damn!" Adam swore. "Part of the reason George has been hiding here is because Queen Victoria is her godmother. George was planning to use the queen's holiday at Balmoral as an opportunity to present herself and explain the circumstances of her disappearance."

O'Brien shook his head. "She can't go to Balmoral. Not if Victor has taken it upon himself to pay the queen a visit." O'Brien paused, then stared at Adam. "You did say Victor wanted to sell Karolya's iron ore deposits?"

"Yes, but Prince Christian opposed it."

O'Brien was silent for a moment. "I heard several men at your sister's reception talking about buying iron ore."

Adam felt a sinking feeling in the pit of his stomach. "Marshfeld. Kirstin mentioned it and Prince Victor, but I didn't connect it with anything at the lodge."

"Marshfeld isn't the only one. There are others. They were forming a business whose sole purpose was to provide a market for the imports."

"Son of a bitch! I can't help feeling that this is all my fault," Adam admitted. "They were safe at the lodge until I arrived and began a massive and very public transformation of the place from an isolated hunting lodge to a fashionable gentlemen's club."

"You couldn't have known that a princess on the run for her life would choose to hide in the hunting lodge you won from a rich Englishman in a poker game," O'Brien pointed out. "And they couldn't have known ownership of the place would change hands or that you would decide to use the property for anything other than what it had been used for. It was fate, my friend. And you can't change fate."

You cannot save me from my duty, Adam. Or protect me from my fate. Giana's words came back to Adam in a rush of emotion. "She wasn't fated to die, Murphy. If she had been fated to die Max wouldn't have been able to save her from her cousin's assassins. No matter how it happened, the fact is that she was safe until I showed up. My job is to keep her safe."

"This Bountiful Baron business has gone to your head, my friend," O'Brien told him. "I know this one is blond and beautiful, and she's definitely been betrayed, but she is also a princess. You're in over your head, Adam. You cannot save them all!"

Adam stared at his friend. "I have to save this one. She's my future."

"Not necessarily," O'Brien protested. "You said it yourself, Adam, and you were right. This one may be the death of you."

"So be it." Adam caught O'Brien's gaze and held it with his own. "I would gladly die for her. She's worth it. But if that happens, promise me you'll keep her safe." He looked around—at the clubhouse situated at the end of the golf links, then back at O'Brien. "This is the safest place on the estate. It's stone and it has a wine cellar. If Victor should happen to find her, bring her here and keep her safe. Promise me you'll stay with her as long as she needs you."

"We're not just talking about protecting a princess here, are we?"

Adam shook his head. "We're talking about protecting the woman I love."

He loved her. Adam had no trouble coming to terms with that. But he couldn't help wondering: would his love be enough?

She had asked him to think about taking on the role of prince consort, if she was able to offer it, but Adam wasn't sure that was something he could do no matter how much he loved her.

One morning of loving did not make a marriage—no matter how wonderful it was. And marriage to a princess came with a set of problems all its own. Even when the prospective bridegroom was a prince—and Adam was no prince.

Marriage to the sovereign head of a nation required a huge sacrifice on the part of the spouse, and Adam knew that in some ways his sacrifice would be greater still because it meant giving up his homeland. It meant leaving everything that was

Adam McKendrick behind and becoming someone else. It meant giving up his freedom.

And giving up his freedom was a sacrifice Adam wasn't sure he could make. He wasn't the same man he was a month ago. He was different and the new Adam McKendrick had fallen madly in love with a woman of incredible strength, love, courage, and an awe-inspiring loyalty to the people she loved. But even the new Adam McKendrick quaked in his boots at the thought of everything he would have to give up in order to be with George.

But he couldn't ignore his responsibility to George any more than she could ignore her responsibility to her country. He knew that in order to offer George some measure of protection, he ought to marry her, but marriage to the heir apparent of a country is not something any man with a healthy measure of self-respect and self-preservation would choose. And he had both. Marrying George meant forfeiting his American citizenship, and giving up control of everything he had worked so hard to gain. It meant allowing someone else to manage not only his property but also his life. Adam frowned. It meant living in Karolya, far away from his family and friends, giving up everything he'd ever known in order to occasionally stand at George's side, but more often than not, it would mean standing in the background, playing second fiddle to George and to any children they might have for the rest of his life.

Could he give up his way of life for George? Could he live with himself if he did?

❧

"You were correct in your assessment, my lord." The marquess of Everleigh stood before his friend and mentor, Andrew Ramsey, the sixteenth marquess of Templeston, in the private study of Lord Templeston's London home and related the details of his audience with His Highness Prince Victor of Saxe-Wallerstein-Karolya.

Templeston frowned. "I'm sorry for that." He looked up at Ashford Everleigh. "I fear, sometimes, that I have lived too long. That I have outlived my usefulness. The world is changing, and I don't envy you the challenges with which you will have to contend." He sighed. "I've seen so much greed and envy and malice—within families and among friends—that I am never surprised anymore." He looked sad, remembering. "We are about to enter the last quarter of this century," he said. "When it began, we were fighting Napoleon—and now, we have this young pretender to the throne of Karolya to defeat."

"Prince Victor is no Napoleon, sir," Everleigh pointed out.

"That is true," Templeston agreed. "Ambitious geniuses like Napoleon appear but once in a lifetime." He propped his elbows on his desk, steepled his fingers together in thought, and breathed a heartfelt prayer. "Thank God. But petty tyrants like Prince Victor are just as dangerous as men who aspire to conquer and rule the world—perhaps even more dangerous."

"How so?" Everleigh studied his mentor. He had known Lord Templeston all of his life, having been at school with Templeston's son, Kit. There wasn't a finer man in all of England, and Everleigh was proud to be among the few chosen to work with him. Templeston still had a great deal of knowledge to share, and Everleigh was eager to absorb it.

"Men like Prince Victor are cunning and subtle and devious. They present a charming face to the world and to the people around them. They are evil disguised as angels. People rarely see them for what they are and most people would deny it if you told them. There was nothing subtle or devious about Napoleon. He was straightforward. He set goals and did what was necessary to attain them, but he was a soldier and everyone recognized that. He was a tyrant—a charming tyrant—but the whole world knew him for what he was. He amassed armies and proclaimed that he would conquer the world, and the worlds he would have conquered knew that the only way to keep from being conquered was to form an alliance and defeat him. Napoleon was a large, lone rogue wolf. Prince Victor is a wolf in fashionable sheep's clothing." He turned to Everleigh. "Do we know if Princess Giana is still alive?"

"No, sir. But I took the liberty of requesting a copy of the Karolyan Charter through our ambassador, Lord Sissingham. I learned from reading it that a coronation must take place within a year following the death of the reigning prince. In order to be crowned, Prince Victor must possess the Karolyan Seal of State and proof of Princess Giana's death. And he must marry. Our sources in Karolya tell us that Prince Victor offered for his cousin's hand in marriage, but Prince Christian refused."

Lord Templeston smiled. "Then she's still alive. Prince Christian has been dead for more than five months. The planning and execution of even a small coronation will take the better part of six or seven moths. If Victor had the Seal of State, he would most certainly have produced it by now. If he doesn't have it, it must be because someone else has it. You investigated the murders and followed the trail of the anarchists. Any sign of them?"

"No."

"No declaration of grievances against Prince Christian's government. No manifestos? No demands? No threats of violence against other royal families?"

Everleigh shook his head. "Nothing. It's as if they disappeared from the face of the earth. Just like the princess."

"The difference is that we know Princess Giana existed," Templeston reminded him. "We cannot say the same of the supposed anarchists. I suspect Prince Victor forgot to complete the fiction. Forgot that anarchists must leave a trail."

"That's because he's accused Lord Gudrun."

"Who also existed and who also disappeared from view." He thought for a moment. "What of the kidnappers? Have we heard from them?"

"No," Lord Everleigh replied.

"So all we have is Prince Victor's version of the story."

"That is correct."

"And, sir, I know Maximillian Gudrun. He did not murder Prince Christian and Princess May or incite anyone else to do it. He was as loyal to his prince as I am to you. He did not kidnap their daughter. Nothing would ever induce Max to betray his prince or his country. Certainly not forests of virgin timber or vast iron ore deposits."

"Ah, the rights to the timber and iron ore deposits. Who has them and who wants them?" Templeston mused. "They should belong to the people of Karolya. They should be held in trust and protected by Princess Giana. But we cannot find her to ask, so we need to ask who is in a position to sell them and who is willing to pay to get them?" He glanced over at his younger protégé.

"His role as regent gives Prince Victor the power to sell them—provided Princess Giana fails to return to Karolya and claim her throne," Everleigh answered.

Lord Templeston clapped his hands together. "All right then, let's look at Prince Victor. Do we know his plans? Where he is going and where he's been?"

"He's here in London," Everleigh reported. "He left Karolya shortly after I did."

The sixteenth marquess of Templeston grinned. "Yes, I read in yesterday's papers that he was planning a trip to Scotland to see the queen. Tell me, Lord Everleigh, since Prince Victor did not announce his arrival in London through the proper diplomatic channels or request an audience with Her Majesty, who is he visiting and why did he come?"

"He's visiting the viscount and viscountess Marshfeld," Everleigh replied, also grinning. "Just down the street. And our sources tell us that the viscount Marshfeld's name was recently added to the roster of businessmen who have formed a consortium in order to purchase and import raw materials necessary for the building of railroads—including virgin timber and . . ."

"Iron ore." They spoke in unison.

"Why Scotland?" Templeston asked. "What, or shall we say, who, does Prince Victor want to see in Scotland?"

"Besides the queen?"

Templeston nodded.

Everleigh shrugged. "I haven't the foggiest."

"We need to find out," Lord Templeston said. "For I suspect she has done a Margo."

"Pardon?"

"Princess Giana has done a Margo." He looked at Everleigh, expecting him to recognize the name and when Everleigh failed to do so, Lord Templeston explained. "Years ago my wife had a pet fox named Margo. She had reared Margo from a kit, and Margo was as tame and nearly as well mannered as a pet dog. That often made it hard for us to remember she was a fox. But whenever Margo felt cornered or threatened, she behaved as any threatened or cornered fox would behave. She went up a tree or to ground. Now, if our missing princess sought to escape her enemies by going up a tree, she would have turned to her godmother, our gracious queen. But if for some reason, she couldn't go above her enemies, she would have to go to ground, to hide and bide her time. Princess Giana has gone to ground."

"How do we go about clearing the way for the princess to come out of hiding?" Everleigh asked.

"We kennel the hounds," Templeston answered. "Pay a visit to the Marshfelds and extend an invitation to visit the queen at Balmoral. She begins her Scottish holiday in a sennight and Victor won't be able to resist an opportunity to present his case."

"Sir?"

"Don't worry," Templeston said. "I'll arrange it with Her Majesty. Just remember that any kenneling we do must take place on Scottish, rather than English soil."

Lord Everleigh frowned. "The Act of Union unified England and Scotland as Great Britain, a single nation under one rule— the rule of our gracious queen."

"That's true," Lord Templeston agreed. "Our gracious queen rules Great Britain, but she is first and foremost, Queen of England and the Queen of England must not be perceived by other countries, or the sovereign heads of those countries, as meddling in Karolyan affairs or assisting in the overthrow of Prince Victor's government. He may be a murderer and a thoroughly despicable male specimen, but the rest of the world isn't privy to that information. The rest of the world only knows that Prince Victor is the last surviving male member of the Karolyan royal family, acting regent, and heir presumptive to the throne. We cannot kennel the hounds in England, but Scotland retains a measure of autonomy in its domestic laws and policies, religious practices, and its system of education that can be used to our advantage."

"Meaning?"

"That a usurper like Prince Victor is guaranteed a certain level of protection under English law that does not necessarily have to be extended to him in Scotland."

"What about Princess Giana?" Everleigh asked.

"As the queen's goddaughter, Princess Giana will be guaranteed protection throughout the whole of Great Britain." Templeston sighed. "Provided we locate her before Victor does."

Chapter 29

In years to come, women of the West will sing the praises and tell the tales of the Bountiful Baron the way Englishmen sing the praises of King Arthur and his knights of the round table.

—THE SECOND INSTALLMENT OF THE TRUE ADVENTURES OF THE BOUNTIFUL BARON: WESTERN BENEFACTOR TO BLOND, BEAUTIFUL, AND BETRAYED WOMEN WRITTEN BY JOHN J. BOOKMAN, 1874.

It had been three days since he held her in his arms. Three long miserable days he had given himself to consider her offer.

He tried to stay away, to give himself time to think about her proposal, but Adam couldn't look at George without wanting her. He couldn't pass her in the corridors without wanting to kiss her, to take her in his arms and promise her everything would be all right. But he had no right to make promises unless he intended to keep them.

"Sir?"

Lost in thought, Adam looked up to see Max standing beside his desk. "Yes?"

"A telegram marked urgent was just delivered from the village." Max held out the telegram.

Adam frowned. Max's manner had become distinctly cold and distant during the last three days. There could only be one reason and Adam decided now was as good a time as any to broach the subject. He set the telegram aside.

"Your pardon, sir, but the telegram from London is marked 'urgent'," Max repeated.

"It's not as urgent as the topic I need to discuss with you." Adam smiled. "Close the door, Max."

Max did as instructed.

"I want to thank you," Adam said. "You have my undying gratitude for saving Princess Giana's life."

Max turned so white, Adam was afraid the older man would faint from lack of blood.

"S-s-sir?" Max stammered, not quite certain if Adam were fishing for information or if the princess had confided in him.

His worst fears were confirmed when Adam replied, "George told me what happened."

"Happened, sir?" Max's voice trembled.

"In Christianberg," Adam told him.

Max groped for the leather chair in front of Adam's desk as his knees threatened to give way.

Adam stood up, rounded his desk and ushered the older man onto the seat. "What I say to you now goes no further than this room. If as Giana says, Victor's spies are everywhere, I cannot promise that some of them aren't working here now. I can promise you that I haven't spoken to anyone about this except O'Brien—"

Max groaned. Why was it that gentlemen felt compelled to tell their secrets to their tailors and valets?

Adam meant to set the older man's mind to rest, but may have succeeded in upsetting him further, so he hastened to add, "—who is not a valet, but is my closest friend and a detective with the renowned Pinkerton National Detective Agency in America. Murphy O'Brien is the very soul of discretion."

Adam paused, allowing Max a moment to digest that bit of information. "She told me everything. I know about Prince Victor and Prince Christian's dying request that you take the Seal of State of Karolya to Giana and that you protect her with your life. I want you to know that I have seen the Seal of State suspended from a gold chain that encircles your princess's waist."

Max leapt from the chair. "You have seen . . ." He sputtered. "How is that possible?

Adam lifted one eyebrow.

"You, sir, are a scoundrel!" Max's body shook with outrage. He removed one of his white gloves and slapped Adam across the face with it. "You deliberately set out to *seduce* an innocent!"

Adam didn't flinch at the insult. He didn't move a muscle. He simply accepted the old man's right to demand satisfaction. The way Max said it, seduced sounded shoddy and lecherous. Something of which to be ashamed. But he wasn't ashamed. Seduced was a word that had nothing to do with what had happened between him and George. "No, sir, I did not."

"How would you characterize it?"

I made love to her. The thought popped into his brain, but Adam wisely kept it to himself. He straightened his shoulders, pulling himself up to his full height. "However I characterize it, it is between Princess Giana and me." Adam looked the older man in the eye. "I'm not defending myself or excusing my actions. What's done is done and I will not embarrass your princess by discussing the intimate details of our relationship with you—except to say that I did not know she was a princess until after . . ." Adam let his words trail off, then cleared his throat and tried again. "Had I known, I could have prevented . . . But there was nothing I could do after the fact."

The older man gasped and turned even paler. "She revealed her identity after she allowed you to . . . ?"

Adam nodded. "Now that you understand, shall we face off with pistols or sabers drawn at dawn? Or will you help me?"

Max began to pace and wring his hands. "You do not know what you have done." He stared at Adam. "Prince Victor will kill her if he finds out."

"That's why I came to you," Adam told him. "I need you to help me make damn sure Cousin Victor doesn't find out—until after she's safely married and beyond his reach."

"Married?" Max was stunned. "Princess Giana cannot get married."

"Why not?"

"Prince Victor will never allow her to marry anyone except him and Princess Giana would never marry her parents' murderer."

"Why does she need Victor's permission to marry?" Adam asked.

"Because she is female. Under Karolyan law, females may not marry without the consent of their nearest living male relative," Max explained.

"Even princesses?"

"Especially princesses. Because there is so much more at stake."

Adam swore beneath his breath. "What if there is no living male relative? Who grants consent?"

"The Ecclesiastical court. But everyone knows that Princess Giana has a living male relative in Victor."

"Victor is her cousin, right?" Adam knew the answer, but he needed confirmation.

"Yes."

Adam smiled. "Tell me, Lord Gudrun, what do you know about George Ramsey, the marquess of Templeston?"

Max was genuinely shocked. Only Princess May, her parents, Lord and Lady Barracksford, Prince Christian, the fifteenth marquess of Templeston and he had known the truth about Princess May's conception. Princess May had insisted that her future husband be told before they married and Lord and Lady Barracksford had complied with the request. As Prince Christian's private secretary, Max had been asked to record the audience and to file the papers in Prince Christian's private archive. In the unlikely event that anything happened to Prince Christian to force Princess May or any of her children to request assistance from the marquess of Templeston, she would have the locket as proof, but she would also have a document to prove to the Karolyan people or government or any other court or government that Prince Christian had been made aware of her heritage before he married her. Max had retrieved that document from Prince Christian's private archive the night the prince was murdered. He had kept the bloodstained document hidden safely inside the heel of his boot in the event that the princess needed it.

Max had never breathed a word of what he knew and everyone else who had known was dead. Except, it seemed, Princess Giana. Max was stunned. He had had no idea that the princess had known. "There is a likeness of George Ramsey, the fif-teenth marquess of Templeston inside the locket the princess wears about her neck."

"That would mean that the fifteenth marquess of Templeston was her maternal grandfather and that the current marquess would be her uncle."

"That is correct."

"An uncle who could grant her permission to marry?"

"Yes," Max confirmed.

"Where do we find him?" Adam asked.

"In London. He is one of Queen Victoria's most trusted advisors. But having permission to marry is not the only re-quirement our princess must meet in order to marry. If she chooses to marry any member of a royal house, Princess Giana must undergo a doctor's examination confirming that she is a virgin." He looked Adam in the eye, challenging him. "As she is no longer a virgin, who can we find who would marry a princess knowing that she is not a virgin, knowing that she may be carrying someone else's heir? What man would be willing to give up his personal identity in order to marry a princess who would have complete and utter jurisdiction over him?"

"I will," Adam said.

"You do not possess a title, sir," Max told him. "Under Karolyan law, the princess may marry a titled commoner, but not an untitled one."

"Will a baron do?"

Max frowned. "A baron ranks below a viscount, an earl, a marquess, a duke, and a prince in the order of precedence. On state occasions, a baron would be required to walk behind all personages above his rank."

"I don't care about any of that," Adam said. "Can she marry a baron?"

"Most assuredly. The style of baron is an ancient and hon-orable one." Max faced him, his expression, unreadable. "What baron did you have in mind?"

"The Bountiful Baron Adam McKendrick."

"I'm sure that will be most acceptable."

"To you? Or to the people of Karolya?" Adam asked.

Maximillian, Lord Gudrun, grinned. "I was charged with one last request by the late Prince Christian. A request I was not certain I could manage. But Princess Giana came to me two nights ago and told me that while she was quite prepared to do her duty to the people of Karolya, if her proposal went unanswered, she wanted me to help her find a way to follow her heart. When I asked what she meant, she told me that she had chosen you to be her prince consort and that if you wanted the position, my duty would be to convince the Karolyan government to accept you. If you refused her offer, my duty was to find a way to help her abdicate, for you were her heart and she was bound to follow you." Tears sparkled in Max's eyes as he faced Adam. "Her father's, Prince Christian's, last words to me were: *'Tell Giana never to be afraid to follow her heart. Promise me, Max. Promise you will help her find a way.'*" He smiled a satisfied smile. "I have fulfilled my promise and done my duty."

Max picked up the telegram and handed it back to Adam. "I took the liberty of sending a telegram in your name to the marquess of Templeston yesterday morning. You received this reply this afternoon."

Adam opened the telegram and read: "The marquess of Templeston will be arriving at Balmoral, Scotland, as a guest of Her Majesty, Victoria Regina, by the Grace of God, Queen of England in two days time. He invites you and the members of your senior household to travel to Balmoral under the protection of Her Majesty, the Queen, where you will be granted an audience. He is most eager to view the locket, your documentation, and discuss your request. Signed Ashford, Marquess of Everleigh." Adam looked over at Max.

Max stood at attention and clicked his heels together in the military fashion. "I should like to accompany you, sir."

Adam smiled. "I should like that as well," he said, gently, "but I'm afraid it's not possible."

"I am a senior member of the household," Max said.

"You are, indeed," Adam answered. "But you are also the only witness to the murders. We cannot risk your life. You must stay here with the princess where it's safe."

"Who will you choose to accompany you, sir?"

"Gordon," Adam answered, "and Josef."

Max gave a quick nod, then sat down on the leather chair. "You will require this documentation, sir." He propped his left foot on his right thigh, then bent and twisted the heel of left boot. It swung open to reveal a hollow compartment filled with bloodied parchment paper. Max carefully lifted it out and handed it to Adam. "Might I suggest that the princess also compose a letter of introduction for you that contains her signature and official seal?" He didn't have to mention the seal still locked around Giana's waist to convey his intent.

Adam understood. "Her official seal might be hard to manage," he answered.

Max met his gaze. "I am sure she and we, may rely on your discreet assistance."

Giana joined Adam in his bedchamber later that evening. Adam looked up as she entered the room. She was fresh from her bath and the scent of orange blossoms clung to her hair and to her nightgown.

Wagner entered silently behind her. He, unfortunately, did not smell entirely of orange blossoms, but of a more pungent odor of orange blossoms and wet dog. Adam wrinkled his nose at the smell.

"I bathed him, but it is raining outside. He will smell better once he dries."

Adam wasn't as certain, but he pretended he believed her.

She looked at him. "I tried to stay away," she said. "But I could not."

"I'm glad you didn't," he said.

"I promised myself I would not try to persuade you into accepting my proposal, but . . ." She glanced down at her bare toes, unable to finish her sentence.

Adam reached out, took hold of her hand and pulled her toward him. "It's all right, Princess," he said, kissing her eyes and cheekbones and throat before finally kissing her lips with a passion that left her breathless. "I've made my decision."

Giana was so nervous her breath caught in her throat. "Have you?"

He nodded.

"And . . ." She prodded.

"And as a result, I've been invited to Balmoral for the weekend," he said.

"Why?"

"I've a meeting with the current marquess of Templeston."

Giana gasped, then waited on pins and needles, for Adam to continue.

"I've decided to accept your offer, George, and I'll need your locket so Templeston can authenticate it." Giana didn't reply. She simply stared at him until he reached over, gently took her face in his hands, and leaned down to kiss her. When he finished kissing her, he said, "I'll also need a letter of introduction with your signature and seal. After my meeting, Victor won't be able to hurt you, and you won't have to worry about him anymore."

"You want to be prince consort?"

She stared at him.

He grinned. "If the offer's still open."

She wrinkled her brow. "Are you certain, Adam? Are you certain you wish to take on the responsibility? I have yet to secure my throne," she babbled. "I may have to fight to secure it. And it is possible that I will not succeed it securing it at all. Do you understand?" She stared into his eyes. "If I do not succeed the throne, I cannot keep my promise and reward you with the title."

"Are you trying to talk me out of it?" he asked. "Because I warn you that it won't do you any good." Adam shrugged his shoulders. "Until I met you, I never cared much for people with titles."

Giana opened her mouth to speak, but words failed her. Her mouth formed a perfect O of surprise.

Adam took advantage, leaning down to kiss her once again. "I want to marry you. The only promises I'll hold you to are the ones you make on our wedding day."

"Oh, Adam!" Giana unfastened her locket and handed it to him and promptly burst into tears.

"Is that a yes?" Adam dropped the locket into his pocket for safekeeping moments before Giana wrapped her arms around his neck, pressed herself against him and kissed him again and again until he was dizzy with the scent and feel of her.

He wiped her tears off her cheek with the pad of his thumb. "You know I've heard it said that genuine princesses never cry."

"Who is crying?" she demanded, taking his hand in hers and leading him toward the bed.

"You are, Princess."

Giana shook her head. "Those are not tears," she answered. "They're exclamations of joy."

"In that case . . ." he whispered in her ear, "spread the joy. Let's consummate this deal."

Adam followed her down onto the mattress, then rolled over to find Wagner resting his head on bed. He watched as the dog lifted a paw, and attempted to settle in beside them.

"Oh, no, you don't," Adam said. "Off!"

Giana giggled as Wagner retreated ever so slowly and walked around to the foot of the bed. "I think you hurt his emotions."

"Feelings," Adam translated. "I may have hurt his *feelings*, but he is not sleeping with you tonight. He'll have to learn to get used to it."

"We are not going to be sleeping," she informed him. "We are going to be practicing."

"Practicing what?" he asked, curiously aroused by the inflection of her words.

"The skills I learned the last time we shared a bed."

"You're going to be a very busy woman," he said. "For it takes time to perfect those skills."

"Wagner is going to be very busy as well," she said. "As soon as you issue his orders."

Adam snapped his fingers and pointed to the door. "Wagner! *En garde.*"

Wagner trotted to the door and lay down in front of it.

"That is better," Giana said, lifting the hem of her night-gown and pulling it over her head. The light from the lamp reflected off the gold at her waist and around her neck as she crawled onto Adam. "Have you any orders for me?" she teased.

Adam snapped his fingers and pointed to the member that was already standing hard and erect. "Princess! *En garde!*"

Chapter 30

The Bountiful Baron is the ideal American. He journeyed west to find his fortune and succeeded where others failed. He is a self-made man. A millionaire, a gentleman and a frontier hero.

—THE FIRST INSTALLMENT OF THE TRUE ADVENTURES OF THE BOUNTIFUL BARON: WESTERN BENEFACTOR TO BLOND, BEAUTIFUL, AND BETRAYED WOMEN WRITTEN BY JOHN J. BOOKMAN, 1874.

Four days later, Adam boarded the express train from Kinlochen to Balmoral for a journey that would take half as long as the journey to London. O'Brien had wanted to accompany him, but Adam asked him to stay behind and look after George. Just in case.

O'Brien had agreed, so Gordon and Josef went in his place.

The three of them were escorted off the train at the station and driven to the castle. They departed the coach at the front door where they were allowed admittance by a butler.

"How do you do, Mr. McKendrick? I am Lord Everleigh, Lord Templeston's associate." Everleigh greeted Adam at the door, then led the three men to the marquess of Templeston's temporary office.

Gordon Ross and Josef Sommers remained outside the room, waiting beside the door to Lord Templeston's office while Lord Everleigh ushered Adam inside.

"I shall be down the hall should you require my assistance, sir," Everleigh spoke to the gentleman seated at the massive desk, then quietly withdrew, leaving Adam alone with the other man.

"Good afternoon, Mr. McKendrick. It's a pleasure to meet you."

Andrew Ramsey, the sixteenth Marquess of Templeston, was a big man, older than Adam expected, and still quite handsome and youthful despite his advanced years. He pushed himself to his feet and came around the desk to shake Adam's hand.

"Likewise, sir." Adam sketched a low bow.

"You have come about the missing princess." Lord Templeston returned to his chair.

"Yes, sir," Adam replied. "I have come on her behalf."

"Princess Giana is claiming to be a granddaughter of my late father?" Lord Templeston's inquiry was more statement than a question.

"Yes"

"I suppose you have proof?"

Adam reached into his waistcoat pocket, retrieved the gold-and-diamond locket, the document Max had given him, and the letter George had written and affixed with the State Seal of Saxe-Wallerstein-Karolya. "Her Highness sent this to you and a note for her godmother, the queen. She asked that you read her letter first." He handed the letters, the proof Max had given him, and the gold locket to Lord Templeston.

The marquess studied the wax seal binding the edges of the letter together, then opened it and read:

> *My lord Templeston, I have entrusted my most precious possessions and my life to the man you see standing before you in hopes that you will grant me my heart's desire. He carries my locket—a locket I am certain you will recognize. My grandmother presented it to my mother when my mother came of age and my mother, Princess May of Saxe-Wallerstein-Karolya, presented it to me along with instructions to present it to the sitting English marquess of Templeston or his representative should I ever find myself in need. I send Mr. Adam McKendrick to present it to you today, because I find myself in desperate need of assistance in regaining my homeland.*

You may know that my mother was born Lady Caroline Frances Alexandra May Barracksford, daughter of the marquess and marchioness of Barracksford. What you may not know is that, my grandmother, the marchioness of Barracksford, was once a Parisian actress . . .

Lord Templeston closed his eyes, vividly remembering the day he had stood in the study of his London town house and listened as his father's solicitor, Martin Bell, had explained the terms of the codicil to his father's will. It had happened so many years ago—more years than the young man standing before him had been alive—but the memory was as fresh in Lord Templeston's mind as if it had happened yesterday.

"There is a codicil to your father's will. He named several. There were more than one."

"More than one what?" Drew had asked.

"Ladybirds." Martin cleared his throat.

"On the yacht?" His father and his father's latest mistress had died in a yachting accident and Drew remembered wondering how many more mistresses he might have aboard and how many more of his father's mistresses might need to be buried in the family cemetery.

"Oh, no," Martin reassured him. "On land."

He had breathed a sigh of relief. "How many?"

"He mentioned five. In addition to the young opera singer, there's a milliner in Brighton. An actress in Paris. A seamstress in Edinburgh. And a young woman in Northamptonshire."

The young woman in Northamptonshire had turned out to be Kathryn Markinson Stafford, the current marchioness of Templeston, and the love of Drew's life. The actress in Paris had married another English marquess—the marquess of Barracksford—and had given birth to a daughter who had married a prince and who had given birth to a daughter of her own—Princess Georgiana of Saxe-Wallerstein-Karolya.

The daughter of his half-sister. A daughter who had been given a feminine form of his father's name. Georgiana. Drew opened his eyes and turned his attention back to the letter the princess had written.

I have known for some time that I had family in England, but my grandmother's, mother's, and my own, great source of pride was that we had never needed to call upon you for assistance. Were it not for the murder of my parents and the situation I find myself in today, I am quite certain that I would never have called upon you and would have carried this family secret to my grave. But today, dear sir, I require an extraordinary favor. Karolyan law requires that a Princess of the Blood Royal receive permission from her closest living male relative in order to marry.

As my uncle, you are my closest living male relative, and today, I ask that you grant me permission to follow my heart and marry the man I have chosen to be my prince consort—Mr. Adam McKendrick. Such a marriage would fulfill the requirements set forth in the Female Provision of the Karolyan Charter and would allow me to fulfill my duty and obligation to my country by reclaiming my rightful place on the throne of Saxe-Wallerstein-Karolya.

Her Serene Highness Georgiana Regina
Princess of the Blood Royal of the House of Saxe-
Wallerstein-Karolya.

Beneath her signature was the wax impression of the Karolyan Seal of State.

Lord Templeston carefully refolded the letter and laid it on the blotter beside the letter addressed to the queen and picked up the remaining letter. All three letters bore the wax impression of the Karolyan Seal of State, but only one carried the signatures of the late prince and princess. Only one was stained with blood.

Lord Templeston raised an eyebrow in question.

"Lord Gudrun assured me that the blood was his," Adam said. "He secreted the letter inside his waistcoat pocket after he was injured and unfortunately, bled on it. He transferred it from his waistcoat pocket to a hollow compartment in the heel of his boot during the journey from Christianberg to Laken and it remained there until he presented it to me."

Templeston read the document from Prince Christian's private archives. It confirmed everything Princess Georgiana had written. The only thing left to authenticate was the gold-and-diamond locket. Lord Templeston scooped it off the desk and opened it, revealing the tiny likenesses of the marquess and marchioness of Barracksford and of Prince Christian and Princess May and the infant Princess Georgiana. It came as no surprise to Drew to discover that the marchioness looked enough like his mother to be her sister. All of George Ramsey's mistresses bore a striking resemblance to each other and to his dead wife. Drew studied the likenesses, then carefully slipped the portrait of the Barracksfords aside and found himself staring into the handsome face of his father, George Ramsey, the fifteenth marquess of Templeston. He looked down at his father's face, then carefully closed the locket and turned it over, searching for the jeweler's mark he knew would be there. "I haven't seen one of these in a very long time. It's authentic." Lord Templeston closed the locket and handed it back to Adam, then removed a document from a sheath of papers on his desk and gave it to him as well. "This is a copy of the codicil to my father's will. Please give it to my niece."

Adam glanced at the document. "May I?"

Lord Templeston nodded. "Please do."

Adam finished reading the codicil and looked up at the marquess. "He must have been an exceptional man."

"Yes, he was," Templeston agreed. "As you can see, Princess Giana is entitled to a substantial sum of money and . . ."

"She isn't interested in the money, sir, just in the permission," Adam told him.

"Permission granted," Lord Templeston said. "I'll put it in writing in case the question of permission arises once she returns to Karolya. Good luck to you, my boy," the older man said. "I'd gladly give my permission to protect Princess Giana from the likes of Victor—even if she weren't my niece. You're in luck, you know, because you're in Scotland. You can be married right away. Today if you like by the local vicar."

"Thank you, sir."

"My pleasure, my boy. Welcome to the family." Templeston

stood up, walked around his desk and clamped his hand on Adam's shoulder.

"If there is anything I can do—" Adam began.

Templeston smiled once again. "Before you go, there is someone who would like to speak to you." He rose from his desk and walked across the room where he opened a door, then stood back to allow a small, round figure completely dressed in black except for her lace collar and widow's cap to enter.

A tall, brawny Highlander entered with her. Adam watched, in fascination, as the Scotsman moved into position, towering over her as he stood a few steps behind her, quite obviously guarding her back.

Lord Templeston closed the door, then bowed to the queen, and made the introduction. "Your Majesty, may I present Mr. Adam McKendrick?"

The queen held out her hand. "Mr. McKendrick."

Adam bowed over her hand and briefly touched her fingers the way he'd seen Lord Templeston do. "Ma'am."

The queen walked over to a chair and sat down, then motioned for the gentlemen to do likewise. Once they were seated, she wasted no time in getting to the heart of the matter. "You are an American?"

"Yes, ma'am."

"From Texas?"

Adam shook his head. "From Nevada Territory, ma'am."

"We understand that you have gained ownership of a hunting lodge here in our beloved Highlands."

"Yes, ma'am," Adam answered. "Larchmont Lodge near the village of Kinlochen."

"I see." She studied Adam for a moment. "We understand that Princess Giana sought sanctuary in your hunting lodge before you took up residence there."

Adam nodded. "Yes, ma'am."

"As an American, you had no idea she was a princess?"

"No, ma'am. She was disguised as a chambermaid."

Queen Victoria laughed at the idea of Princess Giana disguising herself as a chambermaid. Once, many years ago, be-

fore she became queen, she had delighted in disguising herself
and appearing for dinner dressed in all manner of costumes.
"So, you have come to Balmoral as her representative?"

"Yes, ma'am," Adam acknowledged. "She asked me to deliver this letter to you." He glanced at Lord Templeston who
retrieved the letter George had addressed to the queen from
the desk before presenting it to her.

The queen didn't open the letter, but held it on her lap while
she looked at Adam, and asked, "How is our goddaughter?"

"She is an extraordinary woman, ma'am," Adam answered.

The queen smiled. "Of that I've no doubt. But how is she,
Mr. McKendrick? How is she coping with her terrible bereave-
ment?"

Adam stared at the tiny woman, still grieving for her husband, still wearing her widow's weeds and white mourning
cap and understood what the queen wanted to know. "Her
Highness is coping as well as can be expected in light of her
tremendous loss—of her parents and of her homeland. She
dresses all in black, ma'am, as she mourns her loss. But she
bears her grief as one would expect of a princess and sheds
her tears in private."

The queen nodded her approval, then broke the wax seal on
the letter, unfolded the paper and read the note Giana had
written. When she looked up again, she pinned Adam with her
sharp, no-nonsense gaze. "Tell me, Mr. McKendrick, do you
know what is in this letter?" She tapped the paper against the
edge of her chair.

"No, ma'am."

"How do we know this note is from Princess Giana? How
do we know you did not write the letter and seal it with a
stolen seal? How do we know you are not in league with her
kidnappers?"

Adam met the queen's steady gaze. "You've only my word,
Your Majesty, and the word of Princess Giana."

She smiled at Adam, then glanced at the note again, and
laughed. "Princess Giana's message was as well-chosen as her
messenger. She, alone, knew that we would understand."

The queen turned the letter so Adam and Lord Templeston
could see it.

Adam was clearly surprised. The letter wasn't a letter at all. It was a drawing. A pen and ink sketch of Wagner asleep in the center of Adam's bed—head comfortably pillowed, back curved, and all four paws pointing toward the ceiling. A cloud-like bubble above the dog's head contained sketches of a tea table, complete with cakes and whole salmon, and bore the caption: *Wagner Dreams of Iced Teacakes and Salmon, 1874. To Our Beloved Teacher, V. R from her grateful student. G. R.*

"We taught her to draw and paint when she was no more than four or five," the queen explained. "And we have continued to exchange drawings from that day until this one. Mostly of dogs and horses." She looked over at Adam and at Lord Templeston. "Princess Giana excels in the drawing of dogs. When she visits, we pack picnic lunches that always contain salmon as the main course and teacakes for dessert. We drive out onto the moor and sit together for hours in companionable silence, with our trusted Mr. Brown looking out for us." She nodded toward her Highland Servant. "While we sketch."

After carefully refolding the drawing, Queen Victoria rose from her chair and walked over to the Scotsman. He nodded once, then rang the bellpull suspended from the ceiling. When the maid arrived, the Highlander repeated the queen's request and waited at the door until the maid returned with the queen's latest sketchbook and a box of pencils, and a small silver-framed photograph of the late prince consort.

The Highlander presented the sketchbook and box of pencils to the queen and kept the framed photograph in readiness as he returned to his position at her back.

"Please sit, Mr. McKendrick, as we shall return Her Highness's message in kind."

With those words, the queen took out a pencil and began to draw.

When she finished, she presented Adam with a sketch of Wagner wearing a top hat and tails and a much more elegant female wolfhound wearing a veil and a wreath of orange blossoms. There was a Gothic arched window above the canine pair bearing the Karolyan coat of arms and a circle of bulldogs, wearing the emblem of queen's Coldstream Guards, stood guard around them.

Adam was amazed by the queen's talent and by the symbolism of the drawing. The caption read: *Long life and felicitations from H.M.V.R. to H.S.H. G. R.* He looked up from the drawing and met the queen's sparkling gaze.

"We kept our drawings secret," she explained. "Sharing them as a form of secret code known only to us. Something special to be exchanged between a royal godmother and a royal goddaughter." She handed Adam the other drawing.

It was an amazing likeness of him signed by the queen.

She smiled at him and Adam caught a glimpse of the young woman she had been.

"To thank you," she said. "For providing comfort and shelter to our goddaughter."

"It has been an honor, ma'am," Adam said.

The queen turned to Lord Templeston. "We should like to send a number of our own Coldstream guards to Mr. McKendrick's hunting lodge to escort Her Serene Highness and Mr. McKendrick back to Balmoral. If you have no objection." She looked at Adam. "We should like to see you married. We shall arrange for the ceremony to be held here at Balmoral in two days' time. You shall honeymoon here as my guests—"

"But, Your Majesty," Lord Templeston interrupted. "Lady Templeston and I were hoping that Princess Giana and Mr. McKendrick would spend time with us at Swanslea Park."

The queen turned her attention to her adviser. "You and Lady Templeston shall join us here. It's been too long since we have seen our dear Wren and we so much enjoy our art lessons."

Templeston nodded.

"Two days, Your Majesty?" There was no way to disguise the note of uncertainty in Adam's tone of voice. "What about Prince Victor?"

The queen frowned. "We shall handle Prince Victor," she said. "We shall take great pleasure in seeing that particular royal usurper squashed like a bug." She motioned for her Highland Servant. "And we shall take great delight in arranging the princess's wedding while we await her arrival. Please give these to our goddaughter with our great love and tell her that it would please us greatly for her to wear the cameo our dear Albert gave to us." Queen Victoria reached up and unpinned a black onyx and mother of pearl cameo from her lace collar and handed it to her servant who handed the pin and the silver-framed photograph to Adam.

"Thank you, ma'am," Adam replied.

"You are most welcome." The queen rose from her chair.

Adam and Lord Templeston bowed as she walked past. Moments later, she and her servant had disappeared through the massive doors.

Adam stood staring until Lord Templeston clapped him on the back: "Congratulations, my boy! The queen doesn't present a photograph of Prince Albert to everyone. The fact that she did means she approves of you and of the marriage."

"I don't care about the queen's approval," Adam said. "We don't require her approval—only yours."

"Her approval of your marriage will go a long way in dissuading Prince Victor from continuing his pursuit of the princess."

Adam shrugged. "As long as the princess is safe."

"She will be now," Templeston told him. "Prince Victor would have to be insane to defy the British Empire."

"A sane man would not commit regicide," Adam reminded him.

"Quite right," Templeston agreed. "But now, Prince Victor has more to lose."

"How much more?" Adam asked.

"His life should you decide to end it." Lord Templeston's reply was matter of fact.

"You're granting the princess permission to marry me and granting me permission to kill the royal cousin?"

"If needs be." Lord Templeston met Adam's gaze. "And neither I nor the queen are condoning murder," he said. "We are simply reminding you that you're an American. While Her Majesty's government would frown upon its soldiers or citizens taking arms against a member of a royal family who happened to be visiting our country, it would certainly understand if you, an American citizen residing in Scotland, found it necessary to protect yourself—and your bride, Her Majesty's own goddaughter, from Prince Victor's murderous wrath."

"I see," Adam said.

"I thought you would," Lord Templeston answered.

"You can't touch him. Even to protect the princess."

"The Coldstream guards can protect the princess, but they cannot kill Prince Victor in order to do so, whereas you . . ."

"Can do whatever I need to do to protect Her Highness from harm."

Lord Templeston nodded. "Quite right."

"The idea of waiting two days to get married makes me uneasy."

"Then don't wait."

"But the queen said . . ."

"Yes, she did," Templeston agreed. "But there's no law that says you can't have multiple wedding ceremonies. You can marry the princess when you get home and marry her two days from now here at Balmoral."

"I can't thank you enough—" Adam began.

Lord Templeston cut him off. "We'll be here when you arrive for your second wedding." He grinned. "In the meantime, I'll set things in motion by telegraphing the vicar in Kinlochen. I'll have him waiting at the lodge when you arrive."

❧

The journey home was uneventful, but Larchmont Lodge was in chaos when Adam arrived. Lord and Lady Marshfeld and entourage had arrived for a surprise visit four days before the date of the postponed preview of the lodge and the household had been thrown into disarray.

Adam knew something was wrong when Henri, dressed in his best imitation of a butler's suit, opened the front door. "Good evening, sir, it's nice to have you home again."

Adam stared at him. "Where's Albert?"

"Gone," Henri replied. "They're all gone."

"What do you mean gone? Gone where?"

Henri shrugged. "They left. All of them. Including Mr. O'Brien who was very disappointed not to get a game of golf in. He said he particularly liked the eighteenth hole."

Adam looked askance at Henri. Murphy didn't play the game of golf. He did, however, know where the clubhouse was and the clubhouse had wine cellars. "What about Ma—?"

Henri shook his head and put a finger to his mouth to signal Adam to shut up, then spoke in rapid French. "Lord and Lady Marshfeld have arrived with a gentleman from London and the Prince Regent of Karolya."

"Bloody hell!" Adam said.

"Adam! Surprise!"

He turned around to find his sister Kirstin gliding the main staircase. "What are you doing here?"

"We decided to surprise you." Kirstin was bubbling with excitement. "We were invited to Balmoral and decided to surprise you."

"We?"

"Marshfeld and your father and Prince Victor and I."

Every word she spoke fell like a hammer blow to his heart. "Marshfeld, Prince Victor, and my *father*?"

"Yes," Kirstin said. "Isn't it exciting? I've found your father!"

"Who the hell asked you to meddle in my affairs? Who the hell asked you to find my father?" Adam demanded.

"I did."

Adam turned. "Lord Bascombe, what are you doing here?"

Bascombe smiled. "I came to play golf with my son."

The world seemed to be spinning the wrong way on its axis. Adam sat down on the nearest chair to keep from falling. He looked at Bascombe "You?"

Bascombe nodded.

"Why?"

"It was a chance for me to get to know my son."

"You son of a bitch!" Adam jumped to his feet, raked his hands through his hair, then drew back his fist and punched Lord Bascombe in the nose. "You had twenty-eight years to get to know your son! Where the hell were you when I was growing up? Where the hell were you when I was labeled a bastard and forced to fight to defend my mother's reputation?" Adam shouted, standing over Bascombe, looking down on his long lost father. "I needed you then! I sure as hell don't need you now!"

Bascombe pushed himself to his feet and wiped the blood from his nose with a white linen handkerchief, wiggling the cartilage to see if Adam had broken it. "Maybe not." He stared at Adam. "But your sister does."

"What?" Adam looked from Kirstin to Bascombe.

"Prince Victor, Adam. You warned me about Prince Victor, but I . . . I . . ." Kirstin began to cry.

"What is it, Kirstin? What has he done?" Adam demanded.

"His Royal Highness Prince Victor of Saxe-Wallerstein-Karolya has designs on your sister," Bascombe told him. "She came to me because she was afraid you'd think she was crying wolf and because Marshfeld is encouraging her to pursue a— shall we say—friendship with the prince."

"M-M-Marshfeld w-wants me to go to Karolya with Prince Victor and pretend to be that missing princess," Kirstin sobbed. "But something happened to her and I'm afraid that if I go with the prince something bad will happen to me . . ."

Adam blanched. His face lost all color as he turned to his father. "Oh my God!" He shoved Kirstin into his father's arms. "Where's Victor?"

"When we arrived your wolfhound was in the garden. Prince Victor said the dog reminded him of home. He said he'd been confined long enough and he wanted to see the countryside. He borrowed a horse from your stables and rode out. Marshfeld went with him," Bascombe answered.

"Where's the dog?"

"Prince Victor followed him toward the golf links."

"Jesus!" Adam nearly panicked. "If anything happens to that dog, George will kill me. I've got to go!"

"Adam!" Kirstin shouted. "Who's George?"

Adam didn't answer. He simply took off in the direction of the golf links. Bascombe and Kirstin exchanged looks and ran after him.

Adam's long legs ate up the distance to the golf links. He ran the entire way, approaching the eighteenth hole only to find it empty. There was no one about. He turned toward the clubhouse and caught a flash of light from the window.

Murphy O'Brien unlocked the clubhouse door and allowed Adam entrance, but slammed the door in Kirstin's face.

She pounded on the door, loudly voicing her displeasure until Adam reluctantly nodded to Murphy to open the door.

"You're in," Adam snapped when Kirstin and Bascombe entered the clubhouse. "Now, stay the devil out of my way." He turned to Murphy. "What happened?"

O'Brien glowered at Kirstin. "Lady Marshfeld and her guests took us by surprise," O'Brien admitted. "But Josef recognized Prince Victor when he came into the stables demanding a mount saddled. Josef hurried to the lodge and warned us. Gordon went for help."

Isobel, Albert, Brenna, Josef, and Max stood before him—Max, resplendent in full dress uniform and sword—but George was no where in sight. "Where's George?" Adam demanded.

"She's fine," Murphy assured him. "We've been watching for you. What took you so long?" He pocketed his watch as Adam entered the main room of the clubhouse. Adam realized that the flash of light he'd seen had been the glint of sunlight off the cover of O'Brien's silver watch.

"I had an audience with Lord Templeston and the queen," he answered. "Where's George?"

"She's fine," Murphy repeated. "Are you armed?"

Adam shook his head.

O'Brien opened his jacket. He was wearing a holster and a Colt revolver buckled around his hip. He made a clucking sound with his tongue, then removed a small revolver from his jacket pocket and handed it to Adam. "We collected Georgiana and the rest of the family and brought them here to wait for you. How the hell did he find her?"

"He didn't," Adam said. "He was invited to Balmoral as a ruse in order to trap him. He arrived early because Kirstin decided that as long as they were in Scotland, they should surprise us with a visit."

O'Brien frowned. "I thought you told her the lodge was for *gentlemen* only," he joked weakly.

"You know Kirstin," Adam reminded him. "She never listens to me. Where's George?" he asked again. But this time, nobody answered.

Wagner trotted over and nudged Adam's hand.

Adam looked over at O'Brien. "Wagner's here?"

"Of course he is. He goes where I go."

Adam turned around to find Giana dressed in black except for the wreath of orange blossoms in her hair coming up the stairs from the wine cellar. He forgot about his sister and his father. He forgot about Wagner. He forgot about Prince Victor. He forgot about everything except George. She was so beautiful she took his breath away. Adam looked at her and said what was in his heart. "I love you."

George burst into tears and threw herself in his arms. "And I love you."

"Where were you?" he asked.

"Downstairs with the vicar," she said.

Adam breathed a sigh of relief.

Giana stared at him. "Oh, Adam! Victor is here!"

"Don't worry, Princess," Adam told her, holding her close to his heart. "Everything will be all right. You're safe here. I promise."

The vicar came up the stairs. "I thought I was invited here to perform a wedding."

Adam ignored the vicar and stared down at George. "Are you ready?"

She nodded.

Adam turned to the vicar. "We're ready."

They exchanged vows in the wine cellar.

"Do you—" the vicar looked at him.

"Adam McKendrick," Adam said.

"Do you, Adam McKendrick, take this woman to be your lawfully wedded wife?"

"I do."

"And do you—" The vicar looked to Giana.

"Georgiana Victoria Elizabeth May."

"Georgiana Victoria Elizabeth May, take this man to be your lawfully wedded husband?"

"I do."

"Do you have rings?" the vicar asked.

Adam turned to O'Brien. "Jesus, Joseph and Mary! I forgot the ring!"

"I have them," Giana said. "I have rings." She turned her back to the vicar.

Realizing her intent, Adam turned with her, protecting her from prying eyes as she reached inside the bodice of her gown and produced the black pearl ring and the Karolyan Seal of State she had hidden in her bodice since the night Adam had cut the chain from around her waist so that she might use the seal to seal her letters.

"Your undergarments are no longer the safest place to keep your jewels, Princess, now that you've given me access to your hidden treasures," he whispered. "However, I do have a strong steel safe in the library. You might consider keeping either your jewelry or your undergarments in it."

"I may need my jewelry to pay for Wagner's damages," Giana replied.

"Then you'll definitely be securing your undergarments in the safe, because you won't be needing them."

Giana refastened her bodice and turned to face the vicar.

They exchanged rings. Adam placed the black pearl ring on the third finger of George's left hand and she placed the State Seal of Karolya on Adam's finger.

"I now pronounce you husband and wife."

Giana had told Max of her decision to give the State Seal to Adam for safekeeping, while they were waiting in the wine cellar for Adam to arrive, but Max still paled when she placed it on his finger. Giana glanced at her Lord Chamberlain and feared he might faint.

"It's all right, Max," Adam assured him. "I'll give it back to her when she asks for it. And I'll die before I'll allow Victor to get his hands on it." He grinned at Max. "And if I die, George will be a widow and Karolya will be safe from an American usurper."

"That may be sooner than you think."

Wagner growled low in his throat and moved to stand beside Giana.

Adam and Giana whirled around. Prince Victor and Lord Marshfeld stood in the doorway, pistols in their hands.

"Prince Victor, I presume," Adam drawled insolently.

"In the flesh," Victor retorted. "And you must be Adam

McKendrick." He turned his cold gaze on Giana. "Congratulations, Cousin, you nearly succeeded in outmaneuvering me."

"I have outmaneuvered you," Giana cried. "Adam and I are married."

"Not quite."

She gasped as Victor aimed the small silver pistol at her.

Adam moved to stand in front of Giana, but Victor stopped him. "I'll kill her," he warned, moving the derringer closer to Giana to show that he was serious.

"You can't kill her," Adam growled. "You need her."

"I did need her," Victor admitted, "before I met your sister. Now, all I need is the Seal of State. Hand it over."

"What does my sister have to do with this?" Adam demanded.

"She bears a strong resemblance to the princess, does she not? Strong enough to fool the Karolyan people from a distance," Victor said. "And luckily for me, the altar of the Christianberg cathedral is a long way from the pews. Once she dons a veil no one will know the difference."

"I will know the difference," Giana snapped.

"And so will I," Kirstin cried, tears starting to run down her face.

"It won't matter," Victor told them. "Because you'll be dead," he nodded toward Giana. "And you will be within my reach." He nodded at Kirstin, who shuddered.

Adam studied the prince regent. He was shorter than George by an inch or two and although there was a family resemblance, Prince Victor's looks were a pale imitation of his cousin's. Adam snorted in contempt. Prince Victor was dressed in an immaculate uniform complete with dress sword, but his only distinctive feature was the dueling scar that bisected his cheek.

Adam tensed, every muscle ready to spring, as Victor cocked the hammer of the derringer.

Wagner reacted instantly, leaping at Prince Victor's wrist. Adam followed on his heels.

Victor fired as the dog reached him. Wagner yelped in pain as the first shot grazed his side and Adam swore as the second one burned a path across his upper arm.

"Adam!" Giana screamed and rushed toward the fighting. "Wagner!"

Victor shoved Giana aside and pulled his sword. "Come, McKendrick!" Victor taunted. "I'll slice you to ribbons."

"I'm unarmed," Adam told him. "Will that even the odds for you?"

Victor glanced at Max. "Give him your sword."

Max looked to Adam for confirmation.

Adam nodded. "Give me your sword, Max."

Max unsheathed his sword and handed it Adam.

Adam glanced at O'Brien. "Whatever happens, remember your promise." Turning back to Victor, Adam invited, "Shall we?"

Although dueling was forbidden under English law, Scottish law prevailed. "If you're ready to die," Victor replied.

Victor backed out of the clubhouse and onto the lawn. Adam followed.

"Keep her safe," Adam ordered.

"No!" Giana protested, but O'Brien did as Adam ordered.

"Come with me, ma'am," O'Brien told her. "He has to know you're safe or he won't be able to defend himself." Giana resisted, but Murphy hooked an arm around Giana's waist and lifted her bodily out of the main room and carried her down to the wine cellar, then he went back for Kirstin, who was weeping noisily, and the wolfhound. The rest of the household, with the exception of Max, followed.

"Wagner?" Giana sucked in a ragged breath as O'Brien carried the wolfhound down to the wine cellar and placed him on the stone floor. He took off his jacket and placed it under Wagner's head while Isobel inspected the wound.

"He'll be fine, Your Highness," Isobel told her. "The ball scraped his ribs, but it didn't enter."

Reassured that Wagner would live, Giana rushed to the small cellar window, frantically looking for Adam.

"Give me the seal, McKendrick," Victor ordered, "and I'll kill you and my cousin quickly."

"You won't kill us at all," Adam retorted.

"I'll kill you," Victor boasted. "I am an expert swordsman."

"Good for you." Adam sneered. "Because you're a lousy

shot." Adam knew he was taking a chance in taunting Victor. He wasn't a fool. He'd understood the significance of the dueling scar on Victor's cheek, but he wasn't a novice. He'd studied fencing during his tour of Europe. Only this time, they would be fencing with swords instead of foils and to the death instead of until first blood. Adam had no doubt about that. Victor would give no quarter. "Choose your second."

"Marshfeld." Adam's brother-in-law stepped up and accepted the role of Prince Victor's second.

"Be careful of the company you keep, Marshfeld," Adam warned. "Live by the sword. Die by the sword."

"I will serve as McKendrick's second." The earl of Bascombe stood at Adam's side.

"En garde!" Victor shouted the traditional warning, seconds before he attacked.

Adam reacted quickly as the blade of Prince Victor's sword sliced through his jacket and barely missed cutting into his side. He was bleeding in a dozen places within minutes. Christ! A gun would have been better. He was a good shot and he'd have a better chance. And having Victor shoot him was preferable to being sliced to ribbons.

"Adam!" Lord Bascombe shouted. "Don't try to overpower him. Dance with him. Listen to me. Thrust! Parry! Feint! Move!" Bascombe called out the commands, desperately trying to anticipate Victor's moves, in order to keep his only son from being sliced to bits.

"O'Brien! Do something! Victor is killing him!" Giana could feel Murphy struggling with his promise to keep her safe and his anguish for Adam, and she knew she could no longer just stand by and wait for Adam to die. Before Murphy could react, Giana reached inside Murphy's jacket, grabbed his gun and began firing at the two men dueling on the lawn.

"Son of a bitch!" Adam shouted as a shot glanced off his thigh.

Victor roared in pain as a shot hit him high in the shoulder.

Giana cringed when she realized that she'd accidentally shot her husband, but gave a triumphant little squeal when her next shot found a mark on Victor's shoulder. She turned the gun on O'Brien. "Let me out of this room."

"I can't," he said, simply. "Adam will kill me."

"*I* will kill you if you do not," she retorted. "For if we do not stop him, Victor will kill Adam."

❧

Hands slippery from the blood running down his arms, Adam lost his grip on the sword hilt and dropped his weapon. It was over. He had failed her and now he was about to pay for that failure with his life. Thank God for O'Brien. He would take care of Giana. He would make certain Giana gained her throne.

But Giana wasn't safe. Adam looked up and saw her running across the green, a silver Colt revolver in her hands.

"Roll!" Bascombe ordered, snatching up Adam's sword.

Bascombe blocked Victor's thrust and another as Adam rolled out of danger. But Victor outmaneuvered the earl on the third thrust and the blade sliced into his shoulder.

"Move!" This time, Adam shouted the warning to his father. He drew his revolver and fired as Victor lifted his sword for a final thrust. Giana did the same. She raised O'Brien's gun, took aim, and squeezed the trigger.

They would never know who killed him, but as Adam, suffering from blood loss staggered off the green, supported by the earl of Bascombe, Giana rushed to support his other side. "Adam, you are hurt!"

"Yeah," Adam agreed, grimacing in pain. "And you shot me."

"You were already hurt," she protested. "That is why I shot you."

Adam stared at her.

"I could not help it," she explained. "I have never fired this kind of weapon before."

Adam managed a slight laugh. "Well, you're a damn sight better shot than your cousin." He slipped to his knees, took hold of George's hand and slipped the State Seal of Karolya onto her thumb. "I love you, my princess George. I will love you, walk behind you, and defend you until the day I die."

"Which will be today if we don't get you taken care of."

The earl of Bascombe lifted Adam to his feet and helped Giana carry him into the clubhouse.

*"How's the beast?" Adam asked when he was ly-*ing safely ensconced in his bed at the lodge, allowing Isobel to tend his cuts.

"He'll be fine," Giana assured him.

"He can sleep on the bed from now on," Adam said.

"No, he cannot," Giana protested.

"But he saved our lives," Adam said. "Prince Victor was wearing a ring like the seal. He intended to kill us and use Kirstin as a substitute for you whether he got the real seal or not." He looked over and saw O'Brien, Bascombe, and Kirstin standing at the foot of his bed. "Thanks, Murph, for protecting my wife."

O'Brien shrugged. "I only protected her until she began protecting you."

Adam grinned at his friend, then turned to his sister. "How are you, Kirs?"

"I want a divorce from Marshfeld," she said. "As soon as possible."

"I'm sure that can be arranged. Can't it, sir?" Adam looked at the earl of Bascombe.

"It can indeed."

"Thank you, sir, for acting as my second and for saving my life."

"I helped give you life," Bascombe said. "I wasn't about to let Victor take it." He shrugged his shoulders. "Besides, it was the least I could do for the infamous Bountiful Baron—and my son."

Adam groaned. "Oh, Jesus, you know about those stories?"

"Of course I do," Bascombe told him. "They're what led me to Nevada, what led me to seek you out. I read about the first adventure of the Bountiful Baron and I knew I had to find you. And Baron is a misnomer. As my son, you are entitled to be called Viscount Kennisbrooke. But the Bountiful Viscount doesn't have quite the same ring to it."

"How does your family feel about that?" Adam challenged. "Because if you are who you say you are, I'm your bastard son. The product of your annulled marriage to my mother, remember? And as far as I know being a bastard doesn't give me any rights to your titles."

"My family approves," Bascombe said. "My wife died six years ago and my two daughters—" He looked at Adam. "Yes, that's right, you have two more sisters, each of whom have sons of their own—urged me to find you and make things right. I drew up papers to make you my legal and legitimate heir when my wife died. Like it or not, you are the Viscount Kennisbrooke."

"I knew you were a bloody English lord the first time I laid me eyes on ya." O'Brien burst out laughing. "The only one I ever liked. Until now."

"I am Adam McKendrick." Adam narrowed his gaze at the man who claimed to be his father. "I'm not quite sure who you are, but my father was Benjamin McKendrick."

"I *am* Benjamin McKendrick," Bascombe told him. "It's our family name. I didn't become Viscount Kennisbrooke until my father inherited the title of earl of Bascombe and I didn't become Bascombe until he died eleven years ago."

"Nobody had ever seen or heard of the Bountiful Baron when I met you."

"I had," Bascombe smiled at him. "Because one of my American holdings publishes those dime novels."

"You're John J. Bookman?"

"No, that's the *nom de plume* of one of my correspondents." He winked at Kirstin. "I'm the man who pays those correspondents to create legends. One of those legends turned out to be the son I never knew." He stared down at Adam. "Ask your sister, she'll tell you who I am. My sincerest hope is that you will allow me to get to know you."

Adam hesitated, but Giana did not.

"It may take time, of course, but Adam will learn to forgive you. He has a most generous heart and our children will have great need of a loving grandfather." She rushed to Lord Bascombe and hugged him.

"Will you?" Bascombe asked, staring at his son.

"It won't be easy," Adam admitted, "but I'll try."

"Thank you."

"It's the least I can do for the man who made me the Bountiful Baron and helped me win a princess." He extended his hand to his father and when Bascombe shook it, there were tears in both men's eyes.

"That is enough," Giana said, shooing everyone out of the room a few minutes later. "We are on our nectar moon and Adam needs to rest."

"*Honeymoon,*" Adam corrected gently. "And resting has nothing to do with it."

"But you are hurt."

"Yes, I am." He took hold of her hand and pulled her down for a lingering kiss. "And if you're a very good princess, and take very good care of me, I'll allow you to kiss me until everything is all better."

❧

Adam and Giana celebrated two more wedding ceremonies and two more honeymoons before they settled down to life at the palace in Christianberg in Karolya.

The second wedding, held at Balmoral, two days after the duel on the golf links, was a small, intimate affair that took place in the chapel under the watchful eyes of the Queen of England, the marquess and marchioness of Templeston, the earl and countess of Ramsey, the marquess and marchioness of Everleigh, and the earl of Bascombe and Lady Marshfeld as well as all the members of the staff of Larchmont Lodge and the contingent of Coldstream guards who had escorted the couple to the queen's Scottish castle.

The second honeymoon also took place at Balmoral, but fortunately, the wedding guests did not expect to catch more than a glimpse of the participants or to have any say in the proceedings.

The same could not be said of their third wedding ceremony. Held in St. Vincent's Cathedral in Christianberg, four months after their original wedding, the state wedding fell subject to all the rules of etiquette and protocol and contained all the pomp and circumstance, all the spectacle any princess bride could ask for.

Thousands of Karolyan citizens, kings and queens, princes and princesses, dukes and duchesses, heads of state of sixty-eight countries, and the groom's mother, father, and five sisters and their families, attended.

Murphy O'Brien stood as best man in all three weddings and Brenna Mueller served as maid of honor. Archbishops performed two of their three weddings and a local vicar performed the other one. Crowds of commoners rubbed elbows with royalty as they packed the cathedral to witness the exchange of vows between Her Serene Highness Princess Georgiana Victoria Elizabeth May and Adam McKendrick, Viscount Kennisbrooke and Baron Bountiful in a ceremony that lasted over two hours.

At the conclusion of that ceremony, the royal couple journeyed to the palace at Laken where they spent a good deal of their honeymoon recovering from the wedding.

And they needed the time to rest and recover, for the planning of Princess Giana's coronation and preparations for the birth of the heir began immediately after the wedding.

Adam sold the Queen City Saloon and Opera House, and the Queen City Hotel to Murphy O'Brien, but kept Larchmont Lodge. It had, after all, been in his father's family for centuries. It became a world famous gentlemen's club and golf resort except for the one month in August each year, when Adam and Giana and their family and friends gathered for a holiday.

Epilogue

A Princess of the Blood Royal of the House of Saxe-Wallerstein-Karolya deserves a happily-ever-after. Her birthright should always be the love and respect and protection of her family first and then of her people. She is her family's and her country's greatest asset for she is the future and the future should always be filled with love and happiness.

—Maxim 1: Protocol and Court Etiquette of Princes of the Blood Royal of the House of Saxe-Wallerstein-Karolya, as decreed by Adam I, Prince Consort to Her Serene Highness, Princess Giana, 1875.

Christianberg Palace, Karolya
ONE YEAR LATER

Adam finished noting his suggestions for revisions to the Female Provision of the Karolyan Charter, a document only a tyrant could love, and set them aside. He picked up the blue leather-bound volume Max had placed on his desk and leafed through the gilt-edged pages. "What the devil are these?"

"What?" Giana looked over at him from her position in the middle of their massive bed. She sat propped against the headboard, a mound of pillows behind her back as she held their infant daughter, Caroline Alexandrina Margaret, to her breast.

Adam held the book up so she could see it.

"You must be looking at the maxims in the book of *Protocol and Court Etiquette of Princesses of the Blood Royal of the*

House of Saxe-Wallerstein-Karolya. They are the rules by which a royal princess must abide."

"Christ, I thought the Female Provision was bad, but this . . ." Adam flipped through the pages once again, stopping to read several before tossing it aside. "Why didn't you tell me?"

"Because you got so upset when I told you about the Female Provision," she answered.

Adam had to admit that he hadn't reacted well to the news that marrying him had limited her ability to govern her country. "Where are the rules for Princes of the Blood Royal?"

"There aren't any," she answered. "Princes of the Blood Royal are beyond reproach."

"The hell with that!" Adam burst out, unable to keep from shuddering at the memory of the last Prince of the Blood. If Victor had been a product of that philosophy, there was plenty of room for improvement.

"Adam!"

He got up from his desk and moved to sit on the edge of the bed. Leaning over, he kissed George on the lips and touched his daughter's cheek with finger. "If Princesses have rules, then Princes must also," he said softly. "We can't allow one sex to rule over the other. Not when they've equal attributes and strengths to offer." He smiled down at the baby. "At the moment, Alex is the heir presumptive to the throne because she's a girl. If she's our only child or the eldest of a palace full of girls—which, in our families, is likely to be the case—" He gave a little laugh. "There is no problem. As first-born or as an only child, she inherits. But according to the Karolyan Charter, if we have a son, he inherits." He paused to catch his breath and swallow the lump in his throat as Princess Alex reached up and grabbed hold of his finger. Adam stared at the woman he loved more than life itself and the daughter they had created. "That doesn't seem fair to Princess Alex or to her father. What about her mother?"

Giana thought for a moment. "I think she should have the right to choose. She did not ask to be born or to have this responsibility thrust upon her—nor will she have any say as to whether she has brothers or sisters, so I think that as first-born, she has earned the right to choose whether or not she wants the job of running the country. But," Giana cautioned her husband, "we do not have the power to change the order of succession. Only Parliament can do that."

"Right," he agreed. "But as sovereign, you *do* have the power to rewrite the Female Provision."

Giana laughed. "Actually, *you* have the power to rewrite it."

"Exactly." He snapped his fingers. "And that's what we want to change. You are the hereditary princess, you should have more rights in your own country than I do, but because you're a woman, you don't. I want that changed, George. And I intend to work to see that it's changed . . ."

Giana shook a finger at him. "I warn you," she teased. "You will have only yourself to blame when you limit the powers you have over me."

"I don't intend to limit all the powers I have over you," Adam said, in the deep, husky rumble that sent shivers of anticipation up her spine. "Only the constitutional ones." He traced the top of her breast with the tip of his finger. "And I fully intend to exercise all my other powers as soon as you grant me permission to do so."

Giana giggled as he waggled his eyebrows at her and gave her his cat-that-ate-the-cream look.

"I want to make the changes, George," he continued. "So that Alex will never have to worry about losing her inheritance simply because she chose to marry. I want her to be safe."

"So do I, my love." Giana shifted against the pillows and leaned close enough to touch his lips with hers. Sometimes she couldn't believe her good fortune in finding Adam McKendrick. And although she hated to think of Victor and the murders he had committed in order to gain control of the crown, she couldn't help but think that if it hadn't been for him and his incredible greed, she would never have met Adam or fallen in love and married him and she would never have given birth to the miracle that was Alex. One day, she hoped to find it within her heart to forgive Victor for the destruction he'd wrought, but until that day arrived, she said a prayer for his soul along with her prayers for the souls of her parents. And she gave thanks for the gift of Adam. And for the love he gave her. Victor had many crimes for which he must answer. But she had much for which to be grateful.

In the end, Giana supposed it all balanced out. Victor had taken the lives of the two people she loved most in the world but his actions had made it possible for her to have two other people to love most in the world.

"George?"

"Hmm?"

"Pay attention. This is important."

She smiled at his serious expression. "I was thinking of something more important," she told him.

"Oh?" He raised his eyebrow in the gesture she loved so much.

"I was thinking of you and Alex and how very much I love you and all the reasons I have to be thankful."

"I know," Adam agreed. "And that's why we've either got to revise the current version of the Karolyan Charter—especially the Female Provision—to make it more equitable or come up with a book of maxims for princes."

"Does it have to be either or?" she asked.

Adam grinned. "You're the hereditary ruler of this country, you tell me."

"Let's do both."

Four days later, in a ceremony to celebrate the coronation of Her Serene Highness Princess Georgiana Victoria Elizabeth May of Saxe-Wallerstein-Karolya and the birth of the heir-presumptive Her Highness Princess Caroline Alexandrina Margaret of the House of Karolya-Kennisbrooke-McKendrick, His Highness, Adam, the prince consort, declared before the people of Karolya, and his family and friends, that the Female Provision of the Karolyan Charter would be revised in order to limit the powers of the husband over the hereditary ruler.

The hereditary princess, he declared, should be granted the singular right to reign over her country, her subjects, and her husband, with courage, wisdom, and love. Especially love. For love is the saving grace of all husbands and princes.

Turn the page for a preview of

ALMOST A GENTLEMAN

The next novel in the
Marquess of Templeston's Heirs series

Coming soon from Jove Books.

Prologue

Continuous as the stars that shine
And twinkle on the milky way.

—WILLIAM WORDSWORTH, 1770–1850

INISMORN, IRELAND
SUMMER 1824

The stars sparkled like finely cut diamonds
spread out on a background of black velvet. A solitary
figure huddled against the wall of the crumbling tower of Telamor Castle. She sat with her back pressed to the rough, moss-
covered stone and her neck tilted at the optimum angle for
stargazing through the battered crenellations. Below the tower
lay the beach and she could hear the low roar of the ocean
and the occasional sound of voices, but she ignored them. Her
attention was focused on the heavens as she studied the array
of constellations visible in the northern sky, reciting the fan-
ciful names her mother had taught her. She stared at the bright-
est star, then breathed a reverent sigh as one of its lesser
companions streaked across the heavens.

"I wish that when I grow up I can marry a rich, handsome
prince and live in this fine castle," Mariah Shaughnessy prayed
with all the fire and fervor a six-year-old could muster. "That
I can have dogs and cats and ponies to ride and that I can sit
in the tower and eat cakes and biscuits and look up at the stars
every night until I die." She took a deep breath before continuing her litany of wishes. Falling stars were rare. They didn't

happen every night and Mariah had learned to make the most
of their magical powers. "And . . ."

"You'll get fat if you eat cake every night."

Mariah sat up straight and stared into the night. A boy stood
holding a lantern on the top step of the spiral stairs that led to
the tower.

"No, I won't." Mariah stuck out her bottom lip and dared
the intruder to contradict her.

"Of course you will." He left the top step and walked over
to sit beside her. He leaned his back against the stone wall and
slowly slid down it until he was sitting beside her. He trimmed
the wick on the lantern so the light wouldn't interfere with her
stargazing, but he kept the light burning low. "And then no
prince will marry you."

Tears welled up in her eyes. "But I like cake," she replied.

He gave her a disgusted look. "Everyone likes cake."

She sighed again. "It was good."

"That's why they call it cake," he told her. "If it tasted awful
they would have called it turnips."

"Will I get fat if I just wish for cake and biscuits every
night?"

He shook his head. "No," he promised. "Wishing for cake
won't make you fat. Only eating it."

She shrugged her shoulders. "Can you get fat from eating
it once?"

"No."

"Then I guess I'll never get fat."

"You've only had cake one time?" He was genuinely surprised.

She nodded.

"How come?" he asked.

"The sisters don't believe in spoiling us."

"How many sisters have you?" he asked.

She giggled. "I don't have any sisters."

"But you said . . ."

"The sisters at St. Agnes's Sacred Heart Convent where I
live."

The boy shuddered. He knew what convents were. But he
had always thought they were reserved for nuns and old ladies.

He had never heard of little girls living in there. "You live in a convent?"

"Yes," she answered. "Down the hill and beyond the wall. I come here after evening vespers so I can look at the stars. See there!" She pointed through the hole in the ancient stonework. "That's Draco, the dragon."

"Why don't you just look out your window?"

"My room doesn't have windows."

"Oh." He was thoughtful once again, almost unable to comprehend the idea of a room with no windows to look out. "How do you get out?"

"It has a door, silly," she replied in a tone tinged with superiority. "I'm very good you know. And very quiet. As long as you're quiet no one pays much attention to you, so I sneak out after everyone else goes to bed."

He eyed the little girl with new respect. To sneak out of a convent and come all this way without a lantern was an enormous feat of bravery.

"Where are your mother and father?"

"I don't have a da," she told him. "And my mummy's in heaven. She's a star. See that one up there? The shiniest one?"

He nodded.

"I think that one must be my mummy 'cause she used to wear lots of sparkly things." Tears welled up in her eyes once again and her voice quavered with emotion.

He reached over and covered her small hand with his own, stunned by the magnitude of her loss. Life without his mother and father was unthinkable. "I'm sorry."

She sniffled, then wiped her nose with the back of her other hand.

"Here, take this." He reached into his pocket and pulled out a clean handkerchief.

"Thank you."

He shifted uncomfortably against the wall. "Is that why you come—to wish on the stars?"

She nodded once again. "My mummy said that if you wish on the stars God hears your wishes and if you wish on a shooting star God grants the wish."

"Do you always wish to marry a handsome prince and live

in this castle eating cake and biscuits every day?"

She shook her head. "No," she answered truthfully. "Most of the time I wish for my mummy to come back down from heaven and get me. But sometimes I wish that I'll grow up and marry a handsome prince and live in this castle and have cake to eat whenever I want it." Her voice broke and she quickly covered her mouth with her hand.

"A handsome prince might marry you," he said, offering what comfort he could. "And give you cake to eat. As long as you don't eat it *every* day."

"My wish won't come true now," she answered softly.

"Why not?"

"They don't come true if you share them with someone else. They only come true if you keep them all to yourself."

"Kit!" A loud masculine shout echoed through the ruins from the ground below. "Your mother's finished. Time to go."

The boy shot Mariah an apologetic glance. "Papa's calling me," he told her. "I have to leave now. My mama and papa were collecting sea creatures from the beach for my mama to draw. Papa only let me come to the ruins because the grounds-keeper swore they were safe. We're going home tomorrow and I wanted to see the old castle."

"Oh."

She sounded so bereft that his heart went out to her. "Will an earl do?" he asked.

"Huh?"

"I'm not a prince," he explained. "I'm an earl. But my mama says I'm handsome, and one day when I'm all grown up, I'll come back and marry you if you like."

"Truly?" she breathed. "You would come back and marry me?"

"Sure," he answered with a nonchalant shrug of his shoulders. "I have to marry someone. It might as well be you."

"All right." She smiled up at him.

He pulled her close and planted a kiss on her lips the way he'd seen his papa do to his mama. "Then it's settled," he pronounced.

"Kit!" His father's voice sounded louder, closer. "Son, where are you?"

"Coming, Papa," he called down the stairs, then glanced back at the girl. "I have to go."

"You won't tell anyone about this?" she asked. "If the nuns find out . . ."

"I won't tell." He turned and started down the stairs.

"Wait!" she whispered urgently. "You forgot your lantern." She picked it up and held it out to him.

"You keep it," he said. "And use it to find your way to and from the tower in the dark." He smiled at her once again. "Now that we're betrothed, you have to take care of yourself."

"You won't forget?"

"I won't forget," he promised.

He waved once more and then he was gone.

Chapter 1

A mother's pride, a father's joy.

—SIR WALTER SCOTT, 1771–1821

SWANSLEA PARK
NORTHAMPTONSHIRE, ENGLAND

"*Talk him out of it, Drew. He's too young.*"
Andrew Ramsey, the sixteenth marquess of Templeston, stared down at his wife. Tears shimmered in her beautiful eyes and her voice held a barely discernable note of panic. Kathryn was on the verge of bursting into tears at any moment and Drew felt powerless to stop it. He had been her husband for nineteen years and he ached to see the pain in her eyes. There were streaks of silver in Kathryn's hair, but she was every bit as beautiful to him today as she had been the first time he'd seen her. And he loved her more than he thought possible, but he loved Kit, too, and Drew would not—could not—forbid Kit to pursue his destiny. He didn't have that right. Not even for Kathryn. "He's old enough to know his own mind, Kathryn. Older than you were when I first proposed to you."

His words and his tone of voice sent shivers of anticipation up her spine. After nineteen years of marriage, he still had the power to take her breath away and to reduce her to a mindless, quivering mass of anticipation without so much as a touch. All he had to do was speak her name. *Kathryn.* Only Drew called her Kathryn. The rest of the world called her Wren. "That's beside the point," she insisted.

Drew shook his head. "It *is* the point, my love. Kit is two and twenty years old. He's not a child anymore. He's a grown man and he wants and needs a place of his own."

"He can have a place of his own here," she said. "He needn't go all the way to Ireland for that."

Drew laughed. "Are you suggesting I give him Swanslea Park just to keep him at home?"

Swanslea Park, the country seat of the current marquess had been handed down to Drew from his father, the fifteenth marquess of Templeston, who had gained possession of it through his marriage to Drew's mother, the only child of the earl of Munnerlyn. The Ramsey family estate lay farther north, too far from London for convenience and the fifteenth marquess and his wife had chosen to live and raise their son at Swanslea. Drew and Kathryn had continued the tradition.

"I would if I thought it would do any good," Wren admitted.

"Well, forget it." Drew laughed again. "Because I'm not ready to turn over the keys to Swanslea just yet." The title of marquess of Templeston and the keys to Swanslea went hand in hand and although Drew had already given Kit his lesser titles of earl of Ramsey, Viscount Birmingham and Baron Selby, he intended to keep Swanslea Park awhile longer.

"But, Drew, Swanslea Park is Kit's home, too. And it's large enough to accommodate his desire for privacy." She looked at her husband. "He can have the whole east wing to himself and come and go as he pleases. It has a private entrance."

"Yes, it does," Drew agreed. "And a household staff who will note his private comings and goings as they go about their daily activities and those remarks will reach Newberry's ears who will report them to me even though I've no wish to infringe upon Kit's privacy." Drew reached out and enfolded his wife in his arms, hugging her close. "I'm the marquess, Kathryn. Everyone answers to me and nothing goes on at Swanslea Park without my knowing about it. He wants to go to Ireland, Kathryn. He delayed his departure for a year because he didn't want to upset you, but he's eager to take possession of his inheritance. Kit needs to be his own man and the lord of his own domain in a place where the staff answers to him instead of to me."

"I wish Martin had never delivered that letter to Kit," Wren said.

He frowned at her. "You don't mean that."

"Yes, I do," she replied. "If Martin hadn't delivered that letter, we all would have remained in blissful ignorance and Kit wouldn't be moving to Ireland."

The letter their solicitor, Martin Bell, had delivered to Kit on his twenty-first birthday, was a letter informing him that he was the sole inheritor of Telamor Castle and the surrounding estate in the village of Inismorn in County Clare through his maternal grandfather. Drew and Wren weren't Kit's natural parents. Kit was born the illegitimate son of the fifteenth marquess of Templeston, half-brother to Drew and twenty-eight years his junior. Kit's natural mother, the fifteenth marquess's mistress, had died shortly after giving him life and his father had died in a yachting accident three years later.

George Ramsey, the fifteenth marquess, had taken his infant son to Wren Stafford and given Kit to her to rear as her own. Drew had married Kathryn and adopted Kit, making Kathryn the marchioness and Kit, the twenty-ninth earl of Ramsey, the marquess of Templeston's legal son and heir. They were the only parents Kit had ever known and neither of them had been aware of Kit's inheritance.

Castle Telamor had come as a surprise. When he died, the Irish earl of Kilgannon had left it to his only living heir— Christopher George "Kit" Ramsey. Martin Bell, a lifelong family friend and solicitor had held it in trust until Kit reached his majority. Martin had presented a letter from his maternal grandfather and the deed to the castle and the estate a year ago and Kit was eager to inspect his Irish castle and set up housekeeping on the property.

"Swanslea Park came to us through *my* mother," Drew reminded his wife. "You are Kit's mother. There is no question about that. You are the woman who's loved and nursed him and molded him into the wonderful man he is today. Fate robbed Kit of one mother's love, but it granted him another's when my father loved him enough to place him in your care. Nothing will ever change the way Kit feels about you, but he carries the blood of the woman who gave birth to him in his veins. He wasn't granted the opportunity to know that woman, but he has a chance to know the place she called home. Shouldn't we, the parents who love him the most in the world, give him the wings he needs to fly and encourage him to use them?"

Wren choked back a sob and nodded her head in agreement. "But I don't want him to go. A lot of things can happen in a year. And I'll miss him so much."

"I know you will," Drew soothed. "So will I. But we always knew this day would come some day."

"It's come too soon, Drew," she whispered. "I thought I would be ready, but it's come much too soon."

"He won't be gone forever and we'll still have each other and the girls. The time will pass faster than you think." He planted a kiss against Kathryn's forehead. "Remember that Iris has her London Season coming up." He reminded his wife that they had two other children—daughters, seventeen-year-old Iris and twelve-year-old Kate—to think about. "And you have paintings to complete for the new exhibit at the museum. There will be lots of things to keep you busy and before you know it, Kit will be back to visit."

"What if he doesn't come back?" she asked, giving voice to her deepest fear. "What happens if he decides to remain in Ireland?"

"Ah, my darling . . ." Drew leaned down to kiss her soundly and to chase away the tears. "If Kit decides to stay in Ireland, then we'll visit as often as he will allow."

"Allow?" Kathryn wrinkled her brow and narrowed her gaze at the suggestion that Kit might not welcome them with open arms every time she felt the need to pay him a visit. "Why wouldn't he allow his parents to visit?"

Drew wanted to bite his tongue, but it was too late. Kathryn had latched on to his promise to visit with all the tenacity of a terrier on a rat. He had expected that. But he hadn't expected her to balk at the idea that Kit might not appreciate long visits at regularly scheduled intervals. "What's the point of setting up housekeeping and becoming lord of your own castle if you have to answer to your mother and father while doing it?" He reached out and tilted Kathryn's chin up with the tip of his index finger so that she was forced to meet his gaze. "We have to let him go, Kathryn. We must let him become the man he's meant to become. *We* need it and more important, *Kit* needs it."

"*You* didn't move to Ireland to escape your father's realm of influence in order to become the man you were meant to become," she said.

"That's true." Drew's voice took on the harder tone. "But only because *I* went to war. I joined Wellington and went to Belgium to fight Napoleon." He caressed Kathryn's cheek. "My character was refined by heartbreak, betrayal, and war. I became the man I am today because I survived the horrors of war. I would rather Kit build and refine his character in the relative safety of the Irish countryside as lord of Telamor Castle. Wouldn't you?"

"Of course, I would!"

"Then do your best to pretend to be excited and happy for him." Drew grinned. "For heaven's sake, Kathryn, the boy inherited a castle!"

"A crumbling castle," she retorted.

"The tower may be crumbling, but I was told the new castle is quite livable. But Kit won't care if it's old and crumbling, too," Drew said. "It's his castle. Just as Lancelot was his pony. Remember?"

Wren smiled in spite of herself. Lancelot was Kit's first pony. A shaggy old Shetland with a white blaze on his face and black coat mottled with flecks of white and gray. Lancelot had been destined for the rendering pot when Drew bought him. Kit had loved him instantly and the two had become constant companions. Even now, Kit refused to part with Lancelot. The ancient pony still held the place of honor among the thoroughbreds in Drew's magnificent stables. "What should I do?"

"Help him pack, wish him Godspeed, and don't let him see you cry."

Kathryn lifted herself up on tiptoe and pressed her lips against Drew's. "How did you get to be so wise?"

He smiled. "My father was an excellent judge of character. I inherited the gift from him."

"Is that so?" she teased.

"Yes, indeed," he answered. "You see, I once fell in love with a woman thought to be a most notorious mistress."

"Was she?"

Drew laughed. "Of course she was. That's why I married her."

Chapter 2

INISMORN, IRELAND
ONE MONTH LATER

Kit Ramsey, the twenty-ninth earl of Ramsey, topped the rise in the road that led to the tiny village of Inismorn and gazed out over the land surrounding it. Standing in the irons, he surveyed his inheritance. Everything except the village and the convent was his. All of the land as far as the eye could see—twenty-six thousand acres of it—including the castle rising above the mist in the distance belonged to him. His land. His castle. His place. And by Jove, but it was beautiful!

He grinned. The tower to the right of the castle, perched on the edge of the cliffs, was all that remained of an ancient Norman fortress. A newer, more modern castle had been built farther inland, but the tower remained to mark the spot of the original castle and to serve as an observation post and guardian for the new castle. There was a clear view of the beach below the tower and of the miles of ocean stretching beyond it. And although it was currently shrouded in clouds and mist, Kit knew that it was possible to look through the holes in the massive moss-covered crenellations and see the stars sparkling in the night sky like finely cut diamonds spread out on an infinite background of black velvet.

Kit smiled at the memory. A few miles down the hill, inside the wall, facing the coast road sat the slate-roofed gables and spires of St. Agnes's Sacred Heart Convent. Once, long ago, one of the residents of St. Agnes's crept out of her room every evening after vespers, climbed over the stone wall surrounding the convent grounds and made her way up the hill along the coast to the crumbling tower of Telamor Castle in order to wish upon the stars. And once, long ago, an eight-year-old boy had accidentally discovered her hiding place and impulsively proposed marriage.

Harlequin® Historical
Historical Romantic Adventure!

Imagine a time of chivalrous knights and unconventional ladies, roguish rakes and impetuous heiresses, rugged cowboys and spirited frontierswomen— these rich and vivid tales will capture your imagination!

Harlequin Historical... they're too good to miss!

HHDIR06

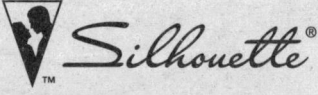

Silhouette®
SPECIAL EDITION™

Emotional, compelling stories that capture the intensity of living, loving and creating a family in today's world.

Special Edition features bestselling authors such as Susan Mallery, Sherryl Woods, Christine Rimmer, Joan Elliott Pickart— and many more!

For a romantic, complex and emotional read, choose Silhouette Special Edition.

Silhouette®

HARLEQUIN®
Presents

**The world's bestselling romance series...
The series that brings you your favorite authors,
month after month:**

Helen Bianchin...Emma Darcy
Lynne Graham...Penny Jordan
Miranda Lee...Sandra Marton
Anne Mather...Carole Mortimer
Melanie Milburne...Michelle Reid

and many more talented authors!

Wealthy, powerful, gorgeous men...
Women who have feelings just like your own...
The stories you love, set in exotic, glamorous locations...

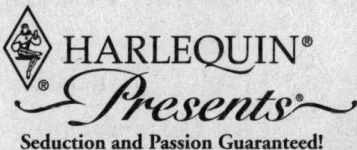

Seduction and Passion Guaranteed!

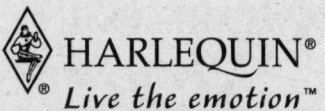

HARLEQUIN®
INTRIGUE®

BREATHTAKING ROMANTIC SUSPENSE

Shared dangers and passions lead to electrifying romance and heart-stopping suspense!

Every month, you'll meet six new heroes who are guaranteed to make your spine tingle and your pulse pound. With them you'll enter into the exciting world of Harlequin Intrigue— where your life is on the line and so is your heart!

THAT'S INTRIGUE— ROMANTIC SUSPENSE AT ITS BEST!

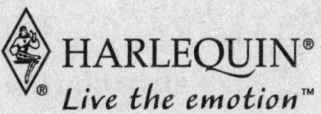

HARLEQUIN®
Live the emotion™

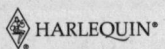
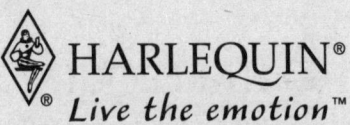

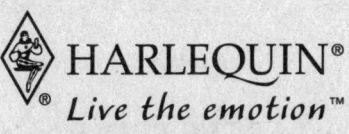

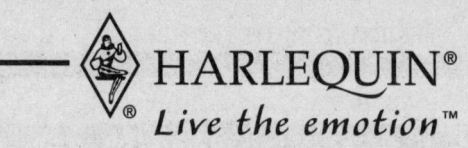
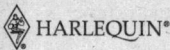
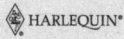

softly. And since he was being honest, he added, "I hope we see each other again."

She didn't say anything in response, only stood silhouetted against the window with her arms wrapped around her in a way that made him wonder whether she was doing it because she was cold, or if she just needed something—someone—to hold on to. In either case, Daniel understood. There was an emptiness clinging to him that he suspected would be there for a long time.

* * * * *

THOROUGHBRED LEGACY
coming soon wherever books are sold!

why I was in Del Mar," he repeated. "I was in Del Mar to win a race. That was my job. And my work was the most important thing to me."

She said nothing for a moment, only studied his face in the darkness as if looking for the answer to a very important question. Finally she asked, "And what's the most important thing to you now, Daniel?"

Wasn't the answer to that obvious? "My work," he answered automatically.

She nodded slowly. "Of course," she said softly. "That is, after all, what you do best."

Her comment, too, puzzled him. She made it sound as if being good at what he did was a bad thing.

She bit her lip thoughtfully, her eyes fixed on his, glimmering in the scant moonlight that was filtering through the window. And damned if Daniel didn't find himself wanting to pull her into his arms and kiss her. But as much as it might have felt as if no time had passed since Del Mar, there were eight years between now and then. And eight years was a long time in the best of circumstances. For Daniel and Marnie, it was virtually a lifetime.

So Daniel turned and started for the door, then halted. He couldn't just walk away and leave things as they were, unsettled. He'd done that eight years ago and regretted it.

"It *was* good to see you again, Marnie," he said

Pacific Classic had been the last thing on Daniel's mind. His loss at Del Mar had pretty much ended his career before it had even begun, and he'd had to start all over again, rebuilding from nothing.

He simply had not then and did not now have room in his life for a woman as potent as Marnie Roberts. He was a horseman first and foremost. From the time he was a schoolboy, he'd known what he wanted to do with his life—be the best possible trainer he could be.

He had to make sure Marnie understood—and he understood, too—why things had ended the way they had eight years ago. He just wished he could find the words to do that. Hell, he wished he could find the *thoughts* to do that.

"You made me forget things, Marnie, things that I really needed to remember. And that scared the hell out of me. Little Joe should have won the Classic. He was by far the best horse entered in that race. But I didn't give him the attention he needed and deserved that week, because all I could think about was you. Hell, when I woke up that morning all I wanted to do was lie there and look at you, and then wake you up and make love to you again. If I hadn't left when I did—the way I did—I might still be lying there in that bed with you, thinking about nothing else."

"And would that be so terrible?" she asked.

"Of course not," he told her. "But that wasn't

THE DOOR CLOSED behind them, throwing them into darkness and leaving them utterly alone. And the next thing Daniel knew, he heard himself saying, "Marnie, I'm sorry about the way things turned out in Del Mar."

She said nothing at first, only strode across the room and stared out the window beside him. Although he couldn't see her well in the darkness—he still hadn't switched on a light…but then, neither had she—he imagined her expression was a little preoccupied, a little anxious, a little confused.

Finally, very softly, she said, "Are you?"

He nodded, then, worried she wouldn't be able to see the gesture, added, "Yeah. I am. I should have said goodbye to you."

"Yes, you should have."

Actually, he thought, there were a lot of things he should have done in Del Mar. He'd had *a lot* riding on the Pacific Classic, and even more on his entry, Little Joe, but after meeting Marnie, the

THOROUGHBRED LEGACY
*The stakes are high when it comes to love,
horse racing, family secrets
and broken promises.*

*A new exciting Harlequin continuity series
coming soon!
Led by New York Times bestselling author
Elizabeth Bevarly
FLIRTING WITH TROUBLE*

Here's a preview!

the waist and pulled her back on top of him. They clung feverishly to each other. "We can't do this to your family, Cesar."

"I know," he said huskily, "but first I have to do this to you. I've only recently come back to life because of you. Humor me, beloved."

* * * * *

He crushed it in his fist before closing his mouth over hers. He couldn't drink long enough or deep enough. When he eventually lifted his head he said, "I should have believed in us, Sarah. What we had was magical from the moment we met."

She raised her hands to his cheeks and pulled his head down to kiss his moist eyes. "It's still magical, my love."

"What a son we made together!" he cried into her scented neck. "I swear when I saw the two of you in my hospital room, my heart nearly failed me."

"Let's promise each other no more heart failures ever again. Well, except for the things Johnny's going to put us through as the years roll by."

"And maybe a Jane."

She laughed. "Where did you come up with that name?"

"In my first English reader. You know. Dick and Jane." His smile turned her heart over.

"You made that up." He chuckled. "For our next child I was thinking something brilliant like Octavia Priestley de Falcon."

"I think we can come up with a better name than that."

"But not now. We've got to get up. You can't ruin your mother's party. She's been living for this day."

"You're right. Just one more kiss."

"No, Cesar. It won't be just one."

She whipped out of bed, but he caught her around